BY THE SAM.

FAT DOG
A Canine Odyssey Across the Human Landscape

CHRONICLES OF RAMPUR

THE MYSTERIES OF RANIPUR

THE SECRETS OF RAJPUR

COVETING THE NEIGHBOUR'S WIFE

KRISH DAY

Copyright © 2021 Krish Day

The moral right of the author has been asserted.

Apart from any fair dealing for the purposes of research or private study, or criticism or review, as permitted under the Copyright, Designs and Patents Act 1988, this publication may only be reproduced, stored or transmitted, in any form or by any means, with the prior permission in writing of the publishers, or in the case of reprographic reproduction in accordance with the terms of licences issued by the Copyright Licensing Agency. Enquiries concerning reproduction outside those terms should be sent to the publishers.

Matador
9 Priory Business Park,
Wistow Road, Kibworth Beauchamp,
Leicestershire. LE8 0RX
Tel: 0116 279 2299
Email: books@troubador.co.uk
Web: www.troubador.co.uk/matador
Twitter: @matadorbooks

ISBN 978 1800463 783

British Library Cataloguing in Publication Data.
A catalogue record for this book is available from the British Library.

Printed and bound by CPI Group (UK) Ltd, Croydon, CR0 4YY
Typeset in 11pt Aldine401 BT by Troubador Publishing Ltd, Leicester, UK

Matador is an imprint of Troubador Publishing Ltd

For
Aaron J. Buckley
&
Ragnhild Dahl Johansen

Thou shalt not covet thy neighbour's wife...
Should not the neighbour's wife covet thee.

I

1

The contract signed with an elegant flourish, he put away the Montblanc, rose to his feet and gave me a well-manicured hand, the palm smooth to the touch. Moving to the tall window, looking out towards the range of smoke-blue mountains and the waters of the lake placid as a mill-pond, he drew a deep breath.

"*Bello!* Some of the older folk still call it by the ancient Roman name Còmm. *Bellissimo!* You'll like it here, I'm sure."

Scenic beauty not always matching the interior landscape, that remained to be seen. No doubt about it, the view was a splendid one. I nodded in agreement. He drew the mitred cuff of his shirt an inch out of the jacket sleeve and turned to me with a smile, warm and amiable.

"But why Como, Professor? If I may ask."

Why indeed? Odd that wanting to distant oneself from the past, one should choose a place that closed the distance in some small measure. A very long time ago, in another life, Myrna and I had visited the town, stayed for several days, Myrna's wish years later to revisit the place denied by her journey's end.

"It's as good a place as any," I replied.

"And better than many," he nodded affably to my lame words.

Outside, as we stepped on the gravel path, Signor Fabbri raised his eyes to look across the garden at the tall, close-knit laurel hedge that shut off from view the adjoining property, a sizeable grande dame of a villa set on extensive grounds. "You have an illustrious neighbour."

"Oh!"

No name mentioned, my mild curiosity less than satisfied, I walked him down to the gate. Pausing, he glanced at the house behind us. With a courteous bow of the head, he remarked with an aloof air, "This place has a history. A secret, they say."

"All human habitats have secrets, I expect."

He nodded with a brief smile. Earnest once again, he said, "You have my number. Call me any time you need."

I strolled back under the warming, early spring sun, no wiser about the illustrious neighbour, the secret history of the house still very much a secret. It would be a while yet before the veil of the estate agent's mannered discretion lifted, to reveal the face of the great man next door, as too the secret silently stalking the house.

Everything about Signor Fabbri bespoke taste and finesse. Reasonably tall, trim, a fine head of dark-brown hair carefully coiffured, the youthful lineaments soberly handsome, it was the smile that made the man, the signature of a cordial and mannered nature. And unusually refined and discerning in dress for an estate agent, with a custom-tailored suit, a silver-grey silk shirt, Bordeaux tie with tiny paisley knit, he had all the air of a gentleman of leisure, elegant and prosperous.

But then, Roberto Fabbri was no run-of-the-mill estate agent. Of little interest to him the narrow-balconied, modest apartments of the concrete box-like condos in the town, his speciality was mainly the mansions and villas along the lake shore and dotting the slopes above, properties much in demand by the new Croesuses cruising the seven seas in their luxury yachts and criss-crossing the skies in private jets.

One afternoon some weeks later, coming across him on the road skirting the lake, following his accustomed amicable greeting and query if all was well, he pointed my attention through the tall, wrought-iron gates at a stolid, château style manor house set on several acres of ground planted with aged palms.

"Gone. Finally!" he said with a breath of relief. "Took a bit of time, though."

Owned by a Milanese banking family since the end of the Great War, he explained, later bought by a German steel magnate, the property had now been sold to a Russian tycoon, one of the many emerged from the woodwork of the Soviet era to find themselves overnight heirs to vast oil and gas fields and mineral wealth.

Some days after, a minor plumbing problem at the villa occasioning a visit to Fabbri in his offices overlooking the embarcadero lined with sail and motor boats, I caught a glimpse of the Russian, a heavy-set figure with a rubicund face, the young woman on his arm in colourful couture wear and overly bejewelled, with all the gait and grace of a night club hostess. Seeing the pair off with hearty salutations, Fabbri showed me in, as he wearily indicated his secretary through the glass panel.

"Franca was told by the young lady that she wears only Dolce and Gabbana. Down to her underwear, presumably. Dolce and Gabbana!" he exclaimed laconically, settling into his seat across the desk, And then, letting fall a mannered sigh, added quite as drily, "These folk are the future."

The morning-long visit of the Russian couple to settle the final details of the sale must have been oppressive. Fabbri loosened his tie a notch and his talk took on an unexpected loquacity.

About a year ago, visiting Como, out for a stroll one morning, the Russian woman had set eyes on 'my' villa and it was love at first sight. Nothing denied the young bride, and the going price the merest grain of gold in the husband's treasury, Fabbri's office had arranged the sale. The paperwork proceeding with utmost haste, the preliminary contract drawn up, due process and formalities carried out, hour and date scheduled at the notary's office, a mere week before the final signing the buyer withdrew. Somehow snatches of the 'secret' had reached the couple's ears.

"First dog in space, very first man in space, a nuclear arsenal to flatten the earth many times over. But... *dio mio!* These Russians are a superstitious lot."

The modest initial deposit, mere beggar's coins for the nabob of Novgorod, forfeited nonchalantly, part of the estate agent's commission happily paid, Fabbri was directed to search out another property, possibly larger and more stately. Worth many times over the Villa Serena, the German steel magnate's mansion had recently come on the market, and it fitted the bill.

Fabbri held up his hand, index and middle fingers crossed. "Hopefully no skeletons in Villa Frieden!"

I wished Fabbri well, but one never knew. With their unsavoury sympathies and generous donations to the Führer's cause, many a German industrialist was known to have had whole cupboards full of rattling skeletons! Indeed, much later, I saw in a corner of Fabbri's office a large, framed photograph he had removed from Villa Frieden just prior to the sale. Of the German steel mogul seated at a banqueting table, with the corpulent figure of *Reichsmarschall* Hermann Göring looming above him raising a toast.

Meanwhile, I myself was still no wiser about the secret lurking in my villa!

2

Settling in was slow and wearying. The Art Deco exterior pleasant enough, it was inside the house that one lost one's way through the maze of rooms, small and large, on the two floors. Built as a family residence, with an expansive hallway, nursery space and playrooms tucked here and there, oversize bed chambers, a dining room for a numerous gathering, a spacious kitchen with vintage stove and oven still in place, claw-footed tubs and old tapware in the baths, the place was outsized for a single person. But the rent was surprisingly modest, the peace and quiet of the surrounds especially welcome, and Fabbri's suave, persuasive voice had done the rest. No regrets, but if the settling in was slow, perhaps in part the fault was in the unsettled spirit of the new tenant.

The Foundation had been generous, overly liberal in funding me a whole year to put my thoughts on paper in a locality of my choosing. A welcome recess from the mundane academic routine, the interminable talk among colleagues about tenure and oversight, it was more a sabbatical from oneself, a retreat from private grief to a quiet corner for a time of convalescence. Familiar with the country, with a passing smattering of the language and local habits, the distance and new air, one thought, would be balm for the healing. Hopefully, the writing too would proceed apace. It would not do to inform the Foundation that in the twelve months I had merely fattened myself with Signora

Maria's cooking, even less that I had coveted, and more, the neighbour's wife!

Fabbri had arranged for Signora Maria to come in daily to cook and generally keep house. "I've known Maria since she was a young woman. She'll take good care of you," he assured. That she did, and amply, I soon found.

No longer young, in her sixties, Maria was the now increasingly rare, archetypal Italian grandmother, with vanishing housewifely skills, energy to shame many a youngster, both stubborn and benign, with a tart tongue when the occasion so required. Inherited from her mother and, possibly, mother's mother, her culinary skills a family heirloom, the offerings she put on the table, less art, more succulent substance, might have roused the envy of not a few of the many-starred chefs increasingly populating the gastronomical firmament.

Not only brisk and skilled with pots, pans and skillets, she also supervised one's dining, coming in from time to time to cast a stern eye, admonishing the meagreness of the eater's appetite, saying, "A man must eat if he is to work." As though, rising from the table, I was meant to set out for the fields for a long day's labour. And once, patiently witnessing my combat with a marrowbone, she remarked drily: "The bone is to meat what the soul is for the body." As fine a culinary epigram as any!

A younger cleaning lady, Romanian, came in twice a week. Pleasant-faced, bright and sprightly, a deal more vocal than the cook, but only when spoken to or in-between sips of her mid-afternoon coffee, Alina, I noticed, occasionally paused briefly in her task to look out of the window of the small room upstairs I had chosen as my study. No drama of particular interest playing out, it was merely a clear view of the neighbouring house.

One afternoon, coming in to fetch a guide to the eateries around the lake, I looked over her shoulder as she stood, seemingly rapt, at the window. No sign of personages illustrious or otherwise, it was merely a still-life scene of a man stretched under a plaid on a wickerwork chaise-lounge on wheels, with a nurse sat by the head, a wooden dining trolley to one side with a gleaming silver tea or coffee set and cups. The dim notes of a piano, barely audible, came over the air, the source hidden to sight. Sensing my presence, Alina turned, shades of a wistful recall in her expression.

"When I was a child in Romania, one of our favourite pastimes was watching the rich," she said with a quite smile.

"Oh, why would you do that, Alina?"

Tilting her head to one side, she turned back to the window. "They had everything, we others nothing at all."

Back home, her family had scratched a bare living from a couple of acres of land in the countryside around Târgovişta, her father a sometime bricklayer and invalid. Not far-off lived one of Ceauşescu's cousins in a palatial residence set on extensive grounds. In the hot summer months, free of school and footloose, wandering idle across the fields, Alina and her brothers often peered over the ancient stone wall of the compound, their infant eyes held still by the magical sight of men and women in apparently regal wear sat outdoors, in the shade of diaphanous linen overhead, at tables spread with silver platters and porcelain dishes heaped with foodstuffs never seen by the youngsters even in their dreams. Then, late one year, when Alina was barely in her teens, the paradisical vision had dissolved in thin air, the mansion shuttered, the grounds empty. Later she learnt the truth. The storm gathering unexpected force and the regime in peril, escaping from the besieged presidential palace in the capital, Ceauşescu and his wife had flown to Târgovişta, possibly hoping to find refuge in the cousin's country estate. But the cousin himself had already fled to destinations unknown, and a day later Nicolae and Elena met their summary end in a mean backyard.

After the Revolution, Alina had trained as an infant school teacher, but the salary barely enough to maintain even a mere infant in life, she had drifted westwards, finally settling here in a lake shore village and, some years later, marrying a fellow countryman.

Alina's brief telling of her childhood made me think as I sat at dinner that evening, while Maria wordlessly forced on me yet another of her creamy cannelonis. Several lives compacted into a single existence, the exterior seldom revealed the truth. Alina was no common cleaning woman nor, evidently, her husband Bogdan, once a minor civil servant, now a mechanic in an auto shop. As soon, too, I was to discover that Fabbri's genteel and gentlemanly air concealed a past murky and distressed. Nor was the illustrious neighbour the man the world had known and lauded, even less so the handsome creature in the guise of a nurse sat by the recumbent figure through long afternoons.

Each a mask, that could lift to reveal yet another face, other faces, lineaments of lives that lay unseen and out of sight, but all too real and present for that. To think then that so very often one appraised, weighed and judged unawares of the shadows lurking behind the affable figure and amicable smile. Not much different, either, this house, with what unquiet spirits inhabiting the woodwork I had yet to learn.

3

In the chiaroscuro patchwork of images of my lost year, one of the more comforting ones was that of Maria as she sat in the mid-morning sunlight at a small table by the kitchen door, the aged but still nimble fingers stringing the beans and stripping the greens from their long white stems. The ample girth sheathed mostly in black, the snow-white head bent on her task, wordless, somehow it was an assuring presence, of domestic well-being and motherly calm, around which my yet vacant days revolved. The aromas from the kitchen recalling attention and appetite, the sound of dishes and the tintinnabulation of cutlery stirring the rooms into life, meals served punctually, Maria's silent bustling and brisk steps making of the house something of a household, gradually I found myself at ease with the surrounds, no less with a spirit hesitant, uncertain of starting anew.

Maria had loaned me her dead husband's ancient Bianchi and some mid-mornings I set out to explore the narrow lanes and alleyways of the old town. Occasionally, the lungs filled with the crisp spring air perfumed with the early blooms of the oleanders fronting houses and gardens, I rode the Bianchi out on the road winding around the lake.

One day, the knee bumping into the stone wall of a narrow passage, I stopped at a small pharmacy to ask for a mild analgesic. The elderly pharmacist in a pristine white coat behind the counter, something of a linguist evidently, halted my less than fluent request.

The pills were out of stock. "But we'll have some in this afternoon," he assured me with a courteous smile. "Are you staying far?"

"Just up the road. Villa Serena."

His expression changed to one of surprise. "Oh!" He held me in sight through the sparkling crystal lenses for a long moment, as though contemplating some weighty matter, to repeat quietly then, "Villa Serena."

"Is something wrong?"

"No!" he shook his head emphatically. "Just that… no one stays there. I should say," he corrected himself, "no one has stayed there for a long time." The brief moment of hesitation passing, he returned to his cordial manner. "I'll have the tablets for you any time you want to drop in."

I would do so, I told him and, on that note, he wished me good day and I took my baffled leave, Villa Serena on my mind as I mounted the bicycle.

"No one's been in this house a long time," I said to Maria as she brought in my lunch. "So the pharmacist told me."

"Farmacia Monti? Old man Monti is a born gossip! The house… yes, this place has been vacant ever since… The kitchen sink tap is so rusty, the water comes out only when it wants."

Less than forthcoming, she hurried away, saying, "I've not brought you the cheese."

Never loquacious, sparse words spent mostly on matters practical, Maria hardly ever engaged in loose talk. Her silences, if not grave, were somehow weighty, seemingly burdened with thought. Not reticence perhaps, but a certain reserve marking a distance, one hesitated to engage her in any exchange other than those to do with the small details of the quotidian.

Back from my morning ride one day, hearing her discreet hum of some local folk tune and encouraged by the less than customary sober look as she dusted the stains of flour from the heavy apron at the kitchen door, standing at the bottom of the steps and casually surveying the house, I remarked off-handedly, "Signor Fabbri tells me this place has a secret."

"Secret? No secret at all." A wry smile flitted across the heavy face. "Everyone in town knows about it. And not only in the town."

She said no more and, smoothing the apron, went back in. I thought it better not to pursue the matter further. But some days later, as I sat at table, surprisingly she volunteered the first morsel of revelation. The house belonged to Fabbri, she said. Or at least was in his family.

"Is that the great secret?"

Setting down the salt cellar on the table, she paused to look down at me with a thoughtful air. "If it was only that," she muttered and, pursing her lips, made her way back to the kitchen.

In the weeks to come, my well-mannered patience was duly rewarded. It came in bits and pieces, disjointed and episodic, the chronicle of another time, a crimson tale of animus, of love and love lost, deception and infidelity, blood and fatality.

Disparate in provenance and distant in possible destinations, little to share by way of his trade and my profession, Fabbri and I had not yet become friends. Ours was more an acquaintance warmed by his ease of manner and cordiality, as too my need for passing companionship, no less a mild curiosity, perhaps. The old town a small place, from time to time we ran into each other. Then he would ask me into a bar for a coffee, a Campari, or a spritz, a bubbly concoction in fashion lately. Once or twice he insisted on my company for lunch at his favourite trattoria up a narrow, stone-walled street with tables set in a small garden at the back.

Our talk, casual and amiable, mostly away from our persons, I learned little of Fabbri the man, as he was now. A daughter in

Heidelberg, studying medieval history. The briefest footnote on a wife somewhere, separated or divorced impossible to glean from the sparse words. Never the least mention of the past, of which I now knew a vague outline, but obviously a chronicle too weighty and harrowing to be touched on in the presence of a relative stranger. Only once, later, he dropped an oblique reference, perhaps inadvertent, possibly a mere rumination spoken out loud.

Sat out together on the lakefront one early evening, seemingly unaware or, perhaps, in no way bothered that I had heard something of his family history, Fabbri set down his glass, to say with a distant air, "Did anyone ever find out the real reason why Cain killed Abel?"

Less a query, sounding more the voice of the passing curiosity of an idle hour, still and all an odd matter to wonder. He looked out across the water and the Easter holiday crowd loitering in the fading light. The Biblical explanation fabulistic and not entirely plausible, but the subject too close to the bone, I shied away from offering whatever version I might have had in mind.

"Love or money, the one or the other. Possibly the first." Pausing, he raised his head to look up at the distant gleam of the first stars in the twilight sky. "What else is there to kill for?" With that, he turned to me with a quiet smile, to enquire politely if I had as yet met the distinguished man next door and his no less distinctive wife.

I told him I had yet to make their acquaintance. "Oh, you will. Be patient. The lady has the long reach of an ivy." He made her sound like a member of the black widow spider species.

Fabbri walking me part of the way back to the house, something read a long time ago about the legendary Biblical brothers inexplicably came to mind.

"About your friends Cain and Abel… Did you know, Roberto, they might not have been full blood brothers?"

"Oh! That's new. Weren't they both mothered by Eve?"

"True. Only that it was the serpent, not Adam, who impregnated Eve with Cain."

"Who'd have thought! But possible, I suppose," he nodded. "After all, it wouldn't be the only mysterious conception in the Bible."

"So the circle comes around. Fall and redemption. Man's destiny determined by the two conceptions, the Satanic and the Immaculate."

"Neat," Fabbri smiled. "And what do we do with the apple, Professor?"

"Just a metaphor."

A boyish grin lit up Fabbri's face. "Never tried it myself, but I've always thought it takes more than an apple to seduce a young woman."

On that light and cheerful note we parted and I made my way up to the Villa Serena.

4

The final pages of the war written nearby, with the capture of the Duce and his lover in the vicinity, memories of loss and suffering in slow recession, the days of hardship drawing to a laborious close, the town had begun to wake once again to calm and life. The toxins of rancour and revenge, the inheritance of the years of blood and death, gradually thinning, the uneasy peace of the early years giving way to hope and expectation, the inhabitants picked their way through the debris and ruins towards restoration and return to the burdens of everyday life.

The hive of industry starting up anew, the shops and stores began to be stocked again with the produce of farm and field, articles and artefacts of common use. Many of the elite of the older order returning, some from exile, to reclaim position and property, the villas and residences around the lake and up the hills began to open their shutters, the hum of affluent bustle appearing again on the promenade, stately sedans and sleek speedsters, Alfas and Avants, dusted and polished and brought to purring life, gliding over the flagstones, sober elegance once again seated at the tables of the finer eateries and bars. The economic miracle brought, too, the up and coming, bankers, entrepreneurs, the elected of the new order, new money desirous of asserting its right to luxury and high living, buying up manors and mansions abandoned by families impoverished by reversal of fortunes during the years of war.

Standing in the cobbled yard of his auto repair shop with a cigarette between the lips and wiping the grease on the hands with a woolly rag, Bellini had watched the to and fro of the ever increasing numbers of upmarket cars brought in for checks and repairs, a bent fender here, a broken tail-light there, as the shining new Aurelias and Abarths navigated the narrow streets through a swarm of scooters weaving in and out of the traffic. Some of his father's old clientele were back, bringing in their ageing sedans and sports cars for topping brake fluid and antifreeze. Mostly soft-spoken, their dress and manners set them apart from the newcomers, younger, brash and loud, risen and rising from humble stations, the recent enrichment written large on their persons, their autos less for use and utility, more extensions of their new-found status as they off-handedly unpeeled large bank notes and set them down in front of the young woman who made out the bills and receipts.

One afternoon, stretched out under a blazing red two-seater that had run into and run under a parked Lambretta, with oil dripping onto his chest from the gear box, Bellini's mind absented itself momentarily from the work at hand. It came to him that the time might be ripe for a better way of earning a living than lying day long under the chassis of a car, with his young wife wrinkling her nose at the smell of lubricant when he arrived home in the evening.

Sat and stood beside his father, cleaning spark plugs and connecting battery cables under the watchful eye of the elder, through almost childhood and youth the small roadside garage had offered better schooling than the classroom. Possibly more familiar with pistons, valves and crankshafts than parts of his own body, his ears in time able to fine-tune an engine with the precision of a piano tuner and tell one car make and model from another from the hum of the engine alone, Bellini's skills went well beyond that of a mere car mechanic. The years of apprenticeship long over, in his early thirties now, he thought it time to try his hand at something beyond the narrow confines of the small repair shop.

His father finally calling it a day and looking in only for the odd hour or two, the garage moved to the spacious shed of an abandoned silk mill on the outskirts of the town, taking on a young apprentice and an ex-army vehicle mechanic, Stefano had set up shop on his own. His good-humoured air assuring, his expertise with things mechanical offering service reliable and punctual, the list of faithful clientele ever longer, trade prospered.

Meanwhile, Stefano had married, with a second child already on the way. The couple lived in the old family farmhouse, with the father and mother, and a younger sister. Business brisk, the improved finances in no way altered the habits of home, the evenings gathering around the kitchen log fire above which hung the blackened metal pot with a steaming rustic soup, the food on the plate what the mother had always put on the kitchen table, bed warmers tucked between the sheets in the cold season.

There were minor alterations to the family's old routine, with the parents staying home to watch on the recently bought Philco the grainy images of whatever the fare the single channel offered. While of a Saturday evening Stefano and his wife, sometimes the sister, went into town to watch a film at the old Astra. And often on weekends, squeezed into the Fiat 1100, they drove out to some country trattoria for lunch. Modest recreations and occasional outings apart, the frugal habits of the past still governed domestic habits. When there was talk of a brand new frig, the mother said no, she had fed the family well enough without one, bottled conserves in brine and vinegar for winter months, meats, ham and sausages hung in the small cellar under the farmhouse.

When one day Stefano mentioned the bank loan, the father looked wary and puzzled. A slight limp in one leg but otherwise intact, returned from the Great War, he had opened the roadside garage some years later when a new, tarred road was laid to the lakes. Working with an old lathe, a small press and essential tools, he had made good, as well as one might in troubled times when money was short and the thought of a loan beyond imagining. Nor was it different now. "Why a loan, Stefano?" the old man asked in quiet voice. Since turning over the garage to his son, he had never once meddled in the day-to-day running of the business. Nor was it his intention to do so now, only that indebtedness, private or to a bank, went against the grain and touched his pride.

Stefano knew his father and refrained from laying out his detailed plans in the open. But the idea gaining ground and confidence in his mind over the past year, he had done his footwork and, looking about at the new energy in the air, the tide of well-being perceptibly settling on the new-born country, certain that he was not far wrong, he set out on the venture with his accustomed spirit of labour and single-minded will. Notice given to none, neither at home nor to his hands at the garage, over the months he had driven down to Milan in his Sunday best to meet with the importers of foreign brands. His good-humour and confidence assuring, he had persuaded his listeners and won over their assent.

But measured as ever, not wishing to stumble with the first steps, he chose three marques, the MG and the Jaguar sports, to feed the vanity and appetite of the newly affluent, and the recently unveiled Morris Mini, a more elegant and comfortable alternative to the small Fiats crowding the streets. The showroom he had already identified, a spacious locale a stone's throw from the lake-front.

Bellini's dealings with the bank sound, accounts in place and grown sizeable with regular monthly deposits, the loan was easily procured. But the family was ill at ease, the father silently troubled. A man was to live within his means, the day's earning sufficing for his needs, with nothing to beg or borrow, or be beholden to another.

Stefano's wife knew of his intentions but was little privy of the details. She was not one to pry and probe, yet sensing the shade of anxiety that had begun to settle in the air at home and watching her husband's thoughtful expression lately, she could not help wondering.

"What's to happen to us if it doesn't…" she hesitated to ask one evening after putting her two little boys to bed.

"If it doesn't work out? It will. And we'll still have the garage."

Drawing near, putting out a hand on his shoulder, she looked down at him as he sat at the little table in the far corner of the kitchen, busy with the stub of a pencil on a sheet annotated with a column of figures opposite spare words in a rough hand. Come from the fatherless home of family grocers, Anna had had schooling, read books and magazines, knew something of the wider world. But her aspirations limited to Stefano and her children, ever calm and patient, rarely crossing her husband in word or thought, she was satisfied with what she had, trusting whatever he deemed best. Resting her face on his head a brief moment now, as though in renewal of her faith in the only man she had known and loved, softly she called him to bed.

~~~

One day accompanying me down a wide street to a shop specialized in old maps and postcards, Fabbri paused before a long glass-panelled frontage, the offices of an insurance company. "This used to be our car saloon. Some afternoons, after school, my father brought me here. Once, running my hand down the sides of the new cars, I managed to scratch the shiny paint with a toy. Was I told off! Papà would have given me a thrashing hadn't it been for grandfather."

He pointed ahead, where the road turned at the lake front and, diving through a short tunnel, climbed up a hill and down again, a short distance from the frontier check-posts with the tricolour flying at one end and the Swiss white cross on a field of red at the other.

"The money road," Fabbri chuckled. "That's the route some of the wealth of this country took on its way out. Often a customer would come in to pick up the new Mini he'd ordered and drive off up the road to deposit a bagful of cash in some bank just across the border. Always after midday, when the customs police went off for lunch. And almost always a Mini. Not a rich man's car, nothing to raise the eyebrows."

"Why only British cars?" I asked.

He tossed back his head with a smile. "That's another story. Don't really know. Years ago, after he was gone, one of the old garage hands told me that for a time grandfather Stefano was much taken by an English woman. The wife of a writer or painter, who spent winters here. She used to bring her sports car to the garage for repairs. A svelte car and a svelte lady, apparently! Just a story. More likely, there were no dealers in this area for those British marques. Hard to imagine Stefano's head being turned by some beauty."

Not only the head refusing to turn at the sight of some seductive sight, in Fabbri's telling his grandfather was little given to revelry and common recreations. Not for him hours idling in the bar joshing, exchanging joke and banter with the other habitués, tradesmen and workmen, nor sat at table with a glass at the elbow, dealing out and slapping down cards. Nor joining the older folk at bowls in the yard behind the bar. Work and home, home and a long days work, morning mass on Sundays with the family in the small church down the road, the weekly cinema evenings at the Astra a rarity after the children had come, almost the only outings were the weekend lunch in the countryside. A cousin once remarking on the Spartan routine, he had replied, "Work's a pleasure if you like what you're doing." The cousin himself sat behind a desk yawning in the land registry office, with Monday mornings heralding a work-week of virtual death.

A big man, tall and broad of physique, Stefano was no less broad of heart. If his build was imposing, without excessive show of muscle and brawn, his generosity, too, was without flourish, discreet and unconditioned. It happened at times that an elderly customer bringing in a car quite as aged found himself in straits when handed an unexpected bill for repair or a replacement, gearbox or suspensions, a major overhaul. Taking the client aside, Stefano would say quietly and out of hearing, "Pay me when you can." Most did, a few vanished, but Stefano never wavered when called on for a helping hand.

When the apprentice taken on years earlier, now grown, married, Stefano met part of the expenses for the wedding feast. "Why invite the whole village when one can hardly feed oneself," his old mother had grumbled.

Stefano fondly caressed the grey head. "It's not everyday that one gets married."

"Some do nowadays."

The mother looked at the merriment all around, the bride in virgin white lace-work, the fine net headdress swept back over the bouffant hairdo, the groom awkward in an overly tight worsted suit, the carafes of wine passed from hand to hand down the table amidst the vociferous diners raising their glasses to sudden peals of cheer and laughter.

She looked at her own family, seated around her, Anna cutting up a slice of roast too stubborn for her arthritic fingers, the grandchildren, now youngsters, sat beside her, Stefano on his feet saluting a late guest. A sigh of contentment escaped her aged lungs. She had lived for this, her whole world, the days of hardship through the long years of the war far behind now, the older grandson planting on her time-worn face a kiss with greasy lips, the memento of a closing season of life of satisfaction and fulfilment. A family close and warm, she the heart.

    A sunlit scene, a lifetime in the making. Perhaps it was just as well that she would not live long enough to see the cloudburst make its sure way towards this small world of hers.

5

Tall and slender, the long blond tresses cascading and curling down on to the shoulders, features pronounced and lips with a slight pout, she was as much of an attraction at the Bellini car showroom as the sleek sedans and sportsters spread across the shiny marble flooring. Passers-by paused to look through the glass frontage, their attention held by the long, turned legs below a knee-length tartan skirt moving brisk with sure steps as Gabriella showed visitors the model of their particular interest. Some of the male onlookers thought the young lady could be put to better employ than welcoming customers in an auto saloon.

"A pretty face turns heads no less than a shiny new car," one of the importers in Milan had cracked, slapping Stefano on the back and directing his gaze towards the showroom receptionist, a vampish creature bosom heavy and with a shimmying walk.

Who better than Gabriella, then, a cousin of his wife, her aspirations to be an airline hostess defeated by the extravagant height, the staff selector muttering under his breath that the airline's onboard hospitality didn't stretch to hostesses sticking their '*culos*' in passangers' faces when serving drinks and dinner. "He himself wouldn't have much minded if I'd stuck my backside in *his* face!" Gabriella blurted half in tears on returning home, dismayed that her innocent derrière could be cause of ruin of her heart's desire.

The next best thing was the typing school. That not only chipped and cracked the nails on the slender fingers, but also offered a most dreary prospect compared to the long dreamt of days flying about through the clouds in the company of the elegant and affluent heading towards destinations colourful and exotic. Stefano's unexpected offer came as a godsend, that would allow her to open her flighty wings. Got up in a pink or violet silk blouse and skirts that moulded to perfection her high rear, a smile enchanting, both angelic and seductive, she welcomed customers and draped herself on the shiny new cars as Stefano showed the would-be buyer around the saloon. "The young lady is an optional, I expect. Not included in the price?" one middle-aged industrialist jested, momentarily distracted by Gabriella's languid pose from Stefano's earnest declamation of the virtues of the five-bearing crankshaft.

Stefano himself had undergone a sea-change. Approaching mid-age, broader in girth with a prosperous middle, the jowls heavier, hairline in recession, good-natured and good-humoured as ever, money and success had changed him little, if at all. But if previously his daytime uniform had been that of a garage-hand, a checked cotton shirt or turtle neck sweater for after hours at home, a baggy suit for Sunday service, weddings, baptisms, and funerals, now his habitual dress had become a well-cut, double-breasted suit and a regimental tie, classic tan brogues always polished to a mirror-shine. All in all, the appearance of a well-heeled business figure, calm and assuring, with an intimate expertise of nuts and bolts that persuaded customers they were in good and trusted hands. Out for a test drive, he would silently gesture the precise moment to shift the synchromesh gear, to lend ear to an unfriendly engine sound, all of which impressed especially younger buyers.

A respected figure in the community, member of the local Chamber of Commerce, often present in public ceremonial events, celebrations and commemorations, Stefano was seen as the archetype of a generation that had risen from the ruins and made good, the epitome of success that heralded the rebirth of the country. But unlike many of his kind, gain and fortune had not changed his persona. Prosperity worn light, manifest only in his wear and appearance, his workday habit long as ever, shuttling between the salon and the old garage, pleasures and pastimes measured, the odd short weekend foray with the wife to the small apartment he had bought down on the coast, the summer break, when business shut down, on the Adriatic seaside with the boys, he could not have imagined or wished for more than the blessings that had come his way.

    The father gone, the mother following a few years later, the old childhood house was still home, renovated and enlarged to accommodate the growing sons, with heating installed and a pensioner coming in to see to the garden and tending the vegetable patch, whose produce still supplemented the family's diet. For the rest, evenings at home, dining at the same table where he had sat as an infant, settled by the kitchen fire with Anna, at ease and peace, recounting some small event from the day: a down at the heel noble man, baron or count, coming in daily to eye sadly an expensive roadster; the repeat visits by a factory owner, as also several other middle-aged men, calling at the showroom more to inspect and court Gabriella rather than buy a car. "More a matrimonial agency than an auto saloon!" he laughed.

    The two boys come of age, Stefano in his mind had already charted the course of their future. The dealership highly remunerative, the ever increasing car sales countrywide keeping the garage busy round-the-clock, with a couple of new hands added to the workforce, there was place for both the sons in the family business. Not only profession, his designs for their lives also provided for how and where they were to live. A disgraced banker, brought to his knees by graft and scandal, disposing of his properties in haste, Stefano had bought up the Villa Serena at less than half its value. There the families of Lorenzo and Leonardo would reside, when finally they came to marry.

~~~

Lorenzo and Leonardo were as unlike as two brothers could be. Lorenzo, named after his mother's father, had taken after Stefano, in build and nature, tall and sturdy, sunny in disposition, mild-tempered and good-humoured. Leonardo not only bore Stefano's father's name, resembling the grandfather in stature and appearance, he also carried the imprint of a sober and thoughtful mind, not particularly gregarious nor much given to the pleasure and leisures of the young.

Rising at first light, pulling on his boots, a small half-cup of scalding coffee sipped in haste, Lorenzo would silently leave the house with his Beretta Savage shotgun underarm, to join a few friends and scale the slopes towards the wooded heights overlooking the lake, to sit silent in a leafy shooting station in wait for the flocks migrating down from the cold autumn air towards the warmth of the south. Leonardo preferred to stay in bed, rise later, wander down to the news stall, and sit at table eyeing the local paper. His brother coming in late-morning with the haul, a dozen wagtails, a score of songbirds, that his mother would be serving up at dinner, Leonardo could not help wincing at the sight of the heap of bloodied feathers. "Whatever else he might decide to do, Leo won't be doing doctoring," his mother said to Stefano, when time came to decide if the boys were to go on to higher studies.

Less than studious, his profit at study little more than meagre, some of his teachers' favours earned with amicable discounts when their autos came to the garage for repairs, Lorenzo enrolled at the local technical college. With his interest in motors and engines, he did better with the rudiments of mechanical engineering than with the doings of the ancient

Romans, the poems of Catullo and the long-winded prose of Manzoni studied at school. Afternoons he often passed at the garage with the mechanics, soiling his hands and gaining practical knowledge of the textbook learning gleaned in the classroom. In this, too, he had taken after his father. Stefano approved, thinking then that when the time came, the business would be in sound hands. Easy-going and taking things as they came, with never a serious brush with his father, nor a trace of the customary rebellious gesture of the young, making free with the girls in town but never settling with anyone in particular, never hesitating to put out a helping hand when called on, Lorenzo seemed the son that many a parent might have wished for.

Slender, with finer lineaments drawn from his mother, Leonardo had sprung more from his grandfather's mould. Not reticent or withdrawn, instead thoughtful and measured in speech, mild of manner, Leonardo had more a mind of his own. Seemingly not over keen on the family business, with no marked interest in cars and their workings, only very occasionally he dropped in at the showroom briefly, to be teased and tickled by Gabriella who, in her usual mirthful manner, announced to anyone present, "Here's the family thinker!"

Lorenzo was presented on his eighteenth birthday with a used Lancia Fulvia coupé traded in by a customer, on which he would roar down the road winding along the lake with some pretty young playmate of the moment. Leonardo declined when came his turn and offered a similar gift, preferring a battered Autobianchi that had sat in a corner of the garage neglected and abandoned. Dissembling with a hearty pat and saying, "Thank heavens we have someone frugal in the family," Stefano masked whatever rebuff he might have felt, and wondered.

He had never knowingly made a distinction between the older son and the younger. Their clothing bought in pairs in the same store, footwear near identical, the money in their pockets weighing the same almost, his gaze filled with the same luminous warmth when his eyes came to rest on them. Nor was there a discernable distinction in his mind when he thought of their future, the Villa Serena that had come into his hands to be shared by both and their families, the business an even partnership, the one seeing to the nuts and bolts, the other managing the finances and paperwork. Never even in his dreams would he have imagined that he could entertain partiality and preference.

"Sometimes we think we are fair. Without the least bias," said Fabbri with a distant air, as one afternoon we walked about through the rooms of the old family home, now enclosed with scaffolding and undergoing major renovation. Once among the fields, the house surrounded by farmland, over the years the town had invaded the countryside, cementing large patches with residential property, workshops, small factories, warehouses.

"Grandfather Stefano was even-handed with everyone," Fabbri went on, his eyes scanning the squat, square villas with washing hung out in the small gardens planted here and there with gnomes and statuettes. "No different with his sons. How does one choose between one child and another? It's not a conscious choice, I don't think. My father was his double in every way, in looks, habits, tastes. Yet grandad had a soft spot for Leonardo. Maybe because he was different."

He shook his and, turning back from the bright noon sunlight outside, added, "I don't know. I was very young. And then it was too late."

~~~

When the call-up came, Stefano went to work to allow Lorenzo to wriggle out of the two-year military service. Anna thought he ought to go, less a sense of patriotism, but that it would make a man out of him. Her husband thought the two years wasted, idling in ramshackle barracks in some provincial town in the company of illiterate youngsters from the south, a rag-tag army barely able to tell the butt of a rifle from the muzzle, that was meant to hold up the Red Army that would one day sweep down from the East. Besides, the boy was man enough already, had talent and interest in what he did, and had begun to ease into the business without undue effort.

By then Stefano was known in the town, the auto salon and success opening doors to rub shoulders with those who counted. A familiar face in the municipal offices, on friendly terms with the mayor, acquainted with officers of the finance police and the Carabinieri, it did not take undue effort to obtain the release from conscription. Despite the young man's robust frame, sound heart and keen hunter's sight, the army doctor found Lorenzo's physique less than fit for military endeavour.

A year later, the papers arrived for Leonardo. Postponing plans to take up law studies, he said he would go. For almost the first time a shadow fell between father and son. Stefano was pleased, and proud, at the thought of a lawyer in the family. It would help with the occasional legal tangles encountered in the affairs of the showroom, saving too the often outrageous honorariums charged by lawyers and law firms for merely drafting a letter or notice. Besides, there was time enough if one day Leo decided to come into the business.

The choice of honouring the military service was quite another matter. A waste of time, talent, and the energy of youth. Sustained by his mother, Leonardo would not be moved. Nor did he want the underhand stratagems employed for his brother. It was not in Stefano to put out a heavy hand, not at work nor out in the world, even less so with his boy. With reluctant heart, he gave his paternal consent. Even so, dropping after dinner into his seat by the fire with a sigh, he said, "You know Anna, two years at Leo's age is equal to ten at our time of life." In any case, he added, the family had paid its dues towards the fatherland, meaning Anna's father who had perished in the Russian wastes.

With his schooling, Leonardo was qualified to enrol in the junior officer class. Stefano urged he do so, thinking it better suited his mind and mild disposition. A desk job, quiet and undemanding, easing the rigorous of barrack life, offering time, too, for his love of books and habit of solitude. There, too, Leonardo said no, he preferred the life of the foot-soldiering, common conscript.

Not one to linger long over a grievance or misgiving, Stefano accepted with good grace his son's wilful decision, rethinking instead plans for the future. Nothing much changed, merely a delay of a couple of years. Returned from military service, law studies completed in Milan, Leonardo would article as clerk in some local law office, finally setting up on his own with a legal firm in the town. Meanwhile, should he decide to wed his pretty Laura, the Villa Serena was ready to lodge the couple and the offspring to come. Meanwhile, too, Lorenzo would be taken on as associate partner in the auto business, along with half the villa at his disposal whenever he decided to call it a day in his flirtatious romping to settle into married life.

There was this in Stefano, faith in the future and trust in providence, life a succession of days to be lived with good cheer and without undue concern, taking things in their stride, the well and the ill as they came. Never chiding nor censorious, yet Anna did at times think her husband lived in a world of ever unclouded skies.

One late autumn morning, then, they set off across the flat northern plain shrouded in a mantle of impenetrable fog through which men and machine crept at the pace of a blind snail. Turning south finally, the air clearing and a tepid sun breaking through, they drove towards the small town on the slopes of the Apennines where Leonardo was to be stationed.

The new conscript received and registered at the barracks, they made their way towards an eatery for a last family gathering.

Oddly named *Clinica Gastronomica,* half-concealed in a clearing in the wooded hills above the town, the restaurant's over-rich and bounteous offering was more likely to necessitate a visit afterwards to a medical clinic. The spread along the length of the bare, hardwood table a veritable feast for the eye for both gourmet and gourmand, they stood back in wonder at a sight never seen where they came from. Eyeing the platters heaped with cured meats, boar and venison, fowls of the air, thick-sliced rounds of salami and anise-flavoured sausage, fresh wood mushroom grilled and conserve of artichoke hearts, it was a long minute before they took their seats, Lorenzo reaching on the instant for a thick-cut piece of bread freshly baked in a wood-fired oven by the side of the stone building.

Lorenzo could not help noticing, as well, the peculiar yet seemingly familiar appearance of the host. "It's him. Adolf!" he whispered under his breath, to the puzzlement of the family.

"Adolf who?" Stefano looked around, thinking Lorenzo had seen a known face.

"The one and only Adolf. The Führer. So this is where he's been hiding out all these years."

And, indeed, of middling height and rounded girth, with a snatch of short-trimmed dark hair swept half-way across the high front and a tooth-brush moustache under the pointed nose, the resemblance was startling. No less the manner, cordial but reserved, movement measured and martial, ordering about with a martinet air the young couple who served the guests. "Wine!" he snapped his fingers, pointing to the Bellinis' table.

The amusing discovery lightening the weariness from the long day's drive, they settled down to the cornucopian feast, Lorenzo's never less than hearty appetite working its way through the several hot courses that followed, Leo ever moderate but basking content in the familial warmth.

Not quite the Last Supper, but perhaps it was the very last time they would be as they had always been, close-knit, without reserve or restraint, minds open and hearts unconditioned. Nor could they have imagined that in the not too distant time to come doubt and suspect would worm their way into their lives, the toxin of hurt and spite spreading through the veins, infecting mind and being, demanding reckoning, if not blood.

Some month and a half into my stay, invited to his elegant apartments overlooking the waters of the lake, sipping an after-dinner drink, Fabbri's eyes lingered briefly on the photograph in a slender silver frame on the side table, a black and white print, hazy, of two young boys in shorts stood under a leafy tree.

"Sometimes God's forgiveness is easier to come by than that of men," he said with a knowing nod, a faint reminiscence of sorrow tingeing the even tone.

Orphaned in childhood, the sole offspring of the Bellini family and heir to its fortunes, there was an oddity that made for curiosity. I had it in mind to ask why he had not inherited the family name. But lowering his head, his gaze lost in the liquid-gold in the cut-glass crystal, he appeared to have retraced his steps to a distant past. For the moment I doused my intrusive interest with a long sip of the sweet liqueur.

6

The heart now sank as I leafed through the several note pads and the dairies of journeys, encounters and meetings, the pages packed with annotations, comments, references and reading lists. A long year's labour sitting in libraries, delving into archives, shifting through papers and documents, burning the midnight oil reading up narrations contemporary and of the past, the dry as dust accounts of academics and savants. All to what purpose? It was not as if the world at large waited with bated breath for yet another biographical record of the wanderings in the metaphysical universe of a Dutch-Portuguese Sephardic Jew in search of a new God.

    The project had been well received by the Foundation and the liberal grant was endowed without much debate or discussion. Neither dry dissertation nor a run-of-the mill biography, the narrative was meant to trace the wandering footsteps of Baruch Spinoza's short and frugal journey towards the demise of medieval faith and, unwittingly, in favour of an all-pervasive Vedantic deity. Friends and associates approved, my sister Mya more dubious, her keener female perception reading into my flight a hasty escape from an altered existence. Breathing now the pristine air coming down from the range of mountains, beginning to savour once again the small pleasures life offered, it began to dawn on me that possibly she was not far wrong.

Our acquaintance gradually easing into a friendship of sorts, drawing on his classical lyceum education, one day Fabbri put it succinctly. He had dropped by to look into some dislodged tiles that let in water into one of the rooms. A distracted air about him and, gazing out at the creaseless waters of the lake receding in the distance into the sunlit haze of a late spring day, he said quietly, as if to himself, *"Καινούριους τόπους δεν θα βρεις, δεν θάβρεις άλλες θάλασσες…"* Stepping away from the window, offering me a thin smile, he shook his head briefly. "How true! No, there's no new land, no other shore."

There were times, I discovered, when he appeared to absent himself from the hour, his thoughts briefly wandering off into regions misty and, apparently, undecipherable to the listener as he dropped a few words, a remark apropos of nothing, unrelated to the task at hand. But knowing now something of the hinterland of his life, I thought I understood the momentary absence from the present. The deranged theatre that had moulded his childhood and youth was a shroud he had seemingly never quite managed to shed, an ectoplasm that at odd moments came alive, briefly woke to sentient life a sense of stoic desolation.

No new land, no other shore. If, for Fabbri, they were the syllables of an echo from a past that refused to depart, perhaps they were quite as pertinent to my state of affairs, but in an obverse manner. My loss was not mired in blood, the destitution infinitely more mundane, merely grief at the abrupt absence of the companion of a lifetime, a common enough occurrence that made for the parting of friends, lovers, man and wife. And yet, overwhelmed by the sudden and unexpected obliteration of the habitual latitudes of a long and settled existence, groping in the darkness of hours and days without purpose and destination, I had thought to seek temporary refuge in the existentialist contortions of Spinoza's tortuous journey of the mind. A sort of cerebral hermitage, that banished the sentient, love and loss, pain and sufferance. Thinking back made one wonder if the feint and play-acting would have been better served by donning the saffron robe and retiring to some mountain cave!

Fabbri knew little of my own circumstances, merely the bare facts of my recent widowerhood and the year's sabbatical to author a book. Moving now from room to room to inspect the ceiling for traces of the leakage, he threw me a thoughtful glance, to say, "This place is too big for you. I ought to have offered you an apartment. There are several near mine."

"Thank you, Roberto. I happen to like it here."

"Maybe then you should get yourself a family. An instant family!"

Going down the corridor, he peered into the little room that had become my study. "May I?"

I moved aside to let him in.

"This was my nest. I must have been two or three then." He surveyed the disorder on the writing table. "A man at work!"

"Not much. Life's too pleasant here. Far too comfortable. And Maria's cooking…"

"Be careful! You'll be doubling your weight by the time you leave!"

Following in Alina's footsteps as she went about her cleaning chores, I too had taken to watching the rich and idle. Summer at the door, the days lengthening, defeated by friend Spinoza's insistence on divine presence everywhere and in all things, at times I rose from the table to stand at the window whole long minutes, to gaze at the unchanging view next door. The colours of the first summer blooms on the grounds of the mansion softening in the late afternoon light, the sick man reclining motionless, as ever, on the chaise lounge, the tall nurse stooping over him or sat by the side, perhaps reading a book. A comforting and picturesque postcard view of a clinic or nursing home.

Fabbri and I now stood together looking down in silence. "Moribund," he snorted. "One of these days the bastard will be taking his leave. And he's not going to heaven, for sure!"

"Not many do these days," I managed, more than a little taken aback. "The nurse…"

"Nurse! The only thing she's ever nursed is a male between her legs."

Startled, I stared at Fabbri. Ever mannered and urbane, measured in speech, never a word out of place, crass or gross, it came as something of a shock to hear him now. True to his habit, he uttered the words, offensive, calumnious possibly, in his ever even tone, without the least air of spite or malice. If at all, there was a trace of acid in the voice. For all that, he might have been remarking on the weather, casual and in passing.

Turning away from the moment, I asked if he knew of the man on the chaise lounge.

"Göttner. Armin von Göttner. You may have heard of him."

It did ring a bell, but not quite loud enough. I shook my head.

"Genius, maestro, conductor sans pareil. Wagnerian. And quite as nasty a character. A proper bastard."

"Really?"

"Obviously the obituaries will be sanitized. Only eulogy, homage and praise, from colleagues and critics, most of whom wouldn't have minded sticking a knife in him in a dark alleyway."

Rolling the name on the tongue, it came to me after a moment. A behemoth on the musical scene once, if I remembered right.

Fabbri met my recall with a deprecating laugh. "More a brontosaurus now! And almost extinct."

Myrna was the music-minded in the family, faithful subscriber to the season's offerings and inveterate concert-goer, and appreciably able, too, at the keyboard. Not quite philistine, nor much familiar with the nuts and bolts of double flats and the octave clef, I went along for the ride and the glass of wine in the interval between suite and symphony, and an enjoyable evening was had by all. A lifetime together, breathing the very same air, tastes and preferences close and entwined, music was perhaps the one interest that kept us slightly apart, hers a consuming passion, mine more amateur divertissment. Myrna once chided me severely when after the performance by a visiting East European ensemble, I remarked that the orchestra must have been in a hurry to get to dinner to have cut short the time of the Beethoven symphony by several minutes. Musicians, whatever their standing, stood tall in her pantheon of heroes and dieties.

Göttner I had never perhaps seen wave his baton, but it was a name heard bandied and repeated in vociferous discussions at the dinner table between Myrna and her like-minded friends as they cited the giants and titans of the classical musical world, Walter and Furtwängler wedged between the hors d'oeuvres and first course, Toscanini held in store for the equally honest caramel flan or tarte tatin. Lending scant ear to whether Mahler would have lent himself to the new atonality had he lived, I helped myself to a second helping of whatever the pudding or dessert.

"The world's forgotten him. And just as well," Fabbri added dismissively, turning away from the window.

On the way out he revealed that it was he who years ago had arranged the purchase of the mansion by the celebrated musician, almost his first big sale after starting the estate agency. "And I've lived to regret it ever since," he said with a ponderous sigh.

I could not understand the vehement detestation for the illustrious figure. Some misunderstanding over the transaction, perhaps. Hardly warranting, though, such harsh words so long after.

And what of the less than subtle and malicious innuendo reserved for the woman? It carried something of the bitter after-taste of the private and personal. But it was more than that, I was soon to discover. Ursula von Göttner's short operatic career might have ended in a provincial theatre amidst derision and laughter, but her lead role of femme fatale in the final act of the Bellini family drama would surely have earned a thunderous standing ovation.

7

The two-year military service over, Leonardo returned home to an unexpectedly changed scene. The parents well as ever, the business still prospering, Lorenzo now at the helm alongside his father, the townscape finally healed from the last scars of the war with new apartment buildings, hotels and shops, no major or visible alterations otherwise in sight, and yet the earth threatened to give way under Leonardo's feet.

He had first met Laura at school and the years at the lyceum had made them inseparable, seemingly made for each other, with eyes for no one and none else. Puppy love, the family thought, Lorenzo occasionally teasing, to say, "And when are you bringing the bride home?" Leonardo did not mind the ribbing, it was his brother's way.

Not one for depths and the designs of the interior, Lorenzo himself could not understand the bonding between the two. Admittedly, Laura boasted an uncommon beauty, slender and bosomy, but it was the face that drew attention and could take the breath away, the lineaments of a Renaissance virgin, the dark gemstones of the eyes under stencil-drawn brows setting off the snow-white pallor of the skin.

Virgin she might have been, graceful and with the stare of a deer, but with a liveliness in look and speech that infused life into the air around her. So different and apart from Leonardo's meditated manner and meagre words that Lorenzo could find nothing in common that brought and kept them together. Then, too, Laura found relish in the good things of everyday life, food and dress, evenings out in company, mirth and merry-making. If at all, dropping in of an occasion at the Bellini's, she found common cause with Lorenzo, sharing his hearty inclination at table, the ease and simple talk, the good-natured banter with the parents.

Of modest stock, like the Bellinis, the Fabbri family's fortunes had taken wing after the war. Metal working in the blood, the name Fabbri earned by some ancestor beating out horse-shoes over an open fire, the once small workshop turning out mainly bicycle wheel spokes and nipples had grown to a modern factory with a workforce of several dozen, the imported cold wire drawing German machinery working round the clock to meet the ever growing demand of the rapid industrialization across the north of the country. Alongside, a second plant turning out narrow gauge steel tubing had come up in recent years.

If the origins were similar to that of the Bellinis, the new wealth was worn differently by the Fabbri family. An expansive villa of uncertain architectural ancestry, part Mediterranean, part hacienda, with a touch of late-Baroque here and there, housed the grand-parents and Laura's parents and brother. Surrounded by ample grounds planted with fruit trees, the two storied villa itself was crowded with faux antique hardwood furniture, paintings of local artists covering entire walls, costly bric-a-brac, coloured mirrors, imitation Greek urns, statues and statuettes. A home décor that bespoke more new-found wealth, less taste and discernment.

The Fabbris' living and habits were no less conspicuous. Laura's father drove a Mercedes, her brother a Lancia Fulvia coupé, their jackets and suiting in Ermenegildo Zegna fabrics. The mother had her hair coiffured weekly and went outdoors in flowing Como silk. Winter breaks found the family in

Cervinia or Courmayeur, summer in a spacious villa on the Italian Riviera. At home, a couple of local women, a cook and a maid, saw to the household chores. And at the lyceum Laura's small Gucci shoulder bag was the envy of her school mates.

If ostentation it was, at times bordering on the showy and redundant, it was also the naivete of innocence, of those who had made good with toil and ingenuity. The fruits of the new affluence relished without practised flair or particular finesse, it was seen as recompense and conquest for those whose feet had ever trod the mud and earth, bare lives of hardship and fatigue that had never known ease and the comforts of well-being. But as yet unaccustomed to the amenities of the creature comforts that money could buy, habits and inclinations not overmuch changed, they were still and equally at ease if called on to forego the fine linen and silver table ware and dine on bareboards with the wooden ladle doling out the broth. So Laura found nothing much amiss when sat with the Bellinis at a meal, the simple fare served on rustic ceramic crockery rather than bone chinaware. Nor did her parents narrow their eyes with censure when Leonardo came calling in his battered Autobianchi to take Laura out for the evening. Only once, the father teased the young man, pointing to Leonard's jalopy, to say, "I'd not noticed that model in your father's showroom!"

The elder Bellinis were content with Laura's presence beside Leonardo. A fitting companion, they thought, who could infect him with her liveliness, drawing him out of his halting silences and what they took for his timid and distracted air. And, indeed, Leonardo did appear to come alive when in her company, at greater ease with himself and the world, relishing more the joys of the young, an evening out on the town, an afternoon's outing with Laura's brother in his small sail boat. Some holidays, taking the ferry down the lake, they would be away for the day.

Not surprisingly, then, the two families quite expected that with Leonardo's military service over, their studies completed, the couple would settle into marriage. Leonardo, however, never failed to make a wordless face when, in the manner of provincial life, Laura was called his fiancée. Whatever his inclinations and designs for the future, not the briefest thought on the matter ever escaped him out loud. When once or twice his father mentioned the Villa Serena as their future home, Leonardo could merely nod with a wan smile, as though indifferently assenting to some vague detail. And when, more light-humoured than reproachful, Anna remarked that Laura's culinary skills might have to go beyond boiling potatoes and making coffee, he eyed his mother with a look both gentle and aloof. "Yes, a man's palate makes of the wife a cook, they say" he pronounced vaguely, as though wanting to distance the talk from the personal.

During Leonardo's absence, in the early months of the call-up, they wrote to each other weekly, his letters lengthier and more weighty, Laura's mainly half a sheet, mostly jottings about her time at the local institute training in book-keeping and accounting. Not overmuch a lovelorn exchange, it might well have been a correspondence between friends. It was not in Leonardo's veins to offer floral tributes of romance, nor did Laura give the impression of the maiden pining for her absent swain. Sober and measured, he wrote of his surrounds, the habits of the small town perched on the hills, of the haughty air of senior officials, a race distinct from the raw young recruits from the south, barely literate and speaking a tongue largely indecipherable for the northern ear, a ragtag soldiery with outdated weaponry, that was meant to hold at bay the hordes who would one day come pouring from the Russian Steppes.

Leonardo's weekly mail arrived punctually, constant and unfailing. But with the passing months, Laura's correspondence became halting and erratic, failing by a fortnight, for several weeks. She offered cursory excuses, examinations at the institute, the autumn flu, the grandfather's failing health.

Leonard perhaps noticed, but made nothing of it. Trusting by nature, unable to espy bad faith, not the least suspicion or alarm disturbed his thoughts. He had been home on leave a time or two, meanwhile, and his Laura had appeared very much as she had always been, warm and gregarious. And if there were stretches of silence between them when alone together, he was sightless to the breach, putting it down to her thoughts for the future, some dissent in her family.

Nor did he discern the faint, premonitory signs, the reticence of his parents in mentioning Laura by name. The changes becoming increasingly visible and noticeable during the end of his first year of service, Leonardo merely wondered in passing at idle moments. Home on a week's leave, he was surprised by her fleeting presence, ever in a hurry and merely stopping over bare minutes for a perfunctory greeting.

Lorenzo, as well, seemed distracted and vaguely ill at ease at times, and not quite the free-wheeling Romeo out carousing in the town evenings and nights with friends and the kissing mate of the moment. Leonardo did not ask or question, putting down the brother's unusually ruminative mien to the looming petrol crisis and falling sales at the showroom.

If sight and insight failed to discern the family air tinged with reticence, the furloughs, brief and welcome though they were, he found oddly dreary and tiresome. Ever glad of the presence of his mother, to sit at table waiting for her to bring in the steaming bowl, the dish with the rich sauce waking appetite, the benign gaze of his father across the board, warm with an affection unspoken, yet something seemed to have gone amiss during his absence. Changes slight and barely noticeable, some writing on the wall, barely illegible, that might have drawn the attention of a suspect mind, not Leonardo's. Ever trusting in the good faith and goodwill of man, it was beyond him to conceive that there might be secrets within the walls of home, that were kept out of his view and reach. If at all, Laura's spare presence and unaccustomed reserve at times made for mere passing notice. It was Nature's way, he accepted, that a young woman's thoughts should turn to the future, marriage and home-making. After all, not a few of her age were already on their way towards the bridal vow.

~~~

The years of military service saw Leonardo draw down the shades ever more, keeping out the light of day, turning inwards, his own thoughts the food for his mind. Nothing in common with those around him, difficult possible communion with the other conscripts, unlearned young men, infantile and juvenile, who passed long, listless afternoons cleaning and polishing obsolete weaponry under the martinet gaze of some bloated sergeant major, while waiting week-long for the brief, Sunday airing out of the cage, to wander the cobbled streets of the ancient town with a loose-change allowance that barely sufficed for a packet of cigarettes. Not surprisingly, Leonardo made no friends, free hours immersed in the pages of the handful of books he had brought with him, Suetonius's *Lives of the Caesers*, Tacitus, Cellini's *Autobiography*. Once in a while, one or two of the young men, farm hands from the islands, dictated short missives to their families, that he wrote out in a neat hand.

His own correspondence had fallen by the wayside. Each fortnight he punctually put pen to paper for his parents, calling home, too, when out in the town, over a crackly line from a telephone in some bar. Laura he could rarely find at home at the given hour. Her letters, as well, had gone missing months ago and he himself wrote spare lines on a rare occasion.

Home for Easter the second year, he found she had gone skiing with her family to Cervinia over the holiday break. And Lorenzo with them. She had not told him, which was odd, knowing as she did that he'd be home. Odder still that Lorenzo should have accompanied the Fabbris. Learning of the absence from his mother, there was a long silence. He did not quiz her, merely retreated into himself, papering over the unexpected surprise with spare talk of life in the barracks, enquiries into the father's trade. No further mention of Laura, nor of Lorenzo, by him or the parents, nothing more was said for the rest of the short stay.

Taking leave of his parents for the return, he felt curious to be glad to get away. Watching from the carriage the countryside roll by as the ancient carriage trundled at an infirm pace by the small villages increasingly turning into townships with new residences and newer factories, he felt an odd sense of estrangement. The place of his birth, the familiar old streets with their little family shops, the baker and butcher, the bars and news stands, the enchanted view of the lake ensconced between the cliffed ridges rising to the sky, all now seemed the tiresome frame of a tedious existence, the monotone of provincial life where ignorance and banality reigned supreme, the talk infinitely repetitive, rumour and gossip ever the same, all eyes peering and prying into the personal, with little or nothing private, nothing spared or sacred. And now, dirt poverty banished, indigence a fading memory, the new wealth preened and paraded in a brazen show unaware of its own loud and risible ostentation. Laura's family came to mind, and it made for unease.

It was not as though he had gone off to some shiny metropolis, a city of life and lights, had beheld sights and wonders to take the breath away. Nor had the distance over the past year and a half lessened in any measure his love and loyalties, to his parents, to Lorenzo. Nor had his designs for the future changed perceptibly, the path charted out towards a legal career, marriage to Laura one day when his studies were done and he could stand on his own feet.

If there was change at all, it was to do with an increasingly restive unwillingness of the heart to settle back in the town, to live a whole life within the narrow confines of parochial small-mindedness, petty talk and petty envies, the discord and disputes of the past still lingering in the air. One day, out in the street, he had overheard two women looking at his father at talk with a customer in the showroom, the elder saying, "Just look at him, giving himself grand airs." And once, in a bar, Lorenzo raising his hand in reply to a half-inebriated sneer at the card table by a municipal clerk: "We all know where the Bellini's come from!" That Stefano had made good was intolerable to many. It was the way of small-town life, and Leonardo wanted no part of it.

Some months later, it was a day that would stay with Leonardo. A long Indian summer, with an unusually warm autumn afternoon, the woods on the hills still in leaf, burnished reddish green and russet, he had wandered aimless in a daze down the narrow cobbled streets hemmed in by squat medieval stone houses, the town dormant at the hour, with only a few elderly about, shops dimly lit, the bars empty save for small group's of conscripts on their Sunday outing.

The mail delivered the previous day, somehow the correspondence had sat overnight on the commanding officer's desk, the letter handed to him only late morning. Tucked deep in his uniform pocket, it had all the weight of a boulder that had swept down the mountain and laid waste his very existence. Leisurely tearing open the envelope, his eyes had settled on the unexpected and never imagined, nor imaginable, his senses awash with confusion. Unable to grasp the sense of the spare lines, he had read and reread the contents, as though the words had drifted onto the paper by chance and would lift and disappear any moment.

It was not the usual spare lines the parents wrote him each fortnight, with odd bits and pieces on the family, snatches of news from the town, the passing of one of his teachers at the lyceum, the birth of a baby girl to one of the garage hands. Usually, too, it was his mother who wrote, but this time Anna's hand was absent. Stefano had put down with the lettering of his uneven scribble a message that was less a fatherly missive, more a terse and formal communique. To say that Lorenzo and Laura were engaged, would marry sometime in the spring, the date yet to be settled. No more, nor less, it ended as it had begun, brief and abrupt. At the bottom of the sheet, as though meaning to ready a balm for a wound that was about to open, a few lines in Anna's flowing hand had added:

Dearest Leo,
The light in this house has been dim in your absence. When soon you're back, to stay, our days will be brighter. Your father and I have missed you every single day and each moment we wait your return home. We love you with all our heart, now and always.
Mamma

There was this about Leonardo, never to slump and seek shelter. As a child, vexed or hurt, he had never run into his mother arms, never sought solace in his father's sturdy embrace. If tears there were, they fell in solitary drops, away from public gaze, never crying out or moaning, drawing into himself, making private and unseen whatever the pain. Where Lorenzo was loud in his remonstrance, he preferred to retreat into a corner within, putting away in storage the injury and misery.

It was no different now. The body-blow suffered, there was no outpouring of blood, the desolation of abandonment seeping in, to gather in a recess where it lay alive but dormant, never stirring into life, nor calling for retribution or revenge. Nor was he much given to recall, ruminating over grievances of the past, the wrong suffered simply a ballast carried in silence. In the days to come he never once voiced reproach or odium for the reprehensible fraternal act, shutting the betrayal out of sight, and apparently out of mind. Provoking curiosity among friends, his parents, Lorenzo himself, it also made for a rift that would endure till the end. The past falling away, loosening familial ties, distancing him from the place of his birth and the scenes of youth, he thought he would make his life elsewhere, a divide to leave behind the loss and pain.

8

There was something theatrical about the woman, not forced or obvious, more studied and meditated, gestures limited but eloquent, the eyes mimicking the movements of the hand, the head tilting back with the short burst of a laugh, the smile seductive, ironic or mocking at times, accompanied with a gaze intent. There was, then, the hyperbole, unexpected, in the midst of sober talk. "Always looking for a woman's entrance," she once abruptly veered off briefly from the doleful recounting of her father's lubricious habits and the long years of violation suffered. Or, again, speaking of her years at the clinic nursing men in the last throes of life, "Sometimes one found a dead man's hand up the skirt and between the legs!"

    The presence, posture and mannerisms recalling to mind some figure from the past, she could well have been a diva of a bygone age, a Dietrich or Rita Hayworth, fluid in movement, filling the eye and wakening the senses to recondite cravings. Not quite willowy, figure full and lineaments strong, northern, bones more pronounced, lips heavier. Tall, a head higher than most men, statuesque and stately, both grace and boldness in stride, one could not fail to notice when she entered a room or swept past, proud, almost regal. When first she gave me her sure hand, I was unsure if simply to take it, or bow, as well. "Ursula von Göttner." And then, in a voice low, somewhat throaty, "We have been waiting to meet you." The tone denoting almost a patient expectation of a long awaited event. When she chose to do so, Ursula made one feel earnestly welcome, getting off her high horse and offering warm access to her home, to her person with some.

Unexpected and something of a surprise when Maria handed me the envelope addressed in a neat, cursive hand and I extracted the note on the white laid letter paper embossed at the top with the von Göttner family coat of arms, a medieval crucifix set between crossed swords in a dark red escutcheon crowned with a horned Teutonic helmet, the motto beneath reading *IN SANGUINE FIDES*. It said simply:

Dear Neighbour,
It would offer much pleasure to have you
with us for the evening this coming Friday.
Dinner is at 9 pm, but do come earlier, if
you possibly can.
We await your word.
Ursula von Göttner.

Recalling friend Fabbri's damning words about the great man next door, no less the less than complementary description of the lady, I felt at sea for a moment. Yet where was the harm. Merely a good neighbourly gesture. Some baked a pie and sent it over to the newcomers, a token of courteous welcome. Or else, a simple invitation to dinner to get to know the strangers and satisfy whatever the curiosity. If anything, Fabbri had aroused my own curiosity, even as at times I briefly watched from the window the still-life scene of the sick man stretched on his chaise lounge and the woman in the guise of a nurse, complete with nursing cap, sat alongside through long afternoons. There were two other female attendants in white tunics who in turn came and went, directed by the seated figure to fetch and carry, she herself never far or absent. It had not occurred to me to ask

Fabbri why the lady of the house should be got up in nurse's uniform, and the peculiarity made for added interest.

Down at the wineshop, a well-stocked emporium with epicurian foodstuffs, a select choice of cured meats and legs of ham, an impressive display of cheeses and long shelves crowded with wines native and imported, I enquired of the stout, ruddy-faced owner if he had German clientele and their preference in the line of spirits. "Oh, beer mostly. But… they'll drink anything alcoholic at hand! This should more than do," he nodded, expertly wrapping in vine-printed paper the two boxes of overly pricey champagne I had set down on the counter. "And if they don't like it, the worse for them!" he said cheerfully, tying the gold ribbon into a bow with a flourish. The following afternoon Alina kindly dropped off the bottles next door, along with my note of acceptance and thanks.

The gate opened soundlessly at the touch of the button. Walking up the drive, I saw her appear at the entrance, silhouetted against the brightly lit interior, the entire ground floor illuminated for once. The notes of a live piano floated out in the early evening air, gentle and mellifluous. Clara Wieck, more likely Chopin, but the distinction beyond my musical expertise.

She came down the few short steps, elegant in a flowing ivory pant-suit with a sequinned jacket, that appeared to add to her already considerable height and trimmed the slightly rounded girth of mid-age to reasonably youthful proportions. The face carefully made up to mask the imprint of time, lips a bashful red, the burnished shoulder-length locks of the rich head falling in soft waves with a curl here and there. The upright and commanding presence was accompanied with a smile of studied surprise, but warm and welcoming.

"Ah, here at last! We've been waiting for you." She gave me a firm hand, a large ruby on one long slender finger. "Ursula von Göttner." I gave her mine.

"I thought we ought to meet." She raised her head towards the upper floor of the Villa Serena. "After all the times you've looked down on us!"

Evidently, she had eyes also at the back of her head. "It's a splendid place you have here," I stammered.

"You're not our first visitor from the Villa Serena," she said in a voice oddly low, as she took my arm to lead me up the steps.

That I was not, I knew already, albeit hoping for a fate very different from that of the one who had preceded me through these doors.

Halfway up, pausing to look me up and down, she put out a hand, slipping a finger down the lapel of my jacket. "Oh! But why so formal? It's only an evening at home."

"First impressions, they say."

"Don't I know! First impressions. And they never leave us. When my husband first saw me, I was in a nurse's uniform." She tossed her head back with a light laugh. "And I'm still there, with my nursing cap. You'll have seen that from your window perch, no?"

Her English was pluperfect, albeit slightly harsh, the 's' tending to a pronounced 'z'." No polyglot myself, but it was easy to detect a hard, German undertone.

My Villa Serena was a modest habitat in comparison to the Göttners' mansion with its wide and ample spaces, chambers large enough to seat comfortably a score or more, gilt-edged stucco work on the high ceilings, ornate Second Empire fittings, original or faux it was hard to tell, long velvet drapes and lacquered furniture with floral figures and oriental figurines, damask upholstery on settees and sofas, marbled table tops. Crystal drop chandeliers, large and small, hung from the tall ceilings, thick Ottoman rugs and carpets underfoot. It was hard to imagine from the outside the opulent interiors of a bygone age.

The sumptuous entrance avenue-wide, the shiny marble flooring ran down the mansion, opening out to a spacious hall that then led to an ample terrace with a view of the lake and the town below. A grand piano sat angled in one corner, with a figure head bowed at the keyboard, playing the gentle notes I had heard. Out on the terrace I caught a glimpse of the host stretched on the chaise lounge, much as I had seen him from my window.

Ursula von Göttner and I paused by the piano, until the piece came to an end with a decisive trill and the player lifted a hand high in the air, holding it motionless an over-long moment in a theatrical pose.

"David, come and meet our new neighbour."

The figure rose, mimed a small bow, and came forward. Of middling height and fashionably casual in a light woollen jacket over a collarless beige shirt, in his mid-forties, or thereabouts, lineaments pleasant and boyish, lips sensuous, a head of short, dark blond curls, it was a face I might have seen somewhere, but beyond recall.

He gave me his hand, smooth and warm to the touch. "David Davidovich." I told him mine.

"Sorry about the alliteration," he added, in a voice suave and playful. "Names are the one few things in life not of one's choice."

"David's an old family friend. Lends eminence to our modest home," Ursula smiled, her tone curiously humourless. "May I leave you together? I've to see to Armin's dinner."

Davidovich's eyes followed her as she went out to the terrace, to confer with a nurse leaning over the recumbent figure. "Our host prefers to dine apart," he remarked slightly tight-lipped before turning to me.

"Ah, so you're the new neighbour. Nice little place you have there. I wouldn't have minded it for myself… if Armin and Ursula weren't neighbours!" he chuckled. "And what are you doing in these parts?"

I told him. A year's sabbatical for research. No mention of Spinoza. A name too weighty for an informal evening with strangers!

The ageing man servant, a butler of sorts in a striped jacket buttoned to the neck, long in the face and seemingly long-suffering, appeared silently behind us, holding aloft a silver tray with a couple of long-stemmed glasses well-filled and with pearly bubbles rising to the top.

"Ah, Silvio!" Davidovich greeted the man, picking up one of the crystal flutes and directing me to the other. "Silvio is the clock in this house. Never chimes but punctual at the strike of the hour!"

The man servant half-nodded in acknowledgement and left as silently as he had come.

The name had a ring and a thread of memory took me back some years to a concert hall. "I may have seen you on a stage. Sorry, just can't remember where," I ventured uncertainly, after he had raised a brief toast to our hosts.

"Oh, that! It was in another life."

David Davidovich had been one of the rising stars in the classical firmament, a youthful prodigy and, later, one of the names lauded universally, wherever he sat at a keyboard, at concert halls grand and renowned or of lesser fame, with a repertoire for all preferences, at ease with Scarlatti as much as with Scriabin. Something of a growing legend, about ten years ago he had abruptly disappeared from view, the name still dropped among music lovers, but an enigma and never seen on the stage again.

Here he was now, in flesh and blood, very much alive and whole, no less hale and hearty. Curiosity stirring, a brief pang shot through me. To think that I could have told Myrna of this meeting in person with the great artiste in exile.

"Do you come here often?"

"More often than one might want. And some welcomes are less so." Taking a sip, he clicked his tongue. "Can't be helped, though. It's the maestro's wish. Written into his will, if one can believe it." He turned to address Ursula as she approached. "Excellent fizz, this. You've been saving it for the neighbour, I expect."

"It's the neighbour's fizz!" She gave me a bright smile. "I've not thanked you yet for the kind thought." She took my arm. "Shall we go in?"

The dining room, no less ornate than the rest, with marble-topped lacquer cabinets to one side, pastel water colour still life brightly lit with Art Deco wall sconces, was laid out with a long table offering seating for a dozen or more, but now set for only three, with fine gold-rimmed white porcelain, heavy silver and etched crystal glassware.

Davidovich and I flanking her at one end, Ursula turned to me, declaring in a matter of fact tone, "Armin is unable to join us."

"But never absent," Davidovich nodded.

Both present and absent. In fact, the slumbering host was wheeled in by the nurse. Setting him at the far end of the table, she fussed for a moment drawing the light plaid over him and tucking in the sides. His hearing vaguely intact and coming alive at times, apparently he liked the sounds of the dining table, the chime of silver and crystal. Briefly unnerving, if not macabre, to have a lifeless figure alongside while one supped and drank. Difficult, too, not to turn a glance from time to time towards the silent presence. Neither Ursula nor Davidovich appeared to notice. It was an accepted habit of the house and, in time, I too took it in my stride, though not without a flutter in the heart when, later, Ursula's overtures became more intimate and pronounced.

~~~

The dinner itself was spare, wholesome if not sumptuous, the fresh perch from the lake in butter and herbs delicate and surprisingly filling, the flan with the season's Amarena cherries pleasing on the tongue with its bitter-sweet after-taste. The young Chasselas Davidovich had brought from his winery on the slopes of Lake Geneva was a friendly accompaniment with its light, floral air. He had inherited the small estate from his parents, the mother's family having worked the vines for several generations. Vocation and career abandoned in midlife, rather than musical notes he now cured the notes of his wines through part of the year, with the help of an architect companion.

"And what's Gabriel up to these days?" Ursula asked.

"His usual self. Idling as ever. Thankfully no longer dreaming of becoming a second Corbusier. Not even Botta!" Davidovich turned to me. "Gaby is my live-in partner."

Putting down his glass, he let out a short sigh. "Correct me on this, Professor, if you will. It's more in your line of work, I expect. Shouldn't there be a fixed tax on dreams? To discourage people wasting away a lifetime dreaming the impossible."

"We are what our dreams have made us," said Ursula with a slight twist of the mouth. "Or unmade."

"You'd know that better than most," Davidovich remarked pleasantly, but with something distinctly acid in the tone.

That first evening at the Göttners', all through the dinner, I caught a hint of caustic undertone in their exchanges, the jabs and thrusts of ill-humoured sparring partners under the patina of conviviality. The talk light and conversational, nothing overt or consequential, yet a veiled animus seemed to infect the casual give and take. They were like a couple who might once have been close, shared time and memories, bound now not by personal choice or volition, keeping forced company. Not making for unpleasantness or open hostility, it simply left the impression of some unhealed wound hidden from open sight.

The meal coming to an end, Silvio and the young maid clearing the table, the nurse came in to wheel the sleeper away.

Ursula excused herself, rose from the table, and walked around to accompany her husband, to lay him to rest for the night.

"Armin refuses to go, but he'll not wake again," Davidovich said quietly when we were alone. "After the stroke, when things looked really grim, we thought the doctors would raise the white flag and recommend palliative care. You know, the last station. A few weeks, another month or two, and he'd be finally gone. But not Armin, he was made of sterner stuff. The arrogant tenacity of old Prussian nobility! He decided he wasn't going anywhere. Before the move to the palliative clinic could be arranged, he came back to life. Not quite hale and hearty, but alive enough, heart ticking regularly and the rest. And here he is now. Minimal Consciousness State, they call it."

"A sort of persistent vegetative state?"

"Not quite. Still minimally alive. Vaguely conscious, to what degree no one knows." He looked at me thoughtfully. "But not enough for the trip to Zürich."

"Why Zürich?"

"Assisted suicide. You may have heard of it. But the Dignitas people in Pfäffikon expect you to inject the stuff yourself. And Armin's just not up to it."

"Is that what Ursula would want?"

"Heaven knows what she wants. Yes and no. Meanwhile he's trapped her in a cul-de-sac, well and good. So like the man. Probably enjoys it, too. Well, all else failing, there's this lake." He chuckled to himself. "Half a kilometre deep in places, they say. Not even cars fallen in the waters can be found!"

"No prospect of recovery at all?"

"It was a massive stroke. The sort that carries away normal mortals. And he'd had a couple before that, years ago. Nothing life threatening, those first episodes, just minor ischaemia. That's how he met Ursula. This last one felled him. In the early days, when he gained a trace consciousness, it was hoped he'd come through. Possibly an invalid condition, wheel-chair bound. Now… he's been absent too long."

"This could last indefinitely?"

"Oh, if for that, he could outlast us all! Doubtful, though, that he'd like it, to return among the living with severe disabilities. Armin was a man for perfections. Shirt cuffs ironed just so, the morning egg poached with chronometric precision. The number of times I've seen him smack a First Violin's cheek with his baton, for merely dropping a note. And it wasn't a caress, I can tell you."

A hollow laugh escaped him. "At the end of one performance he burst into the dressing room frothing at the mouth. Absolutely livid. I was changing trousers. He came up and stuck a finger up my ass, bellowin 'You bastard little Jew boy!' All because for the briefest stretch in the Chopin Piano Concerto I hadn't kept time with his baton. That was Armin for you!"

"Yet adored universally, if I remember right. One of the great batons of his time."

"No doubt about it, the world was at his feet. Sheer adoration. The critics, the crowds, women half-swooning as he strode down the aisle. He had this peculiar habit, never gaining the podium from the wings. The grand entrance was down the middle of the theatre, a hand sometimes briefly caressing a bare shoulder. The sacred touch of the prophet. I expect the lady of the turn went without showering for weeks, not to lose the pat of the perfumed glove!"

Davidovich looked up at the ceiling with a mirthful expression. "Once… and this is not hearsay, I was there. Just before the performance, he had a flying fuck with a young woman in the chorus, buttoned up, made his grand entry and gave his unwashed hand to the high dignitary, President of the country I think, seated in the front row. It made his day. A favourite pastime of his, putting people down, pleb or well-born. Sure, he was the darling of the musical world. We others, in the trade, saw the warts and pimples. And worse. Some would have gladly stuck a knife in him, if given half a chance."

"Really!"

"The nastiness one had to put up with! Irascibility, the say, is the birthright of the genius, but Armin von Göttner…" He paused, to look around the dining room thoughtfully. "Armin is one of those you love and also hate to love. Personally, I didn't really mind. Besides, one was young then. Always his little Jew boy."

Seeing my expression, Davidovich shook his head. "No, it's not that. If at all, his anti-Semitism was skin deep. More the old Prussian hauteur of the lords of the land. Rancour, too, for the lost world, the vast family estate he grew up in. All gone after the war. Besides…" he smiled, "besides, with Wagner as his God, a little bit of Jew-baiting was not out of tune. In any case, he was half right. My mother was Swiss Calvinist, father a Jew. Russian at that." He looked at me with an impish grin. "Difficult mix, the Torah and the Psychopannychia."

Ursula was still busy putting Armin to bed. Leaving the dregs of the coffee, we rose from the table and walked out to the terrace. Davidovich lit a cigarette. We looked down in silence at the lights of the town and the faint glint of silver on the waters of the lake stretching away into the dark.

"Ah well, another evening at the morgue," Davidovich sighed, taking a deep breath of the cooling night air.

Seeing me glance at my watch, he seemed to come to himself. "Do you like it here?

"It's quite, if nothing else."

"And comforting, I dare say, with Ursula's neighbourly presence." He looked me straight in the eye for a brief moment, something severe in the gaze, counselling or forewarning, it was hard to say.

"Well, I expect I'll be seeing you again. My visits here are foreordained! But anytime you happen to be in Montreux or in the neighbourhood, do call me up. Gabriel would love to meet you. He's a philosophical architect. Much philosophy, less brick and mortar!"

I said I would, shook hands, and on that note turned back into the house to meet Ursula, who had come down meanwhile. She walked me to the entrance and down the drive towards the gate.

"Just a simple evening, but it was very kind of you to come." She slipped an arm through mine, her nearness redolent with a faint, floral fragrance, iris and patchouli. "I hope you didn't mind David being here."

"Not at all. An interesting person."

"One could say that, I suppose. Not that one can always choose one's visitors. He's a regular, every other month or so. Homage to his master and mentor. But you'll come again, will you not."

"Gladly."

We stopped at the gate and she touched my cheek with a light press of her full lips.

There was a coda to the evening. A couple of days later I ran into Ursula in the town. We crossed the street together to the old café, where the well-heeled came in for their late morning drinks, and found a corner table in the brightly-lit, wood-panelled interiors.

Ursula had a radiant air, with an unexpected aura of youth, youthful spring in her steps, fresh in a face lightly made up, lips done pale pink and hair loose and flowing. Looks to make heads turn.

"I'm so glad you came over the other day. Thank you," she said, touching my hand with almost accustomed familiarity. "It lightened the evening." She paused as the waiter put down our coffees. "David can be oppressive at times. I suppose we know each other too well. And both in the service of the same man."

"Oh!" she took a hasty sip. "By the way, he rang to say that he's sending you some bottles of his wine. I think he's taken a shine to you. David likes older men."

She smiled seeing my raised brows. "No, nothing like that. Nothing intimate. He's always been in search of a master and guide, someone to obey, serve. Armin fitted the bill. He always knew how to enslave those around him." She primly dabbed her lips with the serviette. "But never mind David. There was something I wanted to ask you. Shall we go?"

I handed the slip at the till and paid. We walked out into the bright sunlight and she took my arm. "I'm off to Zürich for a couple of days. Money matters. Would you mind dropping into the house for a few minutes while I'm away."

"I'll do so, if you tell the staff."

"Silvio has been with us for years, he knows the drill. But the nurses… They work at the hospital and come on their off-duty hours."

"Moonlighting?"

"You could say that. At times they're late or fail to turn up. Would you just keep an eye."

I assured her I would look in. And then she said something that rang a bell, calling to mind what I had briefly heard from Maria.

We were on our way up towards to my place. Nearing, she looked up at the Villa Serena a long moment. "I'd not have bothered you if… In the past Signor Fabbri used to lend a hand when needed. We've not seen him for some time. A touchy person, Fabbri. Some grudge… to do with his family."

Grudge, she said, papering off lightly a drama of ultimate passion and extreme consequence. What little I had gleaned from Maria, Fabbri himself was to fill in later. Recounting in some detail the fate of his uncle Leonardo, he said, "Her operatic career may have been negligible, farcical. But Ursula von Göttner still mistakes life for opera. Singing with blood on the hands!"

9

"If you think about it," said Fabbri, "one might see Ursula and Leonardo making their way towards each other even long before they met. A fatality already written. Both prisoners of a past of high drama, both victims. And you could even hazard that it could end no other way than it did. An operatic ending. Less Romeo and Juliet, more Werther, perhaps. Though poor Leo could hardly be called that."

"Odd!" Odd, Fabbri thought, that one such as Leonardo, always calm and collected, should be drawn to women strong and spirited, red-blooded. "Laura, Eleonora, Ursula…"

"The attraction of opposites," I suggested.

There was, apparently, something in Leonardo that burned within, a slumbering volcano, unquiet and smouldering. Only once had it erupted, the brimstone consuming and laying waste to what should have been a life of promise. Even after years shut out from the world, the fires had remained dormant and unspent, to flare up in a fatality that finally brought to an end an existence solitary and, seemingly, born in an exile of one's own choosing. Had it not been Ursula von Göttner, it would have been another and, possibly, the destination the same or similar. As it was, it was Ursula, femme fatale, a witch and a bitch for Fabbri. Small surprise, then, that half blind to his uncle's tortured soul, he should lay the entire blame at her door.

On his return from military service, there had been nothing particularly visible in manner or speech to signal whatever the upset or distress caused by the forthcoming marriage of Laura and Lorenzo. Yet the parents, especially Anna with her finer, maternal perception, felt the changes, unseen and subterranean, as always with Leonardo, and they were glad and relieved when a mere fortnight later he moved to Milan to begin his law studies. An hour away by road, but distance enough to veil from view the sight of Laura and Lorenzo ever together, seemingly inseparable as the wedding approached.

A bitter winter, quite as gelid as the chill that had settled on the Bellini family. Gregarious but never prolix, the Lombard reserve holding at bay verbosity and effusion, they had never been given to wordy and windy eloquence. Affection enclosed in a look, amity in a smile and accord in a nod, the verb of sentiment reached out mostly in silence.

Leonardo had always been more silent than most. Even Lorenzo, often given to larking and cavorting, never exposed to daylight his innermost depths. But the frigid air that now wafted through the Bellini home made for unaccustomed distance, separation and estrangement. Lorenzo seemed divorced from the life of the family, as if wanting to keep out of the way. Long days at work and spare hours with Laura, a curtain falling between him and the parents, the spare presence shadowy, possibly rendered remote by guilt or shame. Leonardo himself never once, not even at the weekends, made the short journey by train. It was left to Stefano to go over every other fortnight, to lunch with Leonardo, pass a couple of hours in talk mostly away from the intimacies of the family, recounting merely affairs in the car salon, in passing Anna's health, that for the first time had begun to be frail.

When the day came, Leonardo was not present at the wedding. Neither rebuff, nor was it a convenient diplomatic absence. Cycling to classes early mornings in the damp chill of an unusually cold spring, he had come down with a severe case of pleurisy. Admitted to the nearby hospital, visited daily by either Anna or Stefano, he had lain half-comatose for a week. Leonardo had not inherited his father's form and physique, nor had the robust stamina of his brother, the slender build taking after Anna. The doctors decreed that he was to remain in his hospital bed for another week, or more.

One late afternoon, a couple of days before the wedding, Lorenzo finally looked in. Recovery slow, fever receding, the pain in the chest in abeyance, but weak in limb and breath still laboured, Leonardo's eyes opened through the drowse to find Lorenzo stood by the bed contemplating his recumbent figure. Drawing up a chair from the wall, Lorenzo sat down by the bedside, the flicker of a smile, hesitant, passing on his lips. It was a smile Leonardo had seen other times, in childhood when, after a severe scold, Anna would reach out a hand to take his in a gesture of mute, motherly affection.

They had not seen each other these last months since Leonardo's move to Milan. Nor on his return from military service, in the short weeks at home, had they had many words together, Laura's name never once mentioned in the sparse syllables of their exchanges. Neither knew what one might say and, not wishing to add insult to injury, Lorenzo said little or nothing. Never particularly vocal, Leonardo himself had been short of speech more than usual. But Laura's absent presence permeated the air of home, an unseen apparition that had taken up residence, ubiquitous and omnipresent, inhabiting the rooms, nooks and crannies, the minds, thoughts and meditations of the living. Only once, briefly, with Lorenzo out of the house, had Stefano mentioned in passing that Laura's brother had recently come to the showroom to order a sports car.

"Day after tomorrow," Lorenzo murmured, head bowed, voicing more an admission, a confession, than the proclamation of a joyous event. What else could he say. The strained silence in the small room faintly redolent of disinfectants seemed to resound with thoughts that Lorenzo could neither conjure nor utter even as he felt Leonardo's sleep-laden eyes looking up at him from seemingly an immense distance. Many long minutes later, Lorenzo got to his feet and, wetting his lips, was about to say that he would come again after the wedding, when he remembered that, following the festivities, the next morning he and Laura, man and wife, would be setting out for Capri. Leonardo's arm lifted slowly to take his hand in a weak grasp, in a gesture of mute felicitation and, perhaps, final parting.

During the fortnight the newly-weds were away on their honeymoon in the south, at his mother's insistence Leonardo came home for a week's convalescence. Now that it was done with and over, there was a visible air of relief in the Bellini house, Stefano almost his usual self, Anna more at ease and moving about as she had always done, cooking, caring, tidying up.

Debilitated but on his feet again, Leonardo returned briefly to his habits of the past. Rising a little later than the parents, going down to the kiosk at the corner, to sit then in a corner of the kitchen with his morning coffee and the day's paper. From time to time Anna glanced at him from the corner of her eye, a sense of comfort coming over her at the sight of a scene from other days, knowing well that the life they had known was now gone forever, little to reclaim, nothing to salvage save the retentions of the past and the dim Ferrania colour photographs in a couple of shoe boxes, of outings and holidays, the boys on the steps of the church in their first communion tunics, the infants cradled in their grandmother's arms, Lorenzo holding aloft a prize partridge with the hunting gun slung underarm. Mementoes and memories of happier times. But her Leo was still here, with her now and, not wanting to admit it, distractedly she knew that if for nothing else, life had been worth living for this child of hers alone.

On their return, Laura and Lorenzo would reside at the Villa Serena, and Stefano busied himself part of the day overseeing the last touches to readying the house. At home, meanwhile, Anna saw to sorting and putting aside Lorenzo's clothes, hunting gear, his books on birdlife, odds and ends that he would want to take with him. One afternoon Leonardo walked up with his father to the Villa Serena. A couple of workmen were still busy in one of the baths on the upper floor fitting a new sink.

"A big place just for the two of them. The heating bill in winter…" Stefano stopped mid-sentence, as though having bitten his tongue. Moving away, he pointed to the mansion next door. "They say the place is up for sale. Can't be many buyers in these times."

~~~

Admittedly, times were bad. Trouble in the land, turmoil in towns and cities, strikes, demonstrations in the streets, kidnapping of the rich and famous in broad daylight, the Red Brigade knee-capping, maiming and killing in their murderous crusade for a better world. Stefano's car sales come to a near halt, the garage remained the main provider for the family. In no manner impoverished, finances still solid, a time or two Stefano himself had driven up the hill and down to the frontier, crossing the check-post to make sizeable deposits in some bank on the other side. Money increasingly mere printed paper, it was best to set aside what one could in a safer corner.

One day Leonardo dropped in at the show room. Times might change, but Gabriella remained untouched. Smart and colourful as ever, in a tartan skirt well above the knee, the figure still trim, smile scintillating and walk shimmying, the thirty odd years were little visible, if not for the fine hair lines under the eyes, if looked at close. Still single, still flirtatious, her looks and manner made one wonder why no man had yet claimed her. There was a casual hint dropped under breath by town gossips that there was something between her and Stefano. Not one to lend ear to idle talk and knowing his father as he did, Leonardo found the hearsay difficult to credit. All work and little play, Stefano would not have had the time, nor had he the talent for seduction and surreptitious liaisons. Years ago, courted insistently by a wealthy young widow who had taken to visiting the showroom every other day, he had said to Anna with a puzzled brow, "Can't understand what the woman wants. Not interested in buying a car…"

Gabriella wrapped her arms around Leonardo. "*Caro, ragazzo!* You've forgotten your Gabriella! How long since you came to see me?"

"With half the town courting you, what chance for me?"

"Ah, no." She made a sad face. "Not many knights in shining armour around any more. And they don't come on white chargers. Mostly Fiat 600s. Besides," she added, brightening and reaching for his hand, "I've been waiting for you!"

The fond smile, Leonardo noticed, was edged with a faintly melancholy air as they looked around at the mere handful of vehicles sat here and there in the half empty space, looking out of place and out of time, yesterday's models, aged and dated. British cars no longer in vogue, the gleaming sedans and open-top two-seaters once crowding the salon had all gone, with no shiny silver chassis of a Triumph or Jaguar for Gabriella to drape herself on with her seductive come-hither look.

"Pity you couldn't come to the wedding. Laura was a splendour…" She stopped short, half holding her breath. "Stefano told me you were unwell. But now that you're back…"

Leonardo never went back. Years later, passing by the street, he noticed the wide glass frontage boarded up, with an estate agent's FOR RENT sign, the name Bellini still in place above the frontage.

Nor did he see Gabriella again, not until she appeared at the trial. Often present in the crowded public gallery in a cumbersome fur coat, mink or silver fox, her gaze intent on Leonardo sat head bowed between a couple of Carabinieri, she was accompanied by a stout male companion. She had finally found her man, married a widowed butcher a dozen years older, who had made good and traded his small family shop for a wholesale meat business supplying hotels and restaurant chains.

Much later still, seemingly half a lifetime, when, his dues paid, Leonardo had returned from exile to live in retreat at the Villa Serena, going down into the town briefly he had come across her on a rare occasion. The first time he saw her, she had just emerged from a lake front boutique with an armful of silvery paper carriers. Of matronly girth, heavier in face, still wrapped in fur, the years had little touched the spirited Gabriella he had known in youth. The wide smile still intact, the laughter now more throaty, she threw her arms around Leonardo, planting a resounding kiss on his cheek. Drawing back to look him up and down, after a passing moment of hesitation, she asked how long he'd been back. "Oh Leo! Dear Leo!" she half whispered, holding him in a long embrace, eyes shut, as though reclaiming something lost. The past was a region forbidden, a dark space not to be trod or touched, and no words were exchanged on Leonardo's long absence. It was but a moment, and Gabriella regained herself.

She herself had just returned from a fortnight in Santo Domingo and was trying to persuade her husband to buy a holiday home there. Finally, late in life, she had retrieved the dreams of youth, flying to exotic locations around the world. "Wonderful to sit back and look at the clouds passing by!" she chuckled. "And to be served. To think, Leo, that once I was foolish enough to want to be a waitress in the sky! Much better this way."

Light of heart and blithe as ever, forgetting for a moment, she asked, "And how have you been? Are you alone?" Veering off, taking his hand, she said, "You must come over one day and meet Franco."

Leonardo had already met Franco, aeons ago, as a child, going down with his mother to the upmarket butcher with specialities on his shelves, smoked meats from the Trento, hot sausages from the south. Heavy-built and ruddy in face, a jolly sort, never short of a few earthy words for his female clients, the women invariably feigning mild indignance.

Leonardo thought it was a good match, imagining the good-humoured give and take between husband and wife. But he never went. In the place he had made for himself, he did not wish to relive what had gone before, nor see the faces known and hear anew the distant voices. If the years behind the bars had shut out the world, in time he himself had chosen to shut mind and thought within the small space of his prison cell. A confinement that finally Ursula was to breach, a fatal intrusion and a betrayal one too many. But that was yet to come.

10

There was something about Ursula von Göttner that bothered me not a little. Spinoza now keeping me more amiable company as I found him in his small rented quarters in Rijnsberg, the weather warming, settled in a routine of sorts and the work in progress making some headway, yet as I sat at the table seemingly absorbed in the words before me, Ursula broke in, unannounced and uninvited.

An intrusion that rudely broke mid-thought whatever my ruminations, stealing in silently to oust Spinoza, to hover around me with a wordless smile. The distraction persistent, there was nothing for it but to get to my feet and take the few steps to the window, to look out at the still-life scene of her sat in her nurse's uniform beside Armin stretched out in the tepid light of the waning afternoon. As though sensing my eyes on her, even at a distance, she would at times turn and lift a hand in brief greeting.

The presence insistent, it made me wonder. The bloom of youth long faded, she was not some young thing that on the instant mesmerized one's gaze and attention. It sometimes happened during lectures that the professorial eye, roaming the young faces of the year's fresh batch of students, settled on one longer than might be thought judicious, returning to it again and again, like the pointer of a compass ineluctably drawn to the magnetic north. Years ago, a friend and colleague had wooed and finally wed a freshman first seen in the lecture hall, confessing in private afterwards that the fatal moment had occurred at the very first sight of the young woman at the very first hour of lectures. "No such sweetheart for you," Myrna had gently ribbed me at the wedding, watching the young bride stroll around the lawn with the ageing groom, to fall silent with simpering satisfaction then, at my response that "I have mine already." Evidently treading the straight and narrow, satisfied with what one had, I could not think of a life away from Myrna. But Myrna had chosen to go unseasonably, and here I was now, alone and, apparently, bereft and lost.

If Ursula was no fresh-faced maiden with a bright-eyed smile that set the heart racing, nor was she one to be ignored. Face and figure more than reasonably preserved, age had endowed her with a history that no twenty year old could boast, maturity a sieve that distilled the past into a womanhood of variegated talents, those God-given as also the many drawn from a life on the run from an orphaned heritage into the arms of men colourful and choleric, when not abusive. One was yet to learn of the minutiae of her antecedents, where she had come from and who she might have been. Meanwhile here she was, working her way under one's skin.

It made for unease, if not misgiving. Somehow it did not seem right that so soon after, a year or less since Myrna had been laid to rest, desire and need should stir anew, a yearning yet vague but silently pulsating into life. Deceiving the living was one thing, I mused with a guilty sigh, but betrayal of the dead perhaps infinitely more iniquitous. Dissimulation ever a handy tool, how convenient to think that Myrna would not have wanted me to carry my widowderhood to the grave!

Back from Zürich, she sent over a note to thank me for having looked in during her brief absence. Indeed, all had been well, the nurses in attendance, the household ticking over with clockwork fidelity under butler Silvio's supervision. A postscript suggested that we meet one evening. I replied she was free to choose the time and date. But then, an unexpected event derailed our possible rendezvous. Late in the evening, the day before our dinner up the hill, the call came and I heard clear Ursula's breathless voice asking if I could go over.

Dr. Silvestri was a neurosurgeon, the head of his department at the local hospital. Once every few weeks he came in to look von Göttner over. The patient's condition stable and unchanging, pressure and pulse checked, possible change or variation in disposition ascertained, the consultations were brief and never calling for urgent intervention.

Now the doctor was sat in the dim night-light beside the sizeable, canopied bed in a spacious chamber on the ground floor, that looked out on the lake. Tall velvet drapes descending from the high ceiling curtaining off the view, heavy sideboards against one wall, at the far end a night cot for the nurse, a vague sour aroma of camphor permeated the air. Rising to his feet finally, the doctor walked over to where Ursula and I stood at the door. Pressure considerably down, pulse barely discernable, but not quite bradycardia, he assured Ursula. A temporary lapse, from which Armin would likely recover. In any case, he would be looking in next morning, on his way to the hospital.

Ursula introduced us. The doctor gave me his hand, cool to the touch, but the hold sinewy and strong. Tall and upright, with a short-trimmed greying head, the Roman lineaments handsome, he appeared to have aged gracefully.

He addressed me in a tone polite and firm. "You're staying at the Villa Serena?"

Ursula excused herself, going back in briefly for a word with the nurse. "A friend of mine used to live there some time ago," he said in a quieter voice.

I asked if it might be long before von Göttner returned to his accustomed condition.

"It's not a given. But living beings fluctuate." He looked at me keenly. "And like it or not, the man's still alive."

Ursula, hurrying back, accompanied him to the entrance, stopping on the steps for brief words that I could not catch. Walking back with a tired air, she asked if I could stay for a little while.

~~~

Wrapped in a flowing, lilac-print silk gown, head lightly tousled, care-worn in face but somehow not quite showing her years, there was about her a listless weariness, a spirit fatigued, that came through in voice, less in words. It was the first time, by no means the last, that I saw Ursula unmasked, the woman I would come to know, shorn of her public grand dame manner, the ringing tone and theatrical pose. Sometimes, in the hours after dark, after we had been together, stretched out on the bed beside me, more lifeless than languid, breath cold, her presence curiously distanced itself, as though she had withdrawn into the penumbra of a dim space within. "No, it's not you, good man," she once said. Revisitations, she told me then, the past returning and refusing to leave well alone. The ogres and beasts waking once again in the blood, seemingly.

No phantoms about this night, we sat out in the garden under a clean, starlit sky, the air tepid, not warm enough as yet for insect life to be about. "I bothered you needlessly," she said, handing me a brandy snifter. "It was a bit of a panic. He'd stopped breathing, not even Flavia could find the pulse. And she's a trained nurse. For that matter, so am I. Dr. Silvestri was at a dinner and took some time answering."

"I'd not have been of much help. My medical knowledge is non-existent. Apart from a vague idea of the location of the heart."

"Ah, the heart," she repeated with a sigh.

"Dr. Silvestri thinks…"

"Silvestri's a good man. Renowned in his field. But…," she stared into her glass. "Ever so clinical. Not a touch of warmth, empathy. Even his hands are cold." With a wan smile, she took mine. "At times, it's the presence that matters."

She looked around at the grounds with a desolate air as we sat on in the half dark, the night still, soundless save for the distant beep of cars down in the town, dim voices of passers-by down the road. Wordless, then, she laid her head on my shoulder.

"When Armin bought this place," she said in the voice of a reverie but somehow edged with gloom, "I thought finally we'd have a life together. Something we'd never really had. Surrounded always with his friends and musical associates, the adoring crowds, dinners, receptions. And then the concert engagements. The high days of his glory were gone but he wasn't forgotten. And I, always waiting in the wings…"

She shook her head, falling silent for a moment. "Later, when he bought this place, I became a virtual widow. Months and months alone here. In the early years he was mostly away, flying around the world, on engagements that brought money but little else. Conducting Brahms in Bombay with a second rate orchestra wasn't exactly worthy of his name." Head tilting back, she looked me in the eyes. "But why am I telling you all this?"

"It's in my line of work. One's used to listening. An occasional custodian of confidences, so to speak."

"Custodian of confidences!" Unnervingly, she pressed her lips to my cheek, her breath aromatic from the digestif she had been drinking "You sound more like a priest. Did you ever train as one in some seminary."

"There was a time when I thought I might become one. But there were irreconcilable appetites."

"Irreconcilable appetites!" She threw her head back in a quiet laugh, for a moment bringing to life her accustomed self. "Do you still have them, these appetites?"

The moment of lightness gone, the dejection returning in voice, she laid her head back against my shoulder. "All those out of the way places, where the public could not have told a violin from a cello and a cello from a horse's backside. Audiences bursting into applause after the first crescendo, with the conductor's baton still in movement. That sort of thing. Once… can't remember where it was, he was conducting Tchaikovsky's 1812. At the sound of the artillery cannonade, even before the brass finale, the public was on its feet, stomping and clapping. He left the stage, went straight to the hotel, packed and headed for the airport."

"*Triste!* Sad, really," Ursula went on in the same melancholy tone. "The way he allowed himself to be humiliated in those years. The same man who'd conducted at Bayreuth several times. Not only. Once, during the staging of Lohengrin, even told Wieland Wagner to mind his own business. Actually, he told him to fuck off! Armin just couldn't stand Wieland's minimalist preferences."

"Oh! But why travel to those remote…?"

"Musically insignificant places? Simply trying to get back where he belonged, reclaim his place on the pantheon after squandering his reputation trying to make of me another Schwarzkopf, improbably a new Callas. I was to be the elixir, the magic philtre for him to regain his halo. The young have dreams, the ageing illusions, I suppose."

She paused, to inhale deeply the night air. "He heard me sing *Edelweiss* or something in a hospital ward and thought he'd found his Lucia and Violetta. Armin was still a god at the time, and gods have their very own creations. Zeus wanting to mould his Pandora! But I was only a *Krankenschwester*, nurse Ursula Füssli, who sometimes sang lullabies to dying children in a clinic."

Human truths are seldom short of *omissis*, some convenient abridgement or adulteration, and that night Ursula did not recount the whole truth, or even part of it. Understandably, perhaps. We were still strangers, and it was neither the hour nor the moment to confess to the murky past of a life corrupted and blighted.

Still and all, the sketchy frame ill-matched the portrait. A wife abandoned, a medical attendant singing at bed time to infants about to depart life? A touching cameo, that artfully veiled where she had come from and who and what she had been. Neither Lucia nor Violetta, a frail maiden warbling her operatic grief. Nor was there a word or hint of her other, inborn talents, for drama and play-acting, not least the blaze she could fire in men, as she had once stoked the embers of von Göttner's waning satyriasis, as later she was to fan the flames of the conflagration that had finally consumed Leonardo Bellini.

11

Opening the shutters, once Leonardo too would have seen her, walking around the grounds or sat hours in the summer garden, in solitary splendour, and splendid, as well, her person. Younger by some ten years, one could imagine Ursula as she was then, at the peak of her prime, effulgent in face, figure full and statuesque, embodiment of womanhood flawless and replete. Raising her head, then, her eyes, aglow with the ache of solitude and hunger, would surely have met Leonardo's gaze. Leonardo himself, aged in spirit beyond his forty odd years, was no less striking in appearance, the good looks of youth settled into lineaments firm and pronounced, sober as ever, but now imprinted with the pain of a life somehow gone awry.

    If they had met and mated, brought together seemingly by chance, it was also perhaps foreordained, an irresistible engagement of two beings poles apart, pasts diverse, peculiarities and preferences disparate, both lives that in their own way had taken the errant trail at the forking paths. Fruit of shame and guilt, Ursula was the misbegotten child of the cruel quirks of history that decreed that she be born in a peasant's log-house rather than a gilded mansion. Leonardo was born to modest inheritance and of common blood, with the promise of a life of attainment and satisfaction derailed on the way. Both victims, Ursula of birth, Leonardo of his own darkness, their common adversity was possibly the only element that drew them together, that then also made for a denouement of pain and fatality.

Thinking of them brought to mind the saying of the Master: *"All happiness or unhappiness is dependent solely on the quality of the object to which one is drawn by love."* Fabbri was more laconic, talking of his uncle one day, his gaze fixing the von Göttner residence. "*Carpe noctem potius quam carpe diem.* Yes, Leonardo preferred to seize the night, rather than the day."

For friend Fabbri, Ursula was an angel of darkness, termagant, turbulent and promiscuous. But I thought it unfair to lay the whole blame at her feet. Perhaps Spinoza's words were more apt, happiness dependent on the object of desire. Leonardo's gaze had always sought out those not made for him, first Laura, then the wife of another during his law studies, finally Ursula. Unhappiness appeared to have been written into his stars.

The years studying law in Milan had taken him ever away from home and parents, the distance from brother Lorenzo a divide unbridgeable. Outwardly preserving a measure of decorum and civility when a rare time he returned on a visit, Leonardo seemed to have turned the page, put behind him the injuries of the past. In appearance, the brief exchanges at table with his brother and Laura were seemingly affable, if polite, as with distant relatives little seen, even less known. Leonardo had never been given to gregarious heartiness, in the family or elsewhere, and his thoughtful silences went unremarked.

Meanwhile Laura had given birth to a baby boy. Malice not in his nature, more in good faith and, perhaps, to ingratiate himself by way of a small recompense for the wrong done, Lorenzo thought the child might be named after Leonardo. Anna thought otherwise and cautioned him against possibly opening old wounds. Lorenzo acquiesced with a silent nod. The child was christened after his grandfather. But once, Leonardo home on one of his rare visits, unable to keep in check his inborn good-humour, Lorenzo plucked the infant from Laura and, placing it in Leonardo's arms, beaming in face, said to his mother, "I told you! Look at the likeness."

With the parents, Leonardo was more forthcoming. On their regular trips to the city, Anna took him out shopping, a new pair of sun shades, woollens as the season turned towards the first chill of winter. His needs spare as ever, preferring to resole his shoes rather than choosing a new pair, making do with the couple of old corduroy jackets in place of the fashionable two-button seen by Anna in a menswear window in the Galleria, Leonardo went more for the afternoon with his mother. Alone together for an hour or two, regaining something of the ease and intimacy of times past, briefly the joints of his spirit loosened enough to engage in small talk, confide in passing his vague plans for the future. Save for some incidental naming, Anna carefully skirted talk of Lorenzo and Laura.

With his father, the exchanges were more general, life in the city, business at the auto salon, that had begun to see a decided upturn. But one day, in the final months of his last year, when Stefano had come alone, Leonardo startled him with words unexpected. More of a confession than mere news, it was perhaps something uncommon to confide in a father. They had lunched together at an eatery in a side street near the university. The small *osteria* half-emptied of the lunch-time crowd, Stefano, replete with the bone-marrow risotto and leisurely stirring his coffee, said, "I'll miss coming over when your studies are done. Gives me a break. In any case, Gabriella has become such an expert car salesman… or is it sales-woman? Who would have thought!"

Silent a long moment, Leonardo raised his head to look his father in the eye. "There's something I wanted to tell you. Perhaps Mamma doesn't need to know." The spare words then hurried out. "I've got a woman."

"Oh!" After the merest pause, Stefano broke into a wide smile, a hand reaching out to pat his son's arm. "Bravo, Leo!

It was high time. All these years your mother and I worrying about you being all alone. Is she from the *ateneo*… studying with you?"

Leonardo looked out of the glass front, the early afternoon light opaque, the narrow cobbled street busy with office workers hurrying back after the lunch break. "No," he shook his head, expression vaguely bemused.

Words halting, he told Stefano. Neither a fellow student, nor one of his age. Older, and the wife of another. Stefano recognized the name, a well-known industrialist, with several sizeable factories in the hinterland making auto and two-wheeler parts, an eminence in business circles, on the Board of a couple of banks. The man was in his sixties, if he recalled right.

"How old is she?" Stefano asked perplexed.

A wan smile passed Leonardo's lips. She was the second wife, he said. There were no children, a son and daughter, grown, from the first marriage. "Eleonora's only 37."

"Only 37! But Leo…" Stefano started. Easing back in his seat, then, he looked at his son in wonder and concern. Uncomplicated, ever simple at heart, after the early marriage to Anna, his head had hardly ever turned to look at another woman. And when it had, it had been no more than a cursory glance, with no thought to follow, nor recondite intention. "And…?" he asked, gathering his wits, more a doubt than enquiry.

"I just wanted you to know."

"Serious, is it?"

"It could be," said Leo, in a voice low, hands fidgeting with the paper napkin. "Elle thinks she might leave her husband. She could, now that the full Divorce Bill is through in Parliament."

"The Bill's through in Parliament, but you're not through with your studies."

Stefano drove back pensive in mood, the past playing on his mind. Less the disparate ages, ten years and more, disquiet clouded this thoughts. He did not know any more than what Leonardo had told him, less than a thumb-sketch. Uppermost in his mind was the concern that Leonardo not suffer a repeat of the deceit and delusion inflicted by Laura.

Keeping faith with Leonardo's wishes, he did not tell Anna. But in the days that followed, he made time to drop by the offices of the local paper. Familiar with some of the staff, he was able to consult the archives, finally digging up old issues with reports and photographs on the inauguration of one of the factories of the Milanese industrialist, not too far out from the town. There was more. A full page given over on the occasion to a laudatory piece on the life and attainments of the man: the meteoric rise from modest origins to wealth and influence, courted by politicians of all shades but without declared political affiliations, prominence in the upper reaches of social life, the lengthy piece accompanied by several photographs. Stefano peered at the black and white images, the wife, Eleonora, constant by the side of the short, rotund figure, she a pale beauty, willowy and a whole head above her spouse, resplendent in a flowing, sequinned gown in the lobby of the Scala on the opening night of the new opera season; trim and radiant in skiing gear on the snowy slops of St, Moritz, the fair locks carefully wind-tossed.

Stefano was at a loss to understand what his son might want to have with a member of this coterie, a tribe enthroned in opulence and glimpsed only in dim images in the papers and periodicals. A world much distant from Leonardo, frugal, almost severe, in his tastes and habits, and certainly without the means to race with the hares and sit at table with the lions of the world.

Alfredo, a friend of the heart from childhood and Stefano's sole confidant at times in matters private and personal, was laconic when told of Leo's affair with the industrialist's wife. "Sex," he pronounced airily. "What else?" adding casually, then, "Not to worry, it'll not last."

Successful head of a furniture business, Alfredo was much less a seer. It did last, longer than might have been expected or hoped for. On successive visits, not wanting to delve and peer, as also timorous, Stefano did not ask, nor did Leonardo make mention, only once in passing dropping her name when Stefano's eyes lingered on the fine silk and cashmere scarf around the neck, to say that it was a gift from Eleonora.

"See, Leo..." Stefano began to say, but not quite knowing what he had in mind that could be spelt out in words, he said no more. What he did notice in Leonardo, or thought he did, was an unaccustomed hardening of tone and manner, if not of words, the impression of an obdurate will. Puzzled, Stefano left with a lingering sense of some subterranean shift, but nothing enduring, he earnestly hoped. Plain of heart, short-sighted of interiors, he preferred to put it down to the approaching final examinations.

Leonardo passed out with *cum laude*. Never less than brilliant at school, it was expected that he would do no less in his higher studies. Stefano had feared the distraction of the affair with Eleonora, but Leonardo did not disappoint.

The air in the austere hall solemn, the graduands for once got up in formal wear, the young men stiff and awkward in suit and ties knotted tight around the neck, the women in sedate, dark skirts and pastel silk shirts, Stefano took in the ceremonial scene, his eyes quietly scanning the groups of parents and friends to find a match for the face seen in the newspaper archives. Evidently Eleonora was not present, which came as a relief. He would not have wished the day marred for Anna, sat beside him replete with a joy and fullness of heart that broke through the pallor of her failing health. Outside, in the bright sunlight, watching Lorenzo snapping Leonardo as he held up the gilded parchment, she nudged close to her husband, to say, "Who would have ever thought, Stefano? We now have a *dottore* in the family."

Who, indeed? Stefano himself was little learned, his studies closing with elementary school, his parents even less, the old mother ever reluctant to put pen to paper, her name a curious wiggle when called on to sign some official form or document. An odd constriction in the throat, heart swelling with pride, he now found himself short of words The youthful years of unceasing labour, hands ever soiled with grease, evenings at home slumped in his kitchen chair with fatigue and, later, long days on his feet at the car salon, not a born horse-trader but having to haggle with customers over discounts and payments, a life watchful and weary. It had all been worth it, he mused, his arm wound tight around Anna. A reward more than ample he could not have asked.

A family again, as they had once been, close-knit and at ease, seemingly themselves again. Laura had not come. Assistant to the head and owner of the firm where she worked, she was away in Tuscany with her employer. But little Roberto was there, a quiet child, a growing boy now, a replica in miniature of his uncle as Leonardo held him aloft between Anna and Stefano, Lorenzo clicking away with his Konica.

The intruder absent, if only for an hour or two, a day, it might well have been a portrait from the past. But much water had passed under the bridge and it could not be quite the same, as when of a Sunday Anna and Stefano used to take the boys out for lunch in some country trattoria. If the web that had once knit the family together had come lose, the changed times and the hard-earned affluence now also offered more refined fare. Stefano had booked a table at the Savini in the Galleria, the meal at the celebrated restaurant a treat for the eventful day. Seated in the plush dining room upstairs under a high, ornate ceiling, they looked out of the arched windows at the elegant shop and store fronts bathed in the suffused daylight filtering down from the immensely tall glass dome. Little Roberto, clasping tight Anna's hand, looked about in wide-eyed wonder.

"I've been there a few times since," Fabbri told me. "But I remember the day well. Mostly because afterwards grandfather Stefano bought me a giant cone of ice cream from their pastry shop downstairs. And I dropped half of it on the mosaic flooring! And cried and sniffled in the car all the way back home."

Fabbri's recall of childhood could obviously not evoke the mood that permeated the table over lunch. Together again, Anna's gaze cradling her boys in a mother's love tender and ineffable, Stefano's eyes embracing them in a hold warm and protective. Yet, somehow, despite the ease and lightness of talk, both young men appeared to slip out of the parent's reach and clasp, each seemingly caught in the meandering depths of private concern.

Outwardly calm and satisfied, Leonardo's thoughts, turning towards the long haul of several years that awaited him training in a law office, were eclipsed with the shadow of Eleonora, their future together uncertain, beyond sight. Not knowing if and how it would end, reason telling him that Eleonora's place was elsewhere, yet he could not find it in himself to let go. Not mere puppy love, nor the first, he had found in her a world never before known, a woman grown and whole, in whose person he had found the sensuality of cravings unimagined, the ardour and thrill of a love illicit, as too the care and concern of an elder sister. It could not last, that he knew. Already on the threshold of her fortieth year and unable to accept less than what she already had, high living and the paraphernalia of wealth, she would one day, sooner than later, return to the wedded fold. The thought made him dizzy with a sense of abandonment and loss.

While Lorenzo, never less than a hearty diner, picked at his food with oddly muted appetite, his usual easy and cheerful presence appeared somehow tinged with an air of something labouring on the mind. These past several months Laura's presence at home had been sporadic, at times fleeting, her return in the evenings often late, one or two weekends entirely absent as she, apparently, accompanied her employer on business trips abroad. Young Roberto left mostly in Anna's care, Lorenzo could not at all understand the late nights and absences. Not one with a suspect turn of mind, he suspected nothing, nor openly spoke or showed his grievance. Glad that she had climbed the rungs from the hum-drum routine of the accounts office to a position of trust and regard, he only wished Laura would attend more to her role of wife and mother. Only once he voiced a passing concern in his parent's hearing. "Laura's ambitious," said Anna, lowering her head. Stefano said nothing, thinking to himself, then, that what Laura had, a husband and child, their discreet well-being, was perhaps not quite enough for her.

 Had it not been for a chance encounter, things might have taken their expected course. Leonardo completing his time at the law firm and setting up a practise of his own, Stefano ageing and gradually passing on the reins of the business to Lorenzo, time distancing and dimming the memory of deception and injury, the brothers might have come together by Anna's dying bed.

~~~

Out on the town one evening to celebrate the winning of a long and hard-fought, celebrity case of uxoricide in the courts, Leonardo found himself once again at the Savini, seated with half a dozen colleagues at a table reserved by the head of his firm. There, among the animated diners early at table before strolling across to the La Scala for some opera, in a far corner of the busy hall he caught sight of Laura with a middle-aged figure, hands held tight on the table, faces close in seemingly rapturous intimacy. Distracted by the jubilant talk and laughter at his table, Leonardo's gaze returned again and again. Until, a while later, the two rose from their seats, the man giving his hand briefly to the maître d'hôtel. Arm in arm, Laura radiant in a sequinned scarlet gown, her companion impeccable in an elegant double-breasted suit and silvery tie, sweeping past towards the entrance, Laura's eyes met Leonardo's, settling briefly, before hurriedly looking away. Leonardo's gaze followed them out, trying to make sense of the sighting.

Impressed by Laura's glittery looks, but not one much given to conjecture or embroidering on the lives of others, he thought nothing more of it. The chance meeting would have passed from mind entirely had it not been for an unexpected call from Laura a couple of days later. Could she come to see him? No reason given, surprised and at a loss as to what she might want, Leonardo assented, spelling out brief directions to his flat on the third storey of a turn-of-the-century building not far from where he had lodged in the years as a student.

She came the following evening. Glitter and glamour shed, no longer the dazzling creature seen at the Savini, sober in skirt and a light shoulder woollen jumper, she entered wordlessly as Leonardo held open the door. Tense in face and features drawn, moving away brusquely as he made to touch his face to her cheek, she took in the sparsely furnished living-cum-study room, a desk heaped with books and papers to one side, a low-slung, tufted velvet sofa opposite, lithographic prints of old Milan on the walls. A mild, early-spring air wafted in from the door giving onto the narrow balcony.

"Can I offer you something? Coffee?"

She shook her head, moving silently to the balcony door, to look down at the small park with poplars in new leaf, a tall magnolia swarming with swollen buds, and beyond the trees a row of imposing neoclassic mansions. Leonardo stood uncertainly by the desk, unable to imagine the purpose of the visit, nor knowing what to say. He had never once been alone with her since her marriage, seen her briefly a few times since, during his infrequent visits home and, Lorenzo and the family present, hardly ever exchanged a word of any consequence.

It was not at all the Laura he had once known, spirited and flighty, her presence never short of the lightness of gaiety. Young still, still slender but with the years filling out the figure with a shapeliness more pronounced, the pale, fine-etched looks of a Renaissance Madonna grown with the maturity of womanhood into a beauty more bold and weighted, the blue of the eyes seemingly several shades deeper, lips less chaste. Leonardo had never asked, nor even wondered why he had been cast aside. The wound silently borne had sufficed as both offence and response.

Moving back, lowering herself on the sofa, she raised her head to look him in the eye, the stare hard and incriminating, less grieved, as she said in a voice throaty and seemingly tinged with spleen, "You've been spying on me, Leo. Why?"

Leonardo came to from his brief reverie. Dumbfounded, he could not find words. "Spying? Why… why would I do that?"

"You saw me the other evening."

"I did."

"You couldn't take your eyes off. And what did you see?"

"You were there. With someone I've never seen before."

"And you were there on purpose."

"Oh, don't be silly! My colleagues at the office wanted to celebrate our win in the Sensi case… you'll have heard of it, of course."

"Never mind the Sensi!" Her voice rose by octaves, the words running into each other. "I suppose you've already called Lorenzo to tell him. It's your revenge, isn't it? You've been waiting for this moment."

Unreason abruptly fuelling some inner panic, a suffused rage spreading visibly, face colouring, she rose to her feet. "They'll take away Roberto from me. You realize that? But that's what you want, don't you?"

"Laura, please…"

Breath suffocating, voice rasping, she advanced towards him. "In God's name, what kind of a man are you? Not a word, nothing, when I went off with Lorenzo. What are you? A coward, a queer! Can't bear to see anyone happy, you little turd!"

Leonardo backed away out on the balcony as, face contorted, rage bursting open with imprecations vile and gross, her raised fists began to rain down on him in manic fury. Afterwards the recall of the moment was shrouded in a haze. Raising his hands to ward off the frenzied blows, moving out an arm to distance her, he had barely seen Laura lose her step, toppling clean over the low-slung stone balustrade. Petrified in a catatonic trance, he had stood there for how long he could not remember, then or later.

~~~

Leonardo was less than collaborative with the team from his legal firm assigned to his defence. As during the initial police interrogation and the preliminary hearings, his lengthy silences, reticence rather than refusal, were only interrupted by the admission that he could not tell if Laura's fatal fall had been accidental or caused by an intentioned act on his part. Confessing to nothing more, nor less, declining to recount in any detail the reason for Laura's visit, seemingly he had shut himself into a space impervious and impenetrable, the proceedings apparently of little interest, the possible consequences of no concern.

Nor was he any more forthcoming with his father during the extended weeks and months of detention before the trial. Anna ailing and frail, Lorenzo never once seen, Stefano was his only visitor. Subdued and withdrawn, Leonardo heard the news from the world beyond, the talk in his home-town, the concern of people known in childhood, the distress of a few friends from youth. Not a word from Eleonora, vanished from his life as though she had never been. Brushing aside whatever the future that awaited him, Leonardo's sole curiosity, and concern, was for little Roberto, enquiring each time about the motherless child. Stefano assured him that the boy was in good hands, staying at home with him and Anna and well cared for.

The trial, many months later, brought to light the soiled linen of a marriage gone wrong, the public mask veiling the sad murk of feeble will and inordinate appetite, incapacity and infidelity. Driven by rage and demanding blood, Laura's family had engaged the services of a famous criminal lawyer to assist and strengthen the prosecution's case.

Leonardo would have wished it otherwise, but his defence had insisted on bringing to light Laura's promiscuity, the long adulterous relationship with the head of her firm, neglect of home and family, the lead lawyer of the team even contemplating resorting to honour killing, no longer on the law books as an admissible plea, but the medieval culture still alive and resorted to not infrequently.

Offering generous fodder to print and press, the extended trial over many weeks, interrupted by recurring public holidays, no less procedural cavils and quibbles, gained national resonance, feeding the public's morbid interest, dividing the country among those who viewed Leonardo as a devious and vengeful spirit and others who saw in Laura the shallow child of wealth, a woman fickle and perfidious, a hard-hearted adulteress who, bent on her own position and pleasure, cared nothing for spouse and child. Reporters from local and national papers besieged the residence of the Bellinis, Stefano himself not spared, at home and in the car showroom. Lorenzo eluded pursuit by leaving the Villa Serena at dawn and returning late at night.

The sorry spectacle of Leonardo in chains, head bowed and sat between two police guards, finally broke Stefano as day by day the private and personal were laid bare for the public to feed on the carrion flesh of family confidences, trivialities of common human failings dragged out from the closet, Lorenzo's high spirits depicted as the habits of a wastrel, a husband envious of his wife's attainments and incapable of fulfilling his marriage vows; Leonardo himself a spoilt child whose over-reaching ambitions and pretensions had led to severing ties from his origins.

Winding its halting way through endless weeks, the trial did finally come to an end, the conclusion seemingly foregone. It was as if Leonardo had wilfully chosen to immolate himself. The insistent prayers and solicitations of his lawyers, of Stefano and well-wishers had done nothing to loosen Leonardo's tongue, his tight-lipped plea of 'not guilty' sounding less than convincing, the reticence and obstinate refusal to be drawn out viewed as an obtuse admission of guilt, the murder of a young wife and mother deemed the heinous act of a cold-blooded and vengeful heart. The verdict of the court could be no other.

Leonardo said, no, he would not lend himself to appealing the judgement. Unbearable the in and out of the courthouse, the long-drawn uncertainty, endless seasons of hope and hope denied. With a casual shrug he accepted the dozen odd years behind the bars, telling his lawyers with a wry smile that it was but a fraction of a lifetime. To Stefano it seemed almost as if he welcomed the reclusion, refusing the world, to walk the streets a free man.

The seasons came and went, the condemned man in his confinement, the parents piecing together the shards of their lives. With much effort and his connections with public figures, no less a few greased palms, Stefano managed to have Leonardo moved out of the squalor of the overcrowded city prison to a brand new jail, in a nearby hill town, devoid of petty thieves and hardened delinquents, populated mostly by white-collar criminals and minor political figures. The single cells neat and clean, Leonardo could have a view from behind the bars of the white-tipped Alpine peaks in the distance. Almost each week Stefano made the short drive, to sit with his son through the visitors' hour, Leonardo calm and silent as he heard head-bowed his father's voice, stumbling syllables of solace and comfort, hope, above all concern for Anna's condition, but holding back on the doctors' words of resignation. And when Anna passed away some months later, Leonardo received the news with an inert calm, lifeless gaze unmoving from the far-off mountain range.

12

Once, lying languid one hot summer afternoon after a long hour of love, Ursula recounted a recurring dream she had years ago. A vision of herself wandering stark naked on a vast, sunlit plain bursting with ripening ears of wheat, as menstrual blood trickled down her legs and insect life from the russet leaves falling away where she walked through the field of gold. She had never quite understood what it might have meant, nor ever dared to mention it to the analyst she had frequented for a brief period.

"Pliny," I said.

"Who?"

"Pliny the Elder. Roman naturalist."

Ursula looked at me somewhat nonplussed. "And what does your Roman friend have to do with my dream?" she asked, tilting her head.

"Apparently, Pliny suggested that life perishes coming in contact with menstrual blood. Wine sours, fruit falls off trees, crops and insects die. Things of the sort. A metaphor for sterility, a barren condition."

"What an encyclopedia you are, Professor. Had I only known!"

Less then encyclopaedic, I had come across Pliny's words in a student's dissertation on blood as symbol in the ancient world.

Thoughtful a long moment, Ursula's voice seemed to come from the depths of a reverie. "It was a time when I wanted a child. Something for myself alone. I had never really had anything to call my own."

Letting fall a long sigh, she looked through the window at the waters of the lake. "For *Mutti*, I was something that ought not to have happened. All her life mother lived with the hope of reclaiming a world she had never known. My arrival derailed her dreams. As for father… best to let him rest with whatever peace a man like him can find in afterlife. And Armin… Armin belonged to the world. I was only a mascot, his hope of late glory. But a child, someone to nurse and rear, love without condition. That would be different."

No mention then of the first adult love of her life, the head of the clinic where she had worked as a nurse. Much later I learned of Dr. Krieger, the man who had weaned her from her cursed past, but one who also tutored her in the murk of appetites perverse and corrupt. More guide and benefactor, with a curious hold on her, the doctor she had never loved, she corrected herself subsequently. Ursula's narrations at times seemed to be written on sand, subject to shifts and alterations, as though never quite sure or convinced of her past.

In her telling, Armin had made clear that he wanted no truck with children. A wife lost at childbirth early in life had put an end to his wish for fatherhood. Ursula thought it was more the circumstances of the loss.

The early after-war years in a provincial town in the east of the country, the Russians still about, the Party tightening its hold, the never-ending shortages, of medicines, food and clothing, shoes, the dearth of shoes, as though the war had wreaked havoc less on human lives, more on man's footwear. The local hospital was ill-provided, equipment scarce and out-of-date, staff with little training or less, the few aged medics left-overs from the Russian front and scrambling like rats for survival in the new order.

Married early to a chamber maid of the house, young Göttner had last seen his wife on a rusty hospital bed, life fled from mother and infant during the strangled birth. He had never loved the country girl with her broad, peasant face and rustic ways, the marriage a mere camouflage for his noble ancestry, an inconvenience, if not a peril, in the oppressive air wafting through the new-born and divided nation and severely intolerant of the privilege of birth and breeding. But the sight on the bloodied sheets had been enough, as he turned away vouchsafing never to set eyes again on a new born, dead or alive. Tramping back through the ruins and rubble under an ominous autumn sky, he had decided that family and offspring were not for him.

Nothing had remained of the past. Parents gone, estate and lands lost, fleeing before the marauding Russian hordes looting and raping, travelling west with his young wife, no older than him, he had thought to conceal his ancestry in the chaos of lives of a people defeated and a world deranged. If he had not loved Irmele, yet he was desolated by her death, she who with her hard-headed peasant sense had brought him through sleet and snow, hunger and pain. It was not the loss of a love, not regret, but the image of the death-bed that stayed with him. Unhealed, the wound had remained, a suppuration of dread and revulsion. Ever after, birth for Göttner was the obverse face of death, quite as repugnant and unsightly. Putting to rest once and for all her hopes of motherhood, he once said to Ursula, "There's nothing miraculous about birth. Mere ejection of a foetus. Little more than putting out another body waste."

The offspring of a deranged household, childhood often a reign of terror, Ursula had for years pined for a family of her own. No matter that for long years her life as a young woman had been buffeted through the storm and siege of the gross cravings of men, always older by several spans, mostly libertine and lewd, the ageing lubricity often cloaked in genteel manners and paternal concern. Her own father's earth-worked hands had, at least, made no pretence of care and sympathy even as they clasped her flesh. Those others, suited in their high professional garb, waist-coated and white-coated, pried and probed with mannered words and manicured fingers, but the intent was ever the same, salacity masquerading as genteel seduction. If men only knew, she said, that after the wining and dining and whoring, at the end of the day a woman longs to carry a life within herself. If Göttner had denied her motherhood, the ache in the vacant womb still remained, stirring to life at odd moments.

Leonardo was not meant to father her child. It was not her intent, not at first. The desire was to dawn later, when she woke to the clock ticking, the hour glass running out. Possibly a little late in the day, but in these times there were ways and means, long-barren females giving birth to twins and triplets, women of grandmotherly age savouring the bliss of motherhood for the first time.

"One day," she recalled, "we were dining out and a couple of children were running about between tables. Italians don't mind that. In fact, one of the waiters picked up the youngest, a curly-haired little girl. He took her out on the terrace, to allow the parents to eat in peace. It came to me then."

She had gazed at the child squirming and giggling in the waiters arms and she looked at Leonardo sat opposite her. Why not? Why not, indeed? He was a man as good as any, in his prime, handsome, courteous in manner and refined in word, never vulgar, never reaching out to what was not offered. True, a shadow hung about him, she had heard, knew something of the errant past. But she had no interest in peering beyond the person he now was, dig and delve into what had gone. Prying into the antecedents of humans, more often than not one came on misdeeds and misdemeanours, buried fault lines, transgressions of the heart if not crimes against the laws of man. What he had been and done was no concern of hers. The Leonardo now seated across the table was the one she knew, the man she wanted, as lover, husband, no less the father of her child.

Besides, too, no call for the acrobatics of seduction and conquest, they were already lovers. She had come to fill in some measure the desolate void he seemed to harbour within, waking him to life as he increasingly clung to her with an aching need to be wanted, desired, loved as might a mother. Outwardly composed and patient, serene almost, only when together, in the hours of intimacy, only then did his recondite hunger burst forth with the effusion of a passion whose tidal wave often overwhelmed her. Familiar and practised she might be in the intricate maze of the cravings and concupiscence of men. But she had never known one like Leonardo, words few and gentle, gaze distant, seemingly pondering a horizon opaque and nebulous. And then, in her arms, pulsing to life and the moment, as if shot with the vigour of a primordial spirit, the slender figure virile with inordinate strength, an almost feline rage erasing sense and reason. So, why not? Why should Leonardo not father the child so long denied her.

~~~

Leonardo had taken up residence at the Villa Serena less than a year ago. Ursula knew nothing of her new neighbour, had on occasion merely heard his voice, low and muffled, drowned out by the housekeeper's firm, almost stentorian tones. One day, she was at her gate, up from an errand in the town, when for the first time she set eyes on him as he left the house. A slender figure, dressed neatly but simply in a light jacket over a polo shirt, reasonably tall, somewhere in his forties, but the youthful looks shaded by a pallor meek and docile, not quite doleful, more a resigned melancholy. Merely a brief sighting and Ursula thought no more of it.

Some weeks later, invited to dinner by Fabbri, she met Leonardo in person. The tristful expression gone, quiet and personable, not much engaging in talk, yet there still lingered a pensive air about him. Most of all, Ursula was struck by the similarities between uncle and nephew, in build and lineaments, Leonardo's face older and more weathered, Fabbri as handsome as his uncle would have been at an earlier age. If anything, they were more like brothers. As often with blood brothers, manner and presence set them apart, Fabbri suave and affable, mellifluous in speech tinged with humour, the material success evinced by the elegant wear and the furnishings of the apartment, the affluence worn with ease. But the older man, likeable though not much given to sociability, small talk and easy exchange, gave the impression of a weightier presence.

Later, when Ursula had learnt something of their past, she recalled that first evening, thinking then with some wonder how the destinies of both men had forked out from the same cross-roads, the woman who left one a motherless child and shut away the other from the world in the prime of life. Odder still that neither ill-will nor rancour seemed to come between them, not the slightest sign or syllable of the least animus. The byways of human sentience taking paths unseen, it made Ursula wonder if the common tie of love had been the healing balm. Years later, Leonardo gone and no love lost between her and Fabbri, she said to me, "Uncommon types, those two. One doesn't often meet men like them."

That first evening, as the maid served and spooned out moving around the diners, the table-talk was light and casual, nothing weighty, above all away from their persons. Fabbri recounted briefly the history of the Göttner mansion, built at the turn of the previous century by an impoverished Lombard nobleman with clerical funds from a Cardinal uncle.

"The Curia looks after it's own," remarked Leonardo quietly with a faint, wry smile.

"You'd hardly expect the clerical high table to be set with the bread and water served the devotees," Fabbri laughed. "I was sent to a Jesuit college and one had to see the stout Cuban cigars the Fathers smoked. We boys weren't much into smoking, but the size of the cigars did provoke impure thoughts! Are you a Catholic, Ursula? If I may ask."

"I wish I knew! Where I come from, in the forest cantons, most are. Catholic, I mean Old Catholic. But in those parts the male is the one true god!"

"Good to hear that. We'd feel at home there. What do you say, Leo?"

"It's mostly our women here," said Leonardo with a slight twist of the face, "who make of us lords and kings."

"In a way Leo's right." Fabbri waited for his dish to be cleared. "Take Maria, the lady who keeps house for Leo. She's of peasant stock, married in her teens to an older man. A drunk and a brute, if ever there was one. Every other day he used to beat her black and blue. I remember her coming to work at Leo's parent's place. Cuts and bruises down the arms one day, a bandage around the head another. One might have thought she lived in a war zone! Once one of the eyes was so red and swollen, I asked grandfather Stefano if she was going blind! Hard to believe, then, that Maria adored the man, would have kissed the ground where the beast walked. You'd not think it, a woman so practical, so sensible. But through a whole lifetime she never did come to her senses."

He paused, to shake his head with a look of puzzlement. "He's been gone sometime now. And still… Every Sunday morning now she's at the cemetery, putting fresh flowers on the grave stone of the dead man. Soon after he died, I met her one day headed for the cemetery with a pot of chrysanthemums. We only greeted each other, but she must have sensed something in my look. 'He was my man after all,' she said and went her way. She sounded almost apologetic, it surprised me."

"Yes," Ursula nodded. "I suppose sometimes it's we who make gods of our men."

Despite everything. A woman's love, she had often thought, quite unlike that of the male, was all encompassing, more akin to Paul's Biblical love, bearing all things, believing, ever hopeful, ever enduring. Thinking, then, of *Mutti*, her own mother, head-bowed and silent, long-suffering, as the man of the house raged and ranted, spat out foul-mouthed invectives, *hure* and *schlampe*, whore and slut the least of the appellations in his armoury of hurtful epithets. And the times his fist rose in drunken rage to beat down on her as she crouched in a dark corner. But then, there had also come the day when, the cup full, heart no longer able to hold the venom at the sight of the brute hand groping her young girl, her spirit had risen to put an end to the years of abuse and assault.

Her mother, an orphan child of history, might have had reason to bear in silence whatever the outrage and violence. But she, Ursula… A lamb willingly led to slaughter! Why had she put up for years with good Dr. Krieger's gross and obscene conduct, all those countless afternoons when he straddled her as she crouched on the ground on all fours, pulling up her nurse's dress and hurtfully smacking the naked buttocks of his hobby-horse with a birch twig. Then lending her out for the night to his simpering colleagues. And if she had been young and jejune then, what of these later years, Armin's wilful offence, neglect, disdain and injurious indifference? Love, all bearing, all suffering and enduring. Paul the Apostle must have had mostly a woman's love in mind.

"We women make our own beds," she repeated as they made to rise from the table. "Often breeding our own monsters."

"Fair game!" Fabbri laughed. "So in the end it's the woman to blame in the court of justice."

That evening Ursula learned little about Leonardo. She gleaned merely that he had studied law, practised professionally only briefly, had come back to town and moved to the Villa Serena after his father's death some years years ago, that he now informally advised poorer inmates of prisons unable to afford proper legal assistance.

Leonardo had remained mostly silent through much of the exchange at table, look opaque with a seemingly resigned stillness in the eyes. Present, yet somehow also absent, it was as though he sat apart, lending his presence yet wanting to conceal himself, become one with his silence and passivity. Very occasionally, he gave laconic voice when called on in person. When, touching on the grievance of women, Fabbri said, "The laws of the land are made by men. Mostly everywhere. Ask Leo, he's the expert," Leonardo nodded. "True," he agreed in a quite voice, adding nothing more.

Ursula came away with the impression of a man grieved. But whatever the hurt, the pain was not worn on the sleeve, remained concealed in recesses buried and out of sight. Holding himself at arm's length, the uncommon reserve, sober, not solemn, was a rarity among males in these parts.

First impressions at times misled, but not with Leonardo, Ursula was to find. Far from garrulous, never once voluble, vocality was not one of his gifts. Words chosen with care, as though each syllable carried weight and consequence, speech always measured and succinct, even the terms of endearment later were uttered with the brevity of musical notes. Once, in the throes of passion, his arms wound around her in a mortal vice that seemingly could never be loosened, he said, "I could not do without you." Even then, in the hush of the dark, the words pouring warm breath as his face nuzzled her neck, through the vaporous haze of desire she felt him still holding back, the brief declamation measured and guarded, lest the flood gates burst into a surrender excessive and total.

In time, Ursula would come to feel that banked up within Leonardo there were waters with the depths of an ocean and the raging surge of a storm, that had never found release in voice or act, freed into the open. Careful never to let go, always treading the earth with steps wary and hesitant, circumspect in contact and uninvolved with the world and its doings, he seemed to prefer to draw back into the shadows, to live unnoticed, unheard. So very different from nephew Fabbri. Sharing no particular and noticeable family trait other than build and looks, Leonardo instead preferred to keep the world at arm's length.

Yet, in their year or less together, Ursula had not been able to gauge to the full the maelstrom alive within Leonardo. *I could not do without you*, he had said. A common-place utterance of lovers, and she had taken it as such, not giving the brief declaration its due weight and unable to imagine the depths from which it rose. Not mere idle syllables pronounced in a moment of amorous fervour, she had not caught the pulsing resonance of the confession, both plea and prayer. And for long, for ever afterwards, she silently cursed the deafness of her heart that had not given ear to the clamouring supplication. How different, then, her days might have been!

13

It was a fallow season of life. Nothing stirred, neither leaf nor branch, within or in the small world of her confinement. Heart withering, desires in abeyance, the hands of the clock unmoving, the days long and solitary, the nights empty, at times the dark hours flaring with scattered dreams of the past, her father's heavy face burrowing into her belly, Dr. Krieger's impotent fondling, the fingers in the surgical glove prying and probing in niche and nook. To wake of a sudden, then, in the cold dawn, alone, the bed empty of the man who should have been beside her.

Exiled in this grand house, long hours looking over the waters of the lake, insensate to the scent of the oleanders in bloom wafted in the air as, vacant in mind, drained of will and desire, in these empty rooms she had waited, waiting long months for Armin to return. A wilful purgatory, atonement for what she had not been able to offer, what she had not become, a promise unfulfilled, a betrayal! The prima donna on the world's stage, the grand dame on his arm to exhibit, to show that he was not done yet, resurrected and returned from the world's forgetfulness, once again the imposing figure of the great maestro on the podium gathering with arms stretched wide the fervid acclaim, the deafening applause of the audience on its feet. She was meant to be his salvation and resurrection, his very own Aida and Violetta, who would swoon and faint at his command. Senescent hope of a blind soul trying to make its tortuous way back to the paradise lost.

And when he did come, for mere brief stays, he was ever careful to deny himself to her. Hardly ever a touch, rarely an intimate closeness or confidence, even rarer the kindness of a word or warm breath. Coming up the garden path and meeting her at the entrance, his arms might come around her in embrace, his heavy face planting lips briefly on her cheek, yet the effusion of homecoming was somehow restrained, arid and mechanical. She merely kept house, to offer him short rest and respite, more a way station on a seemingly never-ending journey. Only over meals would he tell, peeved and carping, an occasional tale from his travels. The cramped lodgings in some far-off capital, he who had been accustomed to residences of luxury and sumptuous hospitality, the attention of the cultured press, city streets lined with man-high posters and hoardings announcing the musical event he was to preside.

Now, arriving in a rundown provincial airport, the reception consisting of a couple of eminences of the local musical association welcoming him in a language indecipherable, to be driven off in a decades old sedan that was more a jalopy with worn and torn leather seats, to be lodged in a once grand, now ramshackle hotel with fraying curtains and faded velvet seating. The skills of the town orchestra uncertain, the cello players sawing away at their instrument with all the enthusiasm of rustic carpenters, the brass making their entry willy-nilly with little respect for the score, the woodwind groaning with dull, ligneous sonority, it was all he could do to preserve order and reign in the impetuosity of the over-excitable ensemble. "Savages!" he would pronounce afterwards with bitter disdain, "The Peruvians' idea of music is the beating of drums and tin cans!" Or else, back from a tour of Australasia, giving vent to a sniggering dismissal of the local musical talent: "They'd have done better to recruit members of their National Orchestra from among their native aborigines."

"Armin, why…" she would start to say, but her thoughts never became vocal. Why submit to such humbling and humiliation, she meant to ask, why the fate in old age of an itinerant musician aimlessly wandering dim corners of the world? What the purpose of such vagrancy? And what of his self-esteem, the vaunted pride that with a look of hauteur had once shrunk those in front of him? His old agent, a major French impresario, might be indiscriminate in his choice of clients, arranging indifferently bookings for circus troupes, magicians and comedians, long-forgotten figures of the stage. But he, Armin, had no need for such peripatetic wayfaring, making of himself a figure of ridicule and derision, calling forth merely pathos in those who had known and loved him, admired his art and reverenced the artist he had been. Money could not be the reason, their finances were sound. In any case, the earnings were meagre for one like him.

What then? She never did ask, never dared. For he would have turned on her, hurled in her face the cause of this senescent obliquity. She it was, who had brought him down in the world, made of him a fool and a buffoon, a caricature of the man he had been, a figure of scorn and pity.

"I'm going to make something of you, *Liebling*," he had once told her in the early days. "Something the world has never seen!" She was to become a nightingale sprung from nowhere, the song and the singer the one and the same, interchangeable, indistinguishable, a voice to go with the splendour of her form, the beauty the lyric of her art, the art the spirit of her body. And he, Armin von Göttner, would rise once again, beside her, as she unfurled her pristine wings to fly the skies resonant with acclaim and glory.

More than once, then, he had conjured up for her visions of when the singer's voice faded in barely audible ripples and the audience got to its feet as one man, the deafening applause threatening to bring down the domed roof of the concert hall as with the clap of prolonged thunder the concert-goers let out from pierced hearts the ringing tumult stirred by the singer's dramatic coloratura. "Believe me, *Liebchen*," he would tell her then, "there is nothing on earth, no joy or ecstasy, that comes anywhere near. That is the hour I have in mind for you."

Folly! The obliquity of a mind deranged by a chimera fed with the madness of passion. Not love, no, not that, more a ravenous sensuous infatuation that seemed to drive him to an oblivion of mind and sense when he held her in his arms, the eye feasting on her body as she lay beside him, the touch of his hand as he pressed, cupped, moulded her flesh seemingly wanting to draw her entire person into himself. Not the mere passing drive of desire, love-making only the mechanical prelude to the possession of her being, her youth, beauty, body and breath, to nourish and reinvigorate his own spirit and soul. In recompense he would offer her name, fame, the adoration of the multitude, the world at her feet.

Young and ingenuous, little knowing the world and no less confused, she had lent herself to the absurd fantasy. He was older by several spans, it did not much matter. All her life she had been at the mercy and behest of older men, her father, the church choir master, Dr. Krieger and his lecherous colleagues, who called her *Schwester* even as their tongues probed her parts secret and intimate. This man was different, neither coarse nor lewd, refined in manner with the innate elegance of the high-born. Above all, a saviour come to rescue her, take her away from the twilight of a life without promise or prospect, mere grovelling servitude to the infantile whims and gross fantasies of ageing males for whom she was little more than a toy for crude fondling. She had loved Armin then, or so she imagined. And thoughtlessly bidding farewell to the clinic, she had followed him, to be led where he so willed.

Coming back now from his vagrant travels every other month or two, to a house that had become for him more of a transit, short of words and keeping her at arms distance, through the short stay he would sit for hours at the piano, the music a wall around him that Ursula dared not breach. Reclining on a gilt-wood armchair out on the terrace, enervated, the sombre notes resounding and wafting out, shading her melancholy with a darker hue, she waited full hours with mute patience for him to rise from the instrument and lend her his presence and attention.

At times, looking through the wide doorway and the raised cover of the Bösendorfer, she had the impression that he had barely aged since the day she had first set eyes on him. Well past his seventieth year, but the silver head still full and worn long, curling over the nape, the face heavier but not much changed, the lineaments seemingly untouched by time and as imperious as the Bösendorfer Imperial, the full lips turned with an edge of conceit, the dawn-blue eyes still and grave. The large frame, still surprisingly unweighted with flab and fat, sat upright as the hands moved over the keys fluent and sure, without the theatrical leap and pounce of many a modern concert pianist.

Handsome in a patrician manner, emanating an air of commanding will and vigour, his was a figure that could still draw a woman, solicit attention, charm and beguile, seduce. Ursula at times still felt the draw, memory of the early days imprinted within, of his manly hold of her body and spirit, the surfeit of satisfaction he could offer a willing partner, both suave and strong his taking and possession, making for a fulfilment both breathless and replete.

Her heart in love, or so she had felt then, she had sometimes mused with a smile that he bedded a female with the same moves and designs of a sonata or symphony, a brief overture that lit the fire, the slow flames fanned by a singing largo that set in motion desire urgent and impatient, until the tremulous body clamouring dominion, grasping and clawing, was led towards the pinnacle with a pace and motion meditated and deliberate, the crescendo of star-burst erasing time, life, the universe.

She had known other men, but a lover such as Armin rare, Dr. Pelosi at the clinic an exception. Otherwise, not a single one, young or older, artless or practised, had known to make of her body a shrine, for most of whom love-making was more often merely animal coupling or pairing, hurried and brusque, at times surreptitious, as though calling for concealment, from self and the world. Armin, instead, was truly maestro, finesse at his finger tips, as he touched the keys of the piano, held the baton in the curve of a supple and strong hand, a hand that worked its way into the secret byplaces and recesses of a woman's being, moving both wilful and wanton, yet pliant and persuasive. Almost as if, Ursula thought later, for Armin love, *liebe, amour, amor, agápi,* call it what one might, had left its residence in the heart and migrated to the fingertips, his hands the caretaker and the caregiver of all that was human in him.

~~~

Now, almost half a lifetime later, here she was, in a place not of her choosing, in a house that had little of a home, friendless and among strangers, abandoned, a wife in name, suspended in time and ever awaiting the return of a spouse whose occasional arrival wafted through the rooms and chambers the chill air of indifference and rejection. Not yet in her fortieth year, desire and appetite still alive under the ashes, there were nights when the craving of the body to be held and loved kept her awake through the hours of the dark. She had known men in the guise of master, mentor, lover, brute and beast, in youth given herself and given away the little she possessed, learning on the way something of the secret recesses in humans dormant with desires unutterable, cravings ineffable. Seemingly it had served little.

Languishing in this arid wasteland, forcing herself out of the house, on occasion she went to a concert, the theatre less, the speech of the stage not always accessible despite her familiarity with the language of the land, a rare time to Milan on a day trip, to shop, a visit to some gallery, a sedate and solitary lunch at the Savini in the Galleria, that Fabbri had once indicated as a comfortable dining venue.

Fabbri himself had once accompanied her to the city, showing her around possible places of interest, fashionable stores and high-end boutiques, with their dazzling wear and footwear, destinations favoured by women from the upper reaches. She had taken it as a prelude to courtship. But, though pleasant and companionable his presence, somehow he had always held her at arm's length, always courteous and affable, as always mannered and formal, refraining from word or gesture intimate. Often with a bemused air, oddly detached, not quite the lover one might have in mind. Ursula felt at times the need for a heedless and impetuous spirit to storm into the desultory stillness of her virtual widowhood. Fabbri failed to fit the bill, had he even lent himself to her overtures.

A rare time she went over to Montreux, for a brief stay with Davidovich. The concert hall long abandoned, he now lived a quiet existence, seeing to the winery and nursing his love for his Gabriel. But the odd day or two with him were less than satisfactory. Both victims, they had only to show, each to the other, the wounds wrought by the same hand. Besides, Davidovich was still in thrall to Armin, ever his master and maestro, the figure who had both made and broken him, the perverse devotion of the victim for his tormentor still alive and intact. Besides, too, not ever voicing it in words, for him Ursula had been largely the cause of the downfall of his god.

Very occasionally she had travelled back to the locality of her nursing years. Much changed now, friends and acquaintances of the earlier days lost to sight, only a companion of the heart from the time at the clinic had remained. But Ilse, married to an anaesthetist, with a growing son and a daughter, was a simple soul in all, practical and with a housewifely girth, little able to understand Ursula's pain and predicament. Commiserating, yet unable to fathom the entanglements of the heart, she peremptorily advised, "I shouldn't do it, girl! Lose all you have at this time of life? It'll pass, you'll see."

It did not pass. Nor the wayward thoughts of leaving Armin for a new life with Leonardo. A step forward, a step back, her mind hovering at the brink, doubt and uncertainty clouded her days. Leave Armin, and what then? Armin had always been generous, never a word of what she spent, whatever the superfluity or extravagance. On her part, she had no resources of her own, nor honest skills to sell, talent or profession.

All these years she had lived too well, with never a thought of making ends meet, maids and attendants at her beck and call. While not acquisitive by nature or given to excess, no second thought was ever called for when taken by a fancy, a new dress suite to augment the abundant wardrobe, a stone-studded bracelet to add to the treasure-trove of jewellery Armin had heaped on her in the early years. Coddled in ease and the comfort of living, she could no longer contemplate an existence strained by the necessities of the quotidian. Could contemplate even less the return now, in mid-age, to the nursing life of the starched uniform and white corridors redolent of spillages and disinfectants, the maimed young and the senile aged recumbent with the still gaze of hope and hopelessness. For sure, there might now not be another Herr Dr. Krieger in wait to grope her behind. Still and all, unimaginable a return, a reprise of the time in another life.

It was the fractured landscape of a long, barren season into which Leonardo had made his entry, stealthy at first, to sprout then, seed-like under new rain, taking sure root, the young shoot furling leaf and branch, rising firm and full to take possession not only of her days and nights, but also mind and thought, spirit and being. Swept off her feet, poise and balance fled, for a time it seemed to her she had no life of her own, void of will and volition, not at all a separate entity, but one with him, breath common, a single being. Not the sensation of giving and offering, more the partaking of one's own flesh, to be consumed till nothing remained.

14

Ursula remembered Armin telling her once of a cellist in one of the orchestras he had conducted from time to time. Something of a macabre tale, it had stuck in her memory.

A musician of some talent, a thorough professional, sober and patient, ever alert to the directions of the conductor's baton, the cellist had a wife a deal younger than him. Half the year orchestral engagements taking him elsewhere in the country, as too abroad, he was away for extended periods. His return home was for the wife an occasion for celebration, as she laid out a lavish table with his favourite meals, invited over a few friends for the evening, planned day excursions to the countryside. All in all a happy couple, childless but with the feel of a family content and harmonious, with never a dispute or voice raised in anger. Moderately flighty and flirtatious, lightening the mood of the house, the woman seemed an apt complement to the husband, a man kind and considerate, but ever pensive with a curious, wistful melancholy.

A dozen years or so into the marriage, the cellist began to notice that the wife's playfulness had begun to give way to an ebullience excessive and a touch too loud for his uncomplicated tastes. The accustomed warm welcome on his return might be one thing, increasingly now it had all the appearance of a festive carnival for the homecoming of a conquering hero. The house crowded with half the flora of a botanical garden, a score of roses on the sideboard, an enormous vase of scarlet peony in the sitting room, long-stemmed orchids hanging in the kitchen and coming into the face when one went in. Increasingly, too, the foodstuffs and bottles set on the table appeared to be beyond the means of the musician's pockets.

The adornment and the table apart, the wife herself had begun to sport items of clothing that bespoke unwarranted extravagance, not all of it to the husband's sense of taste and housewifely decorum. Her normally youthful dress habits had given way to wear more fitting for a showgirl or hostess in a cocktail lounge, plunging necklines on blouses that revealed the ample bosom more than necessary, long skirts slit to a possibly indecorous length up the leg, her person adorned with jewellery and trinkets he had not seen before. No particular change perceptible in her word and manner, she was affectionate as ever, cosseting and caring, pleasuring him, as always, with her youthful vivacity and vigour, if anything even more energetic in their moments as man and wife together. Unable to decipher possible cause for the alterations, he kept his thoughts to himself, but could not help wondering.

One season, then, a concert tour in a neighbouring country called off at the last moment owing to inclement weather and severe flooding, the cellist came home unannounced, to find the wife out, and a guest on the marriage bed. The stranger, a young man slender and passably handsome, was comfortably stretched out on his side, the tall frame bare save a frilly item of female lingerie around the head, eyes shut fast and face in well-earned repose. Dismayed, the master of the house looked about him, his entry not having in the least disturbed the visitor, sunk apparently in unshakeable sleep. The curtains drawn, the room in disarray, the sheets flung aside by some lively exertion on the bed, the wife's underclothes heaped on one pillow, the intruder's clothes, of elegant cloth and cut, were neatly draped on the chair by the side.

After pondering the scene for long minutes, with no visible change in demeanour, the cellist went about the task with his accustomed calm, and with the same meticulous skill when applying rosin and tightening the bow hair before sitting down to play his instrument. A weighty cast iron skillet from the kitchen brought down on the head, with a force carefully measured not to crack the skull but prolong the repose indefinitely, ensured lack of resistance when he heaved the limp figure on his robust shoulders, gathered up the man's clothes and headed to the rear of the house, making then for the old barn across the cobbled yard. Returning, he gave the bedroom the once over, to ensure that no belonging of the guest had been overlooked.

All necessary implements at hand, donning a worn knee-length apron and spreading several old sacks on the floor, he set to work, dismembering the body, starting out from the head. The young man was unusually lean of body and, sized suitably by the sabre wood saw, the anatomical chunks fitted comfortably the cellist's father's old Jacquet double bass case, the legs however calling for further shortening. Packed and covered over with the dead man's silk shirt and fine fabric suit, the calf leather shoes stuffed into the bow pocket, under garments tucked away in corners, the case shut and bagged in its worn canvas holder, the blood-soaked sacks rolled up for disposal, the implements carefully wiped and put away, the barn reordered, he set off with the load carefully laid in the back of the car, heading for the river beyond the wooded hills. The case and the bundled sacks bobbed for a moment before being swallowed and swept away in the waters swollen by the floods in the neighbouring region.

On the way back, a passing doubt had played on his mind, of some item on the bedside table, a tie pin, a watch, left behind when clearing away the dead man's presence in the bedroom. A small shiny article, indistinct, appeared to linger briefly in the eye of his memory. But things had gone as well as they might and he gave it no further thought.

Putting up for the night with a cousin in the neighbouring town, the cellist arrived home the next day. The wife more than a little surprised, taken aback by his unannounced and unexpected return, nonetheless the welcome was cheerful as ever, as she busied herself in the kitchen, fussed with putting out his nightwear in the tidy and ordered bedroom, the bed laid with fresh linen, the slippers on the side. Her accustomed self, chirpy and at ease, as usual she recounted over dinner small local events, the butcher slaying and quartering his brother over money matters, the scandal of the mayor's wife found in the arms of one of the municipal clerks.

Afterwards, a cursory glance at the bedside tables found no trace of the piece the cellist thought he might have overlooked. The heavy padlock on the barn door in place, the autumn sky washed clean, bright and starry, putting out the cigarillo and breathing deep the night air, he turned into the house, to be received in the waiting arms of the wife.

The rooms no longer reeking of the abundant floral display, the table still well laid but without the extravagant delicacies, the wife herself once again, light-hearted but not overly exuberant, as of late, her habits of dress exhibiting less of her charms, the wayward interlude behind them, the couple's life resumed much as before, he calm and kind, as ever, she loving and solicitous, as always. Not a word uttered, nothing ever asked or said, yet the woman's passing infidelity did make a brief appearance, and it unnerved the innate calm of the cellist. Some months later, out for a dinner to celebrate their wedding anniversary, the wife handed him her present, a slender velvet box with a slim silver wrist watch, with the name of a renowned Swiss house, the leather strap new, but the timepiece itself a vintage. The card with the gift read: *For a good man, a loving and faithful husband!*

~~~

Real or apocryphal, the grim tale recounted at such length and in detail had puzzled Ursula. Armin was not one for anecdotes, fables and tall tales for their own sake, unless it was to deliver a moral or a lesson. Usually pithy, concise in recall of the past, he grew impatient with long-winded narration, and the story of the cellist made her wonder. Was it perhaps an elliptical message, a cautionary tale? Lately the director of a renowned theatre, visiting Milan in preparation for an operatic performance, had begun to lay siege to Ursula, courting her in open sight with some insistence. Nothing concealed, even less to conceal, on occasion she had lent herself to the game, the two seen in public together a time or two.

"This cello player… Is it true?" she had asked. "Did it really happen?"

"It might have. Or not. That's beside the point." With a small smile of paternal benevolence, he added, "More important, there could be a lesson to the story, I believe."

"Oh! And what would that be?"

"Women sometimes forget. It's not always the act that counts, but what one does with it." Holding Ursula steady in his gaze, he went on, "Fornicate, if you will, but don't flaunt it. A man might put up with a wife's infidelity, it becomes unbearable when shouted from the rooftops."

"Oh!"

"Dangerous at times to touch a man's sense of worth. Even if the person is of little worth."

"Self-esteem, you mean?"

"Call it that, if you wish. We are rarely as the world sees us. One's sense of worth of oneself, *amor proprio* the Latins called it, may be a man's most precious possession. Belittle that and you're asking for trouble."

Not the sort of trouble Ursula had in mind or ever wanted. The cellist's story had remained with her and came to mind during the long year with Leonardo. *Don't flaunt it*, Armin had said. Liege to his word, she never did. During his brief stays of rest and respite from roving the world, she neither saw Leonardo, nor sent or received word.

But observation still keen, able to decipher at a glance the smallest cypher musical notation on the stave, Armin appeared to sense there was something in the air. Was Ursula perhaps bedding another during his absence? Unsure, yet he was not one to probe or query. A time or two, over the years, the worm of suspicion had caught his passing attention, but the impressions, indistinct and doubtful, had never given cause for sleepless nights. In any case, it did not matter much. He had had the bloom of her youth, it mattered little if she were to offer the faded and wilting remains of the once radiant blossom to another or to others, but only out of sight and away from the public eye. Discretion and decorum maintained, the rest was of little concern. There were things in life now of greater interest than who or what might chance to pass between a wife's legs.

Ursula understood and observed the pact as best as she could. No cause given for suspicion, not the merest hint or word, her outward manner the same as ever, yet she could not help feeling at times that somehow his instinctive gaze had seen through the invisible, albeit in the dark as to who the intruder might be. Her discretion rewarded, as though with tacit accord, a conspiracy of infidelity, with practised indifference he chose to look away, merely saying one day, casual and in passing, as he squinted impatiently over the score of a concert piece: "A blind eye has it's uses." Crossing out then with a brisk stroke of the pencil a redundant tie, he added in the same neutral tone, "And some things in life are best left unsung. Don't you think, Ursula?"

Not a query, seemingly a mere random remark, rhetorical, she could simply nod in agreement. But Armin's forbearance was of little consolation. Tables turned, less an aggrieved husband, it was Leonardo's bitter resentment that at times blighted their hours together. Ursula had not reckoned with her lover's blind animus, little imagined Leonardo's silent rage of jealousy during Armin's short week or two in the house, seeing himself in the mirror as the betrayed, her infidelity to him the duplicity of an uncaring and callous heart. Impervious to reason, brushing aside with brusque asperity her light-humoured claim that it was for Armin to be grieved, not he, impervious to reason, each time Leonardo gave himself to a fit of pique more akin to a child's tantrum.

"But Leo…," she would start to say, her voice silenced by the look in his eyes, both wounded and vehement. Baffled, she had not understood, then or later, the depth of his grievance, so corrosive and obsessive that, in the end, no longer able to reason, sense and sight blinded, his deranged mind embraced the extreme consequence.

The whys multiplying, repeated again and again, at first Ursula could make no sense of Leonardo's tragic exit. Time dissipating grief and sight clearing, she saw better the intricacy of crossed intentions, expectations beyond reach. Meagre of tears by habit, looking back in the aftermath she could not at times help brushing away the damp rising in her eyes at the thought that she had been so blind, unable to decipher the true weight of the silent script that Leonardo had elaborated for their future together. For her it was more the letter of intent of a season of passion, for him promise and commitment set in stone, ineradicable.

Nor had she paused to query her own intentions, a deceit of self, beguiling oneself with a pledge that could not possibly be honoured. In truth, the year with Leonardo had been more a time of make-believe, an extravagant indulgence that offered the illusion of another life, leaving behind the sterility and solitude of an existence without horizon, devoid of prospect or promise. Abandoning a husband, however indifferent and distant, had never been an option or serious proposition. Armin had been the one and only mainstay she had ever known, his hand sculpting what she now was, the breath with which he had animated her the air she still breathed. It was a bond, she knew, whose severance was unimaginable, the parting to be decreed by death alone, as vowed at the alter of the odd little church on a hilltop. The rest was fable, fantasy, daydream, an afternoon reverie.

Her urgent and abrupt departure at the news of Armin's malaise might have been of less consequence, had it not been for the scribbled line or two left before the flight at the midnight hour. The few words ill-chosen and put down in haste finally brought home to Leonardo's mind the truth he might have suspected but chosen to overlook. Ursula belonged to another, a bond indissoluble, Armin the core and essence of her being, the entwining beyond separation; he, Leonardo, merely the bit actor, humoured and indulged but always in the wings, looking in from the penumbra. A sensation not dissimilar to that in childhood when, peering through the chink in the door, he would see his father and mother Anna clasped in a breathless tussle, and wondering why he should have been shut out and away from their wordless play.

The man of imperatives that he was, poised ever between extremes, seeing no way out from the pitch darkness of the bottomless pit in which he found himself, betrayed and abandoned yet once again, making his way in the night to the small armoury of his brother Lorenzo's hunting guns, he consigned himself to a fate of last resort, for sure never again to be deceived, nor discarded.

15

At the dinner at Fabbri's, Ursula and Leonardo had not, seemingly, taken to each other. He withdrawn, she polite, worlds apart, with no common meeting ground, they had remained at arms distance. No more than a casual encounter, a passing acquaintance, little more than a shared evening with few words exchanged and no afterthoughts, without the least premonition of the storm to come, that was to engulf each in the fury of a passion such as neither had ever known.

What was it that drew them together, Ursula had never queried, not then nor afterwards. She a neglected wife, belittled and set aside by a man for whom she merely kept house and appearance, in whose inner life she no longer carried weight. Leonardo in exile from the world, more in exile from himself, fit in limb and body, yet living a mid-life almost senescent and indifferent, as though already well on the way to a dotage untimely.

In appearance neither betrayed the scars and stains of lives gone awry, no cicatrice visible to sight. Ursula an alluring beauty in her late prime, vivacious in company, Leonardo the figure of a man at repose, calm and unruffled. Together they might have been a couple years into a marriage comfortable and complementary, the one lightening the gravity of the other, he wordlessly holding at bay her sometimes showy liveliness. As it was, their encounter brought into the open the fires smouldering within, the delirious release of needs and cravings long suppressed, desires unfulfilled, hunger unmet.

Nothing planned or premeditated, they met by chance in the streets of the town, he on a brief morning stroll by the lake, she out on an errand, at the gates of their residence, he admitting with a brief smile and nod her cheerful greeting. A few weeks later, running into each other once in a book store, she to buy some new maps for her trips once in a while to friends in the Thurgau, he browsing the shelves with law books, they walked back up together.

"It's the price one pays for living in a place like this," said Leonardo with a wry smile, in response to Ursula's lament about the streets overflowing with the early summer tourist crowds, stout Russian women jostling, backpackers nudging people off the sidewalk.

Nearing their gates, on an impulse Ursula asked, "Will you come for dinner one evening, Signor Bellini?"

Taken aback, avoiding her gaze, Leonardo looked about briefly before lowering his head. "I have Maria," he said in a halting voice. "You may remember my nephew talking about her. She takes good care of me. Expert cook, too," he added softly.

"Well, then, perhaps you can ask *me* over sometime. To taste her expertise!"

Leonardo met her eyes with the look of one puzzled and wary, unsure of her purpose and uncertain of himself. Unwilling to let go, yet unable to decline and offend what might after all be mere neighbourly courtesy, defeated, he nodded assent. *"Si, grazie."*

"One evening this week? When you're free."

Coming across each other in the streets by chance, yet rarely were they out of sight of each other. Stepping out into the garden, looking up, Ursula often caught a glimpse of him intent on a book at the upper floor windows of his place, their gaze at times meeting, when she would raise a hand in greeting. The brief exchanges, wordless, working like yeast, leavening random thoughts, etching vague designs in the recesses of consciousness, made for an odd familiarity that lingered in the empty hours like unnoticed pollen floating by in the spring air. It was as if they already knew each other, sensed the contours of the wish within, merely biding time for the hour and day of encounter and fruition. And if for Ursula the desire was freely admitted in her mind, live and pregnant, Leonardo's hesitance was a barricade too weak and frail to resist the silent assault. Accepting the invitation, he felt himself surrendering to whatever might lie in wait, an inevitability foreordained.

Serving drinks out in the garden, butler Silvio's brow creased briefly. A local man, he knew the history of the Bellini family. Buying armfuls of gossip magazines at the news-stand, his wife had heartily followed Leonardo's trial and incarceration. He himself dubious about the man's guilt, the wife's ironclad certainty had overcome whatever benefit of the doubt he might have been willing to concede. The lurid reports in the press faded with time, the wife's attention moving on to other breath-taking scandals, memory was briefly revived only when Leonardo came to live at the Villa Serena. Taken aback now by the visit, Silvio could only wonder. What might the lady of the house want with one who had spent years behind bars? Keeping his thoughts to himself, removing the large bouquet of flowers Leonardo had the florist send up to the house, he set out the bowl of olives and the tulip glasses.

"Would you prefer something else?" Ursula asked as Silvio busied himself undoing the wire cage from the bottle top.

"My nephew's the connoisseur. For me, just a glass of wine at table. Thank you." He took the glass Ursula held out. "Your Italian is fluent, if I may say so."

"Do you think so, Leonardo? May I call you Leonardo?"

"I've been called worse," he smiled, a quiet smile that

seemed to put Ursula at ease, easing out also Leonardo's own awkward timidity.

"My husband once said that Italian is to opera what honey is for the bee. It was the language to learn if I was to sing. A whole year of lessons during my voice training. Wasn't easy."

"Opera?"

"I began late. And… it ended early!" She pressed her lips with faux resignation. "No, an entire opera score was beyond me. Just short concert pieces, *bel canto* arias, classical songs."

"Oh. Where did you train?"

"Milan. Two whole years of prison life," Ursula laughed as they stood on the terrace with their drinks, looking down on the town and the lake pellucid in the late summer light.

"Must have been difficult!"

"A gilded prison with an old satyr who passed for voice teacher. Actually, he was famous for having trained some of the great names of the past. When it came my turn, Farinetti was a doddering old man. But lecherous as ever, always hovering about touching and fondling. I was meant to hold the note while he held on to my bosom. And his skeletal fingers pressing my abdominal muscles. Just that his idea of the abdomen was well below what we call the stomach!"

"You put up with it?"

"In the name of Art. My husband insisted. According to Armin, Farinetti could turn the croak of a frog into the trill of a prima donna."

The hour before dinner out in the garden a prelude of formality, Ursula cheerful in the ironic belittling of her own talents, Leonardo lending ear with curiosity and wonder, it was as if the talk was merely a pretence, the words a camouflage to conceal from sight the slow, subterranean surge drawing each to the other, Ursula making her way towards him, Leonardo waiting with silent foreboding, resigned with a passivity both curious and concerned. It made for brief moments of awkward silence, broken by Ursula's girlish laugh, the strained timbre of Leonardo's voice.

At table Ursula noticed that Leonardo kept away from the private and personal, more at ease when their exchange touched on matters away from himself and his life, saying only, "You must have been in Milan when I was studying law at the University."

"A small world, Leonardo!" she exclaimed, her hand reaching out to his for a moment. "And what a heady world."

"Drunken times," he nodded agreement. "They were years when the country appeared to be partying non-stop. With never a thought of the cost. And the consequences."

The shared memory loosening tongues, Ursula recalled her youthful days in Milan, not only Farinetti and his busy hand, but also the evenings and outings with a friend training with the Scala ballet school, the late night parties and gatherings with young models seeking their fortune in the fashion world, the men trussed in elegance waiting to scoop into their laps girls barely in their teens, prey and predator caught up in a whirlwind chase of merry-making, dining and wining, dancing the night away and snorting with noses pressed to crystal table-tops.

"We were the fourth or fifth industrial power in the world then," Leonardo reminisced thoughtfully. "The economy booming, money growing on trees, money to be made and spent, the newly rich throwing their wealth in the air like confetti. Parents dressing their school-age children in Armani and Prada. Think, even shop girls went to work in mink and fur!" Putting down his fork, he looked up at Ursula, lips pressed in a melancholy half-smile. "The madness could not last. And soon enough the emperor found himself without clothes!"

"A good time to have been young."

"For some." Hesitating briefly, he continued. "My brother was a little outgoing, the rest of the family… Our father started as a garage hand, set up a car showroom later. But money never went to his head…"

The flow of words halted abruptly as Leonardo veered off from the personal. "Much of it was bad money. One morning the country woke to find the bubble had burst and then you had public figures in high office being led off from the dining table in handcuffs. A sorry spectacle. A nation corrupted and impoverished, but worse than ever before. The Government even had to break into children's piggy bank accounts to save the sinking ship!"

"I think by then I had finished my voice training with old Farinetti. After that many months in Vienna. With a woman from the Staatsoper, to teach me movement, poise and posture on the stage. But I missed Farinetti, a real character. When I left, he said, 'Girl,' he always called me *ragazza,* he said, 'Girl, my only consolation is that I'll not be living long enough to see you on the stage.' His parting words, more or less. He died a couple of years later. Just as well!" Ursula laughed, a wistful trill in her voice. "I really think he would have died a second time hearing me sing in public!"

Puzzled and wary, Leonardo did not know what to make of Ursula. Sat out in the garden under a slate-clean night sky made almost starless by the lights of the town, he looked at her as butler Silvio fussed about pouring the coffee and setting down the liquor glasses.

He looked and listened, lending ear and attention to her words. Yet for long moments his mind slipped away, to contemplate from a distance his mostly solitary existence. Apart from Maria's muted presence in the house and his weekly trips to the city for *pro bono* assistance to prison inmates without means, he rarely saw another face or company, nephew Roberto once in a while, a drink with some childhood friend met by chance in the town.

~~~

Leonardo did not mind the solitude, his own choosing, the life for which he had trained through the time in prison. Always accessible to fellow inmates, filling in forms, drafting an appeal, writing letters home for those little familiar with the alphabet, yet save for passing familiarity and acquaintance, he had made no friends, keeping himself to himself, listening to the silence of his own voice. Staying aloof from the world and its affairs had become a habit, briefly interrupted later by short-lived liaisons, that had opened no door, let in no light into the emptiness within. Ursula's voice in his ears now, he wondered at the wisdom, were it to happen, of an entanglement so close by, at the door step, the sight of one another through the day, the nights together, perhaps. Having held life at arm's length so long, he was no longer sure how one might bear an embrace so vicinal and neighbourly.

If he had lost his way in the world early in life, what of this woman, truly a splendid creature in her late prime, a face and a figure to turn men's heads a second and a third time, with the gift of a chameleon, effortlessly turning laughter into a sigh of hurt and loss, the deep-set violet eyes above high cheek bones holding one in a steady gaze that one moment seemed to burrow deep into one's thoughts, the next turning distant and absent with some unuttered grief or yearning. The engaging cadence of her voice, the trill of her laugh in his ears, Leonardo felt she might have done better on the theatrical stage. From the snatches of her talk, bits and pieces of the past, halting words at the mention of her husband, he had the impression of a life lived between the swell and the deep, at a loose end now, possibly seeking anchoring and headed for what harbour he could not imagine.

Nor could he much imagine the purpose of his presence this evening, in these still waters in which she passed her days, in this grand house, pampered with all the comforts that money could buy, ever waiting solitary in a suspended widowed interrupted briefly by the arrival of a man who seemingly chanced to pass by. He had caught fleeting glimpses of the husband, a tall imposing presence, heavy in face and silver-headed, as he stepped out in the garden for a brief stroll, the sturdy arms wound around the wife, as though lifting some feather-weight off the ground, meaning to whisk her away.

Long years ago, attending some evening a concert with Eleonora, who for a year or two had gifted him a season ticket for the theatre, he uncertainly recalled having seen the figure a time or two on the podium at the Scala. Seemingly a lifetime ago, when he would have dismissed as risible fantasy if told that one day he would be sitting at almost intimate distance with the great man's wife, her nearness redolent with the vaguely floral fragrance of some perfume, but also the musk of a body's silent, impatient longing. Her voice in his ears felt more a distraction, his own words forced and redundant.

In the time since his release from prison Leonardo had met and known women, in truth few and far in-between, encounters of little weight and even less consequence. Only once, the door briefly ajar and heart stirring, he had come close to a commitment of sorts, to let in the world and the pleasure of company and companionable warmth. An erroneous choice, as so often with him. The young woman magistrate, engaging enough, but as severe and peremptory in private life as with wrongdoers in the court, was at times much too overwhelming for Leonardo's retiring manners and habits. Unable to meet her fervid demands and unwilling to rearrange his life around her hectic workday and routine, he had simply let go, her parting words true enough yet wounding: "You are old before your age, Leo!"

There was then, also, a brief, desultory affair with the wife of a minor banker, a woman in mid-age, unhappy beyond words, craving his attention at all hours of day and night, calling at first light to whisper words of desire and despair, her hand reaching out in public to fondle him intimately when they met in a bar or seated in a restaurant, as though the aggressive intimacy was meant to assuage her seemingly immemorial infelicity. He was expected to be at her disposal whenever the fancy took her, or her misery drove her from husband and home, whatever the hour and whatever his own inclinations. It could not last, nor did it. Too old for such unpredictable whimsy, unable to lend himself to the fitful and fevered possession, he had called it a day. Wondering, too, why he should so often draw to himself and be drawn to females wayward and unreasonably capricious.

And now this woman beside him. So different from all the others he had met and known, some loved for a time. Not much given to dwelling on the past, but a rare occasion he had asked himself if there was a person right for a particular time of life. A glove for all seasons. Improbable.

In prison an elderly uxoricide had befriended him, a giant of a man, but a quite and, to all appearances, kindly soul. The Frenchman had had three wives, the last one he had murdered, not in a fit rage, out of simple despair of frustration. Or so he claimed, confiding to Leonardo that he had found it unbearable that all three women were near identical, in habits, tastes and preferences. He had had the impression of marrying the same woman over and over again, an intolerable dilemma put to an end by his oversize, farm-working hands closing around the last wife's neck one night. "*Les saisons changent, mon ami!*" he explained. "And not only the climate. So too the seasons of a man's life. The palate of youth is different from that of age. Try eating a wood mushroom in winter. Tastes of nothing! No different with our expectations, preferences, as we age." Apparently, the third wife had been much too unseasonal!

Leonardo felt timorous, alarmed less by Ursula, unnerved more by his own hesitant gait, as though sensing his own shadow, artful and devious, move with halting steps toward her. They had met only briefly, knew each other hardly, neither with the sheen and sparkle of youth to make them fall into each other's arms after a night on the town. And he could not understand this undertow, like an insistent tug at the sleeve, drawing him towards her. He did not wish to replicate the time with Eleonora all those years ago, nor the short season with the banker's wife. One man's wife might be another man's distraction, but the tentacles of marriage were often buried too deep to make for a spirit pure and free, pristine. Yet now the persistent voice in the blood would not leave the veins, whispering that Ursula was different. Fruit seasonal for this time of life, to use the Frenchman's metaphor of savour.

He was glad, then, and relieved when, the evening late, it was time leave. The couple of hours gone in a daze, lending attention to Ursula's talk, nodding, assenting with brief interjections. But save for her laugh, the ear of his memory retained little, his senses more alive to the beckoning voice within, fear and desire making for unease.

It could have ended there, a companionable evening, nothing more nor less. He would see her again, no doubt, run across her in the town, watch from the window as she sat in the grounds. One evening she might even come over, to dine under the watchful eye of Maria. Neighbourly amity, an imagined friendship. Less than little imaginable, he well knew even then.

She walked him down towards the gate, halting before he let himself out, to say in a voice soft and low, almost a caress, "It's been a good evening for me. So glad you came, Leonardo…"

He made to speak. But one hand on his shoulder, her face close, touching his in amicable farewell, yet the lips pressing into his cheek refused to let go, burrowing, as though intending to meld into his flesh, refusing separation and parting. And with the warm breath on his face, a flavour of something faintly sweet and heady, senses giving way, his arms came around of their own volition, to hold her girth in a seemingly inextricable vice, never to loosen and let free, his own lips probing through the silken fall of her hair, to bury their moist buds, limpet-like, on her neck, a seeking and a surrender concealed from sight and the night.

Wordlessly they held each other an infinite minute. Bodies palpitant, shot with tremulous expectation, but the breathless embrace, an encounter and incursion unforeseen, was itself a finality, of assent, consent and yielding.

And in the warm night, the odd passer-by in the street glimpsed through the intricate ironwork of the gate merely a couple in the shadows locked in a love-lorn hold, not for a moment imagining then, neither they nor Ursula and Leonardo, the tumult and drama of fatality in wait.

16

Her impassive expression betraying nothing, words spare as ever, yet Maria was bewildered. She had seen him as a child just out of his diapers, little Leonardo scuttling about the house, taking shelter between her legs when teased and taunted by brother Lorenzo, his arms around her neck and snivelling with pain as she gently nursed the bruise on the knee from a fall.

She had known him as a youngster, warm and protective, partisan when some sharp word to do with a household chore escaped Anna. Much later, hearing the malicious gossip of the neighbourhood wives during the trial, she had never for a moment given credence to Leonardo's alleged villainy. Travelled little, a time or two to the seaside in youth, a summer week or fortnight in the mountains after marriage, she knew little of the wider world, even less of legalisms and the laws of the land. The world might judge otherwise, not she. "Not our Leonardo," she insisted with an emphatic shake of the head. "Wouldn't hurt a fly!"

Placid and sweet-tempered, with a child's winsome smile, his delicate lineaments had remained in her memory clear as a photographic print, a portrait she had carried down the years. With always the possessive, 'my Leonardo, 'our Leonardo,' when his name came up, in lieu perhaps of the male child she had never had. When, then, a year or two after his release, Leonardo came to live in Villa Serena and Fabbri asked her, she did not wait to be asked a second time, coming to keep house and care for 'her Leonardo.'

Maria might not have known desires compelling, but abundant in devotion, she had faithfully obeyed and served a feckless husband through more than half a lifetime. Even now, years later, Sunday mornings saw her make her way to the cemetery to lay a small bouquet of chrysanthemums, a cluster of white roses on the dead man's tomb. Never mind the abuse and neglect suffered, it was part of her faith, the vow taken before the cross, *'to be faithful, in joy and pain, in sickness and health, to love and honour…'* Nor, afterwards, would she hear a word against the dead man. A rare time the elder daughter's dredging from the past of some hurtful act of the father met with the reprimand: "Remember, girl, it was he who brought you into this world!"

A regular church-goer, week days and Sunday mornings, too, rain, shine or snow, she was never once absent from service, never failing to receive the Host, imbibing the blood and savouring the body of the Saviour with bowed head. The Commandments she knew, though perhaps unable to recite at a moment's notice and in the given order. But she well knew that coveting another man's wife, the neighbour's or other, was not the done thing.

So that, merely askance at first, her thoughts creased with anxious unease to see Leonardo increasingly in the company of the lady next door, often close and touching, indiscreet, seemingly heedless of the eyes of the world. Her own season of passion brief and far distant, but it did not take long for her to sense something blustery in the air, the wind swirling in the undergrowth before a storm.

A man in mid-age, a life seasoned by the vicissitudes of an errant fate, Leonardo was no longer the child in her heart and it was not for her and not her place to peek and peer, query, even less counsel. She could only look on as, opaque of sight and distracted through the hours, impatient, unusually brusque at times, he seemed to come alive, gain height and spirit only in the presence of the foreign lady, as though hers was the only breath of life that could animate him, release the blood in his veins. Soon enough, too, the adulterous intimacy left its hand in open sight. Going up to make the bed one morning, the nocturnal exertions wafted from the linen a woman's presence, a scent of lilac and furze.

Maria's trepidation grew by the day. On and off she had caught a glimpse of the husband, an imposing figure with a high-born, courtly presence. A man of great fame, she had heard, well known to lovers of music and song. Of the little she had seen of the gentleman's mien and carriage, she did not think he would take it well that his wife should be flaunting her infidelity openly on his own doorstep, and it filled her with concern for Leonardo's well-being, if not life.

If Maria watched with ever deepening anxiety, on the other side of the fence butler Silvio was perplexed and disconcerted. Turning a deaf ear to the sly words under breath of the maid, ignoring the thin grimace of the old man who came to do the garden, he looked on with alarm as the lady of the house entertained the neighbour evenings and late into the night. What could she want with one such as Bellini? Did she know of his antecedents? Innocent or otherwise, but judged a felon by the law, a dozen years behind bars with rogues and common criminals.

Submitting his dismay at home, he heard the wife forecast a perilous future for the lady. An inveterate reader of feuilletons, heady tales of doomed lovers and domestic carnage, she had not the least doubt. "He's done it once, he'll do it again," she announced with oracular certainty. "A dog that bites once, will bite again and again. But you be careful. Don't want to see you called up in the witness box."

Silvio hung his greying head in thought. Worried less about having to testify in court, his disquiet had to do more with what might happen when Signor Armin returned, as he did periodically, to find his wife abed with the man next door.

~~~

Armin did return, after a month long concert tour in minor capitals. Himself as ever, extending distracted effusion as he gathered up Ursula in his arms before subsiding in his seat on the terrace.

Putting out a hand to grasp hers, he looked about sniffing the air. "What's new, *Liebling*? What have you been doing with yourself? Has David been over to see you?"

"It's you he comes to see. I'm not on his map of local attractions."

"You would have been, had he met you in youth."

"Oh, I didn't think…"

"You think wrong, lady. There was a time when David would have gladly bedded anything that moved. Man, woman or animal of the field."

"Oh!"

"Ah yes, poor David!" he nodded with distant commiseration. "Bipolar, bisexual. And by-passed! But what could one expect? A Calvinist mother soused in wine half her life. And that Russian father of his. Did you know that almost the only thing with him when he fled Kiev just before the Germans arrived was a solid gold menorah. Don't suppose he'd have bothered had it been in brass. And the only thing he left David. That and a confused brain."

Never merely a simple word, ever the sympathy tinged with a sour note when Armin mentioned Davidovich, Ursula had never understood what it was that made for the attraction and repulsion between the two. For David, Armin was cicerone for the sights of life, always master and mentor no matter the slights, cuts and flagellation received. For Armin, protégé, disciple and acolyte. But there was something more that escaped grasp and sight. Perhaps the son he had never had, she had wondered at times. Not an easy person to love, David, lost in the byways of life, maimed in spirit, erratic in inclinations, still and all the child Armin might have wanted. The undercurrent tug-of-war, the pull and push of affection and dismissal she could not otherwise explain.

If Davidovich's visits were infrequent at this time, Ursula had made sure Leonardo keep out of sight, though no way out of mind. She herself stepping with utmost care, watchful of word and gesture, uneasy of her husband's keen hearing overhearing the tugs of her heart, the strain and refrain of the body's longing, Armin appeared to notice nothing out of place, if not to remark as she undressed before bed that she looked more rounded, with a good-humoured query of no weight, "And what's the cause of the new prosperity?"

Pulse missing a beat, she looked at him with a wan smile, the comment calling for no particular reply, albeit unusual for him to comment on her person. Rare now, if ever, a word from him on her looks, shape and figure, even rarer still his intent of possession. The sap no longer running, once in a while he took his uncertain pleasure merely with the fumbling play and foreplay of age, the enervated self-gratification of a hand fondling her swells and mounds, fingers parting the folds of her flesh, incursions tentative and tenuous, her satisfaction of no consequence nor of interest to him.

She did not know, nor ever asked, if there were women during his travels, fugacious couplings, rather than love-making, in theatre dressing rooms and hotel suites. Sometime ago he had made fleeting mention with apparent distaste of an aspiring singer offering herself in Bogotá, or perhaps Brasilia. Bogotá or

Brasilia, aspiring songstress or streetwalker, wherever and with whoever he might find his hour of cheerless relief, it did not much matter. Nothing for her to gain or lose, Ursula wished him well in whatever passing indulgence and satisfaction he might be able to harvest in this waning season of life.

For her the marriage bed of roses was well behind, his once insatiable tenancy of her body mere memory. Man still, to all appearances vigour intact, his carnal will on the spousal bed had subsided into indifference, if not rejection, after the debacle of her singing career. Letting him down in more ways than one, a reverse aphrodisiac of sorts, bringing on an impotence of spirit, if not entirely of the flesh. If in the early years, her voice had been for him, seemingly, the philtre that woke and aroused, renewed youth and set the gush of blood coursing, curiously the failure of her career had estranged his desire, for all purposes emptying the marriage of its intimacies. Man and wife still, down the years, but the mine abandoned, the vein of gold already mined, for him she seemed to serve no purpose other than her presence.

If Armin had along the way mislaid his earlier ardour, the marriage bed largely vacant of both presence and desire, not so Ursula. The youthful impulse of wantonness subsided, she now instead often sensed an undercurrent of love, silent and deep, that his neglect and slack failed to discourage, he still her her one and only man, his support and comfort still her mainstay, her yearning to be boarded and bedded still alive enough for a hand to reach out to him, to draw him to her to take possession of what was his.

In time Ursula had learnt, too, of the curious and mysterious byways of the seductive enticement that lured him into her arms. On occasion she would wear her nursing uniform, the body bare beneath, the cap tilted half-way back on the head. It was his first sight of her ever, at the Grünewald clinic, in starched white, albeit with underwear and underclothing, an image that seemingly had stayed with him, imprinted on the weave and woof of his desire. Ursula might have wondered, but never paused to ask why when, in earlier days, he sometimes draw her to himself, to say, "Will you be nurse Füssli this evening, Ursula?" Nor did she ever quite understand how a simple white buttoned apparel, without frill or flounce, could call forth heat so scorching and sudden, the blind furore of a rabid beast falling on the prey without mercy, to devour and extinguish the last breath of life.

But age, wearying want, paling a passion in recession, the dare and provocation seemed no longer to swell the veins and summon the insatiable haste even as she stood above him, the abundant nudity draped in white. He would then merely draw her down on his lap, winding arms around her, a quiet hand working its way under the cloth to caress and probe the one secret inlet or the other. And then much later, sat by his side as he lay stretched out on the wickerwork chaise lounge, still and quiescent, she sometimes hoped that his eyes flickering open for a mere instant, recall and recognition would dawn in his dormant mind at the sight of the white uniform encasing her, the nursing cap like a halo around the flaxen head.

~~~

On and off, Ursula had had lovers, short-lived affairs if not quite one-night flings, with men whose greater delight at times seemed less to do with her offerings, more with having bedded the spouse of a figure of some renown in the world, like mendicants stealing a few morsels from the seigniorial table. Liaisons in which each took what one could, a brief barter that in passing satisfied in some measure her still youthful appetite, the partner of the moment indulging his own needs. Neither replete nor fulfilling, they were merely engagements incidental, leaving behind in the aftermath no particular savour on the tongue, nothing particular engraved in memory.

Now, with Leonardo, for the first time Ursula found herself at the cross-roads. Swept up in the whorl of a vortex, a passion late and deliverance unexpected, it was like a recompense overabundant for the days and nights of an existence arid and empty. She had thought of herself as no longer capable of a madness such as this, the parched earth avid and greedy for the wash that came its way, the body's craving so brazenly intemperate, rapacious and carnivorous, the lioness feeding on her mate, as though wanting to consume both brain and brawn, to become one, meld into a single being. And it frightened Ursula.

The breathless tussle and battle between the sheets was one thing, the urgency of the flesh and the body's needs, however delirious and voracious, were finite, the journey hour-long or day-long merely momentary in time, as one fell away in a halo of damp and heat, both consumed and replenished, as the light of day returned and the lungs drew new breath. Love-making of itself was neither the problem nor the panacea. She had held others in her arms, many a male loin wedged between her legs, known the hectic, short-lived or long, to and fro within her of other sinews pulsing with blood. Mere ephemera, fevers of the moment. Suddenly, with Leonardo there was more, a deal more, something perilous and damning, that could tear away her existence from the hinges of the life she had.

Of an idle moment, sight cast backwards over the peaks and valleys of the past, Ursula felt at times an odd distance, estrangement even, from all those she had known through the course of a lifetime, the figures on the peripheries and those who had mattered, still mattered and populated the reams of her memory. She suspected, with a dryness on the tongue, that she had never loved another being, if to love meant, in the Pauline sense, to give of oneself, without condition or reserve, without expectation of a return, regret or remorse.

She had bourne the burden of a mother stifling and smothering, endured the abuse of a father given to violating her childhood. Trusting, she had consigned her youthful years in the hands of the head of the Clinic, hands that Dr. Krieger had used to demean her person and body. With Armin, hopeful of the salvation offered, she had persevered to make his impossible dreams come true. Endurance, trust, hope, but love perhaps never. The curse of a heart possibly stillborn.

The hands of the clock inexorable and feeling the passing brush of age, some days, standing a long hour by the window as the weather broke and the rain beat against the glass with a monotone thrum, her sight grew opaque, the mind clouding with the thought of an existence never infected by the rhapsodic elation she had sometimes witnessed in others, women young and older swept off their feet by love real or presumed, newly-weds on the deck of the ferries playing the waters of the lake, forgetful of the world and clutching each other as to life itself. A sensation that had always eluded her, no matter who the man of the moment, her inert spirit unable to free itself and fly into the lovers arms without restraint or reserve.

But yes, once long ago, with a doctor from the clinic, she had briefly felt the portals of the heart opening out to welcome submission and surrender without condition. Sadly, Dr. Pelosi had not been free to choose, had he even so wished. Over the short holiday he had endowed her with womanhood, an awareness of the infinitely intricate sensations dormant in the pith and sinews of the flesh, the pinnacles of satisfaction and satiety the mind could offer. A mere instant in time, the week of inebriated carnality was what it was, the breathless coupling of a man and a woman out of season and out of time, and nothing had come of it. For the rest, nature contriving that the feral appetites of the body leave untouched the sterility of heart and spirit, the procession of men had come and gone like shadows in the dark, largely discarnate, unsubstantial and ephemeral.

The seasons turning, the prime of womanhood near past, she no longer hoped, nor harboured expectations of some prince charming to come riding to sweep her off her feet, infusing her withered arteries with the lymph of passions never before felt, responses of which she was evidently incapable. So that, now, almost late in the day, with Leonardo, she could not help looking on, like a confused onlooker, at her own figure submerged by the tidal wave of sensations unknown, feelings without sense, thoughts without reason. Was this then what had escaped her grasp so long, that most precious of gifts, that could believe and bear all, think no evil, that could end only with the last breath departing the lungs. Seeing herself in the mirror in the new morning light after a long night's journey with this man, a small girlish laugh escaped her, as at times she wondered why it had taken the span of a lifetime for the release of her soul from the prison cage in which it had been locked, that perhaps she herself had locked from intrusion

If Ursula dared with tremulous heart to glimpse a new life, she did not imagine that for Leonardo she had become life itself, the very air he breathed, the light of day when he woke in the morning. Unasked and uncalled, she had become mistress and chatelaine, keeper of his reason, sense and sanity. Reserved, ever sparse with the syllables of sentiment, without plea or petition he had silently consigned his life in her hands.

Unsuspecting, unaware of the immense, perhaps impossible, burden of carrying within her the fully grown foetus of another human being, oblivious of being invested with nursing the spirit and well-being of the man-child cradled in her arms, she could not weigh the perils of her investiture, not as mere partner and lover, but as something infinitely more, custodian and guardian, as too both care-giver and jailer.

Nor able to imagine the depths of the inroads she had made into Leonardo's being, she could not understand his misery and torment at her merest absence, like a newborn denied the maternal breast. Retreating into long hours of morose silence, retiring into the shadows, he seemed more a wounded animal in the throes of mortal pain. Afterwards, ever after, try as she might, she could not at all fathom why he should have seen her loyalty to her husband at a time of extreme need as dereliction and desertion. And she had never truly found peace within herself that at a single stroke she had lost both, the man who had made her what she was and the only one she had ever loved, the life lived and the life to come.

17

Several years later, the solitary existence of nursing a husband moribund, but refusing to depart, had driven Ursula to indulge in a short-lived liaison with a new neighbour come to live at the Villa Serena. Not an overly passionate and tumultuous involvement, the time well past for such stormy entanglements, more an amicable affair engaging for the mind and reasonably satisfying for the body's needs, Ursula found herself at ease recalling snatches of the past. A widowed academic some years older, on a year's sabbatical to work on some book, a good listener and, apparently, a thinking man, he heard her out, seemingly with interest, trying to piece together and make sense of the often random and out-of-context reflections and recollections.

 Long summer evenings sat out after dinner, now and again at his place, more often hers, with the comatose husband wheeled away for the night, he listened as she picked at the threads of her life, ruminant at times, on occasion a light theatrical recitation in the voice, a rare melancholy mellowness recounting some milestone in a life storm-tossed and, to all appearances, lived at the behest of men mischievous and amoral, if not outright dissolute and wicked. It was obvious she had been places, seen the world, frequented company talented and distinguished, as also known men varied and various in intimacies short or long-lived. But he could make little or nothing of the arid emptiness in the tone when she briefly recalled the time with this lover or the other, mere passing happenstance, until one day, in a matter-of-fact manner, she said, "But, do you know, I was never able to love any of them."

"Only semantics," the Professor smiled. "As we know, Ursula, making love doesn't necessarily call for love. A plumber doesn't have to be in love with plumbing!"

"No, it's not that. I just think I was born incapable of loving. Something to do with my genes, perhaps."

"I don't know much about genes. Nor genealogy, for that matter."

"What then? It comes so easy to most people."

"Hard to tell. Often people lead themselves into believing they love this person or that. Very commonplace, like belief in God in these times. True faith, like love, is something else, a commitment. Somewhere along the way we feel a sort of selfless attachment to a living being, a person, an animal, if you will. We hear people say they could give their life for someone. Maybe once or twice in life one really could. A mother for her child, a man putting his life on the line for his family. That's the sort of devotion, attachment if you like…"

"Attachment," she nodded, curling her lips. "Attachment. I like the word!"

She did not then tell him of Leonardo, as she had not to another living soul. Only once, visiting her old nursing friend Ilse, she had made mention, but largely concealing the depths of the involvement, his manic attachment, her vague and unuttered designs for a future together, the long year of delirium and unalloyed bliss, the blessed moment when finally, for the first and perhaps the only time, she felt the pangs of what she took for love, that for a brief season had stirred in her an opaque longing for motherhood, something of her own creation to hold and call her very own. Confessions that would have been incomprehensible to other ears, however interested and sympathetic. A friend over the years, her only confidant, yet even Ilse, square as she was in her habits and settled into a life of pedestrian marriage and humdrum mundanity, would likely have laughed out aloud.

There were things in life that eluded expression, sense and sensations beyond the reach of words, that human syllables merely diluted and distorted, poetry a pale epigram for passions felt and real, the printed page without much of the whiff and spice of moments lived and folded into the reams of one's being. Ursula did not think she could convey to anyone, much less to one like friend Ilse, or the Professor with his calm and sedated mind, the turmoil within of the months with Leonardo, the unceasing clamour of flesh and spirit that, like yeast fermenting, threatened convulsion and collapse, derailing reason, dislodging the ground from beneath her feet. If was as if perched on the edge of a cliff, she could open her wings and take flight, but the abyss shrouded in a river of mist making the fall perilous, the destination uncertain and out of sight.

"Leave him," he sometimes begged, insistent and despairing. She could only lower her head, pressing her lips to his forehead, to sooth and comfort, as if to erase the words, both plea and demand, her own thoughts confused and wandering in a thicket of doubt and quandary. Leave? How and for what harbour? Neither of them young enough, of an age to imitate innocent cinematic lovers fled to the woods to live on a handful of berries and, breathing their last, expire in each other's arms.

Stuff of fable and romance, she for one had never known innocence, if not only in the cradle and as a toddler. Leonardo himself had emerged not too long ago from the darkness of a past that had robbed him of the prime seasons of life. Each burdened with the weight of episodes and events not of one's choosing, mid-life bringing up to the surface the sediments of injury and pain, the past increasingly colouring the here and now, neither could decipher the other's true expectation and intent.

Leonardo's mind Ursula could never clearly read, a figuration of light and shadows he kept out of sight, with hardly a word plain and lucid on what might lie ahead of them. And, oddly, it was in those hours that there welled within her a recondite longing for motherhood, a fecund offering to seal their union, a living witness of their love as man and woman, lovers, man and wife, whatever, it did not much matter.

Trapped between the extremities of an existence settled and assured, however vacant the nights, the days like water on the tongue, savourless, that, and a journey whose end she could not see, even less imagine, Ursula felt caught in a noose that tugged this way and that, not wanting to let go, allowing neither leeway nor choice. He on his part holding the world at arm's length, the demands of the quotidian, the details small and large of living, preferred to look away, with little concern for the material, money, nutrition and nourishment, the roof over one's head, as though humans could live on air alone, air and the impulse of the moment, the incitement of desire clouding measure and reason.

"Where would you want to live?" she had once asked, in a matter-of-fact tone. "Where would we live?"

"Anywhere. Does it matter?" he replied, impatient and elusive. Trite minutiae of no consequence.

For her it was different. Ursula in her thinking moments did not want to tempt providence with a headlong rush towards a journey whose design and finality she could not see. At the command of others, yet having had to fend for herself through half a lifetime, the design and detail mattered, mattered even more at this time of life. And yet, when in his arms, lying beside him as his warm breath washed over her, his hand gliding down her length, waking each part and particle of her sensate self as though with tiny tongues of flame, reason fled and life and limb caught in a mesmeric delirium, deliquescent and dissolving, she wanted nothing more than to consign in his keeping her entire being, what she was and had been. The choice was not hers to make, that she knew. In the end, it would be others who decided. She, like flotsam, would merely be carried by the tide, wherever and whatever the shore.

She had come some way, away from a past in which she had always moved at the behest of others, in matters small or big, who to bed, the length of hair to be shed, her mother's cautionary words keeping her on the straight and narrow, the good Dr. Pelosi's tongue on her person urging her on to satisfactions never before suspected. To think now that, youth gone and constraints shed, a person in her own right, seen something of the world and the ways of humans, she still remained at the mercy of others, leaving it to other hands to settle the bills of her life, show the way ahead, this path or that, she merely the clockwork figure wound up to move and walk where others wished and willed. So it had been with Armin luring her away from the clinic, so it might be if only Leonardo could force his way through the doorway, for once decisive and adamant.

It could have gone on, she could not imagine how long, the wearying dance of the the tug and pull, like a fisherman's catch out in the sea, netted but refusing to be hauled in. Even had she so wished, she wouldn't have known how to extricate herself, Leonardo's embrace stubborn, Armin's absent hold unyielding. Entangled in the mesh of this unseen web, unable to free herself, nor wanting to break loose, there were times when she felt at the end of her reason. Until soon enough, and as always, life itself intruded to put an end to her quandary and plight.

The summons came one evening, out of the blue, Davidovich's words urgent over the phone. She had just left Leonardo at this place, the warmth of the sheets barely cooling, the aroma of his arousal still clinging to the skin, the frenzied satiètè on the wane. She had yet to dress and make-up, they would be late for the concert down in the theatre. Barely had she washed away the body's clinging effusion, perfumed and readied, when the call came.

Davidovich's voice, usually low and languorous, seemed breathless as in short bursts he told her. Armin had landed in Geneva late afternoon, intending to stay for the night before making his way back to Como the following morning. David and Gabriel had gone over to spend the evening with him.

"I know, David. We were expecting him tomorrow."

Rushed to the hospital following a massive stroke, Armin was senseless and comatose. At the University Hospital the doctors were reassuring, but things boded ill, the cerebral thrombosis evidently unusually severe and life-threatening. One would know for sure after the various tests, still too early for the medics to commit themselves on the recovery or possible therapy. "No, he's not awake. Anyway, they won't let me see him. Not until you come over."

Ursula packed, scribbled a hurried note for Leonardo, and drove away into the night.

II

1

The morning sun playing hide-and-seek through the branches, painting the early summer leaves lucent green, the trees looked ever so tall from where little Conradine sat at the back in the open-top Kügelwagen staff carrier, the mountain breeze keen on her face, sweeping back the pale gold of the flaxen locks of the head. The car winding through the silent woods with a low drone, the narrow unpaved track uneven and bumpy, from time to time Uwe turned to look at this daughter, asking "Are you alright, Süsse? It's not far now."

 A quiet child, never much vocal, the tears silent if on occasion she happened to cry, Conradine had asked her father neither the reason for this journey nor whatever the destination. The passivity of wordless acceptance was a habit with her, holding out a small hand for the gift proffered, obeying with a mute nod whatever the parental instruction, the pale blue of the eyes still when a rare time a small scold came her way. The loss of a mother at such an early age was not much different, the numbing grief suffocated in the depths, finding its way out in voiceless tears that welled in the dark, concealed from the sight of the world. Nature, one might have thought, had nurtured the child for the sorrowful turn that lay ahead, the orphan abandonment at so early an age.

 She had never once asked, nor had Uwe told her of the circumstances of her mother's death, as too that of grandmother

Gertrude. The two women on a brief visit to Hildegard's sister, terminally ill and fading, a stray hit on their car from a RAF bombing raid, in a small village on the outskirts of Cologne. But the air of home ever more close and corrupt, with old man Manfred's bitter rage and rant as each new day brought news of defeat and retreat, Conradine's child's mind unable to extricate friend from foe on the battlefield, she only learnt from her grandfather that the hated English had taken her mother's life, as though in the homicidal act of a common criminal. Once, only once, she had asked her father why the English should have taken her mother from her. The inheritance of mute detestation in the blood was to stay with her through life. Years later, she snatched from young Ursula's hand the little booklet of British nursery rhymes given her by a friend, tearing out the pages and throwing them on the flames in the kitchen fire, muttering under breath, "Not here, not in this house."

Bereft and disconsolate at the loss of wife and mother, the two beacons of his life, Uwe moved through the days drained and unfeeling, as if the sensate part of his being had gone missing. Yet, waking each morning seemingly numbed in mind, shorn of thought, a constant prayer rose silent to his lips, the requital of a grateful heart, that Conradine had been left at home in the care of the old housekeeper and spared the crackling flames that had consumed Gertrude and Hildegard. And woven with the prayer was the desperate urgency that her young life be somehow saved from the vengeful eye that could well come seeking out what remained of the family.

Twined, too, with Uwe's irreconcilable grief was the clear knowledge that if the plot was to go awry, none would be spared, neither man nor woman, no relative, friend or associate, not even an innocent child. No mere hearsay or rumour, he was familiar with the satanic deeds of Himmler and the Gestapo. No quarter given, not the least mercy shown, the last drop of blood would be drawn. It didn't matter much that he was not part of Stauffenberg's inner circle of officials, nor that he was not privy to the precise date and time of the attempt. It sufficed that he had conspired, assented and abetted to betray the land of his fathers, to bring to a close the increasingly futile carnage. An old aide of Stauffenberg had warned him, "One hopes for the best, one must. But… be prepared for the worst. The very worst, Uwe!" He had nodded in silence, the sunlight of hope clouded over with the thought of what might befall Conradine, above all, should things were to go amiss.

Awake in the depths of night, besieged by hope and fear, he had racked his brains, his own safety and survival of lesser consequence, that of the child uppermost in his mind. One dawn, then, tossing and turning through an uneasy doze, it came to him. Farmer Füssli and his wife, their farmhouse just over the border. A sanctuary easy to reach and beyond even the long arms of Himmler's minions. He had known the couple over the years, modest folk, trustworthy. The child would be secure in their care for a while, a week or two at most. All being well, he would return and retrieve her, safe and whole. Should the plot fail… But mind finally finding a measure of relief, blindfully he set aside the possibility of a failed outcome. Failure was not an option, Stauffenberg would carry it through, his design had to succeed.

So here they were now, making their way through the silent woods. Uwe glanced briefly down the slope sylvan with beech and birch, glimpsing through the new foliage the valley below, almost virgin and empty save for the odd, small chalet nestling in the rolling mantle of green and, in the distance, at the far end, the lake like a droplet of mercury, silver in the early sunlight.

How many times they had travelled down this narrow earth track, he and Hildegard, in the early years of marriage. Better days, the world apparently at peace, the land becalmed after the years of hunger and tumult, the country prospering under the tribe of new men wielding the levers of power with their resounding promises of well-being and greatness. A week, a fortnight in farmer Füssli's little cottage, long summer days walking through the woods, afternoons idling by the lake, Hildegard's face restful on his chest as she sighed in the dark for the child that refused to come. By the time little Conradine arrived in their midst, it was over, the spell broken. The world once again on the move, hurtling towards darkness and doom to the boom and bluster of the raucous voices of the same new men, no longer new now, their masks shed and fangs out howling for vengeance and blood.

Clear in Uwe's memory was their last stay in this seemingly forgotten hollow of the world caught ever in the silence of its green slumber, near and yet so distant from the fear and foreboding of what was to come. Somehow they had thought nothing of it, Hildegard's eyes lit with a smile and resting on her swelling front, his ears pressed to the bulging midriff to catch the faint sounds of the nascent life moving in its inland sea. But human events overtaking Nature's calendar, he was not present when Conradine first saw the light of day, learning of the birth as he sat pensive at his desk in ramshackle barracks somewhere in the Sudetenland.

Uwe drew a deep breath of the fresh air streaming in. He turned once again to look at the girl, his small smile an echo of the memory of that seemingly long ago summer, little distant in time, a mere handful of years, with little premonition that the world would soon be turned upside down, countless lives gone awry, the days ahead shrouded in the miasma of pain and loss, the future like the flickering last light of day before the fall of dark.

His eyes fell on the small leather case on the floor of the passenger seat and he thought of his father wandering in as he helped the housekeeper put together a handful of Conradine's clothes and underwear, a few spare items of a child's needs. And, too, a large envelope of foreign currency, collected over time, tucked under the cloth lining, a dower of sorts for the girl's uncertain future, meant hopefully to offer shelter and a roof over her head if by chance he failed to return.

He had told Manfred that he would be taking Conradine away for a few days, a brief distraction after the bereavement of loss, the old man responding with a scowl, muttering that it was hardly a time to go holidaying. Casting briefly a sullen eye as the housekeeper neatly folded the small garments, he looked up at Uwe, the gaze empty, seemingly void of sentient life.

Uwe could not help wondering how he had come to take the errant turn, a man of noble lineage, once upright and honest, liege to King and country, serving with valour long years on the battlefield. How had this same man come to wed the falsity and duplicity of a tribe of upstart figures with their virulent creed of hate and malevolence. Over the years Uwe had seen other converts, but hardly ever one like his father, Manfred's zeal bordering on idolatry, as though wanting to outdo the Führer's most ardent followers. In times recent, trying no longer to be at odds, to cross swords, he had felt more the leaden weight of a sorrow at the sight of a man gradually hollowed out, robbed of the earlier swagger and bluster as the tide turned, voice falling to the pitiable, spasmodic snarl of a wounded beast as news trickled in of defeat on this front or the other. With the woman of his heart gone at a single stroke, now even fatherless for all purposes, Uwe felt a sense of irremediable desolation, orphaned and forlorn. The little girl alone was the breath of life that animated mind and body, the will to live and survive.

The dense undergrowth lining the forest track thinning and giving way, finally the view opened of the short wooden bridge over a narrow stream that marked the unguarded frontier and, beyond, the gently sloping meadow, with farmer Füssli's farmhouse at a small distance. Sat atop a rise above, barely noticeable among a cluster of trees, was the stöckli-chalet on whose wooden balcony he and Hildegard had sat those long summer evenings. Uwe could make out the stocky figure of the farmer's wife leading a heifer along the path winding down the pasture.

"We're almost there, Süsse."

"Will you be away long, Papa?"

"Only a few days. Be good, Süsse. Frau Füssli is a kind person, she'll take care of you."

"You will come back, won't you? Please, Papa."

Slipping out from the farmhouse, to stand by the brook knee-deep in the tall grass and troll flowers, for many months afterwards, and now and again even long after, Conradine had often stood waiting by the old bridge, looking beyond at the bare earth track winding up and away through through the woods. But, promise made and promise betrayed, Uwe never returned.

2

She was named Conradine Ingeburg Wilfriede, the first name in homage to her grandmother, Baroness Gertrude von Stölberg, the eldest daughter of an old Margravian family with considerable estates in the north-east.

Conradine's father was not present at her birth. Busy with the quartering of his regiment in barracks in the woods west of Plizeň after the annexation of the Sudetenland, Uwe von Isenburg, a major in the Wehrmacht, did not see his infant daughter until late spring.

Major Isenburg was pleased and no less relieved. After a couple of miscarriages in the decade or so of their marriage, Hildegard, pale and frail, had finally come through, both mother and child in health, the baby girl, especially, sturdy in limb and strong in voice.

Isenburg's joy was less shared by his father. Beaming with uncertain pleasure as he looked down at the infant at the baptism in the small chapel of the old family mansion in the countryside outside Ulm, a troubled frown creased his thoughts. A girl was all very well, but Hildegard was unlikely to produce another offspring. Without a male progeny, the title and noble lineage would soon perish, and with that a name that had always commanded regard and respect at large.

If Manfred's grandfatherly thoughts were secretly troubled, less so the odd gesture of a close friend and comrade in arms of his, a Party man now and whole-heartedly given to the cause, invited for the event. "For the newly-arrived member!" he announced bowing stiffly and handing Isenburg a small velvet case containing a tiny, black armband with the crooked cross set in a circle of red. Grandmother Gertrude later tucked it out of sight at the bottom of a drawer in the infant's room.

A soldiering family, the Isenburgs had never failed to send one son or another to battle or serve whatever the cause of the fatherland. In the upper official reaches of the new nation the Isenburg name had come to particular prominence when young Bruno Isenburg, an aide to Chancellor Bismarck, had personally drawn up the draft of the offensive Ems telegram that so wounded the French, with Napoleon III issuing the fatal ultimatum that led to the Franco-German war of 1870. The young man's ingenious talent was amply rewarded, with honours and a high diplomatic rank, later an important posting in the German mission in Paris, an irony that made for frequent ribbing by colleagues.

Minor nobility, without hereditary lands and little estate, Isenburg's father, Manfred, had married well, Gertrude von Stölberg bringing with her as dower sizeable wealth from the family's feudal holdings in Silesia, that considerably enriched the Isenburg's modest coffers. Manfred himself had steadily risen through the ranks of the Imperial Army officer corps to become *Generalmajor* at the outbreak of the Great War. The army dissolved and the officer corps disbanded following the defeat, some years later Manfred found employ with Krieghoff, a sports firearms manufacturer in Ulm.

Manfred and Uwe had never seen eye to eye, the father's gaze obfuscated by the past, the son's vision taking in the horizon and the time to come. The nations defeat and humiliation shadowing his days, embittered by the loss of the holdings his wife had brought him, his military upbringing at first finding Hitler's Beer Hall Putsch a risible farce, yet the message of the raucous new voice gradually made its way into his sympathies.

Training as junior officer in the Reichswher, the resurgent new army, Uwe instead had inherited his mother's sensibilities, his disdain unuttered but evident for the brown-shirted and black-shirted little men braying and barking among gaping throngs in the streets and *Stadtplätze*.

On a rare occasion a disparaging word escaped him, much to his father's annoyance, as when he said, "Those crowds would believe it if told that the figure on the podium was the Man from the Moon."

"I'm afraid your son can't see the wood for the trees," Manfred remarked one day with a belittling voice. Baroness Gertrude mostly kept her thoughts to herself, saying merely: "There are other vistas beyond the woods."

Some years later, with the Reichstag burned down and the new men securely in the saddle, the Party keen to recruit to its ranks old warriors with firm convictions in the new order, Manfred's by now open sympathies were rewarded with the position of *Gauleiter* of the district. Back in uniform, trussed in a brown shirt with braided cords on the shoulder and a renewed strut in the booted steps, he often held court in the family house, with loud-mouthed figures at the table, the talk bombastic and at times tinged with an undercurrent of delinquency bordering on villainy.

Increasingly, Uwe found the air of home less congenial. Had it not been for the women of the house, mother Gertrude and his wife, he might have forgone entirely his visits on leave and on festive occasions. Later, the arrival of baby Conradine in some measure compensated for the oppressive rhetoric of Manfred's declamations of a future such as the nation had never seen.

Now risen to full officer rank, Uwe had begun to feel an apartness from the family, unable to air his thoughts in the open, choosing his sparse syllables with care to avoid argument and his father's censure. Nor did he have open support from the women of the family. Reserved and retiring, Hildegard had never been particularly vocal, exchanging merely private thoughts when alone with her husband. Gertrude herself seemed to watch from afar, in silence, her instinct deciphering in her son's few words and, at times, in the set of his lineaments, a silent distaste and distance from the events at large in the country.

At table, if he spoke at all, it was away from the public and the political, matters neutral, about a possible new posting, the hasty pace of training new recruits, the insufficiency of motorized vehicles. Only once, bidding his mother farewell after an Easter stay, his words veered away from the neutral and mundane. "This can't last, Maman."

Gertrude nodded. "Nothing does. Nor will this." Pressing her lips to his cheek, she half-whispered, "All madness has to run its course."

Cordial and courteous by nature, duty bound and precise in whatever the task assigned, regarded by superiors and respected by subordinates, Uwe's career had taken wing, the preparations for conflict earning him significant rank. Uwe suspected that whatever his own merit, his father's name and rising influence in the Party had had a hand in the insignia of *Obersleutnant*. Gertrude thought a discreet word of thanks to Manfred would not be out of place. Uwe refused, remarking "Foot-soldier or *Oberführer*, Maman, the battlefield doesn't choose who's to live and who to die."

It was only following his brief return home after several months in Poland that Gertrude sensed subterranean changes that only a mother's eye could discern. A brittle obstinacy and shifting gaze, words reluctant if asked about his time in Kraków, she thought it had to do with something unpleasant, some discord with a hostile superior, clash with fellow officers. She could not know that, more than merely unpleasant, among a series of brutish scenes of unwarranted ferocity witnessed in the aftermath of the invasion, there was one in particular that had stayed with him, as though etched permanently on the pupils of his memory: a couple of Waffen SS soldiers almost gleefully bayoneting in broad daylight a harmless elderly man pushing a handcart down a street in the heart of the city. Uwe made no mention of the incident when briefly telling his mother of the days in Kraków, limiting himself merely to stumbling words voiced under breath: "War is war. But there are sights that the human eye should not have to watch."

Never particularly gregarious, over the years Uwe appeared not to have close friends among his colleagues. Now, for the first time, Gertrude heard in passing the odd name of fellow officers, of brief stop-overs with their families in Berlin, Wolfsburg and elsewhere. And for the first time, she noticed in her son something elusive, elliptical in answers to simple queries, unusually guarded in naming the names of the small circle he had begun to frequent. Then, too, it surprised her to see him extending to his father a new-found patience and forbearance, hearing him out with a benevolent look as the older man declaimed prophecies of the glory and grandeur that awaited the nation. Watching the two as they sat or strolled in the grounds, instinct told Gertrude that there was something false and feigned in Uwe's new filial docility.

For Gertrude it had been cause for mute pain that over the years father and son should have been wordlessly at loggerheads, Manfred's displeasure at times spilling over in passing words of slight and censure, Uwe's expression, often opaque and bemused, that of a child hearing fables and fairy tales. The recent reconciliatory posture consoling as it was, she knew in her heart that the two had chosen paths not only divergent, but also irreconcilable, Uwe's appeasement ringing hollow, Manfred's bluster and braggadocio louder than ever. She, caught in the middle, a prisoner of love, hoped against hope that with the swift victories on the Western Front and the possible prospect of peace, healing and harmony would descend on the family.

There then followed a long season of quiet, interrupted by momentous news of victories and advances, Rommel's rout of the enemy in the desert, the swift invasion and occupation of lands in the east, the Western theatre subdued and mostly muted. Summoned frequently to Berlin, Manfred came and went, the zeal of the convert solidified to dogmatic certainty that left not the least room for pause or doubt. "This," he told Gertrude, "is our rightful place in the world, what was owed us by history and destiny."

Gertrude listened in silence, her husband's voice less angry or unduly pompous, imbued instead with shades of the ultimate, prophetic truth, as though echoing words of faith from the Holy Book, the new Messiah's name falling from the lips with a reverence she had never heard in his tone when reciting the Lord's Prayer in Church. And she could only wonder what Uwe would make of his father's unconditional prostration before the Golden Calf, the unalloyed surrender of heart and soul to his new god and lord.

Stationed on the Atlantic coast, Uwe's visits were fleeting, more so during his father's presence in the house, as if intentioned to avoid encounter. Leaving little Conradine with Gertrude, he and Hildegard would go away for a couple of days, a week, to some spa in Baden, in summer to an Alpine lodge over the border, in the Swiss forestlands.

Ever more frail, Hildegard seemed increasingly anxious each time Uwe left to return to his posting, clinging to him, not wanting to let go as the car turned into the driveway to take him away. Standing aside, Conradine's little hand in hers, Gertrude watched, afterwards soothing the younger woman with quiet words of consolation: "Thank heavens Uwe's not been posted to the East." Hildegard hung her head, to murmur, "There are dangers as much at home." Words oblique, Gertrude did not ask what she might mean. She did not need to.

For some time now a mother's sixth sense, like an ear pressed to the wall, had been awake and alert to something in Uwe beyond his usual reserve, a reticence bordering on the taciturn. Hardly ever did he now make mention of events at large, the news from the wider world filtering through in dribs and drabs, the hollow ring of the newer victories announced daily on the radio, at odds with the ever more severe shortages, cloth and clothing scarce, the shelves in shops and stores not quite as full, tighter restrictions on civil travel and movement. The Isenburg household itself might be spared the extremes of scarcity, but the want and paucity were evident to the open eye, the rationing more stringent by the day.

One lunchtime, Manfred asking for cream on his slice of cake, Gertrude looked at her husband with a wry stare, to remark quietly, "You forget we are at war."

"Most of the cattle have been shipped to fight on the front," chipped in Uwe, but in a tone without levity.

"Please mind your words, Uwe," Gertrude chided in a motherly way when Manfred had risen from the table.

Less her husband's dogged faith in final victory, that would brook no argument and that nothing, the death and destruction laying waste to the land, could shake, it was concern for Uwe that was uppermost in Gertrude's thoughts. His increasingly rare and ever briefer visits clouded her mind with unease. It was plain to see he was oppressed by some weight hidden from sight, often anxious in his looks, restive in manner, his sparse speech seemingly weighing the syllables, as if the echo of each word carried some consequence.

One day walking down the grounds of the house, Gertrude halted to put a hand on his shoulder where he sat reading under a tree. She caught sight of the title as he shut the book to look up at her: "REGICIDE: THE KILLING OF CHARLES I."

"That sort of thing was easier in the past," she said, her gaze lingering on the cover.

"Never easy, Maman. Not then, nor now. Just necessary, at times."

Gertrude bent forward, to rest her face on his head. "Be careful, son," she half whispered. "These are dangerous seasons."

There were eyes and ears everywhere, she had heard. Housekeeper Ute had recently recounted the local butcher's unexpected brush with the authorities. Meat ever scarce and customers coming in at all hours, insisting on their rightful share, one morning, in front of a gaggle of clamouring housewives, the butcher, exasperated and out of his wits, had loudly voiced words less than prudent: that if this state of affairs was to last the oft-proclaimed thousand years, people might as well get used to eating straw and grass. Early the following day, a couple of plain-clothes men had arrived as he lifted the shutters and walked him out even before he could remove his apron. Bundled in the waiting car, he had returned only later in the afternoon, colour drained from the usual ruddy face, the robust figure seemingly shrunk a measure. The accustomed jollity muted ever since, he only muttered mostly greetings and thanks.

Uwe rose, the fate of Charles I underarm, to stroll with his mother around the wide circle of the gravelled path, faces close, one arm circling her matronly girth.

"We've already lost your father, so to speak," she said in an undertone not quite distressed, merely a touch rueful. "But you…" Nudging her head against his, as though wanting physically to enter his recesses, she paused before gently adding, "Remember, Uwe, you have a family. Lately the days have not been kind with Hilde. She misses you more than she lets out. And Conradine is growing, she'll need your presence when this is finally over."

"Will it ever be over, I wonder."

"It will, someday. When it does, you'll be expected back here. Until then, meanwhile... Do what you need to do, what you think best. But also keep in mind those who'll want you back here."

"I know, Maman. Just that at times the choice is not ours to make. It's forced on us." A faint smile briefly passed his lips. "Let's just say, one has no choice."

From her look, distant, somehow opaque, he knew she had in some-way guessed not the intent, nor the end, but something of the drift of his thoughts. The where, when and how she could not possibly divine. Never once had he dropped a hint, not a single syllable fallen from his lips. Not once made even a passing mention of the meetings behind closed doors, the elliptical exchanges with those who had decided to undertake the same perilous journey, the modest task assigned to him to hold the troops under his command in their quarters and round up the small, local SS garrison the moment the coded word came over the air waves to say that the deed was done. Yet somehow she had sensed an air of cold purpose in him, that she could not express in words.

Months ago, having briefly met Stauffenburg in an officers' circle, sat at table with the immensely tall, one-eyed and one-armed Colonel, Uwe had heard him talk, not in a conspirator's guarded voice, more in a tone easy-going, laced too with a gentle humour, as he raised his left hand with the two missing fingers, to say amiably, "Not quantity, gentlemen, it's the quality that counts!" Uwe would have wanted to tell his mother of the encounter. But he knew merely airing the name might one day beckon who knew what peril.

Halting at the steps up to the terrace, he kissed Gertrude's head, the voice reassuring, the words elliptical. "I'll be back, Maman. When it's done."

3

Hardly ever had Ursula heard her mother call her husband by name. With strangers and casual acquaintances it was Füssli, with Ursula invariably 'your father' in a recriminatory undertone at times, as if she was somehow to blame for having had a father. Only later Ursula came to understand.

For Conradine, farmer Füssli had been not one but several men. At first, Herr Füssli, when one bright summer morning her father had left her at the farmhouse. For sometime, then, it was Jürg. Later, when she had been adopted by the couple, she began to call him Papa Jürg at the behest of Füssli's wife, a rare time merely Papa. Later still, much later, woman and wife, she seldom addressed him directly, telling Ursula, "Ask your father," or "Call your father."

Ursula thought afterwards that not so much a confusion of identity, it was deliberately ill-willed on the part of her mother, a deep-seated refusal to accept Füssli as either father or husband, at best only the man who had sired her child, the sole claim she would concede him. But if there was no love, neither was there any particular detestation. He was simply one more incidental met on the way, a fact of life, like the death of her mother or her abandonment, to be lived with patience and forbearance, with nothing of the heart owed, no commotion of sentiment or feeling. His invasion of her girlhood, the feel and fondling of her budding youth, later the early marriage after his wife's death, she had accepted with stoic acquiescence, merely the rental to be paid for the bed, board and shelter he had provided.

It was a life inert and arid, shorn of dream and drama, the years of toil and drudgery unchanging, without the least relish, devoid of the colours, the impulses and designs of human living. So it might have gone on, merely a life to be lived, she finally going grey with a heart ever mute, had it not been for Füssli, aged and wasted but not quite senescent, reaching out his corrupt hand to young Ursula, in a reprise of what she herself had endured through childhood. Only then did Conradine's being wake to rebellion and defiance. The silent tolerance and sufferance of a lifetime suppurating and rising to the surface, the cup full, one day she had finally put a mortal end to the man who had meant nothing to her, neither as father nor husband, merely an oppressive shadow clouding existence.

Patricide and mariticide at a single stroke, afterwards, in the time that remained to her, Conradine hardly ever mentioned Füssli by name, or mentioned at all, as if he had never been and never trod the earth. Afterwards, too, clear as daylight in Ursula's memory was the look on her mother's face, the eyes like embers ablaze, as arms outstretched she stepped forward with blood-chilling, almost empyreal calm, to push her husband off the edge of the rock-face of the cliff overlooking the valley.

Raised where he was born, Jürg Füssli had never never left the farm. Come to manhood, after his parent's death he had stayed on, doing what his father and father's father had done, raising cattle mainly, supplemented with growing greens and vegetable on a sizeable patch. Later he had built a rustic chalet someway above the farmhouse, to rent out to holiday makers coming over the border in summer months.

He had never travelled much beyond the woodlands and forestlands of the valley, a small world that sufficed for his keep and curiosity. Once a week he piled on the produce, the tubers and greens, cuts of meat, and drove down to the town, half an hour away by horse cart. Once a year he took down to the autumn cantonal fair heads of cattle ready for slaughter. Apart from wheat, oats, salt and sugar, alcohol and tobacco, the Füsslis lived on mostly what they produced. And not much given to non-essentials, frills and fripperies, the earnings from the land and the herds more than sufficed, the sizeable savings in the cantonal bank almost never broken into.

Füssli was in his mid-forties when little Conradine came to the house, his wife some years older. A late marriage, the couple childless, Beate might have wanted infant voices about the house, but now a season too late for her. Füssli did not mind. Solitary by nature and habit, words few and infrequent, nor did he mind not having near-neighbours. Once or twice a year, on occasions of feasts and celebrations, Fasnacht and Sechsilüüte, local folk meets, Beate would brush her husband's preferred bundhosen, take out one of her two ceremonial dirndl and a colourful wool shawl, and the pair would ride down to the town to join the throng merrymaking, with Füssli disappearing among the men roasting and grilling meats, Beate sat quite among the housewives, as the air filled with the sounds of bells and wooden percussion. Late in the evening, her husband inebriated and half-comatose, Beate drove the cart back up to the farmhouse.

A child in the house calling for care and feeding, Conradine's presence was a distraction and disturbance. Amply remunerated by the wad of local currency the girl's father had left behind, for the first months Füssli bore the residence of the newcomer with silent indifference, leaving Conradine in the company of his wife as she went about her day-long chores, milling feed for the animals, weeding the patches, cleaning out the stable, cooking and washing. Nor did he particularly share Beate's concern when the girl sometimes disappeared from view to sit a long hour by the bridge over the brook awaiting the return of her father.

Soon enough, with the passing weeks and months, and no sight of the man coming to reclaim his daughter, Füssli's face at times darkened as he watched the girl move about the house on the skirt tails of Beate, the small voice hardly ever emitting a sound, the flaxen head giving merely a nod when told something, looking up speechless and mute when asked or questioned. "What now?" he would mutter with a groan as, sat by the grate, he drew on his lidded pipe. "This creature will be with us forever."

Beate said nothing, her eye in the dim light on the needle as she mended the ends of his breeches, her thoughts at rest with the quietude of an unuttered satisfaction. Rising at first daylight, she would hurry to where Conradine slept in the small room on the side, above the barn. Contemplating the child's head nestling in a halo of tousled locks, silently she would kneel by the rustic cot, lowering her face to lightly brush the dormant cheek with her lips, the warmth of sleep rising in her nostrils like the aroma of something infinitely rare and blessed, the fulfilment of a prayer that permeated her being with an ineffable contentment.

The time long past for creation, yet the longing had stayed, concealed in the unseen spaces of her days. Something of her own, to hold and love, a young voice to call her name, tender arms to reach up and wind around her neck, this she had thought she was never to know. But now, taking pity for her vacant heart, some angel had brought this child to the doorstep, a gift unexpected, a miracle. Each dawn, opening her yes, she had been filled with dread at the thought of the father reappearing to take the girl away. Each night, as sleep seeped into the work-worn limbs, a silent prayer threaded its way through her abeyant mind.

~~~

Never for a moment straying from the tenets of the faith handed down to her, her God, her man, duty and obedience, modesty and mute submission, never once over the years had she uttered a word against what her husband might say or wish. Füssli her first and only man, she had come to him late, a deal later than many of her childhood companions, already mothers several times over by the time she wed. The marriage delayed from year to year by ill-health and the droplets of blood she threw up with a cough from time to time, her plain looks, stocky figure and awkward gait did little to invite suitors for her hand from among local males. Deemed, too, slow in the head, she had remained on the shelf till her late twenties, until Füssli, indifferent to appearance and drawn by the over-generous dower of a whole herd of cattle, took her to wife.

Her name more a cruel taunt, Beate was less than blessed, entering a home lightless and joyless. Eve sprung from the ribs of Adam, a woman, she had been taught, lived in the breath drawn by her man, his command the final word, his will the law of the land. Füssli was never unduly cruel, nor excessively demanding, a hand raised occasionally when inebriated, a hurtful epithet spat out when finding serious fault with whatever the task assigned to her. *Dummkopf or Schmalzarsch*, Beate was not much offended. She had heard herself called bag, bitch, lard arse and more by her own father grown crabby to still have to feed and keep an ageing daughter about the house.

As husband, Füssli took his pleasure much in the same manner as when tending and branding his cattle, silent and heavy-breathed, falling on her with brusque movement to part her legs, entering without let or leave and vacating with the grunt of a dying beast. Lungs emptied under the crushing weight and thrust, Beate submitted dutifully, one more chore, little different from the washing, cleaning and cooking, never imagining that the few minutes in the dim light could offer pleasure, release and relief. It was, she knew, an act of submission owed to the man, without question or condition. The same passivity that turned her head and made her look away when, years later, her husband's hand reached out to grope and fondle Conradine's budding girlhood.

A whole year and more Beate had lived glancing over the shoulder, dreading the dawn of the day when the girls father would appear to reclaim his own. Putting Conradine to bed some nights, she would clasp the spare frame in a hold tight and long, not wanting to let go, as if waking in the morning she might find the cot empty. A voice weaving through her mind telling her it was wrong that she should seek to possess a life born of the womb of another, yet she could not help shutting her eyes in the dark with the prayer of being granted her this one indulgence, she who had never asked her Lord for any gift precious or rare. And on waking, threading through the fear of loss was the resolve that nothing on earth would make her part from the blessing that had come her way.

Chafing, at times complaining under breath, Füssli wondered when, if ever, the father would come to take the child away. If nothing else, at least for the moment she appeared to earn her keep, he consoled himself. Always beside Beate, her little hands did what they could, weeding the vegetable patches, helping clean out the pens, fetching wood for the stove, silent and obedient, mostly wordless. Füssli could not imagine what would become of her, whether he should tell the authorities and consign her in their hands, to be placed with some family or sent to a home for war orphans. But the thought of his wife stayed his hand. The sight of her clutching the child to her bosom, kneeling long minutes by the little cot at bed time, a smile rare and ineffable through the steam rising from the small wooden tub when bathing the pale little limbs, made for pause, robbing Füssli's quandary of haste and urgency.

No visible improvement in Beate's health evident despite the medications prescribed at the hospital, the dry cough at times bringing up copious gobs of blood, yet she went about her chores indefatigable as always. Never a day in bed, short of breath but ever on the move, up and down the grounds, climbing the rickety ladder to bring down feed for the cattle, washing and cleaning, her young companion like a mascot moving on her coattails. Glancing at the pair from time to time as he himself heaved and dug, piled up logs and tugged at some recalcitrant heifer not wanting to give ground, Füssli could not help reading Beate's distraught expression as she paused in her labours to pass a weary hand through the bright locks of the child's head; nor did he fail to notice her distraction in leaving the stable door open, forgetting out in the sun the day's pail of milk, the supper on the table now oftener under-cooked or under-baked. He would then shake his head to himself, undecided to tell her what he had learned not long ago.

~~~

The war over, there were grim tales about exchanged in the town, anecdote or hearsay but stopping the breath. Among other grisly details recounted by the postal clerk over a stein of beer, Füssli had listened open-mouthed about the scores of Wehrmacht officers rounded up after the failed attempt on the Führer's life and strung up on meat hooks in a slaughter house outside Berlin, as too the summary execution with a bullet in the neck of several scores more.

    Shocked and ruminating as he drove the cart back home, he clearly recalled the words of the girl's father when well over a year ago he had arrived at the farm to leave behind the little girl. Seemingly certain of himself, the officer had assured that he would return in a fortnight to take the child back, adding that things were about to change, with the war over soon. Either he had ended up hanging among the carcasses of dead cattle in the abattoir, or else simply perished at the Front. Füssli had a passing acquaintance with the man from years earlier, when he would come over with his wife, renting the chalet for a month in the summer. A gentleman, quiet and kind, the wife silent but gracious, not at all the sort of people to abandon lightly a child in the keeping of strangers.

Certain now that the child had come to stay, Füssli was at a loss, unable to think how to unburden himself of this uncalled for presence. One day, letting himself down beside Beate as she sewed a child's apron, he decided to tell her. "Her father won't be coming back," he said with heavy breath, glancing around to see if little Conradine was about.

Beate paused in her work, to look up, puzzled. "Why do you say that?"

"More than a year now. Too long. A person like that, a real gentleman, wouldn't just leave a daughter…" He omitted recounting what he had heard, the fate of the conspirators and the slaughter house meat hooks. Beate would not have understood, anyway. "Probably dead somewhere, in the last months of the war," he added simply.

"There's the mother, the family…" Beate suggested hesitantly.

Füssli shook his head. "God knows where they are. Everything bombed and burnt out in those parts. Not a house standing, they say. What do we do with the little one now?"

Beate's heart missed several beats. Not wishing to rejoice at the loss of the child's parents, if what her husband said was right, she could not help feeling the surge of a peculiar elation, part relief, part consoling, at the thought that Conradine would now be hers, would be there on the morrow and in the days to come. Emboldened, her uncertain prayer answered and the unexpected blessing a gift lasting, in an unaccustomed manner, voice firm, she told her husband that the girl was to stay and live with them.

Putting his head down for once, as if bowing to her wishes, yet he could not help protesting. The child had no papers, her age unknown, with no certificate of birth and origin. The authorities would want to know how she had arrived and when. Unusually, Beate brushed aside his hesitation, both firm and pleading. "You know them, the people in town. In the *Bürgermeister's* office. All those best cuts and joints always for them," she reminded him. "Just give them whatever they want."

Füssli looked at her amazed. Never since she had come to him had he heard her voice so firm with intent, words not quite peremptory, yet unwilling to give ground. Beate's mind slow and dull, to all appearances, but storing away what she saw, she knew that over time he had obtained with gifts and offerings large and small favours not always in keeping with the law.

Patting her back, Füssli heaved himself up. Perhaps it could be done. In recent months he had seen small clutches of bedraggled war orphans shepherded through the town by nurses from the Red Cross. With so many lost children about, confusion in the public offices, trays heaped with documents clipped with photographs of wan little faces, possibly little Conradine could be slipped in with the army of stray and wandering young.

In fact, in good standing with local officials, supplying their larders with choice cuts, one or two of the council clerks among his occasional drinking companions, after several months Füssli managed to get the papers, easing Conradine's adoption and, for all purposes, granting him paternity and the claim of fatherhood.

The blue blood running in her veins still, but no longer an Isenburg, a child once high-born to wealth and name, Conradine Füssli became the daughter of a phthisic mother and a father rough-hewn and heavy-handed, a farm girl raised on the land, toiling from dawn till night, herding cattle, hoeing and weeding, unkempt in dress and manner, with dirt under fingernails. True to her ancestry, she grew long-limbed and handsome, both forbearing and headstrong, with a silent will of her own under the pallor of a silken skin. And as fate would have it, she still remained Conradine Füssli when wed at barely sixteen, daughter and wife to the same man.

4

"O Come all ye Maidens,
Virgins and Wenches,
Come ye, come to Grünewald Klinik
Come do and behold him
Round and stout Joachim
O Come, let us adore Him..."

The senior doctors nodding with bemused tolerance, the nurses and junior medical staff bursting in high laughter. The Pastor, invited for the Christmas party, looked on wide-eyed, as Joachim sang in an operetta falsetto, swaying and conducting himself on the platform at one end of the wood-panelled hall.

Come to work some years ago at the Grünewald Klinik, trussed in his white, attendant's jacket, the buttons straining against the barrel bulge of the belly, Joachim was everywhere, in the corridors, in and out of the rooms of the sanatorium wing, quite as often in the children's ward entertaining the young with his round and ruddy face puffed and fleshy lips pouting in imitation of a porcine snout, or else simply stood at a window putting out billows of smoke from hasty drags at a cigarette as he silently contemplated the woodlands around the clinic and the valley sloping down towards the small town in the distance.

A native of the area, large of head with short, burnished curls, rotund in body, hands meaty and arms stout as the shanks served by his mother at the family table, something of a mascot and a favourite with everyone, doctors and nurses, the kitchen staff who slipped him a slice of cured meat if he happened to be passing their way, Joachim was ever at hand, to lend both hands, lifting a patient off a bed effortlessly, as though plucking a feather, pushing with a few fingers a trolley with cumbersome medical equipment, ever on call and ever willing, with never a protest or complaint, a boyish smile on the lips whatever the task.

Endowed with an unlikely talent, Joachim was something of a lyricist, making up ditties and jingles, setting words of his own choosing, at times dubious and risqué, to popular melodies, voicing them to himself as he went about his chores, often entertaining the nurses at table with a brief sing-song, with particular attention for young nurse Hanna, a short, rounded country beauty.

But Joachim's profane setting to the carol at the Christmas eve gathering of the staff was not without consequences. Reprimanded by the head, albeit not excessively, more a scolding, Dr. Krieger feigned a touch of severity, saying, "You realize, Joachim, that the Bishop sits on the Board of our Institute…"

"I know, Herr Doktor. The Bishop has difficulty standing," interrupted Joachim brightly, having seen the high churchman, afflicted with gout, being helped up from his seat when visiting the clinic.

Dr. Krieger let Joachim's facile remark pass with a pressed smile. "It is to be hoped, Joachim, the good Pastor has not reported your little show to the church authorities."

Unlikely, thought Joachim, bowing his head in contrition, seeing how the Pastor had departed the party thoroughly soused with a glass too many.

Krieger did not persist with his mild censure, knowing full well that Joachim's irreverent performance was merely a mild, tell-tale parody of the peccadillo among staff members.

"So, please, no more of all this maidens and virgins, Joachim," he admonished solemnly, waving the attendant away.

Shutting the door behind him, Joachim could not help humming the tune to himself and silently mouthing the words…

…O come all ye young maidens, to the gracious and varied calling of a nurse's life, the noble task of sliding in and removing bedpans, the privilege of tweaking and tugging at will shrivelled male willies to coax unwilling bladders, to feel the gnarled hands of dying men sneak up one's legs for destinations unknown. And if, perchance, fortune happened your way, to be pressed face against the wall in a dim corner of a ward by the night duty doctor straining to seek rear entry under the raised, starched skirt, with the warm breath of mint or tobacco washing down your neck, the stifled groan and grunt of the white-coated beast in heat one with the moan and mumble of the slumbering figures recumbent on their beds.

Much of the fingering and fondling often in play and jest, at times in earnest, many of the young nurses appeared game for the grope and feel by the male staff, a legitimate right of way of man, to be countenanced without undue protest. Together at meal times, one or the other would say amused and under voice, "Me too!" at the peculiar habit of some junior doctor coming up from behind to press his stethoscope to the derrière, with one elderly nurse, a motherly figure life-long at the clinic, protesting "And why not me?," the sisterly conclave breaking into girlish laughter at the unfair partiality.

Most of the young women brought up in canonical belief, with regular attendance at Sunday service, confirmation and communion faithfully observed, less merry was the company at the mention of the old Pastor from the village. Summoned to pronounce the *Viaticum*, the ageing servitor of faith could not help casting a sighing glance at the apple-cheeked trainee nurse as at some forbidden fruit, even as his short arm struggled in vain to encircle the florid hip. But ever a man of God, come to anoint the sick departing their mortal remains, going down the corridor to the bedside of the dying soul he reluctantly refrained from further profane indulgence.

Much too much of a prize catch, a regal beauty, Ursula was largely spared the common touch of the lower orders, the medical assistants, the therapist and pharmacist. Her virtue and offerings were retained as the sole province of a select few senior physicians, mainly Dr. Krieger, his good-hearted benevolence not particularly averse in sharing the largesse with a few older colleagues. Ursula soon discovered that their needs and appetites were not that of the man in the street. They were men of the world, had been married a time or two, or more, had over a lifetime partnered lovers young and older. Now in age, simple carnal urgency long spent, their cravings refined beyond mere boarding and bedding a female, each had some singular urge, rarefied peculiarities that often surprised Ursula. She had never imagined that such tortuous fancies could be lodged in the human mind.

Dr. Krieger's favourite hobby-horse was to straddle her, as she knelt on hands and feet, a slender birch switch in one hand, with which he stroked her bare rear with the skirt raised, stroking too at times inbetween, always gentle, never intent on hurting, even though Ursula's knees hurt as she moved with slow, elephantine gait on the looped pile of the carpet in his study. What pleasure it obtained him she could not imagine, fully clothed as he was, with nothing gross in word or movement, not the least trace of the salacious or lubricious, if not the odd chuckle and a smile of boyish mirth on the lips. She never asked, nor did he ever offer motive or meaning.

Of a slow winter afternoon, summoned to his study with its tall dark-wood cases lined with weighty tomes on man's mortal condition, tall windows that gave on to a view of the snow-mantled valley sloping down and away with clumps of pine and birch, he would take her hands, drawing her to himself in a companionable manner and, inhaling the perfume of her close presence, simply say, "Shall we, Sula?" He might as well have suggested a hand of cards or a game of chess, as he went around the desk to extract from a drawer the slender birch switch, while Ursula partly undressed, shedding underwear but leaving on her nursing cap.

Not particularly unseemly, save for her nudity, it might have been a theatre of infants in the nursery. Whatever satisfaction the doctor might have drawn from the recital, Ursula did not find it unduly unpleasant. If anything at all, in time she looked forward to the weekly summons and, in time too, the early timidity and shame fading, she felt a brief shimmer of something gratifying even as she crouched exposing her secret, nether parts to Krieger's eyes.

Unlike some of the other nurses, who regaled their companions with amused and bemused telling of the mischievous overtures of the males at the clinic, Ursula never made mention of her equine enactment with Dr. Krieger. Her friend Ilse, curious about the regular summons to the doctor's study, one day dropped a vaguely snide remark. "Studying medicine with Krieger, Ursula? Don't expect anything. You'll get nothing out of the old Scrooge."

"Oh! I've not asked for anything."

"And you'll get nothing, dear girl! The only woman in his life was his mother. A famous horsewoman. Won something at the Olympics once."

"Horsewoman?"

Ilse's father had once worked in the Kriegers' stables, grooming thoroughbreds. A disjointed family, Ilse recounted. The father, moneyed, otherwise a good for nothing, chasing the wenches in the village when sober, if ever. The mother, stern and much given to the faith, had lived for her horses alone, and for her only child, reared with a severe hand that didn't spare the whip when the son, a good-natured boy, failed to qualify in the local equestrian meets and competitions. Still and all, she was his world and, save for the years away studying medicine, he had lived with her till the end.

"That's your good doctor!" Ilse nodded severely. "Really, Ursula, can't imagine what you get up to with one like him."

Ursula did not mind Ilse's chiding. The first few months at the clinic she had lodged with Ilse's family. Becoming friends, Ilse, older by a few years, had taken to being something of an elder sister, sometimes a bit of a scold, but warm and well-intentioned. Level-headed for her young years, Ilse herself had other plans for the future, away from these spaces reeking phenol solutions and suffering. She might lend herself cursorily to the coarse pranks and whimsies of the male staff, but had set her steady sight on the anaesthetist, hoping to net in the young man for a life together.

If with her common-place looks, Ilse could pass unnoticed, not so Ursula, her stately figure turning heads, the high-cheeked face with tell-tale traces of a higher lineage and the luminous sensuality of the violet eyes setting in motion in men young and older earthly ruminations. Up the stairways and down the corridors, in the hallways and wards the eyes of both the sick and those in health kept pace with her steps as the erect figure, luxuriant and undulating, passed by. The sick might sigh and despair, perhaps worsening their already infirm condition. The medical personnel, mainly the senior physicians were privileged not only to feast their eyes but also occasionally indulge their ageing appetites, variegated and eccentric.

A lifetime later, in the occasional haphazard recounting of the past, recalling brief episodes from her days at the clinic, it amused Ursula to see her Professor neighbour wince with mute embarrassment. The revelations might be sanitized by time and age, confessions that skirted some of the gross and lurid, human confessions being seldom devoid of exclusions and omissions. Even so, startling and disconcerting, though one had sometimes heard of the hanky-panky between nurses and physicians on hospital premises. What Ursula and her colleagues had been subjected to went well beyond what might be expected of those who had answered a noble calling and solemnly taken the Hippocratic oath.

"And no one protested?" the Professor asked.

"Protested!" Ursula laughed. "What was there to protest? And to whom?"

Where she came from, she said, the dark forest lands, women had always been little more than chattel, sometimes less than a herd of prized cattle, given away at an early age, to live lives silent and forbearing, stand and sit at the behest of the man of the house, bear and rear the young, growing grey and going to the grave within the narrow and narrow-minded confines of the village of birth or the village down the valley.

"Things have changed, but not that much," Ursula added, nodding in recall. "Bear in mind, though, in my country women got the right to vote after man had already stepped on the moon. At my mother's time, especially in those rural areas to the north, you'd think the Dark Ages hadn't passed. Not many real Seigneurs about, but a plebeian version of the old *Droit du Seigneur* was still in practice, by fathers, teachers, masters, employers, the baker and the butcher. Maybe not for the first night, but every other night. Any night and any hour, whenever the man's trousers showed a swell! Wife, daughter or sister, any female was fair game!"

Neither wife nor sister, Ursula was no exception. But not any passing female, her standing at the clinic as something of a favourite with Dr. Krieger had by and large spared her the common harassment and vexation to which some of her fellow nurses were subjected almost daily. The ill-tempered physiotherapist's bug eyes might be glued to the undulations of her derrière as she went down the corridor, the pharmacist's silent gaze mesmerized by her front as she leant over the counter to count the capsules. Otherwise, she was exempt from the wayward hand appearing from nowhere to slide down her dress front. Worse still, to be pushed against the wall in the laundry room with one leg raised as the white-coated attendant clumsily attempted his invasion.

The privileged preserve of some of the seniors Ursula might be, but it was still some time before she could come around to lending herself and her services to their eccentric and out of the way tastes. Though not unduly frail or doddering, they were mostly past the age of youthful, lubricious callisthenics behind hospital ward screens and curtains. Well-remunerated and well-off, with successful careers behind them in institutes of importance national and abroad, they had come to the clinic to positions in part sinecures but that did lend the place the authority and prestige of names known, even illustrious, that in turn drew an affluent clientele, whether for convalescence in the sanatorium wing or to draw their last breath in the comforting peace of the hospice. Ursula's children's wards housed mainly the select young of the better-off, children often beyond therapeutic cure and hope, the avuncular care of the senior medical staff reassuring and offering a measure of solace to despairing parents.

~~~

Neither aged nor particularly avuncular, otherwise amiable and good-humoured, Herr Doktor Hoffman, a paediatrician, specialized in endocrinology, was a favourite with the young, his daily rounds briefly lighting up the infant faces. "When you're better, you'll have a lollipop the size of your face," he might whisper, beaming a gentle smile and smoothing back the gold-grey locks, the child afterwards asking Ursula when she might get better. Bending over another sick bed, seeing the eyes of the emaciated little boy on the large green, paisley-print bow tie he wore habitually, touching the broad silken loops he would say, "Wings to help me fly!"

Soft-spoken and caring with the young, Hoffman was no less polite and refined in his person, dapper in a bottle-green or wine-coloured velvet jacket, the bow-tie well-knotted. Trim and tall, the hair-line receding but the slightly greying egg-shaped head well-groomed, the pale-blue eyes above an aquiline nose alive with good humour, looks deceptive but in fact Hoffman was somewhere in his early sixties. A cheerful word at all times for the staff, his pithy responses often had the sound of mots and aphorisms. Reminded once by the head nurse that a watch on the wrist would prevent his habitual lateness, he remarked, "Time? A precious commodity. Meanwhile our young charges here are running out of their time." Watching Ursula bending over the bedside of a child in the throes of pain, he might remark with a pensive air, "A fairy queen in the garden of infants. For when they arrive in fairyland." Some days, the passing of a young appeared to deject him unduly, beyond the call of duty, the accustomed cheer faded, words ruminant uttered under breath, almost to himself. "Saddening such a short stay in the world." To add with pursed lips, "No less than overstaying."

Consulting head of the children's unit, he never brought to bear his position on Ursula or any of the other nurses, never a risqué allusion or a pointed look-over of the female curves and contours, nor could anyone recall him having ever asked for extra-curricular favours. At first it was thought his preferences were elsewhere, the guesswork soon put to an end by the sight in town one New Year's eve of a young woman on his arm.

They were drawn together not as partners in some tableaux of intimacy, not by what Ursula might have to offer of herself in homage to a man and a superior, but more by a talent that she had, that had gone unnoticed and undiscovered. Going about his visits, late afternoons he sometimes overheard Ursula crooning by a sick child's bed, some lullaby or local folk tune. Until one day, he distinctly caught her voice sing softly a cradle song as she sat by a fevered little girl who likely would not see the week out.

The melody familiar, the words he knew, heard oft in childhood and embedded securely in memory: *Guten Abend, Gute Nacht… Morgen früh, wenn Gott will, wirst du wieder geweckt…* Hardly a child of those times spared the notes of Brahms's cradle song, yet it was the limpid tonality of the voice that caught and held Hoffman's attention. Unforced, a crystalline purity making the words redundant, Ursula might as well have sung about lunch and dinner instead of bidding good morning and good night and invoking God's grace for the infant. That evening, back in his chalet, Hoffman sat at the small piano in the corner of the living room picking out the gentle melody, thinking of Ursula, her voice once again faintly winding its way in his ears.

A few days later, going through a list of medications brought into his office, he surprised Ursula, asking if she would sing something for him.

"Sing, doctor?" she asked, taken aback at the odd request.

He raised his head with a smile. "Singing for a grown up might earn you even more points in heaven!"

"Oh! I've never sung solo in public… only in the church choir. A long time ago."

"Hardly a public here. A public of one!" Hoffman remarked amiably, handing back the list.

On and off, slowing his steps in the corridor, pausing at the entrance, he would hear her as she nursed the young, snatches of some carol, a berceuse familiar or little known, always in the same voice mellow and unforced, soprano or mezzo his musical expertise unable to decipher. One day, coming up behind unheard as she stooped over a bed, tucking in the sheets around a child and softly voicing a lullaby, often sung by his mother to a younger sister, he stood by silently. Sensing a presence, Ursula turned to look up, the words still gently spilling from her lips. At best a voice edging towards the baritone, and not much given to singing, he joined her quietly in a duet: *Schlafe mein Prinzchen, schlaf' ein...*, the little 'prince' on the bed looking up at the duo with sleepy eyes, the night nurse peering from the doorway at the curious sight of Hoffman's face pressed close to Ursula's as they intoned the sleep-song.

It was the start of a friendship of sorts, voice and song an affinity, whatever other allure might have drawn Hoffman's attention. One day, then, he asked if some off-duty evening Ursula might like come over to his place. A courteous and amiable invitation, Ursula could see no ulterior design in his suggestion, no shaded stare of some of the other medics attempting to lure her to their den. Hoffman was different, she had noticed, his hands always kept to himself, no unwarranted physical sorties, no press of his body against hers when stood close by.

Something of a mystery, not many knew for certain of his provenance, what he might have been and why he should have come to the Grünewald some years ago. It was said he had been married several times over, had earned professional laurels, and then some misstep or scandal along the way had derailed the course of life and career. Truth or hearsay, he remained a mystery, living a bachelor's life in a small, rented chalet at a small distance down the valley, from which he cycled to work in clement weather, at the wheel of a small, nondescript car when the weather broke.

It was a companionable evening, that first time, Hoffman serving her a drink before sitting down at the piano, his playing not virtuoso but fluent enough to ably accompany Ursula as she sang pieces from her limited repertoire, mainly some of the lullabies she sang to the children, several folk songs, not overly taxing for her untrained voice but the clarity of her innate melodic sense coming through and lighting up Hoffman's face as he lifted his head from the keyboard, asking her for an encore of the short everyday song *'O du liabs Ängeli'* he had often heard her hum.

Thinking she had been asked for dinner, Ursula was surprised when Hoffman drove her down to a small eatery on the way to the town, apologizing that the elderly cleaning lady, who also kept house for him, was down with fever. Not quite a romantic rendezvous, the Gastätte offering wholesome country fare on bare-board tables, it was a simple and satisfying evening, without frills and fuss. Not accustomed to the glint and glitter of starched-cloth dining rooms, Ursula felt at ease in the unpolished surrounds of heavy dark timber and unpadded seating, no less Hoffman's easy and amiable company. Nothing of weight said, the table-talk mostly about life and work at the clinic, small incidents, the droll habits of some colleague of Hoffman's, the pleasant evening passed with no give-and-take proposed, no overture intimate or otherwise.

Whatever pleasure he might draw from her presence, Hoffman's company enriched her a deal more. Evidently, he had seen the world, been places, savoured pleasures that Ursula found both curious and instructive, she who had seen less than little of the world, had never known the exotic or esoteric. In no way taxing or offensive, his demands on her were more companionable than intemperate, with no design on her virtue other than an odd aberration at first sight risqué and indecent, but in essence innocent, that in no way appeared to ask for more than what it was and not particularly demeaning of her person.

Invited over for dinner at his place once in a while, she would find herself in a large living room, sparsely furnished, with a small piano in one corner, the odd bric-a-brac, a silver antique or two, a cabinet with a record player, a dining table by the wide glazing that looked down the valley towards the small village on the way to town, leather-upholstered seating along one wall. The table laid with foodstuffs that Ursula had never seen, much less tasted, Hoffman plied her with the rare fare, fish roe marinaded in Madeira, a wedge of Epoisses washed in pomace brandy, the festering aroma of the cheese making Ursula hold her breath. Apparently, a friend in France procured and sent over the delicacies.

Not the choice dishes alone, a general air of refinement accompanied Hoffman, gesture and movement, word and manner, the sort of breeding Ursula had not much known and that impressed and drew her to him. Quiet in voice, at times distant, always persuasive and reassuring.

Years later, moving about in the upper reaches of the musical world, once in a while Ursula surprised her husband with her passing knowledge of the delicacies offered at receptions and dinners, as she proffered to his lips a parfait cigar, naming the duck *rilette* inside, or asked for a wedge of Reblochon. "You've had that before?" he would ask, raising his brows in wonder at her nod of assent, wondering where on earth this bride of his from the backwoods might have tasted such delicacies. For a brief moment, then, Ursula's thoughts would reach back to the evenings with Hoffman, with the notes of the music from the record player softly weaving in the air for the after-dinner dance.

Hoffman was an expert dancer, the foot work nifty, the three-step and four-step precise and agile, as too his effortless guiding of the partner, the arm a supple and sure support when turning or gliding. Ursula followed as best as she could, the first few times stiff and awkward, blushing and embarrassed. She had danced with men, but never bare and in only a black négligé draping her to the feet, that hid little or less from view, neither the erect bosom billowing the chiffon, nor the undulations of her rear as she moved.

The ritualistic nudity Hoffman's sole demand and insistence, his hand on the small of her naked back as he guided her firm but never straying, his figure upright and with no gesture or movement other than those called for, they might well have been any other couple on a dance floor. His eyes rarely grazed over her figure, without stare over this curve or that swell, yet it would have been an odd sight for an onlooker. And Ursula, the first few times, catching a glimpse of herself reflected on the glass of a large print on the wall, almost a double, depicting a young woman in dishabille in the arms of a top-hatted man in some libertine cabaret scene, shied away from the image.

If courtship it was, Hoffman never went further than the discreet hold of his arms, with no words of sentiment or endearment, no move to signal designs of possession, nor the short breath of desire. But in time it was Ursula who sensed within herself an undertow, an undefined drift towards acquiescence and surrender had he but merely dropped a hint, tightened his clasp, drawn her to himself and sought her lips with his.

She had never known one like him, not where she came from, her brushes and encounters with men always one of submission to needs and appetites unfeeling and loveless, the heart never enlisted, her fulfilment perfunctory and peripheral, the satisfaction of the male the essence of the engagement, short-lived or long. Easy-going and undemanding, Hoffman seemed a rare sort, never before met. She would not have much minded in giving herself to him, if he had but asked. She thought she would not have minded at all if he had asked her to consign in his hands the days to come and the life ahead. Puzzled and wondering, she could not understand the careful distance he kept, the absence of an engagement more demanding.

It mattered little that she was in her twenties, he decades older. Age was, she thought, what one made of it, and he was still upright, vigorous in movement, head sound and lively, face and figure younger by a span. For the first time Ursula sensed within the stirring of an impatience never before felt, his sometimes temporary absence from the clinic casting an unaccustomed gloom over her day, the sight of him again easing breath. Perhaps for the very first time she thought to find herself in love.

The better part of her young life lived in the shadow of a mother stifling and oppressive, a father irascible and heavy-handed, the blood rising crimson and dark on his face if merely crossed with a word, the low grunt of an animal of the wild when he closed in on her in a dim corner of her room, she had hardly ever known the peace and quite of a home, nor ever much known a man and a human whom to offer what she had, share her needs and share her heart's ease. Finally, now, in Hoffman she thought to have found one who could take her whole and as she was, unlike others, who preferred the meat without the bone, the feathers and outward finery, with neither regard for nor interest in the person, the woman she was.

Yet, there was something in Hoffman that at times baffled Ursula. She could not understand his hesitation, if not refusal, to reach out and take what was on offer and so close to hand. The door ajar, waiting in vain, she had perhaps not signalled and made clear her wanting, not only for an hour or the day. So that, at his place one late summer evening, once again in his arms as he led her through the steps of a slow dance, provoked by her own nudity and an aching desire coursing through the veins, her arms coming around to draw him to her in an embrace seemingly intentioned not to let go, lifting her head and nudging his face, her lips sought out his, warm, both pliant and firm. Yielding to the touch and press, he drew back after a long moment, to look her in the eyes with the breath of a sigh.

"Too late, Ursula," he said softly, in apology almost. "A little too late." Lifting a hand to gently trace the fall of her cheek, in a voice even but edged with defeat, he added, "A journey begun at sunset ends in the dark."

Had it been it his way of telling her, she wondered afterwards, elliptical and opaque, the truth likely already known to him, the diagnosis certain. At the moment she had not known what to make of it. Rebuff or refusal, afterwards it mattered little. Turning away with bitter heart, she had silently inveighed against fate, or providence, or whatever it was that traced and marked the paths of life. If divine will, it was a cruel God to deny her for this once, the only time, she had felt free to choose and offer of her own will what others had taken by force, robbed or inveigled, without her say and consent. In moments calmer, she wondered if she had not reached for a fruit too high on the bough, beyond her station and standing, her worth meagre for one like him, she having little to offer, neither learning nor talent, without skill to hold and keep a man.

One day, some weeks later later, he simply went missing. The first few days of his absence from the clinic she thought he might have taken ill or merely taken a short leave to see to some private affair or, else, away briefly as in recent times, with no particular reason offered on his return. But the days passed, turned to a week, a fortnight, and still Hoffman was nowhere to be seen. Anxious and troubled, she asked the Head Nurse, to be told that the doctor had left.

"Left?" she asked. "Left for where?"

"Gone away, dear. Don't think he'll be back any time soon."

Panic numbing mind, she went through the day in a daze, seeing to her duties with unfeeling, mechanical habit. The hours, interminably long, done and finished, walking with leaden gait, on the way out she met Dr. Krieger.

Krieger had seen Ursula and Hoffman together, at work, out in the town once or twice, had sensed their friendship, perhaps something more. Struck by her fatigued look, the expression seemingly pained, the ever bold, bright gazelle eyes dimmed to an opacity that evaded gaze, he took her by the arm and let her into his study. His hobby-horse, bare-back riding of her apart, a private space for an aberrant indulgence that in no way spilled over into his workday, Krieger had always been kind and generous with Ursula, a paternal eye keeping watch from a distance. Sitting her down now, he himself perched on the edge of the desk, he looked at her a long moment, as though shifting through the syllables, the words to break the news.

"As you may know, Ursula, Dr. Hoffman has left us. It's possible he'll not be coming back. There was no choice. He had to go abroad…" As if abruptly tiring of the skirting and beating about, he cut short the preamble. "Hodgkin's Lymphoma. We've had a number of guests in the hospice in the terminal stage. Thankfully a few survive, not many. One can only pray for the best. It would be wrong, though, to hold out too much hope. I'm afraid we may never see him again."

Ursula hung her head, her voice a mere thread of a whisper. "He never told me."

"Hoffman wasn't the sort to wear his troubles on his sleeve. A good man, never a complaint. One doesn't see many like him. He'll be missed." He took her hand in his, pausing as she brushed away the damp from her eyes. "We have a Dr. Honegger coming to take his place for a few months, until we find a permanent replacement. Honegger's an old friend of mine. You'll like him, I'm sure."

~~~

A fortnight later Dr. Honegger did arrive to take Hoffman's place. An older man, mild and likeable, as Krieger had said. But for long nothing was the same again for Ursula. Her thoughts ever turning to Hoffman, a sense of desolation echoing in the empty hours, she felt abandoned. Drained, arid in mind, at times bitter that it should have ended even before it had begun, she went through the day silent and resentful, keeping herself to herself and shunning the gregarious company of colleagues.

Irate with no one in particular, if at all with herself and the hand dealt her, she lay awake at night wondering if she might have gone with him, to be by his side, to nurse him through whatever his pain.

"Life's not over yet," her friend Ilse comforted in her accustomed no-nonsense, practical manner. "We're still young, Ursula. Hoffman can't have been the only one. There'll be others, there's always some one else. Just wait and see." She made it sound like getting a new ironing board in place of the old. With the flicker of a wan smile, Ursula wished she could have been like Ilse, taking the hard with the soft, shrugging off whatever the hurt and looking forward to the new day.

For sure there would be others, someone else. For the moment it was of little interest to her. Days seemingly without a horizon, she did not know what time would bring. More than ever she felt alone and abandoned, orphaned once with her mother's passing, orphaned yet again, of the only man she might have loved. For the first time discontent clouded her mind, to live here among the sick and dying, as though on the fringes of the living and the outer reaches of the world, with no prospect other than watching morning and night infant faces pale and frail, the soft moan in the ears of young life ebbing and draining away.

It was also the beginning of a season of life when slowly she let herself go, passive and acquiescent, going with the tide, accepting whatever came her way, yielding to singular demands, appetites eccentric and aberrant. Listlessly surrendering will and volition, it was a time that marked the erosion of her innate innocence. No stranger to sins greater or lesser, the knavery and turpitude in men she had seen and met before, early at home, as an adolescent, in the church precincts, later training as nurse, somehow she had come through, her womanhood sullied but spirit untouched, blood little infected and trust in humans still reasonably whole.

Sallying out in the world, she had always risen in the morning glad and with good cheer, curious about what the new day might bring, readily savouring the small pleasures of company, a word, the smile of a greeting, grateful for a gift large or small, and never particularly conscious that she stood head and shoulders above many another woman, the splendour of her looks and impudent figure setting her apart. If the uncommon beauty caught the eye, her good nature also made for access, men handing over in her keeping their innermost and shamed secrets without undue hesitation or trepidation.

~~~

"There are things in humans," she once said, recounting to the new neighbour Dr. Honegger's particular inclination, "that one would never ever confess. Not even under torture. When I think of it, it still surprises me, after all this time."

"That, I expect, is what sets us apart from other living beings," the neighbour nodded with a smile.

"I'm afraid I've never understood that. Many don't mind being called names of one kind or another. Nazi, fascist, thief, murderer. Maybe offensive, but people don't curl up with shame."

"Breaking the Commandments, the Cardinal Sins, never brought the blush on any one's face. Dishonour mother and father, worship other gods, covet the neighbour's wife…daily events. Water off the duck's back. But the appetites hiding in the interstices of the brain, that's another matter. Call them State Secrets, if you like!"

Ursula's trill of laugh rang briefly in the evening air as butler Silvio dimmed the garden lights and came to bid goodnight. "State Secrets," Ursula repeated. "I like that, Professor! You'd not let me into some of yours?"

"Ah, not even under torture."

"You might even enjoy it!"

"Quite possible. One never knows."

The brief smile fading, he looked at her thoughtfully. "They're not secrets in the conventional sense, I don't think," he intoned with a pedantic air. "More like blemishes, bacteria if you like, resident in the recesses of our being. Like the marine life in the depths of oceans, that can't bear the merest ray of sunlight."

"Some things are difficult to confess. Almost unconfessable."

"Confessions almost never plumb to the bottom, especially in the confessional. In writing his *"Confessions"* Rousseau's intentions were honest. But the whole truth, that was another matter. For large tracts he loses himself in self-justification and a litany of misery. In this the great are no more immune than lesser minds. We talk of ourselves endlessly, but most revelations are preening and posturing, justifications, ego-trips, you might say. In these disclosures there's rarely space for candour, as with our toilet habits, the seamy grime… like the dregs at the bottom of the coffee mug."

"Oh, do stop!" she feigned to beg him. "Must say you've a poor view of human nature. For myself, I admit to being a sinner, but also admitting to like it…" The brief mirth fading, she stared long at the night-sky, as though intent on a voice within.

She never saw Hoffman again. A little over a year later Dr. Krieger told her he had passed away in a palliative care centre in France, comforted in the final days by his mother. She had not known he still had a mother. How little she had known of him, almost nothing or less.

"People drift through each other's lives… it was the same with the doctor who took Hoffman's place," she said, returning from her star-gazing.

~~~

Elderly, lean and bony, with a mostly balding head and a face with a patrician cut that still echoed a more or less handsome look in earlier times, Dr. Honegger was retiring and mild of manner, treading the wards and rooms with steps barely audible, as though not wanting to intrude or disturb. Imparting an order, he appeared to be asking a favour. Voice soft, the expression of benevolence breaking into a small smile, never commanding in word, he seemed more a wayfarer lost in the labyrinthine corridors of the clinic. When consulted on some matter weighty and calling for a decision, he cogitated and meditated long minutes, at times hours.

Clumsy with a bottle of capsules, dropping the syringe, he gave the impression of ageing frailty, less feeble of physique, more tenuous of mind. The Head Nurse, brisk and over-busy, losing patience at times, watched with pursed lips as Honegger fumbled with the sphygmomanometer, saying in a barely audible aside, "Heaven only knows in which old people's home Dr. Krieger found him;" or else, "This gentleman should have been registered as patient in the hospice." Ursula looked away, judging her colleague unduly harsh.

When alone, a shade of melancholy appeared to descend on Honegger as he sat half-slumped behind the desk, coming alive and righting himself if one of the staff looked in. Ursula mentioned to Dr. Krieger in passing that the new doctor often looked sad.

"Honegger has much to be sad about," said Krieger in a pensive tone. "Poor man. But a good sort, a likeable person."

More than liking, with the passing weeks Ursula came to feel a sort of tender sympathy. Not only a touch maladroit, but also irresolute, more than once undecided on the best remedy for the young patient, he looked about with an air almost forlorn, as if awaiting the voice of a second opinion from the heavens. Momentarily abandoning whatever the task, Ursula attempted always to be at hand whenever he did the rounds visiting the young, gathering up the medical cards that slipped from his fingers, a hand on the arm to steer his steps that seemed to wander. His mind often appeared to stray, alive enough but listening to voices elsewhere. A distraction that made the staff testy to the limits of rudeness, making faces over his shoulder, the *Oberschwester* departing with impatient breath, muttering, "Let me know, doctor, when you've decided." More and more Honegger came to lean on Ursula, taking refuge in her kindly attention, looking about to search her presence, her smile and nearness reassuring, seemingly.

Looking back, Ursula sometimes wondered why in her younger years no local youth stout and sturdy had claimed her attention, why no dashing and debonair young man had attempted to charm her into his arms, why those of or near her own age had stayed, at best, at arm's length, eyeing her from a safe distance, like an animal uncertain of approaching its prey. The junior doctors at the clinic were amicable in a brotherly way, their taunt and teasing light-hearted, but with never an invitation for an evening out or an errant hand reaching out. They might make free with her fellow nurses, but she was always merely *Schwester* or, more familiarly, *Engel*.

Later, in her husband's circles, there were scores of men, young or younger, musicians, orchestral personnel, associates eminent or less so, many personable and often handsome. But most remained, at best, at a stone's throw, cordial, admiring and respectful, with never a seductive overture or gesture of suggestive interest. At times, Ursula felt something of a china doll on the shelf, not to be touched or overtly coveted. Always, unfailingly, it was the ageing and the aged who eyed her with design, approaching with purpose, often enough making their intent clear. It was as if there was something in her blood that drew to her the elders of the species, like night insects with a marked preference for the blood of a particular species. Seemingly, the paternal lover was her lot.

It was no different with Dr. Honegger. Adrift he might appear at times, but Ursula's presence unfailingly animated his absent air, the opaque gaze brightening, voice coming alive and mind recalled to whatever the task at hand. The chemistry did not go unnoticed.

"I'll get Miss Elixir," the Head Nurse occasionally mumbled under breath, as Honegger hummed and hawed over a dosage or a course of remedy. And Dr. Krieger one day remarked in passing, "Seems you've brought old Honegger back to life. What's the particular therapy, Ursula?" Ursula merely smiled. Innocent enough it might be, but purple and suggestive to an intruding eye, Roman Charity was not something that Krieger or others might have easily understood.

The familiarity came by chance and unforced. The rain beating down, she and Honegger waiting at the end of the day under the cover of the entrance for the sudden summer downpour to cease, Joachim offered the doctor a ride back in his ramshackle car. "May I come with you?" Ursula asked on an impulse, curious to see once again the small chalet where Hoffman had lived and where Honegger was now lodged.

She had heard no more of Hoffman, on and off she still thought of him, missed his lightness of manner and heart, still sensed at times the vacant place he had left in her and wondering, too, what might have been. Memory undimmed, but the resilience of youth helping to climb out of the trough of misery of the early days, she wanted to revisit the scene of their evenings together, Hoffman's quite talk, their voices unison in song as he sat at the piano, the press of his hand on her naked skin warm as they danced.

Nothing much had changed. The personal items had gone, the books and records from the shelves, some of the furniture rearranged, the piano dormant in its habitual corner, the sized logs neatly piled by the stone chimney. It was the wall above the dark-wood mantlepiece that caught her sight and held her with surprised attention.

The cabaret dancer winding sinuous around the top-hatted gentleman had given way to a large, framed painting, both curious and bold, of a frail and infirm figure on his knees feeding at the ample breast of a pale young woman, her hand drawing the cloth over his nudity. Honegger watched as Ursula tried to make out the title in small, uneven wording at the bottom of the frame.

"Bartolomé Esteban Murillo. *Caritas Romana,*" he read out for her. Drawing alongside, he added, "An act of mercy. But you'll not have heard of Murillo. A Spanish baroque painter, not very distinguished."

"Quite old, I suppose."

"Late 17th century. No, not the original," he added, turning away. "A copy by one of Murillo's apprentices."

Not Esteban Murillo alone, Ursula knew little or less of art. Save for a school outing once to some provincial Pinakothek, the odd rustic brushstrokes of landscapes and mountainscapes hung on the walls of local taverns and Gasthöffe, she was largely unfamiliar with portrait and painting. Her mother had one day made a tolerably passable crayon sketch from an old photograph of a handsome man in officer's uniform, telling her it was her grandfather Uwe. Otherwise, she herself had never held a drawing pencil, nor set eyes on originals of oil on canvas. Seemingly taken by Murillo's depiction, she now asked, "Who are they?"

"Ah!" Honegger drew a deep breath. "You may well ask, Ursula. Mythological, Juno and Hercules. Maybe father and daughter. Or simply a maid nourishing a tired old man."

Himself sounding worn and weary, in need of nourishment, Honegger eased himself on the sofa facing the chimney. "Can I get you something?" Ursula asked.

Hoffman had left behind a case of bottles and Ursula uncorked one. Handing the glass of wine to Honegger, she made to leave. "Won't you have a glass yourself?" he asked gently patting the leather of the seat alongside where he had let himself down.

They sat in silence, a little apart, Ursula sipping her drink, eyeing the mantelpiece and the painting above, casting now and again an awkward glance towards Honegger, his head leant back, eyes shut. In repose, yet somehow he looked infinitely tired, as though overcome with the exhaustion of age, of having lived over-long, the high brow lined, the once sensuous lips loose, the day's growing stubble sprouting through the wrinkles of the face.

As if sensing her gaze, his hand reaching out and taking hers, he said quietly, "Thank you. You were kind to drop in. Every bit helps." When she rose to her feet a short while later, he saw her to the door, repeating, "Thank you for coming. Will you look in again sometime?" She nodded and, unthinking, touched her lips to his cheek, feeling the tiny bristles prick her skin. "I will."

And she did. Not quite knowing why, what might be the draw. Unbeknown to her, the yearning of earlier times still alive, dormant in the labyrinths of her being, imagination with a sleight of hand rearranged faces and figures. So that, both in her dreams, a rare time in idle hours, Ursula at times pictured the realities of the past altered and reformed. So that now, at odd moments, she thought to see in Honegger's lineaments the sketch her mother had made of grandfather Uwe, the two far apart in years, but age obliterated, the half profiles near-identical, the same sombre gloom in the eyes.

Was it a silent quest, begun early in childhood, for the father she might have had, not the ogre who had sired her and later assailed her innocence, her eyes often lingering with pining wish on her class mates crossing the *Volksschule* yard hand in hand with fathers at the end of the school day. Not only till much later did she pause to ask herself if it was this hunt and seeking that drew her to men older by many spans, to submit almost willing and without undue protest to their ageing whims and quirks, but for her somehow gestures of filial compliance, of need and care even.

Honegger never appeared to want to ask or demand anything more than what Ursula herself offered. Stopping by occasionally, when off-duty, she might make a meal for him, tidy up if by chance the cleaning lady attending to an ailing husband failed to turn up. Quartered some minutes from the clinic, in a residence for nurses who came from localities too distant for daily travel, Ursula was glad to be away for an afternoon or evening from the spartan surrounds and company of colleagues, their gregarious chatter and din about men, mating and marriage. Her mother gone the year she started at the clinic, the old family farmhouse tumbling and shut, Ursula had no home to call her own. If Honegger's place, more bare and spare than during Hoffman's residence, was not quite home, at least it had the air of one, and his company easy, gentle and kindly.

Neither romance nor affair, it was an odd companionship, far distant in age and disparate in provenance, Ursula's life in its morning, Honegger's marking time to tiptoe towards the sunset. She might have been a daughter of the house, he an elder, mellow and benign, surprisingly affable at times. Reticent in the early days, with hardly ever a word on what and where he might have been before arriving at the Grünewald, gradually and with a cautious finger he turned the odd page or two of his past, once extracting from a chocolate box a handful of old prints. A photograph yellowed with age of him in cape and gown on the steps of the imposing, neoclassical frontage of the medical school where he had studied; a later portrait, as head of the department at a city hospital, surrounded by his staff, stout nurses prim in starched uniforms, a handful of young doctors stood stiff with ponderous looks. Ursula caught, too, a glimpse of a postcard-size colour image of him flanked by a woman and a girl, but Honegger hurriedly shuffled the pack away, putting the prints back in the cardboard box. Later, when Honegger had left, Dr. Krieger briefly recounted Honegger's sad story of a life that had wanted for nothing, success, fame and name, that one day, like the sudden death of the sun, had plunged his days into darkness irreversible and enduring.

Familiarity did not breed the accustomed intimacies, more the well-being of companionable familiarity, Ursula's care and comforting presence received with a gratitude little uttered in words but clear in his look, the smile when she stepped into the house, the thankfulness in his eyes when, sat by a sick bed at the clinic, he looked up as she stood above him. The past chequered and weighty for both, but whatever the pain resident in their hearts, never touched on, the losses and intemperance of time never revealed, increasingly at ease each with the other, neither ever seemed to ask what the other might want, no curiosity about the finality of their odd companionship. Perhaps there was none, no expectation undue or out of place, the drawing together welling in each from what life might have denied or betrayed.

Early that first winter, then, Honegger fell ill, coughing his lungs out, breath laboured, running a fever that seemed to scald the hand when Ursula touched his forehead. Dr. Krieger came down in person, to declare that there was nothing to fear, merely a mild case of pleurisy, made out the required prescription and relieved Ursula for a few hours from her duties at the clinic, so that she might nurse and feed the sick man.

The recovery surprisingly rapid, Honegger was soon on the mend. But weak and weathered, he rose from bed to take a few slow and uncertain steps, slumping then on the sofa, somnolent. Ursula kept house, cooked and fed, the first night night or two staying back to sleep on the sofa, commuting between the clinic and the chalet each day, Joachim giving her a lift into town to buy provisions.

What then happened one day she was at a loss to explain to herself, at the time and afterwards. It had come without thought, as if in the natural course of things, a gesture of no exception, much as when she and Honegger sat to dine together at table, as when she looked in to tuck him into bed for the night.

Thinking back on that time, memory lingering briefly on the peculiar episode of... what might one call it? Perhaps license, voluntary and unrestrained. Ursula thought that all through life, ever since childhood and the adult years into age, there was something that drove her to defer and surrender herself, a submission at times of her own volition, unasked and unsolicited, a recondite will to acquiesce and please, perhaps to gain approval and acceptance. It had been so with her mother Conradine, who in the depths of her heart had denied her as a child of her blood, more an offspring of disinheritance and violation. So it had been with her father, perhaps to keep at bay his appetites perverse and unnatural. So, too, later and always, with Armin, going along willing and indulgent with his senescent vision of her as a great voice on the stage. How else to explain even the innocuous, if not quite innocent, horse-play in Dr. Krieger's study, or the denuded dancing in Hoffman's arms? Gross or otherwise, not meant as acts of seduction, she had lent herself to the varied and various deviant peculiarities merely to gain not favour but approval, that she was a true child of her mother's womb, that Armin had taken her to wife for love and not only for whatever art she might offer. If Ursula thought she had never loved, she often wondered, too, if she had ever been loved, for what she was, a woman, a person and a human.

Perhaps Armin had been right, after all, the words hurtful but close enough to the bone. Once, in the early days of marriage, making love, she had surprised him with a move overly bold and out of sorts for his tastes, her lips still gorging, as though bent on devouring, on his spent manhood, as he fell back trying to detach her tousled head from his loins, her intent merely to please paid with derisive rebuff as he muttered with worn-out breath, "You've got a heart of gold, Ursula, but the head of a whore." Seeking approval by way of acquiescence was a bent that had always come to her unforced, unthinking as second nature.

The late afternoon light leaden and flickering as the busy flakes of snow swirled by the window, the drifts soundlessly settling on the garden sloping down towards the road, the log in the grate quietly crackling with small tongues of flame, sat on the sofa in front of the chimney with Honegger's head nestling silent on her lap, Ursula's gaze fixed and unmoving on Murillo's painting of *Roman Charity* above the mantelpiece, she herself might have been a figure in a still-life scene. Seemingly in hypnotic gaze, her fingers then slowly picked at the buttons of her dress, as if of their own volition. Freeing one breast from its cup, she proffered the pout of the abundant weight to Honneger's mouth, pressing the tip between his slack lips. The epiphany of an act impulsive and without thought, Ursula had the brief sensation of something within her mysterious and indecipherable, unfelt before yet elusive.

The drowsy eyes slowly opening, sense coming alive, some wonder perhaps but with no visible shock or surprise, Honneger appeared to accept with grace what was offered, much as a suckling babe at its mother's teat, quiescent and drawing sustenance. Not a word spoken, Ursula looked down at the thinning head in her arm, the warmth of his slow breath washing up her bosom. She did not know if it was an act of charity, Roman or otherwise. Nor was she certain, even afterwards, what she might have felt. No evident incitement, no wakening call of desire, if anything at all, a sense of incidental satisfaction that gratified the mind more than the body.

Something changed after Ursula's random and impulsive gesture that afternoon. If till then she had been for Honegger an amiable companion who sometimes looked in, nursed him back on his feet, spent an hour or two in the house relieving his solitary bachelor existence, offering a helping hand with small chores, now in his eyes she appeared to have gained the contours of an altered presence, not merely a kindly young person extending sympathy and care, but one with the aura of alluring womanhood. It was as though he had woken from a long dormancy, his senses in hibernation, to discover anew things the mind had set aside or forgotten, the pleasing sound of a youthful voice in the ears, the warmth of another sat close, the whiff of the body's scent, the tactile pleasure of the feel and soft touch of a hand. In public, too, he appeared to have regained the latitudes of the self he might have been once, not youth or vigorous manhood, but more certain in speech and movement, a manner more consonant with an age not overly time-worn or ancient.

The change did not go unnoticed. Watching the surer gait and benign smile as he visited the ailing young, the Head Nurse screwed her face with mild puzzlement. "The Herr Doctor is back from the dead!" she muttered, throwing Ursula a keen glance. "What have you done to him, Ursula?"

Ursula herself was at a loss, surprised by Honegger's firmer tone when dealing with the staff, the fumbling with the sphygmomanometer gone, writing out prescriptions with a surer hand, no longer wandering down the corridors as if in a daze. Returned to the land of the living, seemingly, but Honegger made no ulterior demand of her, no overture or request of greater access to her person, evidently contented of an evening to stretch out on the sofa in front of the grate with his head on her lap, as might a father with a daughter of the house or a man with the spouse of a lifetime, spare words reaching back on occasion to the past, selecting from the reams of memory some incident to do with his profession, at times touched with an air forlorn and of failure. One day he recounted, but at some length, one such episode, that had stayed with him down the years.

It was all a very long time ago. Still young, in his thirties, career taking wing, he had risen in the hierarchy of the Institute, second to the head of paediatric care, with ambitions to make his way up yet further. Personal aspirations aside, however, he often felt invested with a keen sense of mission. So that, as yet single, with no weighty private encumbrances, he gave of himself in unstinting measure, filling in for colleagues, passing long days, often nights, in the children's wards, the failure to retain an ailing child in life at times casting a pall of melancholy on his day. Such was his youthful zeal that had the good Dr. Schweitzer summoned him to his clinic in the heart of Africa, he would have departed without second or afterthought, sharing as he did the great man's conviction that "The purpose of human life is to serve…"

His arm gentle around Ursula as they sat one afternoon before the grate, he lifted his gaze towards the chimneypiece, sight lingering silent on Murillo's painting of the *Caritas Romana*.

"To serve. But to what purpose," he half murmured, with a sigh of resignation, perhaps. "To care is also to court pain. Like love, with its attendant misery." Drawing himself up, he turned to Ursula with a quiet smile. "But why am I telling you this? You are young, Ursula. Time enough to discover for yourself." But he did tell her.

One season, unusually, several young children admitted to the Institute had succumbed, one after the other, to some malaise seemingly mysterious, perhaps as yet undiscovered. The summer sun barely dimming even as evening fell, huddling long hours with colleagues, puzzling over diagnoses and examining reports of laboratory tests, shifting through the sheaves of paper and listening to opinions learned and less so, coffee cups emptied and refilled, no sure prognosis came to sight. Guesswork, trial and error, remedies new and old tried and failed, it turned out to be a season of bewildering infant deaths.

Physically worn and dejected, he had taken a few week's leave. On the welcome suggestion of a colleague, a close friend as well, he had readily agreed to motor down together to northern Spain, to a small town on the Atlantic coast. A welcome getaway from a dispiriting time, as also from a brief private affair come to an abrupt and unhappy end.

He could no longer recall the name of the locality, a small fishing port not distant from Francisco Franco's birthplace. The quiet of the little hotel, the bracing ocean air, the undulating Galician landscape with its gentle slopes and valleys and woodlands, all a world away from the helpless young faces in the hospital wards, did much to revive the spirit. Between invigorating morning dips in the waters of the small bay and leisurely drives into the countryside, stopping over at some small inn or tavern with its simple but hearty and wholesome rustic fare, the days passed unnoticed. Revived in spirit, both men were ready for the return, when a chance incident cast a passing pall of gloom over their days, making Honegger, especially, doubt the futility of his zeal, the sense of mission he had always brought to his calling.

He had never known to distant himself from his work, drawing a curtain between himself and the pain and misery of the afflicted, looking away to pretend that it was a job like any other, as might a bank manager in the counting house counting out the money, the waiter in the hotel serving toast and honey, the music conductor on the podium blithely swinging his arms to Beethoven and Brahms. Skin too thin and porous, much too susceptible to the suffering of the sick and the dying, he at times regretted not having taken up a profession that called for no sympathy or empathy, an academic given to dry, pedantic lecturing, or an administrator, an accountant whose only concern was with the figures in the columns of cost and profit.

One evening, then, with a couple of days to go, the young man who waited at tables at the hotel, knowing that the foreign gentlemen were doctors, approached them with a desperate plea. His sister's newborn in a nearby village had taken seriously ill and the aged paramedic at the rural clinic was all at sea, unable to offer remedy and pronouncing the child would not see the night out.

The village was less than nearby, almost an hour's drive over narrow country tracks through the darkening woods. The fratricidal war long over and the foe vanquished, brooking not the least dissent and enthroned for decades as supreme lord of the Spanish lands, yet the Generalissimo had neglected his own native backyard, the villages on the way decaying hamlets of small, mean medieval habitations lit with oil lamps, thoroughfares muddy, lightless unpaved tracks and trails hard on the bones. The young man frantically gesturing and gesticulating, the ramshackle car borrowed from the hotel manager finally came to a stop below a narrow, dilapidated wood and stone farmhouse raised on stout trunks, with cattle stood or sat on the bare earth below and the living quarters above, under the sloping slate roof, the customary narrow wooden granary rising over the edifice on sturdy stone pillars. Under the cold drizzle, the two doctors followed the youth in the dark up the steps on the side.

More a hovel than a habitation, in the dim penumbra of an oil lantern hung from the beams they saw the young woman, a small slender figure, a dishevelled head of abundant locks framing a once pretty face now seemingly aged before time, eyes darker than the darkness around, gaze frantic. The young man spoke a few words and she hurried forward in her swaddling attire to meet the two strangers. "*O Señor, O Señor Doctor!*" she exclaimed in a barely audible voice, stooping to take Honegger's hand, pressing her lips to it repeatedly *"El bebé no está bien. Ella no se mueve. No, no se mueve. Por favor…"*

Indeed, the infant, bare months old, appeared still-born in its narrow cradle cot in a corner of the room, the rough-knit woollen cover concealing the meagre figure, the tiny face unusually swollen, the sparse down on the head wet with scalding fever. In the flickering light of the oil lamp held close by the young man, Honegger's friend lifted the almost weightless life and, passing a hand softly over the head, felt the slight bulge above the fontanelle. Turning to Honegger, he nodded. They agreed, with few words, that probably it was too late, the bacteria working its way through the brain, the meningitis had run its course. In any case, with no medicinals at hand, antibiotics or other, and too late for remedy, it was not unlikely that the residual life in the tiny creature would fade during the night.

And yet, the vow to his profession reluctant to let go, hoping against hope, Honegger thought the small creature might yet be saved. It was worth a try. But how? Garbled enquiries to the brother revealed there was no pharmacy nearby, the nearest miles away and shut at that hour. The dirt roads in the dark uncertain and impervious, it seemed an undertaking impossible, probably futile. Dejected and wordless, the visitors sat themselves down on two rickety stools drawn up by the bare-board table.

Unable to answer the woman's anxious and querying gaze, they looked about with downcast eyes. The musty odour of the ruminating cattle below coming up through the rough-hewn floorboards, the air chill with autumn damp, the low-ceilinged room faintly redolent of stale, boiled greens and strewn with a few pieces of rustic furniture, a narrow door at one end leading to the kitchen perhaps, it was not a habitation of health and well-being, the infant likely catching its fever from the soiled and unsanitary conditions.

There was no other male about, apart from the waiter brother, no man of the house. Honegger and his friend understood in a confused fashion that the husband had been incarcerated for indiscreet words in public about the Caudillo, was still behind bars in Ferrol after several months. Accustomed to absolute obedience and obeisance from the nation, the great man was especially severe with those of his native land for the least dissent or disrespect.

Offered what little there was in the house, a carafe of wine, a hunk of sour dough bread leathery on the teeth, they kept helpless vigil through the night, the young woman stooping from time to time to wipe the infants heated brow with a damp cloth. Wordless and restive, Honegger and his friend rose to pace about in the fitful light, pausing now and again by the cot to look down at the waning life, touch the fevered brow.

Despairing, a sense of utter helplessness silencing thought, Honegger had had the sensation of nothing making sense, the profession he had chosen, the finespun debates and discussions about cure and care, the strident proclamations of science promising humans eternity on earth. Such claims and so much noise, even as a newborn succumbed to a malaise studied and known in the heart of lands and countries boasting prosperity and well-being for all.

The last strained breath departed from the infant towards dawn. Oddly, there was no scream of lament from the young woman, no scene of catatonic grief. With the still calm of fateful resignation, merely silent tears witness to the heartbreaking loss, she clutched the dead child to herself, pressing the tiny face to her bosom as though meaning to offer renewed life from her teats. Not a word uttered, nor a sound from the lips, only grief dripping from the eyes in soundless droplets, oblivious to the presence of the others, she neither moved from where she sat, nor looked up as the visitors took their mute leave.

Outside, streaks of silver brightening on the horizon above the distant mountain ranges, Honegger and his friend boarded the car and the engine shuddered to uncertain life, breaking the pristine silence of the cold dawn.

"To serve. To what purpose," Honegger repeated the thought like a faint refrain, his fingers smoothing Ursula's hand, reciting then words, almost to himself, of which Ursula could make no sense. *"ὄμνυμι Ἀπόλλωνα ἰητρὸν καὶ Ἀσκληπιὸν καὶ Ὑγείαν καὶ Πανάκειαν καὶ θεοὺς πάντας τε καὶ πάσας, ἵστορας ποιεύμενος, ἐπιτελέα ποιήσειν κατὰ δύναμιν καὶ κρίσιν ἐμὴν ὅρκον τόνδε καὶ συγγραφὴν τήνδε..."*

"One takes this ancient oath, enters into a covenant to cure and save, alleviate suffering and renew the living. But... only one man ever returned from the beyond." Seeing Ursula's surprised look, Honegger smiled. "Old Lazarus. After four days of wandering around among the stars! Or so it's written."

"Lazarus..."

"Didn't you go to Bible class at school, Ursula?"

She did. And as a favourite of Pastor Braunschweig, she more often felt his hand roaming on her than hear of Lazarus and his recall from eternity. Pastor Braunschweig. Ursula pursed her lips and, for a fleeting moment, saw the ruddy face, the dim echo in the ears of the voice soft and silken as, knelt side by side, his plump hand slid from her waist, the fingers like the claws of some prehensile insect settling on the roundness below, as he said, "Shall we now pray together, daughter."

The permanent replacement arriving, Honegger departed a couple of months later. Before leaving, he gently pressed in her hand an ornate silver brooch, studded with blue-green garnet, of a peacock with furled plumes. "A little something to thank you," he said, touching his lips to her forehead.

Unawares and unthinking, Ursula's arms wound around him, in an embrace both filial and carnal, as too a gesture of affection and gratitude, for one in whom, in the few short months, she had found the figure of a father, the kindness of a friend, at odd moments, too, a man to whom, the years notwithstanding, she might have given herself, had he but asked. He never had and, afterwards, thinking of him, her memory evoked only the often quiescent and sorrowful mien of one who seemed to have done with the world, desire and possession defeated by a bruised spirit, some hurt never touched on or aired in words. Only later was she to learn of the affliction that shrouded his days.

One afternoon, unusually foregoing the accustomed horseplay with Ursula, and unusually thoughtful, Dr. Krieger, told her. He had heard from Honegger and the message had kind and good words for Ursula, especially. "I wish he could have stayed with us longer," Krieger mused. Latterly, he had felt his old friend to be finally coming out of himself. After long years of a sort of hiatus. "Not hiatus," he corrected himself. "More like sleep-walking."

"Had he been ill?"

"I suppose you could say that. Wounded, maimed in spirit. You don't drive, do you, Ursula?"

"I've never learnt."

"Well, let's say you've been behind the wheel of a car a lifetime and never a scratch, not even the smallest bump or accident. Then one day you run over someone, not at all your fault. Or someone comes up from behind and sends you towards the edge of a precipice on a mountain road. Still alive, but sitting in the driving seat you are never the same again. You see that with some of the people who come to us here. A long life of perfect health. And then, out of the blue a major stroke, a tumour, threatening to cut short the presumed immorality. A blue sky suddenly darkening…"

Not yet fifty, Honegger had climbed to the topmost rungs of his profession. Head of the paediatric wing of one of the most renowned institutes in the country, lauded by colleagues, amenable to whatever new cures and curatives science had to offer, author of a series of papers published in prestigious medical journals, much in demand in conferences and congresses. And, hand in hand with the professional success and renown, an enviable private life. Married to the daughter of a wealthy industrialist, a woman of some beauty, educated and elegant, finishing school and the rest. A couple of years later, the birth of a baby girl had completed the picture.

"I was her godfather," Krieger added. "Honegger loved children like no one. To have one of his own finally… It was as if he had waited for little Anja all his life."

One could not have asked for more, a life of satisfaction, professional and financial, the happiest of families, the little girl, pretty as a doll, bright and lively, the glint in her father's eyes. His wife sometimes chided him that he would spoil the child. Her words fell on deaf ears. Children were his life, both work and passion.

Krieger broke his narration with a stoical smile. "The trouble, Ursula, is nothing lasts. All feasts end, if not at midnight, at dawn." Honegger's good fortune was, evidently, no exception.

His wife had a house near St. Moritz, a sizeable chalet gifted by the father at marriage. Each winter season, they went down there for brief skiing holidays, some years for the summer vacation. That winter, when little Anja was about six or seven, Honegger, considerate as ever and wishing to relieve some of his senior staff over the holidays, left early, before the New Year. The wife and the girl, left with in-laws, would follow a couple of weeks later.

It was an odd winter, severe weather of heavy snowfalls alternating with unusually mild temperatures, roads frozen over one day, the ice melting to slush the next. Setting out on a clear morning a fortnight later, nearing Chur, the car met headlong a speeding van skidding around a narrow bend. The Mercedes, heavy and stolid but no match for the loaded transporter, bounced back towards the edge of an outcrop, precipitating in a short, steep fall. Nothing much remained of the car itself, nor of mother and child.

Derailed, Honegger never recovered, the still youthful age notwithstanding. "We never expect calamities," Krieger said, getting to his feet and, winding an arm around Ursula, paced to the wide glazing with a view of the woods in new leaf. "The unexpected is always a surprise, at times a tragic one. Humans generally bear whatever the loss, loved ones, wife, children, parents. It's our survival mechanism. Obviously, one remembers, but memory is also a sort of balm. One sheds tears, grieves, but most get over it and pick up the threads of their life again."

Not Honegger. He himself appeared to have departed with the dead wife and daughter, in all but body. He remained at his job but gradually became something of a recluse, shunning friends and company, declining invitations to medical seminars and conventions, passing up the perks of prestige and fame. A few years later he called it a day and retired. For some time after retirement he had offered his services to missionary organizations, going over for months at a time to clinics and orphanages in Africa. Always at the service of the young, as he had been lifelong.

"It was some years before I saw him again," Krieger recalled. "Much changed in appearance, aged. But all in all the same man one had known. Warm, amiable, modest as always. Something, though, had gone missing, it was clear. Like one of those machines made up of dozens of small parts. Take out just one of those little cogs, and the whole thing comes to a standstill, stops working." He shook his head, dismissing the thought. "A rare person, Ursula. You'll not meet many like him."

"No, I don't suppose so."

"But you," he smiled, releasing his hold, "it's time you got yourself someone more your age. Passing your days with all these grey-haired men, you'll be ageing before your time."

Krieger noticed Ursula's cheeks colouring, and it surprised him. He had never seen her blush, nor show any particular trace of timidity, when she disrobed for his equestrianism hobby, taking off her dress and shedding intimate wear with a placid, almost indifferent calm. It was as though, uninhibited, audacious even, in exposing the splendour endowed by nature, her bashful nerve came alive only when touched in matters of the heart.

~~~

It was something that Dr. Pelosi also noticed, the mute shying away, when during their brief time together, after a long afternoon of love-making, he murmured in her ears words of claim and possession. "Stay, Ursula, stay with me. I'll never again want another woman." Not at all the sort to abandon family and home, least his wife's wealth, it was more easy male rhetoric of the moment. Taking him at his word, Ursula started, like a startled stag, and it surprised Pelosi, waking him from the hypnotic daze of satiety.

In the revolving gallery of the past, of all those who had grazed across her days, briefly or longer, Pelosi's was a portrait that had remained whole, clean and intact, distinct from most of the others, faded with time and dim of recall. Clear in Ursula's memory even long after, he had earned his place, her first true lover, so very different from almost all the males she had known, the ageing and old exercising merely elderly quirks, less carnal, more whimsical fantasy. In every way her first man, Pelosi had ushered her through the doors into womanhood, leading her through the labyrinths of desire towards the fulfilment of the body's needs and cravings, to the discovery of the surfeit of pleasures she herself could offer, alongside her own satisfaction and gratification, little known till then.

Pier Paolo Pelosi was the head oncologist of the sanatorium wing at the Grünewald. An odd figure, few knew how he came to find himself at a clinic in the midst of the dark forestlands. If asked, his jocular response with a pleasant laugh was that he might well be the sole, remaining centurion in an abandoned northern outpost of the Roman Empire. Not much of a centurion in looks and manner, the slightly aquiline Roman nose and accent did betray in small measure his Southern origins. Of middling height, a full head of dark brown curls, features pronounced, large eyes with pupils alive and always on the move, all in all a handsome man of fifty, he was distinguished, above all, by a rare refinement in posture and manner, elegant in his sartorial habits under the always impeccable white medical work coat, the fingers of the fine hands sculpted slender and delicate, the permanent olive tan of sun lamps betraying a trace of vanity.

Well liked by almost all, the gossip among the nurses was that Pelosi was a true gentleman, with never a rude or intimate foray into the female presence at the clinic, never a pinch or pat on the rear, always of good cheer, attentive in ear and kind in word, the mellifluous tenor voice soft and reassuring with patients and staff. Only once, nurse Anke, a tall creature with sober good-looks, who sometimes assisted Pelosi, ventured to differ from the general consensus. "A secret Casanova. There's one who really knows how to handle a woman." But she said no more, leaving her audience curious and waiting for more. Anke merely smiled to herself, the Mona Lisa smile of a discovery too precious to be aired in public. Not particularly versed in tales of exotic historical figures, Casanova or Cagliostro, Ursula made nothing of Anke's name-dropping. She was to discover it for herself.

Their paths often crossing, they had become familiar by presence. But Pelosi, seemingly ever on the move, hurrying through the entrance, pausing briefly before Krieger's office door with a thoughtful air, pacing with rapid steps to his shiny red roadster in the car park, there never had been occasion for a pondered encounter, merely a salutation and a brief smile when their eyes had met in passing. Nor was Pelosi much present during staff parties and holiday celebrations, putting in only a brief appearance to greet colleagues, one Christmas mounting the podium to sing solo and unaccompanied, in a voice surprisingly strong and musical: *Dormi, dormi, bel bambino.*

Bowing out to warm applause, then, to fetch coat and scarf and make his way through the drift of snow settling on the silent night. "True Italian," Ursula overheard one of the senior doctors say. "Always and only the family."

That foul autumn afternoon, the thin rain slanting down from low clouds and threatening to turn to sleet, clasping herself and hurrying out at the end of her day's duty, Ursula ran into Pelosi, coming face to face.

"Oh, pardon!" Putting out a hand, he gently drew her under his wide-brimmed umbrella. "Ursula, isn't it? Can I drop you off somewhere? I'm not in a hurry."

Ursula told him she was on her way back to the nurses' residence.

"Oh, only a short way off. But you'll be soaked. Let me walk you there."

Ursula nodded to assent and thank him. Barely had they gone a few steps, Pelosi asked, "Are you free this evening?" To Ursula's nod, again, he said, in a voice light and amiable, "What does one do on an evening like this? Dinner and then climb in between the sheets. What do you say," he asked, with the air of a passing thought, "shall we dine together? Somewhere in town."

Surprisingly unsurprised, yet not often accustomed to urbane courtship and timid with formal invitations, Ursula hesitated for a moment. But the thought of yet another grey evening at the residence, in the company of colleagues and talk of new men friends and imaginary destinations, overcame whatever the reserve. She turned to Pelosi with a smile. "It's kind of you to ask."

Pelosi waved away her words with a short laugh. "Asking is easy. Giving is another matter! You get changed, I'll pick you up in… shall we say an hour. No, don't bother to walk back to the clinic. I'll come to get you."

For Ursula, Pelosi at first sight was an uncommon type, the sort of man she had never known. Forthright, not hedging his words, he appeared to speak what was on his mind, syllables simple, intention clear, shunning the veiled and the abstruse, without much beating about the bush he laid out what was on offer. Invariably light of mood but never loud, witty with a charm that could conquer and overcome, the gift of persuasion seemingly effortless, never straining to convince, one gave in to whatever the request or suggestion, barely conscious of the concession. So it was at work, with colleagues, superiors and subordinates, so too in private, with family, friends, the women he had known, as it was now with Ursula. And, possibly not witting scheme or technique, the asking or invitation, like an unseen and subterranean aquifer merging unnoticed into the flow of a waterway, usually emerged in the course of easy and casual conversation, making the proposal appear inconsequential, of no particular weight.

Whisked down into town in the plush sports car, Pelosi's touch on the wheel light and taking the turns at some speed, Ursula found herself again at the Gastätte where Hoffman had taken her the first time. Helping Ursula out of her coat, seating himself, possibly at the same table where Ursula had dined with Hoffman, Pelosi looked around at the timbered surrounds, a handful of diners in one corner.

"Not my first choice, Ursula. No fine dining here. But better than most others in this town. More substance, less smoke! The first time Dr. Hoffman brought me here."

Ursula avoided Pelosi's eyes.

"Hoffman. You'd have known him, of course. We've not heard from him again since he left. Dr. Krieger may know. Sorry he had to go. I managed to get him over to pass Christmas with us at our place a couple of years ago. A solitary type, but interesting. *Simpatico*."

The waiter coming to take their orders, Ursula was thankfully saved further talk of Hoffman. The menu cards handed back, she looked up and smiled timidly. "Sometimes they call you *Freiherr*. Are you really a baron?"

"Oh that!" Pelosi waved it away with an airy hand, adding with a wry smile, "One has been called many things, better and worse. Baron? Yes, I'm supposed to be one. Can't be helped, *meine liebe Dame*. One can't choose one's ancestry, can one?"

Encouraged by Ursula's easy smile, he went on. "I really have not the least idea how it happened. No Crusaders or warriors in the family tree, no distinguished service rendered to any Caesar or crowned head. And no vast estates and palaces. Only a patch of land and a smallish castle, more a family mansion, somewhere south of Rome. The bit of land is long gone, the castle a heap of stones. There's an old print of the place somewhere. Barren of wealth and possessions, I'm your Baron of Nothing!"

"But the title..," Ursula's began with hesitant curiosity.

"Ah, the title. Of course." Pelosi paused until the waiter had finished pouring the drinks. "I'll let you into a small secret," he winked conspiratorially. "Once long ago, an ancestor must have lent the services of his wife or daughter to some bishop or Cardinal for a night or two. Very likely the origins of the Pelosi baronial family!"

Pelosi's hearty laugh drew the stare of the diners at the corner table. "There you have it," he took a sip, still chuckling. "And you, Ursula? Not a simple *Krankenschwester*, I suppose. Why nursing, Ursula? Please don't mind if I say you don't fit the part?" He rearranged his cutlery with an earnest look. "We all come from somewhere, sometimes we ourselves don't know where. Are you from these parts?"

Ursula nodded, to say she was, and then told him, simply in bare words, a scant history shorn of details. The daughter of a Wehrmacht officer, her mother had been placed in the care of a family across the border in the final year of the war. The father never came back to claim her and she was raised by the farmer and his wife. After the wife died, the farmer married the adopted daughter.

Pursing her lips, Ursula looked up. "There's not much more…"

"And you trained to be nurse? Ever wanted to go back to look for your mother's folk across the border? Maybe there's a family castle somewhere. And a title waiting. Baronin Ursula…"

Ursula thought it cruel of Pelosi, the humour less than teasing. Noticing the shade of a clouded look in her eyes, he reached out to take her free hand, holding it in a warm and firm clasp. "The past is sometimes a rubble. Best not to look back too often."

Ursula could not help a quiet smile. "My mother's words. Never look back, she would say sometimes. She'd tell me of a woman in the Bible who did and became a pillar of salt."

"Ah, yes, Lot's wife. Turning to look at the destruction of Sodom. But tell me, Ursula. Never mind the past, the holidays are around the corner. Will you be going back to your people over Easter, if you have leave?"

"I have no people," Ursula replied stiffly.

"Oh! For that matter, nor have I. That's two of us."

"Your family…"

"Ah, the family. Thank you for reminding me. My wife's in Canada with the boys. Visiting *her* people. She's from Montreal."

"Canada?"

Pelosi smiled at her wide-eyed expression. "A land of everything and nothing!"

"You've lived in Canada?"

"Lived is a gracious word for life in Canada. People there have never decided who they are, Europeans or North Americans…"

"So you've lived there?"

"I have," Pelosi nodded.

Describing the vast distances, the scattered towns and villages, with the provincial air of the past still alive, the wistful hankering of the Québécoise for their European origins, recounting his time there and some of the odd habits of the inhabitants, Pelosi regaled Ursula briefly with the droll tale of the ageing mayor of a small Francophone community on the St. Lawrence river.

Much given to claiming distant but no less noble descent from the House of Valois Orléans, the man ordered from France a young bride by correspondence. "A mail-order bride, you'd say today. Well, the young lady did finally arrive, a creature of some beauty, too. It turned out she was a street-walker from Toulouse, of mixed Guadaloupean stock, speaking a patois little comprehensible to her new husband's fellow citizens. Not a happy end, though!" Much laughed at, shamed and derided, the old man died soon after.

"Age sometimes makes fools of us," Pelosi concluded, with a judicious air. "Follies are best committed when one's still relatively young. But, then, age at times also makes us want to reach out for the unattainable."

Feeling at ease and light-hearted, despite herself Ursula could not help asking, "You weren't mail-ordered by your Canadian wife?"

"Oh! Who'd have thought?" With a hearty laugh Pelosi took her hand to brush it with his lips. "You're a wicked girl, Ursula. Ordered around a bit, certainly, but not mail-ordered! You might not know it, but even penniless barons are worth their weight in gold in the New World."

What Pelosi did not say, that Ursula was to learn later, was that the wife was heiress to a considerable fortune, her family timber barons for a century and more, with lease over vast stretches of forest land in the Northern Territories. Nor, money-matters of not much concern, did Ursula, in her simple-mindedness, pause to wonder at Pelosi's wherewithal during their week together, the sumptuous suite at the Palace Hotel on the lake, the obsequious bowing and saluting of the staff as though a sultan or sovereign had breezed in, the high dining and wining, the costly presents gifted her with an almost casual nonchalance. The salaries of the medical staff at the Grünewald were generous enough, but not quite gold and gilt to be thrown to the winds with blithe insouciance. After their final bout of love-making on the last morning, Ursula's sleep-laden body liquescent as Pelosi released possession and fell back on the bed, lying supine with gaze fixed on the stucco-work of the high ceiling, a hand gently circling the plateau of Ursula belly, he said, voicing a thought as if for his own ears alone, "A gigolo is paid. Sometimes a husband, too, but he's made to suffer." Becalmed in the satiate lull of a dream-like trance, Ursula heard the words, but could make nothing of them.

It was then, the evening at table passed light of mood, Ursula amused and charmed, that Pelosi slipped, into the interlinear of good-humoured tease and talk, his seemingly casual offer, raising his brow in faux amazement that Ursula had never been to Italy.

"See Naples and die, they say. I don't think we want that, as yet. Besides, it's too long a drive. We'll go down to the lake in Como. It's something worth seeing. Three or four days and we'll be back before the week's out." Not waiting for her acceptance, or otherwise, he added, "A bit of traffic over Easter week. If you can arrange your leave, we'll start out early morning."

Neither suggestion nor proposal, an invitation allowing no room for refusal, it was decided and sealed, leaving Ursula surprised, her wide-eyed silence taken by Pelosi as assent. However much in two minds, it had never been in her nature to deny the expectations of another, however innocent or, for that matter, gross and demeaning of her person. To appease and please and earn her bread of approval and acceptance. She had clear memory of one such submission, an unusual acquiescence in childhood.

Among the girls in the village school, she had been the odd one out, the teachers eyeing her with benign pity as the offspring of backwoods parents, the father an aged illiterate with foul, alcoholic breath the rare time he appeared to affix on a form or certificate his name, laboriously signing with an undecipherable hieroglyph; the mother young enough but haggard in face, as if aged before time, silent and with eyes downcast. And little Ursula herself, pretty as a doll and taller than her companions, stood out among the others, her ill-fitting rough woollens setting her apart among the fine-fabric pinafores and colourful *Dirndls*.

Shunned by her class-mates, friendless, she often stood alone in a corner of the stone courtyard, seemingly lost as she watched the mirthful play around her, the ring of the young voices in her ears. One day, then, a girl who sat next to her, who often provoked the others to snub her with snide words, took her in hand. Alone together in the classroom, with the others out in the yard for the mid-morning break, stealing in from behind her hand reached down to Ursula's lap, the small fingers insistently probing through the cloth of the skirt. Sat frozen still, the merest cry barely escaping her lips, she felt Annika's warm lips press against her nape, even as the hand gathered up her skirt to reach bare flesh.

It was the first of many such encounters through the school year and it changed Ursula's standing among her companions, Annika drawing her into her inner circle, a coterie of half a dozen girls always together, whose words and whims held sway in the classroom. Ursula little relished her new-found friend's fumbling seduction. But appeasement and acquiescence the price of approval and acceptance, she submitted in silence, however unpleasant and unnerving the intimate intrusion. So it had been with Pastor Braunschweig, so too during her time at the Grünewald, her indulgence of aged fancies passive and uncomplaining.

Only much later, well into her days, a woman of the world and mistress of herself, did Ursula come to see her charitable forbearance of youth as invitation for use and abuse, men senior and superior wielding position and power to feed on her innate innocence for their unsavoury propensities. In the long backward glance, as though looking through the reverse end of a telescope, the distant scenes of the prank and play of the various Kriegers and Hoffmans, that had once seemed innocuous and devoid of particular malice, appeared for what they were, acts predatory and degrading, and her mind rebelled with dismay and chagrin to think that she herself, wanting to please and pleasure, had with mute submission accepted whatever their wayward inclinations.

Odd, then, to think that Pelosi was almost the sole exception, exempt from the dissolute company, he who had boarded and bedded her with the skill and thoroughness of a topographer familiar with the unseen lie of the land, every dip and curve and rise, inlet and rivulet. In so doing, he had delivered her into the world, reborn, a whole person, a woman, finally awake and aware of the infinite pleasures of the physical realm, the body a quarry with treasures concealed but inexhaustible, able to offer, as also to receive in equal abundance. Her first true man, through a lifetime he had remained also the only one, the one face that stood out and apart in the blur of figures crowding the album of her adult years, distinct and somehow still alive, the handful of days by the lake by his side aeons ago etched in memory perdurable and never to fade. Half a lifetime later, with Leonardo alone, she had been engulfed by sensations similar, recondite and extravagant, not quite a repetition, more a reprise, with the difference that Leo brought to their mating the passions of his tormented spirit. Pelosi was pure matter, primordial, before the divine endowment of the human soul, the body its own temple, desire the sole plasma of the universe.

Ursula remembered Pier Paolo Pelosi as also the most honest of men, devoid of feint and stratagem, without mask or pretence, the sly and wily craft of seduction under the guise of amity and benevolence practised by many a male. Not so Pelosi, his intentions clear, expectations laid out for one to see, the approach without the tortuous meandering of guile and cunning, the usual handful of sweets to waylay the unsuspecting child. It was an honesty that could at first sight surprise, even shock, that only in hindsight did one come to value and cherish. So it had earned him a place of his own in the variegated cast of Ursula's life. Not perhaps a man for all seasons, nor only a good-natured companion and consummate lover, above all a spirit shorn of common hypocrisies and common-garden male conceits.

Arrived and settling into the plush comfort of the gilded suite at the Grand Hotel, stood together at the tall bow window and looking out at the placid waters of the lake in the spring sunlight, the red-roofed villas and mansions rising up the wooded hills on the far shore, he asked, "What do you think?"

"It's another world!" Ursula could only whisper, sight dimming with elation at the enchanted vision.

Steering her away from the cool morning air, holding her by both arms, gaze steady as he looked at her, voice even and unusually sober, the words were clear, their sense leaving no room for doubt. "One thing though, Ursula. We're here for a few days. Whatever happens, there must be no consequence."

Meeting Ursula's puzzled look, his own eyes lowering, tone softening, he took her hands in his. "There's a family somewhere, Juliette and my boys. One has a debt towards them."

Ursula shook her head. "I don't…," she began to mumble awkwardly, still at a loss, meaning to tell him that she wanted nothing, in particular nothing that might rob or wound another.

Coming to his accustomed self, winding one arm firm around her waist and holding her close, his face lighting up with a winning smile, he nodded. "*Lo credo.* Of course, I believe you. Only that, sometimes, we ourselves don't quite know. It's what makes us human, after all."

It had been a long drive, starting out in the slate-grey light of daybreak, down through the sudden curves and bends of the mountain roads under the leaden weight of a low sky, the dark valleys caught fast in sleep, Ursula's heart racing with the car's roaring pace, as though in transport to some magical land, her eyes meeting Pelosi's as he turned to look at her, his smile mirrored in the sparkle of her gaze. It was as if she had never been anywhere, seen little or nothing, never been with one like him, his presence close now in this compact space, touching, quickening the pulse and speeding the blood, she felt within the welling of a sensation never before known, urgent and demanding, desire or hunger she could not tell, a craving to clasp and possess, be possessed. So that had he stopped by the wayside, turned and drawn her to himself, sought out the hurting urge, taken her and assuaged the famished ache, she would have had nothing more to ask, not the morrow, nor what was to come, no promise or fulfilment other than this moment.

Lost in the incandescent reverie, Ursula started when he reached out to take her hand, to say, "We're clear of your dark lands. Look!" Raising her head, she saw a landscape of red-tiled brick houses, factory chimney-stacks rising like tapered fingers, tarred roads winding neat through towns and villages. And, running alongside, a vast expanse of water mirroring a limpid sky blazoned with the gossamer brightness of the mid-morning sun. "Almost there now," he pointed with his eyes, as the habitations multiplied, taller stone buildings, mansions with neat gardens and, ahead, the customs post with flags atop tall poles.

The car driven away to be parked, entering the vast carpeted lobby, Ursula's eyes widened with disbelief. True to its name, the Grand Hotel was truly grand, grander than anything Ursula could have imagined, a relic opulent and extravagant of another age, the outsize chandelier hung from the gilded stucco ceiling outshining the daylight outside, plush velvet seating arranged around coffee tables on clawed brass feet, guests attired in utmost elegance, hats and furs, treading soundless the tufted carpet of the lobby, the mid-aged clerks behind the reception desk in formal suiting and stiff as mannequins, their salutation to Pelosi one of warm and courteous deference. "*Benvenuto, barone!*"

"They know you," Ursula said as the wood-panelled elevator glided upwards soundlessly.

Pelosi nodded. "I've been here before."

When and with whom? Ursula did not ask. She might be curious, but it was not her place, nor was it in her nature to pry and probe. Pelosi was, for her, a man of the world, gone places and seen life. It sufficed that almost for the first time someone had taken her out of the dim corner of her existence, a courtship of sorts, offering new vistas, newer sensations. Guileless she might be, but she well knew the week to come would have no permanence, nothing to build on something lasting, save for what remained between the folds of memory. It was no affair of hers should he have come here before with others, lovers or mistresses, to lie perhaps on this same outsize bed with a quilted headboard, to take his pleasure between these same satin sheets.

And the next few days did indeed remain, etched deep beyond the wash of time, a giddy swirl of sights and sensations that woke to vivid life the five senses, perhaps a sixth and a seventh, the discovery of worlds that might have caught her eyes in passing on the pages of periodicals and magazines, no less the unspelt revelations of her own nature, appetites and propensities, the apparently cornucopian gratification she could offer and the luxuriant fulfilments she herself could attain.

Pelosi laid out before her briefly the banquet that wealth could offer, the fineries that money could buy, the infinitely variegated taste buds of the gourmet's palate. No less the pampered quirks of the better born, the ever so slight twitch of the nostril of the mink-wrapped lady at the counter of the perfume shop catching the evanescent notes of honeysuckle; the young wife or daughter of an aged, heavy-set male at the window table of the restaurant as she smoothed the iridescent mulberry silk moulding her sinuous figure and summoning the waiter with a mere flick of the finger. No less, too, the truckling, fawning and toadying of the lesser born, the doorman, the shop lady at the boutique, the maître d'hotel. Not for an instant did Ursula then imagine that around the corner there lay in wait for her not only such scenes of profusion but a landscape even more extravagant and indulgent. Pelosi might be a baron, but a mere doctor in a backwoods sanatorium, Armin von Göttner was a name in the world.

"Money does matter!" Ursula heard herself say, in wonder almost, as she stepped out from a plush lakeside eatery following a lavish dinner one evening, thinking of the deeply obsequious bow of the waiter after Pelosi had slipped a sizeable banknote under the coffee cup.

"Matters if you have it, and matters if one doesn't. That's the problem with money!" Looking up at the rising disc of the moon in the crystal mountain sky, putting an arm around her waist, he exclaimed, "Money! Probably that's why we say the silvery light of the moon. And sunlight is gold."

And gold it was, too, the slender bracelet in white gold set with a single, small aquamarine topaz, the velvet case placed discreetly by her table-setting at the restaurant. An accompanying note read: *Danke, dass du hier bist!* It was not his only gift for her being there.

It might have occurred to her for a mere instant, but Ursula could not bring herself to think of the presents as payment or reimbursement. There was in Pelosi's giving something casual and natural, akin to laying out a table for a friend unexpectedly at the door, with no return expected, apparently, no particular indebtedness or thanks due.

Taken aback, as he gently snapped the clasp around her

wrist, she said timidly, "You shouldn't. It's a little too much."

"Too little, too much," he smiled sitting back. "Who's to say?"

Pelosi's gifts and giving might have a casual air, but Ursula could not at times help wavering in her acceptance, not wanting to appear wary, yet not wishing to offend. Giving, she knew, called for a return. What could she offer, other than her presence, what she was. A barter too meagre, she thought, little aware that she possessed in abundance, with a cut far superior to most others, what the world saw and expected in womankind, less the four cardinal virtues, a deal more presence and appcarance, form and figure, the body as vessel and vassal of man's primordial intemperance.

Eyes fixing them with insistence, stares of passers-by in the street, lingering glances in bars and restaurants gave Ursula the impression that Pelosi was a familiar figure with most everyone in the town. "Everyone knows you around here," she said as the keen gaze of a group of men followed them across the square.

Pelosi shook his head good humouredly. "I'm not the one turning heads."

"Oh. Why then…?"

"And if you were to be alone, some might also decide to pay you a little personal tribute. Like this," he chuckled, discreetly tweaking her rear.

"Paolo! Why on earth would they do that?"

He could not help breaking out in a laugh. "For the same reason that people like touching a sacred relic!"

Catching Ursula's puzzled expression, he went on in the same light-hearted vein. "See, Ursula, this is a Catholic country, but we are a doubting people. You'll have heard of St. Thomas refusing to believe that Christ had risen from the dead. Not until he had touched with his own hand the stigmata, the wound in Christ's palm where the nail had gone in. Like Thomas, we too are earthy and doubting folk," he added, gently patting the small of her back. "Touching is believing, tasting credence!"

Pelosi could not help marvelling at Ursula's naiveté, not quite innocence, more a childlike ingenuousness, unable to see or attribute malice and ill-intention, blind to the hooded look and the wolf's fangs. As he could only wonder that she seemed little aware of the splendour of her own presence, that could beckon the attention, possibly, even of the dead! Steeped in his work at the Grünewald, little present in after-hours, little privy to the day's gossip and hearsay among the staff of the clinic, it surprised him now to think that some doctor or other had not taken up with Ursula, a common enough occurrence, affairs not flaunted but not entirely clandestine. Perhaps it was her unembellished look, simple country clothing, plain and ill-fitting, the rough wool cardigan a size too large, the skirt of cloth and colour more befitting a farm wife, the rich red auburn head unattended and calling for the hand of a coiffure. A rare bloom in plain brown wrapping, Pelosi had on the very first day decided to take matters in hand. It might not be true of males, but clothes did a woman make!

That first morning, arrived at the hotel, Pelosi had come in from the bath after showering, to stand bemused as Ursula unpacked her small case, neatly folding a few items of clothing and underwear. Picking up from the spread on the bed the pastel grey waist high briefs, stretching the knit cotton, he held it up.

"Oh dear! This is like my grandmother's! That was after the Great War." Shaking his head, he looked at her with a teasing smile. "Ursula!"

Later that afternoon, when the shops had reopened after the long lunch break, he took her down the street a small distance, to a lake-front store with intimate finery in the window. After a few quite words with the middle-aged shop lady, as Ursula looked wide-eyed at the display behind glass of underwear to bring a blush to the cheeks, sheer bridal lingerie the kind she had never seen, half bra cups that revealed more than they held, he turned to her.

"The *Signora* will help you choose whatever you want," he told her, making for the door out.

"I've brought everything I need."

"But not what you ought to have!" With that he made his exist.

Almost half an hour later Ursula appeared at the entrance with several small gift bags, to find Pelosi calmly seated on the bench below the shop window with a cigarette in hand.

"The lady insisted I take these…," she said helplessly. "I've not paid her."

Getting to his feet, relieving her of a couple of the purchases, he casually waved her words away. "Not to worry. She'll be sending the bill to the hotel."

"Everyone here is so trusting!"

"Don't you believe it. Trust is monetary. Money offers credit."

Once again, the casual and airy giving left Ursula awkward and uneasy, the words of her mother's severe admonition coming to mind when she had received some small gift from a class mate, merely a colourful ribbon to tie her locks, a box of used crayons: "Never take, if you've nothing to give!"

What could she now offer Pelosi in return for his giving? He who appeared to have everything, deep pockets for anything that took his fancy, a generosity seemingly without design, Ursula's mild protests met with sparse and carefree syllables, as when on the breakfast tray one morning she found a pair of tear-drop earrings finely chiselled at the edges and set with an opalescent moonstone.

Sleep still pressing down on the eyelids, after a long, late evening of exhilarating ministration of his hands and lips on her person, consuming and ineffable, and an even longer night of infinite oblivion, she could only mutter sounds of feeble protestation, to which he replied with a conversational air, "White gold suits you better. Don't you think?"

The fog of drowse refusing to lift, thinking was more than she could do at the moment. Merely reaching up, she drew his head down to press her lips to his cheek. Mostly passive in her intimacies with men, it was a gesture new to her, unforced and effortless, made as though her arms had a volition of their own. Waking intermittently to the new day, between sips of coffee, she dimly wondered. A child reaching for a flower it could not have, the accretion of a longing beyond reach? Or gestures of recompense for his offhand liberality, drawn from resources unseen, from within, the recesses of one's being. She would have wanted to tell mother Conradine that there were gifts beyond silver and gold, a deal more precious, mined from the heart and inestimable. As the friendship proffered her school mate for the roll of ribbon, the box of crayons.

Watching Pelosi as he moved around humming to himself while he dressed, Ursula's thoughts turned towards avenues she knew she ought not to roam. Beyond the largesse of his generosity, beyond the pleasures, luxuriant and rapturous, he could gift and provoke, what was this man to her, who each day took root and took up residence within her, without promise or surety of permanence?

But that morning Ursula's wistful sigh found little room for despondency or misery as Pelosi walked her around the town to revisit sights and scenes familiar to him from the past. Strolling by the town theatre, up a broad tree-lined avenue, Pelosi paused to look up at a sizeable ochre-coloured mansion, where he had done his internship.

"And then almost ten years as geriatric assistant. There's a wing for the elderly. A good place to die." Catching Ursula's surprised look, he smiled. "It's run by the nuns. Last rites guaranteed."

"You're not a believer?"

"One tries, my dear. Just that life and faith are so often at odds. As my good father used to say, some of those Commandments need updating. Love your neighbour... but not the neighbour's wife? Odd." He stepped back on the pavement as a sleek sports car roared past. "Now that's something one can believe in!" he exclaimed, following the silver streak vanishing at speed. "Which reminds me..."

Walking back down a broad street towards the lake front, Pelosi took her arm and stepped up to the wide glass front of a car showroom. Inside, a tall robust figure with a large ruddy face, trim in a well-cut double-breasted suit, emerged from an office at one end.

"*Buon giorno, Bellini.*"

"*Caro, barone!*" The man clasped Pelosi's hand with the warmth of familiarity. "*Ma che sorpresa!*" They looked at each other, evident old amity in the broad smiles. "When did you return?"

"Only for a few days. But how are you? How's trade?"

"Not the same. Not since you left us! And you? The family, are they here with you..." he began to enquire when he caught sight of Ursula looking about with silent curiosity. "Oh, pardon...," Bellini murmured under breath.

"Ursula, come and meet an old friend of mine. Stefano sold me my first car. A second-hand MG two-seater. Glorious machine!"

"Madam." Bellini lifted her hand with a courteous bow. "No, they don't make them like that any more." With a small, regretful chuckle, Bellini cast an eye around the showroom, at the handful of autos of British marque. "In fact, the English practically make nothing any more!"

"How are your boys?"

"Well, all well. The older one works with me. Leonardo... you remember little Leo? Studying law in Milan, his first year. Helps to have a lawyer in the family in this litigious country!"

Glancing surreptitiously at Ursula looking about, he lowered his voice, hesitating. "And your signora...?

"Oh, she's in Canada with the boys."

"Quite some way," he nodded, with a knowing look again towards Ursula, before calling out to someone in the office. "Gabriella!" A moment later a tall woman in a knee-length tartan skirt, slender and with an undulating gait, appeared at the door. "Look who's here!"

Her language skills somewhat less than trilingual, Ursula gleaned little of the bantering exchange between Pelosi and the owner's secretary, the woman's sing-song vocalise running words into each other and often trailing off in a high laugh. The light-hearted ribbing, in a tone of familiarity, made one wonder if once there had been something more between them. Ursula wished she could understand better, catch the sly nuances.

It had not helped that at school, Italian had been taught with the same lightness as bird-watching, the cantonal authorities treating the southern tongue with benevolent negligence, at best. No surprise, then, that the lanky, ill-shaven and unkempt teacher dozed through most of the class hour after handing around smudged cyclostyled sheets of a crammed text, little decipherable. Ursula had clear memory of Herr Diliberto Soncino coming to life laboriously at the end of the hour, rising with a yawn and a groan to wander aimlessly about the classroom peeking at the pupils' labours, occasionally exclaiming *"O bella fanciulla!"* alternating a rare time with *"O bella figa,"* especially when he stooped over Ursula. Made wise by a companion to the sense of the teacher's words, Ursula could not understand why her class mates usually merited 'beautiful maiden," while she alone should earn the dubious praise of 'pretty pussy.' She had complained at home of the particular address, only to be met by her father's grin and leering remark: "Can't say the man's far wrong!"

A wistful note lined Pelosi's voice on the small boat crossing to the island for lunch. "That old MG that Bellini found for me.

It was a gift from Juliette." The past seemed to surface briefly as he looked across the lake, the flickering sheen of a truant sun breaking through spare drifts of cloud on the move. "We first met here. She was on holiday with her family."

Taking a deep breath, as though trying to inhale the fugitive perfume of something lost, he lifted his gaze towards the mountain range. "It was a good time to be young." Returning to the moment, he smiled, running a hand down Ursula's arm. "I expect any time's a good time when one's young! But just look at that, Ursula," he pointed towards a low neoclassical villa on the shore with a small boathouse on the side. "Maybe I should have stayed on and got myself a place like that."

"Why did you leave? Why the Grünewald?"

"Oh, an old story. I'll not bore you. Some trouble with the nuns." He pursed his lips. "And a young novice sister. The follies of youth." He said no more and a minute later the boat was at the landing of the island.

Seated at a table set with pristine linen, under the gnarled branches of an ancient black mulberry, a tall young waiter moving about briskly taking orders, the voices of diners rippling in the mild spring air with a laugh, a guffaw, a sing-song female voice, Ursula felt a sense of repletion, a plenitude that could ask nor expect anything more than what she had at this moment. The mountainscape all around, jagged and blue-ridged, rising towards a sky pearl-blue and pellucid, mirroring the waters of the lake still with the silence of sleep, the distant chug of a ferry boat gliding almost motionless across the silken plane, the faint sweetness of apple blossom wafted by the breeze.

Years later, seated almost where she sat now, the indelible imprint of the scene almost brought to her lips Pelosi's words on the goodness of youth. Possibly, Leonardo would not have understood. Ursula had the impression at times that Leonardo had never been truly young, the care-free stride of a youthful spirit. And where Leonardo's passion fed on his own being, consuming and cannibalizing self, Pelosi offered a heart *en plein air,* buoyant and uncluttered.

Everything there, that day, the surrounds and the soothing air, no less her own youth, had come together to offer a rare magical moment that she thought she was never again to know. Most of all, above all, this man beside her, so fine in bearing, gentle in word and mellow in mood, courteous in approach and cordial in company, that one might never have guessed the vigour of the spirit resident within, an ardour that could both conjure up worlds unknown and cravings never imagined, as also partake and consume with a leonine voracity, that eclipsed matter and being, leaving finally an ethereal exhaustion that blanked out mind and erased consciousness.

Unbeknown to herself, timidity and reticence giving way, Ursula took his hand to put her lips to the palm, in a gesture of what she knew not, amity, gratitude, exhilaration or passion. Surprised perhaps, but seemingly not taken aback, possibly touched, he raised her face to look into the eyes. "If I were a praying man," he said softly, "I'd pray, Ursula, that one day you meet someone deserving of you."

Pelosi had not quite gauged matters right. Less love, it was more to do with the realms of the physical, that at times bound and enslaved a woman to a male of little worth, even less virtue. Pelosi was no such, for sure, but whatever his other talents, as wooer and lover he was perhaps without equal, peerless in the unalloyed bliss he could gift, the undefinable thrill and fruition that his lips, touch, embrace and possession could endow, like the heady perfume of some secret bloom in an exotic wilderness, that went to the head, sedated thought and reason, an inebriation of the senses exalting scent and savour, engulfing craving and appetite with the tidal waves of delirium that flooded the arteries, surged down nerve and sinew, the heart a percussion of drum beats, consciousness eclipsed, to burst then in the blinding phosphorescence of a thousands suns. Each time he took her, Ursula experienced a miracle of epiphanous starburst, the simple act of love-making both annihilation and revelation. She did not know if it was the host, her own body, that housed the hidden, Delphic glow of the all-devouring conflagration, or this hand, warm now on her cheek, merely the wand, the divining rod, its seeking and touch igniting the spark. She did not know, nor did it much matter.

No, not quite love, perhaps not at all. Simply adoration of his person, the manly presence alongside, as she laid her head on the fine down on his chest that, like a silken fleece, flowed down to his loins firm and indurate, as though set in stone, engorged with desire and pulsing with avid rapacity. And this same hand, that gently now caressed her face, that probed and delved in its covetous search and discovery of the secret locus of her silently smouldering want. In those few days it had amazed Ursula that he appeared to know blindfold what was where, both seen and secret, as if his fingertips, endowed with prehensile hearing and dexterity could catch the cry and call of the tendrils in the labyrinths of her body, the caress and press measured but startling, waking the marrow in the bone.

The few days by the lake shorter than short, returned to work, Ursula was taken aback by friend Ilse appearing to breath unexpected scorn after having heard briefly of the week with Pelosi, the unaccustomed syllables on her lips quite as surprising.

"Fêted and fucked!" she blurted with sibilant derision. "Oh Ursula! Girl, you'll get nothing from him. Nothing! Apart from pokes and a few trinkets," she added, her fingers lightly flicking one of the tear-drop earrings gifted by Pelosi.

"But Ilse… It was only a short holiday," Ursula protested. "Not that I wanted anything…"

"Oh, noble dame! Laying out on the tray the choice bits for his lordship to pick from. Better than liver, better than tripe. No harm in giving, there's more of the same. Give it away and you still have it. Grow up, girl, for heaven's sake!"

"What should I want?"

"What should I want! Oh, really! What should I want?" Ilse mimicked Ursula's voice of innocent puzzlement. "Expect nothing, because that's exactly what you'll get."

"How do *you* know?" Ursula made bold with exasperation.

"No need to know. Open your eyes, woman, and you'll see. The man's got a wife, getting on a bit but still a beauty queen. A couple of kids. And the lady's got money, lots of it, with which to buy you dinner and get you into bed. How do I know? What man would give up all that for…"

Words too harsh, halting, Ilse breathed a sigh of resignation. "Oh, I don't know, Ursula, I really don't. All these men, old enough to be your grandad. Don't know what you see in them. They'll take and take, and one day you'll end up a washed-out rag. If that's what you want…"

What it was that she might want, Ursula had never asked herself, no particular heart's desire, no port of destination where to drop anchor. Around her, over time, many of the nurses had found themselves a companion, a spouse, settled into family life, children and domesticity. Soon Ilse herself would be departing the unwed sisterhood. But she, Ursula, had never been asked, pursued and pressed, never offered the permanence and security of a settled existence. Lending herself without thought to the play and whims of elderly males, the months and years slipping away, her sight had never much kept count of the leaves of the calendar, as if this bloom of effulgent youth, that so caught and halted men's breath, could last forever, this figure of an Aphrodite incarnate withstand the erosion and attrition of the seasons. An indifference and unconcern rooted in the past, she had never given the matter much thought.

Possibly, unknown to her, memories of what had been, a home cheerless and lightless, the long, sullen silences of her mother, the gnarled hands of a father who in drunken intemperance reached out to her in the corners and reaches of darkened spaces, the guilt of the painful finality, this and more had compounded a veiled and oblivious aversion for the life of a housewife, conspiring to keep at arm's length and out of sight whatever hope and musing she might have had of a home, a family of her own. Possibly, too, the outré and awkward intimacies with men twice and thrice her age were meant as flight from the accustomed finalities of love, homemaking and housewifery. But she had never paused to ask herself, nor planned, living by the day and letting it be, leaving the future to its own devices, if not to Providence.

In the weeks that followed Ursula saw Pelosi only a time or two, at a distance, striding brisk across the grounds, running towards his car under a downpour, accompanying a group of visiting medics into the conference room, seemingly ever in a hurry with never a spare moment. Finally, one afternoon they came face to face, as he emerged from the administrative offices with a sheaf of papers.

"I wanted to see you," she said, breath catching.

The cordial smile dimming, brow creasing, he asked, "Is something the matter, Ursula?"

"No, just that…"

Face clouding with an anxious look and with a swift glance at the time on his wrist, taking her lightly by the arm, he steered her towards the end of the long corridor, to step out on the small open terrace. "One breathes better here."

"I've not seen you since we returned."

"No, in fact. It's been a busy fortnight. Several of our older folk have decided to leave us, almost every other day." He shook his head pensively. "A thankless task, trying to keep the ageing alive."

"Will you have time one evening?" Ursula made bold in a small voice.

Pelosi turned to look across the grounds, sight far away,

contemplating the woods in the distance. Inhaling deep the mild air redolent with the whiff of new leaf, he spoke softly, almost as if to himself.

"The family is back, the boys are due at school." Gathering himself, then, he turned to look her in the eye. "You remember asking me why I had come to work here? I think I mentioned the trouble with the nuns at the hospital in Como over the novice Sister."

"I'm not a Sister," Ursula pronounced in a fretful tone.

"Nor a novice, for that matter," he smiled gently. "That was a long time ago. It taught me, though, that the workplace is no place for private distractions."

Ursula could still recall her mother's words one afternoon as she lay in her sick bed, withered and aged, in pain with the malaise that was to carry her to the grave. Told that she was only one of the two selected from the nurses' training school and that the head of the clinic had personally assured her that she would want for nothing when she took up her post at the Grünewald, mother Conradine had looked up with a blank expression, as if working out the thought through the fog of pain. A long silent minute later, pressing elbows back and straining to raise herself, she had fixed Ursula in the eye, the words stumbling through laboured breath.

"Promises," she said, her mind perhaps reaching back to the flickering memory of her father waving to her as he crossed the little bridge over the brook that long-ago May morning. "Men make promises. But they give you only what they want." Stretching out a pale hand and taking Ursula's in an infirm hold, her voice gained a trace of her accustomed energy. "Never let go. Hold them to their word, claim what is yours. Will you remember that, *Engel?*"

Ursula wiped the damp from her eyes, unable to remember when last she had been called angel, if ever. Conradine had never been one for shows of tenderness, in word or gesture. Leaving the room she had wondered why so often humans handed over the heirloom of the heart only when breathing their last.

If Pelosi chose to walk away, amiable and courteous as always, nevertheless firm in his choice, nor did Ursula feel she could have particular claims on his time and attention. After all he had committed himself to nothing, no promise to be broken, for her nothing to claim. What had passed between them was more like a chance meeting in the dark, without prologue and sequence, without the weight of consequence. That there was to be no aftermath he had made clear on the very first day, a notice unambiguous, peremptory even, of which she had been little mindful, not as yet aware of what was to come, the inroads he would have made and the terrain conquered in a few short days, waking in her a dormant self, another being whose newfound yearning and cravings would persist, gnawing like urgent hunger in the pits of the stomach.

Not so much the person and company, in the main it was his living and intimate presence for which her senses clamoured, the throbbing veins of blind desire, the blood coursing warm in limb and loin, the idolatrous worship that a body could inflict, flesh giving way to flesh in ravenous demand, opening out to vistas of fulfilment seemingly infinite, the satisfaction of appetites esurient and without measure. She had known all this, again and again, but all too briefly, in his arms, limbs entangled and bodies entwined, the invasive possession repetitious yet startling each time, as though he had come on her of a sudden, she herself straining muscle and sinew to draw him in ever more swift, ever deeper, as though wanting to host not merely a mere portion, a part or morsel, but his entire being.

One afternoon, neither giving ground through a maddened combat, a tussle and wrestle primordial, a warring of the senses alone, shorn of finesse, bellicose even, when at last, the lungs emptied and vigour spent, they had fallen back from each other, light and life returning, his head pillowed in the dip of her thigh, after a long silent moment Pelosi said, as if meditating on the landscape of crooks and curves: "The body is a miracle. If people only knew, they'd hurry every day to church to light a candle. We know something of how it works, but not why." Adding with a boyish smile, a finger lightly tracing the swell of one breast, "This is merely the icing over the miracle!"

Ursula did not much know of mysteries and miracles, but afterwards she could only wonder about the revelation that Pelosi's touch had brought her. Glancing at the mirror, she saw no alterations, nothing changed, the same statuesque figure, florid, passable abundance here and there, the 'icing,' as he had called it. Matter, the visible, shape and physique, revealing nothing, no alteration, shift or mutation, yet deep within there were volcanic stirrings, dormancy giving way to an arousal sensuous and demanding. There were times, in lonely hours, in bed as sleep seeped in to drown wakefulness, when like a thief in the night stepping out through the portals of the dark, there arose from unseen depths, slow and insistent, the beating echo of an urge never before felt, a distant reprise of the roar and furore she had known bound and trussed in his hold, a transport of fit and fainting down a void. Tossing and turning in restive sleep, the desolate cry to be possessed and carried away reverberating silent in the blood, at times she woke of a sudden, breathless in the first light of dawn, to find the body bathed in a glaze of damp, the savour of salt on the tongue, the inner lips liquescent with moist, as though just abandoned by a phantasmagoric lover after the tumult and convulsion of a furious coupling. To lie there, then, spent and abandoned, unable to make sense of the trespass, the intruder melted away in the light of the coming day.

The brief chapter ended, the book shut and put away, well aware in her mute resignation that Pelosi had gone from her days with the same haste with which he had entered, yet she found it hard to put out of sense and sight this new-born creature he had left her with, lurking beneath the skin and demanding attention and satisfaction.

Suffering Pelosi's desertion, Ursula might have pined for long, endured with aching emptiness the denial of his attention and intimacy, assuaging the loss, in some small measure, with self-satisfaction, had it not been for an unexpected and improbable event a few weeks later, when she found herself at the cross roads that offered a way out of the world she had known till then, towards days beyond her imagining, a life so changed that no soothsayer or clairvoyant could have foretold. But no conscious choice, it was not her hand that picked or discarded; for Ursula was largely incapable of choice and decision, her innate passivity leaving to others the arrivals and departures of her existence, the tide she was to take and the port of destination.

It had always been so, her coming to the Grünewald, ever ready to please and oblige, accepting without protest the night-duty of another, filling-in for a fellow nurse taken ill, the ready indulgence of the outré whims of the seniors at the clinic. So too in childhood, with the invasive attention of her father, the seductive reach of class-mate Annika's infantile groping under her skirt, no less failing to stay the fatal hand of her mother rushing in blind fury towards her man on the edge of the rock-face. Nor could it be different on this occasion, especially this time around, when she found in front of her not the risqué request of some elder or the fumbling touch of a school girl, but the towering figure of a titan who laid out before her with a benign hand and words eloquent the promise of a luxuriant landscape, comfort and well-being, protection and friendship, glory perhaps, love even.

No need to ponder and consider. The offer reluctantly seconded by Dr. Krieger, she had accepted with accustomed passivity, if with an irresolute nod, a small uncertain smile, whatever it was that lay ahead. Nor, mindful of her mother's oft-repeated descant, did she turn to look back as the hour of leaving approached. "Never," she had exhorted on and off down the years, "never look back, girl!" Not much given to the faith, a negligent church-goer, at best, somehow the odd salient event in the Holy Book had lodged in Conradine's memory, so that she would call out in after-thought, "The last time someone did, the woman became salt!" Conradine herself might not have become a pillar of salt, but she knew something of the misery of the backward glance, the corrosive affliction of the heart's endless grief. The years of childhood misted and opaque, yet she herself had never lifted her gaze from the past, eyeing a rare time with a short-breathed sigh, even half a lifetime later, the bridge over the brook where her father had taken his leave, consigning his young daughter in the keeping of strangers.

~~~

One afternoon, the late spring air warm with the sun breaking through with a misty haze, Ursula had sat out cradling a sick child on the balcony fronting the ward. Admitted to the Grünewald a couple of months ago, little Sofie's condition had rode a roller-coaster of highs and lows, veering between hope and hopelessness, the lymphomatous prognosis certain, but the abrupt gains and equally sudden reversals a riddle for the doctors. Over the weeks the girl had taken to Ursula most, quiescent in her arms as she now listened to the infant song, the simple words spelt slow in a voice cadenced, soft and crystalline: *Weist Du, wieviel Sterne stehen...,* Head cushioned on Ursula's bosom, Sofie gazed unblinking towards the sky, as though wanting, in reply to the words, to count the stars in the pale blue swept with quill feather streaks of cloud.

And shifting in the upright seat, to lay the child's head on her shoulder, Ursula caught sight of the figure below on the terrace, the silver head turned upwards, the hands raised towards her mimicking applause with a brief silent clap, before homaging a brief bow, turning then to stroll away.

Looking after him, Ursula asked Head Nurse Merian, stood beside her, who the man might be.

Nurse Merian nodded, to reply in a regardful tone. "One of our most distinguished patients. A famous musician, they say."

"Oh. What's the matter with him?"

"Recovering from a stroke. Nothing serious. They sent him over from the Bethanien, I think, for a bit of rest."

Ursula had not long to wait to discover the rest. Summoned to Dr. Krieger's study the following morning, she was taken aback by his words. "There's a gentleman who saw you outside the ward yesterday. Rather, he heard you sing."

"I'm sorry if I disturbed anyone. I didn't mean to…"

"Your disturbance was impressive, it would appear," Krieger smiled affably. "Do you know who he is?"

Ursula shook her head uncertainly. "*Oberschwester* Merian told me he's famous. A famous musician."

"Don't suppose you'll have heard the name," Krieger explained settling behind his desk. "Not just a famous musician. One of the very great names in the world of music. Armin von Göttner. Well, he appears to be interested in your voice and has asked to see you."

"Oh, I was just singing a little something to Sofie…"

"It was enough for the maestro. I expect he knows what he's about."

Ursula took leave of Krieger perplexed. Apart from a few seasons in the church choir, she had never sung in public, certainly not before professionals, even less a figure so renowned, apparently. What the great personage might want she could not imagine. Lullabies to put him to sleep, she mused with half-amused, vaguely anxious thought.

At first sight Armin von Göttner was impressive, in person and presence. She had seen him briefly and at a distance, now he stood before her, half a head taller, tall as she herself was, broad-shouldered and of muscular girth, the large head silver-haired, the long locks flowing down the nape with slight swirls and curls. Lineaments prominent, a high forehead and lips fleshy, the dark eyes, silent and severe, softened as with a bow he bent forward to take her hand and lift it briefly toward his lips. Straightening, he looked at her with a long piercing gaze, seemingly spellbound. Appearing to regain consciousness, he met Ursula's small, hesitant smile with a voice low and mellow, benign, as he addressed her after a brief glance at a slip of paper in one hand.

"Fräulein Füssli… Ursula. May I call you Ursula?" Indicating the chair by the piano stool, seating himself at the keyboard, his look still keen on her, a faint smile, amiable and teasing, briefly lit his face, as in an undertone he repeated her name: "Ursula. Ursula, the Virgin Saint, if I remember right." No sooner business-like and formal, he straightened himself. "Dr. Krieger will have explained why I wished to see you?"

Ursula nodded uncertainly.

"I heard you sing yesterday. What was it?"

"Oh." Lowering her eyes, Ursula thought for a moment. "Nothing really. Just a couple of lullabies. *Weist Du wieviel…*"

"Ah yes. Not heard that in a long while, a hundred years or more! Would you mind singing it for me?"

Hands fidgeting nervously as von Göttner, nodding encouragement, shut his eyes, Ursula tuned the sleep-song in a small voice. When she had done, he said, "¾ time, I think. Right?" and turned to pick out the notes on the keyboard with a light touch. Then once again, faster, and more pronounced on the long notes.

"This old thing needs a bit of retuning," he noted running a light finger across the keyboard of the old rosewood Schwechten, which was good enough for the sing-song of festive celebrations at the clinic, but less so for the subtle hearing of the maestro. Turning to her, he patted his chest briefly. "Please let go. Don't hold it in. Ready?" More at ease, breath flowing, Ursula voiced the words as she usually did when singing to the children.

"Soprano, more mezzo," von Göttner muttered to himself, as if in some doubt, when the last notes had faded away. Sober in face, he looked her in the eye. "You have a gift, Ursula. Has anyone told you that before?"

Gift? She was unsure what he meant. Whatever it might be, no, no one had ever made mention of it. Her mother had never been one for praise, spare in a rare word of encouragement, more monitory than heartening, cautioning and exhorting to keep her eyes open in a world teeming with perils for a woman, the modest choice of a nursing career met with ill-concealed disdain. "Cleaning up the vomit of the sick and being bedded by dirty-minded doctors," her words of scorn, "What kind of life is that?" Nor was there ever a good word, compliment or commendation, from teachers at school, who saw her as a backwoods farm girl destined for cleaning out the cattle shed, wedded early, to bear a clutch of children sired by a boorish husband, an existence of mute obedience and drudgery, one for whom a passing acquaintance with the alphabet more than sufficed.

Never giving it a thought, Ursula was unaware of any particular grant or endowment, if not the face and figure Nature had bestowed, which, growing up, she had noticed often called the attention of males surveying her with ruminant stares, making for her timidity and unease, at times making her want to withdraw her presence from the sight of strangers. For the rest, with apparently no inborn talent nor skill to vaunt, it had never once occurred to her to aspire to attainment and conquests greater and higher than what she had. If anything at all, it offered her a small measure of pleasure that very often the children who came to the clinic for cure and care were especially drawn to her, her soft-spoken words a caress, the unalloyed warmth of her smile bringing light to the young eyes, the sleep-songs she crooned gently in the infant ears lulling to rest and sleep as they lay quiescent in her arms with heads pillowed on the ample, motherly bosom.

"Gift?" Her puzzled look, querying, met von Göttner's keen gaze.

Taking her hand in his, studying the slender fingers tapering to the light peach varnish of the nails, his voice seemingly coming from the depths of distant thought, he said, "Fräulein, Ursula... Some have gifts, God-given if you will, that remain unrevealed. Of which we know nothing. Like walking on plain ground with mother lodes of gold under our feet."

Letting go of Ursula's hand, lightly hitting the middle C key, sticky and ill-tuned, he turned to her once more. "Let me tell you a little story. Do you mind?

"Long ago, when I was a child, we had a young valet who waited on my father, pressing his clothes, polishing his boots, dressing him. A farmer's lad, he had come to the house as errand boy. When not at work, young Franzl often went swimming in the lake at the edge of the woods down from our estate. What a sight it was, to watch him splash about, floundering, very nearly drowning. And how people laughed at his clowning about in the water. Our father was less than amused. He was fond of Franzl and was afraid that one day he'd go into the water and never come up again. '*Du bist ein Dummkopf!*' he would roar, calling him a variety of names, dimwit, blockhead, mulehead and worse. Even threatening to whip him. But nothing could stop the young fellow making away to the lake on the sly. Well, only a few years later Franzl Ribbeck found himself a member of the national swimming team at the Berlin Olympics. Didn't win any medals, but did have the honour of shaking the Führer's hand. For what it was worth. Franzl the dumb mulehead! Who was to know that an illiterate farmer's boy had this special talent, he himself least of all. Had it not been for the keen eye of a swimming trainer, he'd still be scraping the mud off his master's boots."

~~~

There was this about Armin von Göttner, an out of the ordinary ability to match intention and word, surprisingly suave and seductive when he so wished, waylaying the listener with an aura of cordial admiration, the winning warmth of sympathy. No less cutting and caustic in moments irascible, not infrequent, able to dose insult and injury in measure with matching words that, with an appropriate expression of contempt and derision, often left the hapless victim baffled and bleeding.

And, too, there was the fabulist's pithy recounting, drawing from whatever the anecdote or tale a moral, a forewarning if need be, the parting shot of a monitory intimidation. As when he once crippled for long the self-confidence of an aspiring young conductor with frequent sneering and sniggering scorn, remarking in a snide aside but loud enough to be heard, "A baton in a limp hand makes one as much of a conductor as a drooping prick a Casanova!" Or else jeering in the hearing of the gathered ensemble, "Young man, that hurried downbeat is more like dropping your trousers at the mere sight of the lady!"

Ease of praise was not among von Göttner's habits. But, if a past-master at belittling and putting down, a rare time he could also ably inspire and hearten, restoring faith in oneself, as he once did with a little-known young Bulgarian soprano, who went on to walk the boards in the great opera houses of the world. Ever indebted, Ivanka Stoichkov had repaid her mentor with her florid love for several seasons. No less David Davidovich, a timid and tortured young man, with a magical touch on the keyboard, rising under von Göttner's guidance to become a star in the musical firmament.

The one and the other, the warm and empathetic father figure and the detestable ogreish persona spewing bile, made von Göttner much-loved by some, as also heartily loathed by many, the numbers of the latter swelling as he grew older. The license often granted to genius to hector, bully and browbeat, torment and molest had over the years worn thin, gradually distancing friends, colleagues and associates, theatre directors and seasoned musicians turning away with a shudder at the mention of the name. Davidovich himself, fond as he was of his patron and friend, had often found his palms damp with sweat before walking onstage to perform with von Göttner.

Losing his hold, seeing enemies everywhere, unable almost to distinguish between friend and foe, finally little welcome on the major podiums of the musical world, the season's engagements increasingly limited to the concert halls of minor centres and provincial towns, matters had come to a head when one day, coming down from his Paris offices, Pierre Laurant, von Göttner's agent for half a lifetime, announced as though it was a matter of some pride, the conquest of one of the more impervious peaks in the Andes or Himalayas, that he had managed to obtain the maestro's engagement for a series of concerts to celebrate the fifth anniversary as national capital of the city of Chişinău.

David Davidovich thought afterwards that it was Laurant's news that had brought on the stroke. Crimson in face, stammering "*Où est la baise…?*" he had looked around with eyes wild and bloodshot. Repeating again and again with failing breath, "Where the fuck is this Chisi… whatever?" finally he had collapsed in a heap, half-lying on a sofa by the tall windows overlooking the lake, the bulky frame contorted like that of a beast in its last throes.

Laurant leaning over him, alarmed and confused, called out to Miranda, the long-suffering house-keeper who, hurrying in, knelt at the maestro's feet trying to prop him upright. Face frozen to marbled stillness, he had sat slumped there for long minutes until, raising opaque eyes towards Laurent, with words half-mangled he said, "So the old whore goes to the beggar's brothel. Eh, Pierre?"

Seemingly returned to himself when his personal physician arrived soon afterwards, helped to his feet, he made to walk but the uncertain steps moved sidewards, almost crab-like, unable to decide direction and tilting the body left.

The malaise evident, the doctor nodded and let fall a sigh. "I'll arrange for a room at the Universitaires," he told Laurant on the way out. "Would you see to get him there?" Proffering his hand, he added, "Nothing to worry. Only a minor ictus. Should be up and about in a week, fortnight most."

Speech restored enough for von Göttner to return to his accustomed self, dismissive and cavalier once again, steps slower but certain, tests revealing merely a passing cerebrovascular incident, yet the doctors at the university hospital deemed expedient a period of rest, preferably in some quite locality, with specialist expertise at hand and offering necessary comfort and conveniences. Dr. Krieger had been more than glad to receive such an eminence at the Grünewald, reserving for the visitor a small suite in the sanatorium wing. When told of the move, the convalescent himself had been less than enthusiastic.

"First that Moldavian hell-hole," he grunted, "now this place in the cowpat country." He turned an accusatory stare at his physician, at Laurant and Davidovich. "You're all plotting to kill me."

Accustomed to treating personalities famous and less so, celebrities, divas and dictators, the doctor looked down with a tolerant smile. "The Grünewald is in beautiful country. A couple of weeks there and you'll be on your feet again, better than before."

"Better than before. Before what?" von Göttner grunted, sitting up to take the doctor's hand.

Davidovich fussed and fumbled by the hospital bed. Laurant soothed and assured. *"Repos assuré, maestro,"* he submitted humbly. That very afternoon he would be calling his office in Paris to have the engagements in Chişinău cancelled. *"Même si, la capitale Moldave…,"* he began to say with faint insistence, the louring look in von Göttner's eyes making him desist.

The Grünewald was set in beautiful country, no doubt, the maestro admitted grudgingly at first sight, the mountain air pristine, the views of woods and valleys refreshing. Comfortable in his private suite, well-served, cosseted even, the nurses at his beck and call, respectfully solicitous to whatever his needs, happily lending themselves to his occasional teasing and half-lame flirtatious sallies, yet he could not help feeling somehow hollowed out, an oppressive emptiness gnawing within, making for restive impatience, as too a silent bilious animosity, towards no one person in particular, more towards the world at large. A world to which he had given the many years of his life, his talent and genius, lifting hearts and kindling with joy unalloyed, as only music could do, the multitudes sat rapt in the shadowed dark of concert halls and opera houses.

Wed to music alone, his sole passion and pastime, nothing else had mattered much, marriage considered a distraction, rearing a family an unnecessary burden, garnering wealth vulgar and demeaning, with the fine prints of contracts and monetary details left largely to agent Laurant. In lifelong pursuit of the alchemist's dream, subscribing without doubt to Walter Pater's observation that all art aspires to become music, and wanting to turn music itself into an expression ever more sublime, beyond the mere ear, transcendent, he had received with a worn smile Laurant's words telling him of the substantial earnings from a best-selling recording, murmuring then, "We've managed to turn the divine into dross."

What now? Ingrate humanity and a feckless world. Strolling with slow, reluctant steps in the grounds of the clinic, a nurse trailing the aimless wandering, he felt abandoned. The stage vacant, the musicians departed from behind their music sheet holders, the plush red seats of the theatre empty of the audience springing to its feet even as the last note lingered dying in the air, raising the roof with deafening applause, the accolade and unsparing encomium of critics fallen silent, the great hall now merely resounded in the chambers of the mind with the desolation of scenes never to be seen again, gifts never again to be reclaimed. Gone too, seemingly for ever, the countless seasons basking in the obeisance of the world, homaged and fêted by celebrities, luminaries and dignitaries of public life, even waiters tiptoeing to the table he sat at as though approaching the chancel of some god, no less women young and older, waiting expectant in the aura he shed, preening and cooing, ready and willing to immolate themselves on whatever the alter of his want or desire.

Unable to accept the desertion by the multitude, unwilling to admit the apostasy, he had never paused to query the cause of the reversal of fortune. Inconceivable that a living god could ever be abjured, repudiated. Embittered, a heart acid and rancorous, he could only curse and rile against a world frivolous and villainous, berating Laurant through a long afternoon when the Frenchman came on a visit during his stay at the Grünewald, repeating, "So now the old cow to the slaughter house, the old whore to the beggar's brothel."

Laurant's earnest assurance that the Moldavian engagement had been definitely cancelled bought no peace. "What next, Laurant?" he asked with studied pathos. "A fiddle in the hand and a cloth cap on the side-walk, to sing for one's supper?"

Laurant pressed back a smile, accustomed as he had become down the years to the maestro's moods and moments, a one-man theatre of a superb Thespian walking the boards, now ranting and raving, now crouching with a whimper to call forth in the onlooker pity and sympathy. The Frenchman was certain in his mind that had not von Göttner heard the call of music, he might well have been summoned by some other muse, Thalia or Melpomene, or both, to play out the tragi-comic poses and postures of his own life.

"Nothing dishonourable, maestro, in singing for one's supper," he ventured lightly, raising a wan smile on von Göttner's lips. "One way or another, we all do that."

The long hours cheerless, wallowing in gloom and recrimination, Ursula's sudden appearance on the scene, like the clouds parting on the darkened horizon to reveal the vision of an angel with outstretched arms, lifted him at a stroke from the enervating slough of despondency. Mind confused, imagination running riot, the miracle of a new life, a newer beginning seemed not beyond reach. Seeing her in person, the handsome presence, the striking beauty of lineament and form, the configuration became real, taking shape with plan and project, the future laid out and painted with broad strokes of fantasy. And seeing her in person, too, woke anew a nerve of desire, the sudden and unexpected renewal of an almost youthful appetite, but also the ardour of a passion rare for his nature, the covetousness of possession, to hold and keep.

There and then, within the space of a day, a mere week, he had decided that with this splendid creature it would be different. Most of the women in his life had come and gone with the ease and speed of a revolving door, soundless and leaving little trace, the affairs, short or long, casual and cursory, the parting without regret or recrimination. And if a rare time there were tears of farewell, they were not his. Watching at a distance over the years, Laurant called them *affaires de la longe,* the maestro deeming the term in poor taste. More than merely a matter of the loin, to each liaison he had unfailingly brought generous thoughtfulness, generous with gifts and offerings no less, the lover of the turn often gratified and grateful for the attention of the great man, a bouquet to be cherished and pleasing for one's vanity. Hope notwithstanding, most knew that he was not a man for all seasons, not one seeking the anchor of permanence, more a passing gale, that blew one away in a whirlwind of luxuriant abandon, breathless and panting.

Not so with Ursula. With her he saw himself as creator and author, guide and tutor, taking in his hands matter rough-hewn and as yet unformed, to shape and mould into a figure that could walk tall to the applause of the world; in turn, she by his side, her breath infusing him with new life. A perfect union, he master and mentor, she his very own diva, brought together with single-minded purpose.

If there was doubt, it was a faint blemish on the edges of the silver lining. His seasoned ear perfectly attuned, able to tell from the mere echo a weak note from the strong, the fourth from the first, in the recesses of sense and perception he knew that, now in her mid-twenties, it was late in the day for Ursula to navigate the infinite intricacies of the operatic world. Endowed with a fine sense of pitch and timbre, a rare melodic expression, but the voice untrained, it was half a lifetime too late for her to stride the stage as Carmen or Violetta. But, tutored and trained, the career of a concert artiste with a lighter repertoire could well be within reach. A year in Milan with his old friend Farinetti, the renowned voice teacher, would see to the cutting, sizing and polishing of the rough diamond.

Watching Ursula from a remove each time they met, immersed for long minutes in a trance of fancy and reverie, that obscured sense and reason, his mind conjured up visions of triumph yet to come, scenes transposed on the past, no longer cavernous concert halls thunderous with the soar and sweep of orchestras massed a hundred strong, the bellowing brass and the rolling thunder of timpani. A softly-lit theatre stage instead, with him seated at the piano, she alongside, resplendent in satin and lamé, voicing melodies from song books loved down the generations, Schubert and Wolf, Handel's early Italian cantatas, and why not, promenade crowd-pleasers like Toselli's Serenade.

His mind letting out a sigh of relief, he was finally done with the ill-veiled reluctance and impertinence of music directors and theatre managers, some of whom he himself had brought to prominence, promoting their careers with his name and encouragement. To the devil with the ingrate creatures! Henceforth he would be his own man, impresario, sponsor, director, manager, stage-setter. And Ursula his very own creation, prize and possession, too innocent and guileless to rebel and find her own way in the world, beholden to him, and bound by indissoluble ties of marriage, if need be.

~~~

Von Göttner's stay at the Grünewald nearing the end, Ursula's hours were crowded with confusion and doubt. Undecided, veering between anxiety and acquiescence, never called on before to take a leap so bold into the unknown, she did not know what to think, fog shrouding the broad glittering path laid out before her by the great man's seductive eloquence, by turn benign and paternal, by turn urgent and hurrying.

Distracted through the work day, she sought council, but words of comfort denied her, friend Ilse's voice was one of distant indifference, of an unsympathetic onlooker, with a touch of impatient scorn. "I don't know, girl!" she shook her head. "This geriatric speciality of yours. All these senile old men trooping in line to get between your legs. Don't really know if you'll live to regret it. Hope not. Anyway, do what you think best."

Dr. Krieger was more forthcoming. But if comforting and assuring, it was as if he had been presented with a fait accompli, a matter decided and accepted elsewhere. Leaning over her with a kind, fatherly expression, he held her in a long, thoughtful gaze, saying finally, "It goes unsaid we'll miss you. *I'll* miss you."

A knock on the door and, following a brief consultation with the head surgeon, he returned to the desk. "They've just brought in the Bishop. A midline hernia of all things. Too much bending and bowing before the Cross, I expect." Krieger and the Bishop had never seen eye to eye, the doctor a free thinker and libertine for the churchman, the Bishop excessively orthodox and a bore for Krieger.

"His Lord will see him through," Krieger mused aloud in a sardonic undertone as he returned to his desk. "Coming back to us, Ursula... it's not everyday something like this comes one's way. Von Göttner asked to see me the other morning. An interesting talk. Great men are not always great in their intentions. But he looks an honest type and he really does think you have a future in music. It might not be easy but he's minded to do whatever it takes. That at least was my impression. Obviously you have something that all of us missed. The only music around here are cowbells morning and night!"

He looked away with a small, pursed smile. "I believe he's a little bit taken by you... Whatever happens, Ursula, remember there'll always be a place for you here. Should you ever want to come back. Or need to."

"It's been decided, then." Her words barely audible, free of protest or resentment, she felt a wash of relief, passive in acceptance, not having to weigh and choose, meekly content to go with the tide.

Gathered around a sizeable *Nusstorte*, Ilse cutting the wedges of cake with measure, a hand stealing in to pick at the crumbs of walnut, Ursula's nursing colleagues had come together for a brief farewell.

Ribbing, vaguely ribald, thronging around, they joshed with hugs and kisses, asking, "And will the grand dame come to see us again?"

"Too busy serving her lord in bed, she'll not have the time," nurse Anke laughed, with perhaps the merest trace of envy.

"No," said the Head Nurse, sobering the gathering with her motherly words, "You're not to come back, Ursula. Make something of yourself." And Ilse, perhaps regretful of her earlier coolness, laid her cheek against Ursula's. "We'll think of you. We'll miss you, *Schätzchen*."

The crumbs of the *Nusstorte* lingering in the gullet, for a moment Ursula sensed an odd weight on the chest as her eyes shone with rising damp. These faces around her, amicable presence and voices familiar, this was the only world she had known, however small but intimate and consoling, the cradle that had seen her into womanhood, a home of sorts for one like her, for all purposes homeless. Abruptly to sever these ties and go out the door towards landscapes unknown, the future narrated to her in only airy words, Ursula felt for an instant the ground giving way under feet even as she held fast around her the comforting arms, warm and maternal, of the *Oberschwester*, the older woman's words in her ears kindly and reassuring. "There, sweetie, there, it'll all go well, you'll see."

The chauffeured limousine silently rolling towards the gate, von Göttner beside her, unmindful of her mother's cautionary biblical tale of the wife turning to a pillar of salt as she looked back at the Sodomites perishing under fire and brimstone, Ursula did look back through the rear glass at Ilse with several fellow nurses stood at the entrance, Dr. Krieger and Joachim alongside with arms raised in farewell. Eyes misting, she saw the low, flat-roofed outline of the Grünewald recede as the car speeded up down the long slope until, turning the bend, the past fell away from sight. And a warm hand closing over hers, she felt for a passing moment the airless suspension of a weightless void.

III

1

"Curious" said Davidovich. "Decidedly odd that Ursula never had women friends. You know the sort of bosom friend one confides in. A shoulder to cry on. Possibly more common among women than with males. In all the years we knew each other, I never once saw anyone from her past, from the days she worked at the sanatorium. I remember her mentioning once or twice a fellow nurse there. Isla, Isette… Can't quite remember now. But she sounded more like an elder sister."

Davidovich held up the platter of the Gruyère and bacon swirls, helping himself to a couple. "I could love Gabriel just for these. All his architect's precision in those perfect concentric circles!"

"And yes," he resumed, dusting off the tiny flakes on the shirt front, "I did meet her once, this Isette or Ilse or whatever. It was in the end days. She had left nursing years ago, married and all that. We met the day Armin was booked into the clinic. I think we just exchanged a few words. Looked a sturdy, nononsense mothering type. Don't think she and Ursula could have been close friends. At least, not the Ursula I knew."

"For that matter, David, the world's full of people without friends or friendships," I said.

"True. Possibly, Ursula never had any of the fair-weather sort even. Something in her kept other women at arm's length. Partly it was her grand beauty, looks that belittled others and put them in the shade. I remember a reception thrown by the Consul of some South American country, Brazil or Chile. Half the men were around Ursula and the Consul's wife, no mean beauty herself, looking on and saying, 'What does she have that we others don't?' What indeed? There was something in her that drew men like bees to honey, but distanced her from those of her kind. Can't have been looks alone. A mystery woman! No one knew where she had come from, where the great music-man had found her. In a doll's house, in a brothel, by the way side?

"One thing very noticeable about her was that she never much spoke of herself. At least, not in a meaningful way. She seemed to prefer to keep her past at arm's distance. Not a territory strictly *verboten,* even so vague and hazy. Even after we got to know each other, one hardly ever heard a mention of parents, home, childhood. It was almost as if she had descended on earth fully grown, no antecedents, nothing behind her… except her own splendid behind, if I may!"

"*De Mortuis Ni Nisi Bonum!*"

"Oh, far be it for me to speak ill of the dead! Or even of the living! But no denying that Ursula's rear was her crowning jewel, just as much as her frontage. A sincere attribution from a disinterested admirer like me." Davidovich's light laugh floated away in the stillness of the evening.

We were seated on the broad terrace of the old chalet-mansion, all stone and heavy dark wood, he had inherited from his mother, the front sloping down in a broad sweep towards the waters of the lake and the main road, with an ample acreage of land pleateauing behind, both front and rear planted with row upon row of vines, the stout braided branches running in long lines in the dark like the barbed enclosures of some labour camp. The Indian summer seemingly intending to stretch into winter, the late-autumn air unseasonably mild, the moonless night sky indigo and scattered with sugar crystals, the silence was broken by the dim din and rattle of trains on the line skirting the lake, occasionally behind us the clink and clang of dishes and pots as Gabriel busied himself getting together our supper.

Pensive, his thoughts roaming at random over a season of life come to an unexpected close, Davidovich's recounting was not without a gentle humour, the same lightness of touch he brought when sat at the keyboard playing some song or sonata. His own days entwined over a lifetime with that of a man who had been mentor and master, no less often severe monitor of his talent, and quite as often bully and browbeater, von Göttner's story was in some measure also his own. Stood a step behind, in the penumbra, he had looked on at the journey of a titan from the heydays of fame and glory to a decline imperceptible, perhaps ineluctable, to wallow then in a slough of self-pity, now ranting against fate, now raging against enemies unseen, torment and lacerations largely self-inflicted. Listening to Davidovich, one could not but think that there was in him something of a son, derided and ill-treated but unable to bring himself to sever the paternal tie, a forbearance borne with patience whatever the injury, an affection unfailing.

Collecting himself after a long pause, sipping his drink, he resumed the tale of the wedding. "Armin was adamant that there was to be no publicity. A hushed affair, no press release, no journalists."

Because even then, when his name had almost faded from the billboards, no longer made news in the music columns of papers and magazines, he was not quite forgotten, appearing from time to time in a mention or reference, as though in faded print. As often with stars and celebrities who have left centre-stage, but still there, somewhere, mostly out of sight. From time to time a call would come through from some critic or reporter, asking for his thoughts on some up and coming young conductor who had taken the music world by storm. Usually

Armin dismissed the query with a laconic one-liner: 'If you're asking me if the young man's a new Mitropoulos or Karajan, the answer is no." Than rounding off the terse comment with, 'Not even another von Göttner!'

"So the wedding was to be a very small affair, he had decided. Strictly private, tucked out of sight, with no guests, the only present were to be Laurant, the best man, I was to play the organ. Housekeeper Miranda would be there with her husband Juan. She had come to Geneva as a young woman, working as chamber maid in one of the grand hotels. For the past twenty years or so she had kept house for Armin, mothering and cosseting him, putting up with his tantrums with a muttered *'Paciencia'* thrown over her shoulder. Severe in her faith, never missing mass on Sundays, rain or shine, Miranda was relieved that her maestro had decided to marry in church. Even though it was not *her* Church.

"These people," I remember her saying to me once, "*¿cómo se dice... Luterana, no*? They have no saints, no confession, no Maria. *Nada*! Denying the Mother of the Saviour! What kind of religion is that?"

"What about me, Miranda," I made bold to ask.

"Oh, you're different. *Muy deferente.*" Meaning, outside the pale. She was fond of me and didn't want to say out loud what my people had done to her Saviour!

"Miranda and the bride apart, the only other woman in church was Armin's personal secretary, Christine Laforge. Harassed, hectored, but with a stiff upper lip the likes of which one had never seen. A school ma'am sort, strict and efficient. She was just about the only one who could stand up to Armin. She treated his bark and bullying like the yelp of an infant and in the end she always had her way. I clearly remember the time he was to conduct one of a series of concerts by the Suisse Romande and was invited in advance by a radio station to talk of the pieces he would be conducting. He bluntly refused. Sitting in a glass box, talking to some nincompoop, thirty minutes of an inane exchange. 'No way. I'm not going.' Standing over him, Christine looked down at him through her glasses, very calm, collected. No argument, but her words must have worked their way through his brain. 'Going missing once too often, in the end one is not missed at all. You should go.' He looked up at her with a hangdog look. 'As you like, Christine. If that's what you wish.' I thought then that Christine Laforge would have made a name for herself taming lions at the circus!"

Looking up at the star-littered sky, Davidovich smiled to himself. "But there was more to Christine," he mused. Evidently, she had a heart.

A native of a village across the frontier, near Annecy, she had been brought up by nuns and had come to work in a bank in Geneva. A dozen years later she left, some scandal over an affair with one of the senior figures putting an end to her banking career. Von Göttner had met her at the bank and asked if she would come to work for him. He was then already with a firm footing in the pantheon of the weighty musical figures of the time. Laurant looked after the bookings, contracts and finances, but he needed someone able to take charge of his day to day affairs, engagements, schedules, travel arrangements, correspondence. From Paris Laurant had got him a secretary, a charming young woman, who lasted all of a month, leaving in tears and telling Laurant afterwards that the man was *le dèmon* in person come to earth to torture and torment humans. There were others, able and efficient young women. None of them had lasted more than a few weeks, some months at best.

Christine Laforge, true to her name, was of stronger mettle, instead. She set about taking charge of Armin's days, though not his nights. As far as he knew and could tell, Davidovich was certain. He was unaware of any intimacy between the two over the years. Not altogether surprising. At all times, whatever the occasion, among acquaintances and those familiar, as with strangers, Christine seemed ringed with a circle of razor fencing, which discouraged approach and advance, or any gesture remotely personal or intimate. Averse to touch, for salutations she put out a stiff hand for an instant, bussing her cheeks in her native manner or a warm hug and embrace felt more like the ravishing of a Sabine maiden. Evidently, the nuns had done their work well, the hushed-up scandal of the affair with her senior at the bank merely a youthful and momentary fall from grace. During the years with von Göttner, she had neither a paramour nor fiancé of any sort, not a single courting male in sight. She lived alone in a small apartment somewhere in Cornavin, a rare time going away for a few days, back to Annecy, presumably to see her old folk, of whom she never made mention. If she had a life of her own, it was hard to guess, even less imagine.

"But yes," Davidovich nodded, "Christine did have a heart. Who'd have thought! Armour-clad, severe in dress and manner, words limited to the matter at hand, without superfluities, little or no distraction, moving more like an automata. Yet, she did have a life of her own.

"Curious our common habit of seeing someone plain and nondescript, shallow as the complexion, thinking there's nothing to the person, only to discover one day a storm raging silently behind the blinds. I remember a musician in one of the orchestras that accompanied me sometimes. A tuba player. A cardboard figure, one dimensional, no personality and, evidently, characterless. Only to learn one fine day that the man had been married and divorced several times over, had fathered at least a dozen children, ran on the side an emporium for luxury goods, and went on big-game hunting safaris to Africa. Who'd have thought! Downing one of those huge African tuskers, a couple of rhinos for good measure, all on a morning's outing! A tuba Hemingway!

"So our Christine, tight-lipped and knees close-knit always…"

A beating heart and a life of her own, with hopes and dreams coursing through the veins. But out of sight, never betrayed by a word of even in mere jest, whatever the thought or expectation locked tight in her bosom and never to see the light, until the day of fulfilment. But the day never came.

Von Göttner's erratic profligacy she appeared never to notice. If she did, she chose to look the other way. But it must have been hard to ignore all that random reaching out to some female in passing, the hectic affairs with the woman of his trade and milieu, singers, aspiring young musicians, a stage manager's wife, some middle-aged patron of the arts bejewelled and swaddled in mink, each in turn bedded briefly a few weeks, a month or two, rarely more, treated with Armin's usual lavish manner but never allowed to step through the portals of his life.

"I don't think she ever once protested or commented on what Laurant with French elegance came to call 'affairs of the loin.' Even so, a human after all, it must have been painful for Christine to see this bevy of beauties troop in and out of the house, with their cries of *cheri*, *liebling*, darling, one ageing Italian singer even cooing '*il mio ercole!*' Hercules himself might have been startled to have found in Armin von Göttner his twin! But Christine knew to tell between chaff and wheat, and she waited.

"Poor thing, she waited and waited, patient and forbearing. Through all those years, all the while, brick by hopeful brick, silently building the mansion of her dreams."

From her Catholic education and a short-lived aspiration to be a nun, Christine apparently knew her saints, Augustine and Aquinas, and she knew that human excesses, avidity and avarice, lust and license, were of man's own making, could be overcome with time and love. Time she had, barely thirty when she met von Göttner and, in time, too, there took root in her the shoots of a love, that grew unseen and unheard, putting out over the months and years branches and leaves that one day would bear fruit. The day would come when her man…, in the interstices of her secret heart Armin was then and ever *her* man, would tire of of his libertine gluttony, growing weary of the tawdry engagements of fleeting hours, without savour, without memory. Surely, then, he would turn to her, lover and bride, able to offer satisfactions enduring, swaddling him in the warmth of a passion abiding, granting him without reserve body, heart, mind, all she had, her entire being. So she waited.

"And waited…" Davidovich shook his head, with distant puzzlement. "But Armin never noticed. Strange. Christine was attractive in her own way, tall, slender, an angular face, good features. The dark eyes behind the glasses, intent and severe, could be provocative, seductive for other men. Not Armin. Oh, he was generous enough with her, lavish with his gifts, for her birthday, name day, at Christmas. The one thing she so wanted he never gave. Never a look that betrayed some inner intent, recognition of her as a woman, never, as far as I know, even a passing curiosity about her private life, feelings and sentiment.

"In those years she travelled around with him quite a bit, accompanying him on concert tours, especially on engagements overseas. They'd be away together weeks at a time, staying in the same hotels, together at dinners, receptions, she always within reach, at his beck and call night or day, at times saving his skin and his name. Once, at a summer music festival, Salzburg maybe, after the concert Armin was boarded by an insistent female fan. A svelte young woman, I was told by a friend who was there. The long and the short of the incident was that around midnight there was shouting and screaming in Armin's room. The svelte music fan was asking the maestro for a lordly sum, that he of course didn't have on him. Apart from loose change, he never carried cash. Called to the scene, Christine took the cocotte aside, heaven knows what she told her, and managed to send her away with a small 'gratuity.' It must have been galling for her, truly painful. But then, as they say, love conquers all, bears all. And she put up with that, as well.

"Hard to imagine how it might have ended. I mean the dreams Christine had nursed for so long. My old father, a great expert of the Torah, used to say that sometimes there's a beginning but no end. So one passes a lifetime patiently waiting at the door. And then, bang!, the door shuts suddenly, and there's only darkness.

"A couple of years before Armin had the first stroke, Christine was diagnosed with uterine cancer. They caught it a bit late, Stage 3 or something. Already metastasized, evidently. She was treated back in her place, in Annecy. Once or twice I went down, once with Armin. Painful, not at all a pretty sight. Christine was one of those persons one could never imagine taking ill. Never absent, always punctual, precise, meticulous, muscular in her ways, there was about her something hard and enduring. Yet there she was, shrivelled, the face colourless with the pallor of death, so small, sunk in the tousled spread of a few strands of what remained of her rust-red head.

"Armin was across the waters, in Boston or Chicago, when she passed away. Miranda came with me to the funeral. The small village sloping up from the lake, very picturesque, couldn't have had more than a couple of hundred souls and they seemed to be all there crowded into the little village church. Very baroque, full of gilded *putti* and saints. Christine was a local daughter who had gone out into the world and made good, and they had all come to say their farewell. In the surprisingly big cemetery on the hump of a rise every second name on a headstone was a Laforge. I expect they were all related in some way. We met the mother afterwards. A daunting old lady all in black with a snow white head, tall and ramrod erect, with a striking calm, the grief little visible on the fine features. As if she had seen it all before time and again. Evidently Christine had taken a lot from her. I gave her my hand and all she said was '*Ça arrive.*' Not another word.

"We drove back mainly in silence. Miranda looked through the window when I dropped her off. "The mother's right," she nodded. "It happens. *Si, si sucede.*" Southern stoic patience, I suppose.

"Armin sometimes gave the impression of being indifferent, indeed almost nonchalant about life and death. As something that was of no particular concern for him. When someone he had known for years departed, an old colleague, a fellow conductor who one day went out swimming in the sea and drowned, he might mention the event casually, nothing out of the way, just another incident or accident. Things that happened. Christine's passing away did, I think, make a dent. For months afterwards he'd say, 'She would know how to deal with this,' or 'If only Christine were here.' Or "Laforge had warned me about this fellow.' In the early months, working in his study, he'd raise his head and call out to Miranda, asking for Christine. It was sometime before his absent-mindedness noticed that her presence had departed the house.

"Armin never much showed it, in word or gesture, but he was fond of Christine. Informal though it was, their day to day relationship was also very workman-like, practical, the nuts and bolts of managing Armin's professional life. Christine also supervised the sundry details of the household, bills, insurance, repairs, maintenance. Matters for which Armin had neither the time nor patience. He'd look out of the window, at the patch of green with a tall hedge and a couple of cherry trees in the front of the building, and then ask Christine why there was a man in the garden and what he might be up to. Trimming the hedge, she'd tell him with quite patience, as if explaining the location of the stars to a child. 'Can't remember having seen him before.' Yet the same elderly man had been coming year after year to see to the garden! No head for practical details, time, money, the clothes he wore. Like a baby, needing to be nursed, fed, put to bed. Christine had to even keep track of and insist on his medical check-ups. She really was his angel. Women do things for love, even when there's no return."

Davidovich found it difficult to put in words what von Göttner might have felt for Christine. Love unlikely, fondness or affection it might well have been, perhaps more the sort of unfeeling and mechanical attachment of an aged couple, sympathetic but shorn of the warmth rising from the depths of the heart, neither desiring nor expecting anything more than the presence of the other. He was fond of her but took her presence for granted, much as one might the presence of an old piece of furniture, useful, essential even, that somehow one could not do without. Sentiment, but not sentimental, without any particular depth of feeling. Perhaps just as well, Davidovich mused. Any show of emotion in the attachment would have only added fuel to Christine's schemes and dreams.

"But I was telling you about the wedding…"

"And what wedding would that be?"

Gabriel had come out to top up the bowl of olives on the table. A flowery apron around the front, he stood before us with hands on his hips in a commanding housewifely stance.

"This man talks of weddings, everyone's except ours. When will that be, dear?"

"I'm a law abiding citizen of this great, backward country. We may be ready, but not the law." Davidovich looked up at his companion with a sly smile. "Unless, Gaby, you're still interested in my offer of a trip to…"

"No, no, absolutely not!" Gabriel protested in a high voice. "I'm not having a $50 wedding in Las Vegas, with a drunk officiating as priest in a cardboard church. Will you please tell this man, Professor, that a marriage can't be sanctified with a cheap snake-head copper ring from an Indian reservation souvenir shop." With that he turned on his heels and with brisk steps made his way indoors.

Their back-and-forth reminded one more of the banter in an amateur pantomime, the intimate affection evident in the pretence and play-acting. Davidovich somewhat heavy-set and more weighty in manner, Gabriel light-footed, colourful, something of a butterfly, one a foil for the other, their union could, on felt, survive and endure in time.

"As I was saying, the wedding… Turned out to be a bit of a farce, a bizarre affair. Armin had told Laurant it was to be out of the way, away from the public eye. And believe me, it was. So out of the way a satellite would have found it difficult to locate!"

Having to do with his artistic clients over the years, Laurant had become a past master in satisfying the oddest of whims and rare eccentricities. Armin von Göttner was in fact one of the less demanding among his clientele.

One renowned Indian sitar player touring several European capitals refused to touch food unless prepared by a high caste Hindu, a Brahmin. "A tall order!" Davidovich chuckled. "Where in those days could one find a Brahmin cook in Bonn dishing out veg and vegan?"

Laurant, being Laurant, took up the challenge, managed to dig up a well-tanned Greek from Lesbos or Lemnos, one of those islands, working as waiter in a gyros rotisserie. Dressed up with a sacred string across the bare chest and a few beads around the wrist, forehead daubed with a smear of saffron, the man was presented to the maestro as an expert cook from the Brahmanic tribe. But regrettably, both deaf and mute, he was told. Satisfied that his ancestral dietary constraints had been observed, after several days of tea and toast the sitar master dug heartily into the meal smuggled in from an Indian restaurant recently opened near the Bundestag. Applause all around, the maestro complimenting Laurant between one grateful burp and another before retiring to strum on his sitar, save for an unexpected slip at the last minute, the witless Greek blurting out *'πολύ ευγενικά, κύριε!'* [1] on receiving an over-generous tip. With the upshot that Laurant's list of clients lost its only classical sitar musician.

---

[1] 'Most kind, Sir!'

Operating out of the spacious offices of his company, ARTISTES UNIS, on the Rue la Fayette, Laurant and his sizeable staff left no stone unturned in their effort to meet whatever the request of the clientele, which possibly explained why few, if any, abandoned Laurant's stable. Sometimes over a drink or at the table, Laurant would regale the company with tales of the fanciful, at times bizarre demands of this or that artiste, with no names mentioned unless dead and buried, his experience having taught him that for many a professional performer the line between art and life blurred over, the mask becoming the man, the actor playing Othello through a long season gradually growing suspicious of the wife's fidelity, the public prima donna turning prima donna in private, as well.

"It's the prerogative of the gifted," Laurant would concede with indulgence. "We others live a single life, these people as many as the parts they play."

In his anecdotal reminiscence there was one particularly outré tale recounted by Laurant that had stayed with Davidovich. Possibly because it touched at the fringes of his own private preference.

One ageing rock star, a gold disc winner several times over, whose career Laurant had managed through half a lifetime, earning his company handsome contractual commissions over the years, was known to pick choice cherries from among his clamouring female fans. Mostly one-night stands. *A flying fuck*, the singer called it. A common habit in the pop world, this particular rocker had the extravagant habit of picking up among the groupies and bedding not one but a pair of young women at a time. The glory days mostly over and career on the wane, but the name not forgotten, age taking its toll had made the singing Casanova disinclined to hunt, pick and choose. Besides, too, no longer surrounded by pawing virgins swooning at this feet, he expected his after-concert morsel to be served directly in bed.

"This one you've got to hear," Davidovich laughed, breaking the still evening air.

Laurant's people had arranged with the local organizers during a short South American tour that the old rocker be provided, in the after-hours following the concert, with a couple of young women of the place, whose air was not to betray them overtly as ladies of the night paid for their services. A curious puritan strain, it was the vaunt of the man that he had never once paid for sex. If anything at all, he claimed, it was he who should have been remunerated for his extra-contractual exertions.

All had gone to plan, one city after another, the aged hunk a bit wobbly at the knee but managing somehow to stomp, hop and leap, with his signature wiggle of the hips, the rusty voice emitting the familiar choking barks and rasping shrieks. After a moderately successful performance in São Paulo, dined and wined, he found himself in the hotel suite with a couple of females of dazzling allure with outrageous bumps and curves. Lounging around with a drink as the ladies shed their frilly blouses and dropped the gold lame skirts, his eyes caught sight of rather generous bulges under the stringy tanga panties.

Returned from the tour, the singer mentioned the incident to Laurant. "Ah yes, Brazil," Laurant commiserated. "For that matter, one can't walk the pavements of certain streets in Paris without bumping into a dozen of these Brazilian viados."

"Well," said the rocker, not quite tongue-in cheek, "they were there, I was there, and they were what they were. What was one to do? And why waste an evening?"

No stranger to the often undefined latitudes of human propensities, yet Laurant could not help being taken aback. "Why indeed?" he nodded wide-eyed, never having suspected the man of such easy gender fluidity.

"Nor was the evening wasted," the Englishman had smiled satisfied.

"The thing about Laurant that struck you, once you got to know him," Davidovich said with a thoughtful air, "was his immense tolerance. The sort one might expect of a Buddhist Lama."

Himself no rake, he lived a quiet home life, when time allowed, with his second wife and a couple of daughters. No visible excesses, a love for the table, something of a gourmet, very particular about sausages.

"Moral turpitude in others was water off the duck's back, but sausages for Laurant…!" Davidovich laughed widening his eyes. "Coming over from time to time, to see Armin, also an aunt who lived somewhere in the south, going out for a meal he'd go dark in the face when offered sausage. Ah, the Swiss, he'd say, masters of clocks and the counting house, but still in the Dark Ages with sausages. Once, I remember, when the waiter at a small place brought him some by mistake, he cheerfully tossed the *Kalberwurst* out of the window, saying, Not fit for humans! The shocked waiter remonstrating, '*Mais monsieur, ils sont fait maison. Une Spécialité!*' House made or speciality, he would have none of it. Possibly, Laurant's only intolerance!

"Otherwise, never a word, not the least judgemental remark on the follies and foibles of the tribe whose affairs he managed. Silent even about the well-known penchant of a stage actor of the Comédie Française for very young girls. For some, this looking away made at times for a suspect impression, his neutrality taken for tacit assent. One year when Christine was in Paris with Armin, after an evening at the Comédie for some piece by Racine, with that actor in the lead part, Christine in passing touched on the man's predilection for the under-aged in a vaguely caustic tone, suggesting that Laurant's indifference bordered on moral default.

"More a sort of amorality," Davidovich mused. "I suppose you could call it that. As often with the French. But of course Christine was a bit straight-laced, at least outwardly, often severe in her judgement. Laurant was piqued by Christine's insinuation, though. *'La loi. La loi du pays'* he told her. 'It's for the law of the land, eventually for heaven. I don't have the authority of the one or the other.' Very likely Christine couldn't understand that with a thinner skin Laurant would have had to change his trade.

When von Göttner announced his intention to marry Ursula, Laurant took it in his stride. No questions asked, why the maestro in his condition, so soon after that first stroke, mild though it was, would want to commit himself to an unknown young woman just met, of uncertain provenance, too. It would have been fine just to bed her and have a fling, like all the other times. The possible legal implications of a marriage apparently worried Laurant. Love was all very well, but love passed, and if the union were to be short-lived, she could lay who knew what claims to his money and estate.

Above and beyond their professional rapport, they were also friends, had been together almost from the time Laurant had set up in business. Less interested in the maestro's choice of a wife, his well-being and finances were uppermost in Laurant's concern. He had in mind to suggest perhaps a pre-nuptial agreement, as had become the practice of late among celebrities and names that counted. But in his accustomed manner, he refrained from stepping into the bedroom and boudoir of another. Yet he did wonder and aired his thoughts with Davidovich before the wedding.

He could not help wondering why a man who had lived in the limelight through a lifetime, glad to bask in the attention and applause of the world, should suddenly want to conceal himself from the public eye, as though about to commit something illicit, cause for shame or scandal. Was it perhaps awareness of possible ridicule, the oblique smile and the compassionate look, occasioned by the veritable chasm between man and bride, a span of almost fifty years. Feeble age and blooming youth, decrepitude and maidenhood, entwined in a dance piteous and out of season, without prospect, the tomorrows on the calendar already crossed!

To Laurant, Ursula did not much look a maiden, with the -head preserved, or otherwise. Nor, for that matter, apart from passing aches and chills, and recovered from whatever the visible effects of the stroke, was von Göttner infirm and wasted; if anything, firm, upright and robust, appetites intact, he appeared the equal of any man. The hush and secrecy around the wedding Laurant found inexplicable. But faithful friend and trustee, he executed the maestro's wishes to the letter.

Locating a small village in the uplands of one of the Cantons to the north, he made a couple of trips to the locality to put in place the necessary arrangements. A closed community of a hundred odd souls, the males barrel-shaped and taciturn, the women short and square wardrobes. Low wood and stone farmhouses littered across a shallow valley, a small shingle-roofed church with a tall pointy steeple on an overlooking rise.

"One of those places, Laurant said, that had yet to receive the news of Columbus's arrival in the New World! But very picturesque, totally off the beaten track. One would never have found it on the map. Can't really imagine how Laurant came across it. But then, Laurant is the type who can locate a needle but also a pinhead in a haystack."

The problem, evidently, arose with the pastor. A notable among the Lutheran clergy of the region, ageing and infirm, one eye gone and the other dim of sight, hearing often half-deaf even to a shout, he had begun to bumble and stumble at service and ceremonies, often passing into beatific sleep while the congregation sang, once nearly drowning a newborn at baptism. The ecclesiastical authorities had finally decided to put him to pasture, sending him over to the little village to put both him and the faithful out of harm's way. Enfeebled he might be, but the man was unwavering in his faith, an old school type, abhorring the worship of saints, castigating the inhabitants of the village every other Sunday for their devotion to a medieval folk figure, a certain Ellinus Barbatus, considered a saint of the pasture for having miraculously saved the ovine population of the area from a particularly virulent foot-and-mouth outbreak. The other hobby-horse of the senile pastor's muddled brain appears to have been to harangue the faithful from time to time against bearing the offspring of sodomy, that left the listeners in quiet as much of a muddle.

"Some of it might have been true, but I can't vouchsafe for the rest," said Davidovich raising his hands, adding that Laurant at times was given to baroque embroidery when recounting events and incidents. "Possibly the influence of an uncle of his, a satirical cartoonist for the weekly *Le Canard enchaîné*."

Apart from the bride, the only other women present in the dim interiors of the small church were Miranda and Christine Laforge. "One can just imagine Christine's state of mind. She might have taken some small heart from the fact that, going on past experience, Armin's constancy towards the women in his life was rarer than rare earth. A bit more serious this time around, but when did the marriage vow make a lamb of the wolf! Even so, can't have been easy to stand there watching Ursula beside Armin, a place that should have been hers, dreamt for so long.

"Ah, dreams!" Davidovich exclaimed. "Many of the tragedies of human life, I think sometimes, are caused by the fact that dreams are without border, boundless, without confines. Creating mirage and illusion. Would you agree, Professor?"

I nodded due agreement. Evidently a thinking man, there was more to Davidovich than merely the affable air and able fingers on the piano keyboard.

"And Miranda. Quite a sight, very much a matronly dowager got up in colourful brocade and a fine lace mantilla over the head, her usually concerned expression at ease. Glad, I think, that the maestro had decided to do the proper thing and wed in church, not *her* church but anyway sanctified and blessed by divine fiat."

Laurant, sauve and elegant, got up in a three-piece from some famous men's tailoring house in Paris, stood at Armin's elbow as best man. Armin himself, in an ivory linen suit, exuding a debonair and youthful air, head well coiffured, the long locks in order. No visible trace of the recent stroke, he appeared to have shed years from his great many summers, a groom more mature than elderly next to his young bride. And Ursula was a sight, shedding light in the dim interiors of the church. Wide-eyed and veiling whatever her anxiety behind timid smiles, she was no less than ravishing, the half-sleeve, simple silvery organza sheath with sparse silver thread vines setting off with effect the sinuous and generous de Milo figure.

"I was to play a couple of short airs from Bach, *Jesus bleibet meine Freude* and a couple lesser known from one of the late cantatas. Perched half way up, it was a very tight fit. Had Armin selected any piece calling for more vigorous playing, I'd have toppled over from the console and smashed my brains on the stone floor. But the organ itself...!" Davidovich laughed. "The pipes were probably clogged with age and you should have heard the poor creature, the squeaks and squeals, the sudden shrill bursts, more like a windy intestine letting off air. The pedal drone was more like a buzz. Afterwards Armin let me know what he'd always suspected, that I had no future as a church organist!"

"Gabriel must have loved the curious set-up."

Davidovich shook his head. "No, he wasn't there. He'd not appeared on the scene as yet. I met him a few years later at an architecture heritage party. One of the benefits of having been a minor celebrity is that once in a while one gets invited to tedious arty seminars, but at least with drinks and canapés afterwards.

"So there we were, a warm late summer day, all dressed and trussed, but no sign of the pastor. He had received us when we arrived, ushering each through the entrance with a fluttering wave of the arm. We filed in, took our places, but the old codger meanwhile had disappeared from sight. We waited and waited. Finally I worked my way up to the organ perch and was settling in at the console when suddenly he rose from behind the altar. I can tell you it was a startling sight in that dim light coming in through the narrow, heavily-leaded windows. The sharp skeletal face, the pulpit robe hanging loose on that stick-thin figure, with a cape thrown over the shoulder, he looked more like the Grim Reaper come to harvest us! Stepping forward, he moved up close, squinting at each face. Raising a withered hand, he counted the company. Bride, groom, best man. Then the trouble started, with the hand fluttering mid-air at the space beside Ursula.

"Who was to give away the bride, he asked with a thin croak. No answer forthcoming, he insisted. 'Who authorizes this woman to be married? Who?'

"No one was prepared for this turn of events. Armin looked around wide-eyed, quite perplexed. Then Laurant incautiously announced that the bride's parents were absent owing to a mourning in the family. And that did it!"

Scowling, querulous in voice as if personally offended, the old pastor had launched into an inquisitorial enquiry. No father? Not even a mother? How could that be? An orphan? Was the maiden an orphan?

"Ursula made to open her mouth. But intimated by the one eye with a flickering vision boring into her, she thought the better of it. Unbelievable what followed. Even Laurant looked nonplussed."

Davidovich cleared his throat before launching on an imitation of the Pastor's quivering preachment, more a rancorous cackle. *"Know that a bride is a gift offered to a man, for joy, care, safekeeping. Know too that no soul on earth, if not that of Satan, comes alone. A child is born to a man, a daughter to a father. A human is born of a seed and only he who has planted the seed may give the fruit away."* Voice rising by a full tremulous octave, Davidovich raised his arms to the heavens. "*Divine law so ordains. So it shall be! It cannot be otherwise. Nor shall it be in this house of the Lord!*"

"Or something to that effect. Quite a performance, I can tell you. Everyone stood there looking foolish, stunned."

Exhausted by the stern peroration, breathless and snorting, peering up-close at bride and groom, the best man, his gaze shifted over towards Christine Laforge, Miranda and her husband, as though to ascertain that his stentorian syllables had been heard and understood. It was then that Laurant's quick wits woke and he said, with head lowered and in a tone meek and reverent, "How right you are, Father. How right! Man is truly born of a seed… As it happens, the young lady has a relative waiting down in the village. Please allow me a few minutes to go and fetch the person." Heads turned to look at Laurant, quizzical stares following him out as he made for the entrance.

"Hard to believe, David," I said.

Amused by his telling of the farcical episode, a boyish grin spread across Davidovich's face. "All true. Absolutely! Remember I was there, up at the organ desk with a clear bird's eye view. You could have asked Ursula if… Laurant told me afterwards that as the Pastor spoke, the air clouded over with the heady smell of schnapps. Oh yes, the old fellow was properly soused! And when Laurant left, he straight-away limped back behind the altar, for another swig or two, I suppose. Surprising that he could stand on his feet at all!

"Laurant drove down to the village, heading for the little *Bäckerei* in the square. He had made the acquaintance of the baker on his previous visit, rather impressed by the outsize *Vogelnestlii* in the shop window and taking back with him a whole boxful of the tarts. Well, he rushed in, told the baker in a few words that the bride risked being left at the altar without someone to give her away, and asked if he could drive up with him and stand in as an uncle or some such relative.

"'Oh, the Pastor! Drunk again, is he? Starts at the morning mass, shuts himself in the church and the bottle's empty by lunch time!'"

Sorry, said the baker, but he couldn't help. He was in the middle of the day's bake and he had to deliver several trays for a birthday in the next village. Suggesting that it only needed to offer the Pastor a bottle of something strong, which would do the trick, he turned to poke and pry the contents of the oven with his heavy wooden peel.

Quietly working at a wide table at the rear, the baker's wife, an apple-cheeked, roly-poly figure, shorter than her giant of a husband by a good measure or two, had listened to the exchange in silence as she worked a spread of pastry. At the baker's refusal, she looked up with a girlish smile, rubbed the dough off her hands and said, "'I'll come with you, Sir.'" Without removing the apron over the work smock, the flour-speckled rust red head looking like a fine bridal veil, she came around to join Laurant. The pair exited the shop with the baker's loud jocular words ringing in their ears, "'Please mind that the old fool doesn't marry off my woman instead!'"

All finally ended well, with the Pastor peering down at the baker's wife and raising his dim sight to Ursula's imperious height, muttering "*Mutter und Tochter*? Mother and daughter, good, good!" Filling the air with his short, alcoholic breath, he proceeded with the ceremony, making Armin wince with his repeated "*Dieser junge Mann*" and "*Diese Jungfrau,*" while Laurant gulped to hold back a smile at the mention of the couple as young man and virgin maiden.

After a mercifully short sermon on the sanctity of the marriage bed and the bride's duty to submit to the grooms every wish and caprice, the exchange and the blessing of the rings, prayer and benediction with a deal of humming and hawing, much to the relief of all present, not least the Pastor himself with his exhausted lungs, von Göttner and Ursula were at last pronounced man and wife. Davidovich pounding at the organ console and working the pedals with all his might managed to produce enough squeaks and squeals from the pipes to resemble Bach's cantata air to see bride and groom out of the church. And coming down the steps from the organ station, he noticed the pastor dive back towards the chancel. "Probably for a last celebratory swig from his bottle of schnapps!"

Davidovich sat back, bemused by the memory. Shortly, summoned by Gabriel, we rose to move indoors for dinner.

"Given the bearing of false witness by the baker's wife," Davidovich opined good-humouredly as we took our place at table, "the courts would have likely granted a ready annulment of the marriage. Laurant for one was satisfied with the show he had managed to put on, worthy of a minor impresario. Very grateful, too, for the baker's wife's willing services. Returned to Paris, he sent the good woman a big faïence jar from Quimper filled with Ladurée macarons."

~~~

"*Mettre de l'eau dans son vin!* One heard this refrain through the hot months of summer. My father adding some water to his glass of wine, mother looking on and scowling through the words. Wine might be made of water mostly but, according to her, once on the table, the two did not mix. And it didn't always end there, with a frown of disapproval. Now and again, father would add insult to injury, reminding her that the Lord she prayed to had once added gallons of water to the wine at a wedding? Receiving the speedy retort, 'And he was one of your famous tribe!'

"I used to look from one to the other, wondering, as I grew, how the two had come together, and even more of a wonder, how they had managed to stay together through the years. There's no telling of the choices of humans, even so they were as apart as oil and water, never mind wine and water! Homo Sapiens both, maybe, but heavens, how different two people can be!

"Father…" Davidovich spoke very slowly, as though carefully treading towards something rare and precious, "my father you'd have liked. A Hasidic Jew from Odessa, probably the Jewish capital of the world at the time. Learned, steeped in the pages of his faith, from a wealthy and urbane family, in looks there was nothing Jewish about him, or at least what passes as the Jewish stereotype. Tall, broad-shouldered, light-haired and bluish eyed. No doubt about it, he'd have been certified by Himmler himself as a model Aryan male!

"A pity that ancestral curiosity only wakes when one gets older. I wish I'd asked him for the details, but the lives of elders isn't of much interest to the young. In any case, with the Germans at the gates of the city, at his mother's insistence he made his escape. Travelling across the Ukrainian plains by foot, under haystacks on horse carts, clinging to the wagons of goods trains, he slowly made his way west. Don't know how, but he managed to get a job working for the Red Cross. And finally landed at the ICRC offices here in Geneva. And here too he met my mother.

"In some of the villages, small towns around the lake area, you can still come across women like my mother. Mostly elderly now, modest, laborious, severe in their faith. Good-looking in her own way, slender even in age, mother had the looks of a china doll, delicate and fragile. Appearances can deceive. In fact, she was as strong and stubborn as tempered glass. An unequal match, my father used to joke, because she always had hovering behind her back not only her Lord but also his spokesman Monsieur Jean Calvin to back up any argument.

"As I was saying, I for one never understood what they had seen in each other. As for the magic glue that kept them together… Curious, they really were inseparable. Parting only when the famous bell tolled for the one, then the other! Father went first, mother only a year later. As if her own lungs had begun to empty without his breath beside her.

"One hears sometimes that it's sex that keeps two people together. Don't think so, not over several decades. The physical isn't limitless. The cuddling and copulating has its limits. Just think of Ursula and Armin. Warriors between the sheets in the early years, no doubt. Later, things were more platonic, so to speak. But they stuck it out.

"None of us," Davidovich went on, "friends, old associates, would have bet a florin or franc that Armin and Ursula's marriage would have lasted. A year, a couple of years, at best. Armin just was not the marrying kind, to put it that way. I knew, but not many did, that he'd been married once, as a young man, fleeing the Russians as they advanced into German territory towards the end of the war. The daughter of an old family chambermaid, of all people. Something of a curiosity. She had died at childbirth soon after, apparently. The new-born, as well. Don't mean to be cruel, but maybe just as well. Impossible to imagine one like Armin playing single father, changing diapers, cooing into a baby's ears. It was a time when he could barely keep body and soul together, never mind nannies and help to look after the infant. Becoming a father might be the easiest thing in the world. But not everyone is cut out for fatherhood. Armin certainly wasn't. I once saw him holding Laurant's little baby girl. He'd have done better with a sack of potatoes!

"Anyway, he never looked back. No nostalgia, no sentiment for the son he might have had. The prospect of family and family life out of the way, for the rest of his days he became a swashbuckling bachelor, cutting a swath through the womanhood of the earth. Revolving door loves and lovers, opera singers, would-be divas, comely cello players. No chambermaids, though!"

Mirth in his voice, Davidovich chuckled at the recall of some particular memory of his maestro's licentious living.

"Ah yes, take your pick. Nothing and no one was sacred for Armin, as he lowered his trousers and raised skirts in every capital city of the world! As I told you, curiously enough Christine was exempt from his diligent siege of the females who came his way. To think that she more than most longed for his hand reaching out to her. Poor thing, she'd have given herself body and soul, without second purpose, wanting nothing, just a little attention, a touch of affection. Does it not prove, Professor, that prayers are almost never self-fulfilling!

"But don't get me wrong. Libertine certainly, but Armin was neither a roving Casanova nor a Don Juan. His casual seductions carried no weight, nor inflicted particular damage. But he was choosy, no fling or flirtation much below his station. As also a mortal dread of being tied down. Permanence was not his forte. He lost interest in things that lasted too long. Even a dinner, a party, a reception. Halfway through he'd find some excuse to leave. The only exception was a music score, however long never too long for him. He thought Bruckner's Ninth Symphony still incomplete even after some musicologist added on the missing last movement. For the rest, everything else had to be short, succinct, brevity in speech, at the table, in bed. At times, it made for trouble. At times…

"There was the wife of this doctor, an eminent cardiologist in Bern, head over heels in love with him. Ines, Isabel… I'm poor with names."

Apparently, they'd had a short affair after meeting at some Red Cross charity event. One of Armin's usual fly-by-night encounters. It had lasted a month or so, but the woman refused to let go. Calling him early in the morning, late at midnight, coming over at weekends. With long hours at the private clinic, often travelling the globe for conferences, the doctor husband was not a problem. But no one and nothing would have stopped the wayward lady.

"She'd have paraded nude around the lake had Armin asked," Davidovich chuckled. "She was that besotted with him. Not that it would have been an unpleasant sight, from Miranda's description of her. *Señora muy florida, si muy sabrosa.* Or something of the sort."

At his wit's end, von Göttner had, apparently, taken to hiding in his own house when she came calling. It was Christine who finally came up with the idea, surprisingly malicious for one like her. An anonymous message was mailed to the doctor at his clinic. It was expected that husband and wife would settle the score between them. It worked, but not the way it was meant to. A couple of weeks later the cardiologist presented himself at the house. Miranda and her husband had their day off and Christine was out on some errand. Armin answered the door and got the full blast of the husband's fury. Eminent the doctor might have been but was less so in appearance, short and chubby, half Armin's height, and there he was tearing his throat out, bawling, "You've been fucking my wife, you bastard!" and a whole string of racy terms perhaps not quite in keeping with a cardiologist's profession.

"Some might have suffered a heart siezure, calling for the eminent doctor's services on the spot! Not Armin. Unfazed, he invited the doctor in, sat him down and poured him a drink. What passed between the two we never came to know. But nothing was seen again of the adulterous wife, nor of the cardiologist husband. Armin had this ready talent of both brushing people the wrong way, as also making them inoffensive.

"Don't know about you, Professor, but I'm not up on my Freud and Jung. Possibly a shrink might conclude that for Armin the phallus was an extension of the conductor's baton. Wave the wand, seduce the audience, take the bow and go your way. That was what we others expected of his affair with Ursula. I mean, what was there to keep them together for long, never mind a lifetime. He'd been sent to this clinic in some backwoods area to the north, seen this swell of a creature in a nurse's uniform, got the heats, and laid her. And that should have been the end of it, like all the other times.

"True, the first sight of her was breathtaking. So much so that…" Davidovich paused, pressing back a smile. "Seeing her for the first time, I couldn't help doubting for a moment my own gender preference! Rare, very rare, the perfection of face and figure, curiously innocent and provocative at the same time. Ursula was then in her mid, maybe late twenties, at the height of her bloom. Oddly enough, she remained little changed even through later years. There are those who don't age much until mid-life. Something to do with the bone structure, I once read somewhere. My mother was one of those. At sixty she was as she had been at forty, with a few wrinkles here and there, the midriff wider. The Ursula you met was a passable copy of what she had been at the time of her marriage, just a bit heavier in face and a little more abundant elsewhere. Of course, by then the younger Ursula had dissolved in thin air. Looks apart, she was in no way the same person. Her own mother wouldn't have known her!"

One was struck with the analogy Davidovich employed to narrate the transit from Nurse Füssli to Ursula von Göttner. In her nursing days, he said, she might have been a slab of butter, flat, submissive and mindless. After the marriage, von Göttner had taken her in hand, gradually impressing on the contour-less matter shape and identity, breathing into the inert substance life and character. It was like watching a statuary figure, lifeless and will-less, come alive, move and walk, sure of itself and with a voice of its own.

"And the creator obviously owns his creation. There was no getting away for Ursula, had she even ever wanted to do so. My father used to cite something from the Talmud, that says that trusting in God we live as God desires. She trusted Armin and became what he wanted her to be. There was no way she could ever leave him, even when later through all those years he was stretched out mostly dead."

Davidovich paused briefly, with a thoughtful nod. "There was the other thing father used to say at times. One might turn one's back and deny his God, but believer or apostate, the point of reference was always the Creator. Ursula had affairs here and there, fucked a few other men along the way, but it was always Armin sat like a silent Buddha at the centre of her being. Her centre of gravity... Incidentally, I've always thought that the atheist is the only true believer! His insistent denial is perforce admission of the existence of the divine. Like the little boy adamant that the vanished cream tart was never there!"

"And you, David? A believer?" I ventured. "If I may ask."

"Hard to say," he pursed his lips with a bemused look. "One finds oneself here, just a mite clinging to a clod of earth, in the shadow of a giant figure, peering down, claiming to be your maker, friend and father, Alpha and Omega. Does one have a choice? And then, when through childhood you've had Calvin's beady eyes looking down at you in the living room and your father putting you to sleep with *kinder majses* fables... One of my favourites was about a Passover feast where a goblet of wine magically grows bigger and bigger. At table the next day I repeated it to mother. Only to hear her say, 'Not much of a surprise, Davy. With your father's people multiplying the wine with water, the goblets could even be barrel-sized!' So, yes, I was luckier than most, if you like. Buffeted between two gods, never quite managed to settle on the one or the other!"

A bit of a pity I got to know Davidovich somewhat late in the day, when my time was almost up. One could have done with his amiable and thinking companionship, laced with quite humour and a gentle irony, during the long weeks alone at the

Villa Serena, the evenings vacated by Ursula's increasingly frequent absences, the mind dulled with unreasoned yearning, the work at hand neglected and deferred.

~~~

Davidovich had planned to make the couple of hours' drive to see how von Göttner was 'settling in' at the new palliative care wing of the Grünewald Klinik. I had come over for a night's stay at his place, intending to travel with him, to take a last leave of Ursula, a farewell of sorts. Workmen coming in to see to some fault in the air flow of the wine cellars, our trip had been postponed for the following morning. Gabriel away for the day on an architectural commission in a nearby town, the housekeeper putting together our lunch, Davidovich took me on a leisurely tour of the winery.

The land levelling out behind the château, the broad undulating plateau of several acres was planted row and row with vines, a low stone building at the far end half-hidden by clumps of apple and pear trees, with long underground cellars running beneath. We strolled down the length of the lanes between the lines of gnarled trunks rising from the ground and twisting away along the runners. Picking here and there at the odd grape turned raisin on the leafless branches, Davidovich explained briefly the history of the Gamay vines brought there long ago from Burgundy by Cistercian monks, some of the ones there now arrived later from the time of his grandfather. His expertise as wine-maker provoked a thought I hesitated to put in words, but finally did in a brief lull during his talk of it being possibly a good year thanks to the dry late summer.

Leaning against the fence surrounding the grounds of the stone winery, he gazed thoughtfully over the rows of vines we had walked across. "Why did I give up a promising career? A pertinent question. You're not the first to ask, nor I suppose will be the last. Sorry to say, I've no precise answer. Several reasons, I expect, but the truth is I don't really know. People don't believe that. I've heard it said that I was just trying to be rare and precious. Following in the footsteps of the likes of Horowitz, Michelangeli Benedetti, not that I was ever in that league, or even in the vicinity. Horowitz, Benedetti… Hermit geniuses who sallied out in public every other leap year, gave a concert or two before retreating back to the den again. I was no genius, better than good perhaps, but in no way God's great gift to the musical world.

"One thing though, I did have a certain flair, a fairy touch that often brought the audience to its feet. Personally, it impressed me far less. At times I felt like a cheat, passing off a mere glittery gemstone as a twenty carat diamond. I must have got it from my father. He could make a small slab of meat sound like a royal roast at a banquet!"

Davidovich glanced at the time and hauled himself upright. "The truth maybe is that we are never a good judge of our own talents. There's this doubt that eats away. And you ask, too, if it's a gift in perpetuity? Think of all the child prodigies, the wunderkinds who hopped onto the stool on the concert stage and one day simply disappeared from view. Or the one book author of a great work slipping into life-long silence. Frightening. What then for the rest of one's time here. Like trying to stretch out the first hot, sunny day into an entire summer! So better to take the bow while the applause lasts and tip-toe out through the side door.

"Just the opposite of what Armin refused to accept. For him exit from the stage was inconceivable, unless carried out feet first. Then when he began to be shown the door, his mind elaborated this folly. Ursula was to be the magic stone to raise the roof with hosannas to the once great Armin von Göttner. His name, more than whatever her talent, meant to parachute her into the midst of a clamouring crowd that would swoon at his feet once again."

"It didn't work out, did it?"

"Miracles might be witnessed in Lourdes. *Mais même là, un evénément rare!*"

With that he took my arm and we walked back to the house for lunch.

~~~

At table Davidovich was curiously less his usual jovial self. One soon discovered the reason. The old housekeeper returned to the kitchen and out of hearing, straight-faced he informed me that Céline was averse to excessive mirth at table. Permeated with the strictures of her upbringing, she conformed faithfully to the Calvinistic credo of moderated pleasures, whether of palate or bed, gorging at meals or fornicating at will seen as abuse of the precious gifts of her God. Davidovich still could recall Céline's fury and telling his mother 'boys now, wastrels afterwards!' when one birthday party had got out of hand a bit, with his school friends throwing bits of *cremique* at each other and smearing faces with cream.

Céline had come to the house as a young woman and never left. "She and my mother were two of a kind. Grown from the same roots. The only difference was that we were propertied people, Céline's family worked a small patch of land, with the women employed in the bourgeois houses in the area. For the rest, shared habits of mind, shared beliefs, worshipping together, prudent and penny-wise, there wasn't much of a difference. Perhaps moderate wealth and well-being had made mother a little more indulgent. She had to be, what with father's habits.

"Some of Father's habits… totally out of step from those of my mother, Céline's too." Davidovich tilted back his head, his voice softening in reminiscence. "I remember him sneaking into the house from time to time with boxes of cream pastry and outsize chocolate cakes. There was always a Biblical excuse, some quote from the Exodus or Leviticus, the Feast of Trumpets, the Feast of Tabernacles, a feast of this or that. True or spurious, mother could not know, as she heard him out in stony silence. She would look away, pretending indifference when he opened one of those boxes at the table. In the end she had her generous slice and enjoyed it, too. Then when Céline came to clear up and saw the cream and chocolate smeared plates, mother in turn would repeat, as if in apology, Feast of Trumpets, Feast of Pentecost, Purim. Mother was familiar with the names, if nothing else. But can't imagine what Céline made of it. Very likely deplored once again father's immoderate habits.

"Thank you, Céline. Out, I think." Cordial, but Davidovich's voice was unusually loud, when the housekeeper came in to ask if we were to have our coffee at the table or out on the terrace. Apparently Céline's hearing was not what it used to be. Davidovich thought she heard only what she wanted to hear. "Never been a great talker, now she hears even less!"

He seemed amused, as we took our seats outside, by the thought that the housekeeper's sense of moderation and restraint extended beyond the table, a censorious eye judging even a person's presence and figure.

"It was, I think, a couple of years after they'd been married, maybe more. Armin and Ursula had come over one day for lunch. By then Ursula had changed, no longer the shy young bride, silent and retiring. She was on the way to becoming the diva Armin had in mind. Somewhat theatrical, with an easy laugh and surprisingly vocal. It did not go down well with Céline. Her idea of womanhood required a female, regardless of class, to be prim and demure, soft in voice and speaking only when spoken to. No surprise that she found Ursula a bit too forward, so to speak. A little too loud and showy. Worse still, her sense of propriety was offended by Ursula's figure, a physique overly handsome and abundant. Not often seen where she came from, most of the women laborious and work-weary, wiry in body and frugal with words. One like Ursula was more likely viewed as of suspect conduct and morals. Céline said to me afterwards, but more to herself, 'I wonder where the gentleman found the young lady.' Mother wouldn't have said it in so many words, but would probably have thought it. A bit impertinent of a domestic, but then Céline has been long in the house, almost since I was crawling around in diapers!"

The old housekeeper, said Davidovich, was not the only one to so wonder. Evidently not a few of those who knew and had known von Göttner had their heads turned when first meeting Ursula, for the better part curious where she might have come from.

"It wasn't so much the mismatch of age. Not that uncommon among those from the world of art. There was the 80 year old Pablo Casals with a bride of twenty. And here, closer to home, we had the great Charlie, a prolific father in old age, with a wife a third his years."

Not so much the age difference, in Armin's case, that raised eyebrows. In part, Ursula's somewhat Junoesque presence, but mainly it was her mysterious origins that was cause of the close look. Introducing her, Armin might only add that Ursula was from the north. He left it at that, leaving the listener to guess if it was north of Java or the North Pole. Even more curious was the way he hovered around her. Those familiar with Armin's habits of life were struck by the way he chaperoned her, always close, protective, like nannies with the children of the rich. But also with an evident air of adoration, side by side everywhere, almost a lovelorn youth. It was an Armin they'd never seen before, with no trace of the casual, off-hand manner during the usual short-lived flings with a variety of females. Obviously, neither they nor those closer to him knew of his plans of turning the lady into a diamond whose brilliance would rekindle his waning glory. Plain to see, though, that the alchemist was also utterly enamoured of his matter.

"We didn't see much of the pair after the wedding. They left soon after for Bratislava, I think. Armin had a summer stint directing a couple of operas. One a forgotten work by Meyerbeer, if I remember right. Light stuff, a walk-through for Armin. But Laurant had had to use all his weight to wangle the engagement. Can't have been easy. The truth was that by then Armin had become *persona non grata* with the management and musicians of the big theatres and opera houses. They'd had enough of the caprice and increasingly offensive antics of the old tyrant. Unlike wine, ageing had made him worse. Aged tigers, they say, become even more ferocious. Not much different with human despots, à la Stalin, Mao, Ceauşescu, to name but a few…"

"It's Father Time who helps us dig ourselves in even deeper!!"

"One had heard humans get better with age," Davidovich laughed. "Not true, then?"

"Only hearsay, David. Maybe true of saints alone. Not sinners."

"And what of those of us in the middle? Neither one nor the other."

"Mediocrity never left its footsteps in history. I speak for myself, obviously."

"Somehow it's difficult to think of Armin as being mediocre. Looking back, I think it was also that musical tastes were changing. Armin came from the old classical world, one of the last heavyweights. Out of time and out of place, the last dinosaur still roaming the plains. And dinosaurs have difficulty adapting to changing times. So, lighter interpretations, original instruments, throwing out the frills and ornamentations added in Victorian times, the stylistic solipsism of a bygone age. A new generation, newer perspectives. A bit like Nouvelle Cuisine cleaning up the act, dispensing with lard and rich sauce. And then the late-century mania, the somewhat absurd notion, absurd for me, of trying to reproduce the sounds heard in music halls in Vivaldi's Venice and old Vienna. Especially with all those acoustic panels crowding the ceilings and wings. Not to mention the stress on technique. Technique and more technique, with youngsters in their early teens, baby virtuous, outdoing Paganini's fireworks.

"Talking of changing times, the tonal and atonal were never a problem for Armin. As far as he was concerned, it had all been settled a long time ago, when Homo erectus first appeared on earth. With tonality running naturally in the blood, whether one beats on the bongo drum or runs up and down the sitar scale. The rest was forced artifice, baffling the expectations of the human ear. He rarely pronounced on the matter, but that was about the sum of his thinking.

"So, yes, apart from his personal quirks, Armin had also likely outlived his time. The musical ear does change with the generations. The other day I was listening to one of the renowned sopranos of the great 19th Century Polish School, Marcella Sembrich… something. Long double barrel name. Singing Bellini. Did it hurt the ears! Sounded like a parody. Partly, it was the ancient wax recording. But no doubt about it, voices do change down the ages. No less than styles in underwear!"

In his brief excursion recounting a changing world, what Davidovich did not mention, but I had heard from Ursula, was that about this time his own career had begun to go off the tracks. Davidovich saw Armin's taking a wife as an act of desertion. Or so Ursula thought. Whatever von Göttner might have been for him, putative father, master, guru and guide, Davidovich felt abandoned. It didn't much matter that in his usual manner the maestro often baited and tormented the younger man. No abuse or cruel word could shake the love and loyalty of the disciple. Even long after, talking of Davidovich, there was a hint of envy in Ursula's words, as though harbouring a grudge for the place he had had in her husband's life. That I had noticed myself.

The maestro, on his part, had never shown much sympathy for the disciple's wounded heart. Dismissing it, in his usual offhand manner, as the Jewish penchant for self-inflicted pain, he had once cited the Biblical tale of the priests of Baal mutilating themselves and letting out their blood. For von Göttner, an artist's character had to be forged on the anvil of pain, possibly a reference to his own early years, the loss of family, estate, wife and infant son. Davidovich, like his countrymen, had instead lived in a cradle of milk and honey, a land devoid of high human drama, strife, conflict and combat. Not quite the air that steeled the spirit against failure and despair.

Whatever the case, by Davidovich's own admission the immediate cause was that he had began to lose his touch, the flair and brilliance that had made his name. Until, following a series of concerts received at best with lukewarm words, a performance in some German city had drawn an openly scathing critique in the paper the following day, his playing called *unsicher*, uncertain, his 'fingers abandoned by the Muse.' Abruptly, barely in mid-career, he had decided to call it a day.

"Can't have been easy?" I remarked pointedly.

Davidovich looked away. "No," he admitted with a vaguely pensive air. "But not that difficult, either. I had won a major prize at the Tel Aviv Piano Master Competition and lost my father at an early age. I could execute a fortissimo flawlessly but sex I'd hardly had any. My universe consisted mainly of black and white keys, all my young years I'd lived in a mansion of sound, the world outside silent and unknown. One day, then, I felt the lease on the mansion had come to an end. Finally I walked out into life and the sunlight. Free of mentors and masters, audience and admirers, critics and detractors. My own man, at last!"

Well worded, but whatever he might have meant, the larger significance escaped me. Too close to the bone, some things behind the curtain are best left alone. One had learned that there were wounds in life that never quite healed, pricking and pressing the tender parts merely brought the pain alive. In his person Davidovich was likeable and companionable, and it was not my intention to peer into regions he preferred to skirt.

In any case, of greater interest to me was Ursula's time after the marriage, the lost years of her brief foray on the public stage and, subsequently, unable to meet her husband's lofty expectations, the fall from grace, from *diva futura* to mere wife. She had hardly ever touched on that melancholy season. If at all, cursorily, with some off-hand line of brittle irony, remarking with thin laughter that her Milanese voice teacher Marinetti's going to his grave was timely, not having to suffer hearing her in public. The self-belittling words, that concealed who knew what humiliation and pain, were almost the only reference to her failed prima donna dreams.

Davidovich recalled that he for one had not seen much of the newly-weds after Armin's engagement in Bratislava. They had come back to Geneva once in a while, staying over for a week or fortnight, before flying out again. Teresa kept track of their movements, answered correspondence, took care of things generally. By then she had begun to have troubles of her own, having to go down to Annecy for the preliminary treatment of her cancer. Miranda and her husband were still in service, keeping things ship-shape in the house for whenever Armin and Ursula chose to return.

"Was it Kierkegaard who said that life is best understood backward? Some truth in that, I suppose. At the time, Armin's continuous trotting around the globe with Ursula was something of a curiosity, incomprehensible. Quite out of character. Never a vacation idling in some resort, never a day's holiday. A year-long honeymoon, then. Improbable, knowing the man, his limited patience for anything other than music. What one never imagined was that the travelling and wandering about was merely the first chapter of a much larger design, a sort of Soviet

Five-Year Plan, with target and destination clearly set out. I don't think Ursula's herself was privy to the elaborate programme."

Davidovich's mirth at whatever the recollection startled and sent flying the couple of sparrows pecking around our seats. It was a private laugh, not meant to be shared. "Goodness, when I think back on it!"

That first year, he said, the maestro had given himself to bringing up baby, playing Professor Armin Higgins to Ursula Doolittle. Maestro in bed and maestro in life, he took the country girl in hand, getting her to shed the rough woollens and ill-fitting wear of Nurse Füssli, dressing her up in couture apparel, silk and satin, long gowns and pantaloons that set off stature, curves and contour to startling effect, the statuesque figure hung with white and old gold, not excessively showy, mostly pearl and coral from Boucheron and Bulgari.

The dressing, the bells and whistles, was the easy part, the dressage took time. Von Göttner wanted more than a still-life doll, a woman who could walk and talk, hold up her head in company, exude both glamour and grace, hold attention and engage, in readiness for the day when she would walk onto the stage before a live audience.

Quite a tall order, getting the Venus de Milo to come to life, dance and sing! Not that Ursula was any more ungainly than most, but not particularly comely either. Nursing life was not quite finishing school, with its preparation of gait, poise and manners.

"Professor Higgins-Pygmalion saw to that. Hard to believe, though," Davidovich shook his head, as if still in disbelief. "To take a grown person and change the persona. Plastic surgery can alter appearance, but character… It's one thing to reinterpret Mahler, but breathing new life into a figure of clay! One could only admire Armin's patience and persistence. Of course, he wasn't one who took no for an answer. Always knew what he wanted and usually got it, too.

"Once, I remember, he was especially keen on getting a year's residency with an orchestra. The management had hawed and hummed for months. Then the evening of the premier of the opera he was to conduct, he got Laurant to present the contract, with the threat of the maestro walking out out unless the administrators signed up. Blackmail, but he got his way. He always did.

"But changing Ursula Füssli into a salon lady was a whole different game. Talk of Daphne being chased by Apollo and turning into a laurel tree! Armin had waved his magic wand, turning a *lento* into *allegro!* When they came for lunch that time, in truth I had difficulty recognizing Ursula. I think I said something like, 'Madam, have we met before?' A bit of leg-pulling, but not that far-fetched, I can tell you. Where was the young woman one had seen at the wedding? Awkward, tongue-tied, ready to be frightened by a mouse. I had seen her briefly once or twice since, noticing only cosmetic changes, elegant in dress, a little more sure of herself. Now the difference was startling. The way she moved, looked you in the eye, vocal chords alive with gurgling laughter, charming and seductive. A bit artful, theatrical if you like, but quite sure of herself.

"That was the time Céline asked, '*Le Monsieur l'a trouvée où?*' Not one to be taken in by appearances, not our Céline! Yet… I can't help wondering what she might have had to say had I mentioned what I learned only much later. The soupçon of blue blood in Ursula from her mother, the daughter of old German nobility. So Armin had been told by the head of the clinic where he'd met Ursula. Well, I suppose it's not everyday that, lying on a hospital bed, you discover that the young woman in white sliding out the bedpan from under you just happens to be the descendent of a margrave or marquise. Life offers some strange encounters! Not all of them welcome… Like Ursula meeting a famous Icelandic writer at some reception. What was the man's name? Gunnarsson… Gudmunsson… Can't remember. Someone's son, anyway. A proper Nordic Casanova!"

The year's travelling had taken von Göttner and Ursula to major cities on the Continent and overseas. Schooling for her, to meet the world. For him a walk down memory lane, all the many sites of his erstwhile fame and acclaim. Calling at the theatres and opera houses where he had conducted for several decades, he was welcomed and well-received. Professionally an outcast, with hardly a single management willing to offer an engagement, yet he was no pariah, his name still carrying weight and evoking in memories the many triumphs that had over the years also helped the ascent of the careers of not a few singers and musicians, managers and administrators. At the dinners and receptions, Ursula caught a glimpse of the man he had been once, not so long ago, the place accorded him at table, the presence that silenced a room when he entered, the cordial respect with which his words were heard out.

Basking in an aura dimmed but not quite faded, von Göttner appeared to gain a renewed lease of life, seemingly shedding years in look and manner, easier of mood and freer in speech, limber in movement, intimate appetite in bed endowed with a vigour that for a fleeting moment or two awakened in the dark Ursula's memory of Pelosi's unrelenting grasp and embrace, less ardent, more driven by some primal esurience.

In those months of roaming Ursula discovered that Armin von Göttner was more, much more than the man she had married, a deal more than she could have imagined. Demanding and exacting, assertive and not infrequently short of tolerance, yet under the ancient embers she glimpsed grace and a finesse of spirit, generous beyond measure and a leniency concealed beneath belligerent syllables. And always by her side, a light hand guiding her around, protective and reassuring, ushering her through the company of figures more or less eminent, or at least important, men and women of talent and achievement with a secure foothold in the world of music, art and letters...

"That Icelandic writer I mentioned," Davidovich tapped his forehead. "For the life of me I can't remember the name. Gustavsson, maybe. Quite an acclaimed figure in his country, I was told. For years on the short-list for the Nobel. His new book was just out and he was here in Geneva for a reception offered by his publishers at the Palais Wilson. Ursula gave me the book later, after a quick read! Beyond avant-garde, definitely.

This Gustavsson had followed literally, to the letter, Kierkegaard's observation that life reveals it's meaning only when read backwards. The first page had the word 'ENDE' in block capitals, the last page a dedication to the latest of his several wives, preceded by the quote from Kierkegaard, *Life can only be understood backwards.* No text inbetween, 200 odd blank pages that you were meant to fill in yourself. Because, the blurb on the cover explained, fiction being make-believe and essentially fake, the sole reality the self, the one and only universe known to a human, each of us had to write our own story. Something like that. Nordic humour, I expect. Nothing new, of course. You might remember the blank white canvases with a slash here and a cut there, in vogue not long ago. Or wandering an art gallery hung with empty frames.

"Ursula was quite taken by it. 'I can do that,' I remember her giggling in my ears. I told her she certainly could, except that it took courage, perseverance, and a bit of a po-face! Her copy of the book is somewhere in the house, autographed by the author to a *Divine Goddess.* Well, that evening this goddess just about saved the author's skin!

"Armin was usually very liberal with Ursula receiving attention from other men. Maybe less of her, but he was very sure of himself. After all, who could dare prise and make away with the Kohinoor from the Queen's crown! He knew what was his and I think he quite enjoyed it, amused to seeing males flocking around her at those parties and receptions, flirting and courting, Ursula gradually learning to lend herself to the facile talk and banter common on these occasions. In fact, that's what he wanted, for her to stand alone, meet people and make her way through company. Part of her training to become familiar with the world in which he moved.

"It was quite a sight, I tell you, to watch her enter a room, tall and radiant, heads turning, half in disbelief. One could read the wonder in the eyes, as to where the Maestro had unearthed the splendid creature. Awkward and tongue-tied at first, Ursula learned and learned fast, speaking little, listening with a coy smile. Not too difficult, after all in the world of art people tend by habit to be verbose. All quite harmless, if a bit tedious. And whatever they might have had running in their heads, with Ursula most of these admirers were mainly flirty and playful.

"Not this Gustavsson chap. He overdid it, clinging like a limpet the moment they met, presenting Ursula a copy of the book, steering her around with a firm arm as if holding on to a prized possession. A proper satyr in high heat, under the effect of the several glasses of fizz he had downed. Halfway through the evening, drawing Ursula behind the heavy window drapes at the far end of the hall, the pair disappeared from sight. Armin and I were chatting with a couple of the other guests and I saw him catch the abduction, so to speak, with the corner of his eye. Excusing himself, he hurried across, to find Ursula pinned against the wall as the randy Norseman's itchy hands pawed her up and down.

"Armin could be unkind and odious, impossibly irascible at times. But his temper and tantrums were limited to words, language that could and did wound and draw blood. In all the years, though, I had never seen him raise a hand against man, woman or animal. Something there must have given way as he saw Ursula struggling to break free. The molester was big and brawny, but Armin was bigger, and he took the man by the neck of his white jacket, half-dragging him through the startled crowd out onto the terrace. After delivering a couple of resounding slaps across the dazed face, he would have toppled the man over the balustrade had not Ursula run out in time to hold him back.

"Drawn by the ruckus, people had drifted towards the glass frontage and caught part of the scene. The wretched author hurriedly slithered past me as I came out on the terrace. Ursula's arms were wound tight around Armin, holding him still. It made a certain impression, to see them that way, looking inseparable in the chiaroscuro half-light. Entwined, a single entity, like trees one sees in the woods sometimes, grown too close and the trunks joined. And it made me think, afterwards."

Watching them there that evening, Davidovich said, wound together, inseparable, somehow he felt that there would be no parting of ways for the two. Contrary to his initial expectations, and of those who knew the man, Armin would never leave Ursula. Nor she him. Laurant who had seen marriages galore among his famous clients, often wedded in March and parted in April, thought Ursula had come to stay. Armin he was less sure of, having seen him discard a gallery of females over the years. Like a child plucking the petals of a flower!

"Ursula, evidently, was no passing fancy, to be bedded and abandoned. Unusually for him, with her he was visibly paternal, possessive but also protective. Letting her loose, but never much out of sight. She in turn was submissive and obedient, going along with whatever he decided. Never a hint of dissent or complaint. Perhaps it was her upbringing. She might have told you about her father. Her mother, too. Hard, severe and dominating. In any case, for once I was right. They stayed together through thick and thin, together till the end.

"I'm obviously no expert in these things. Only what I saw as a boy. You look in from the outside, through a window pane, watch the two figures moving about, hear dimly the shouts, the sounds of loathing, and you think its the end of the road for the man and the wife. I remember how it was with my parents, with me sleepless in bed, dreading that father would up and leave. But something escapes us, that one can't see or sense. Must be the mystery of marriage. Something indissoluble, but impossible to read from the outside, even when the marriage comes unstuck, and however bitter the breakup. The chap who composed the marriage vow was spot on. *Till death do us part...*

"Yes, the Elizabethan Book of Common Prayer, from the ancient Latin *donec mors nos separavit...*"

"Maybe after all there's some truth in what they say, that marriages are made in heaven. A knot that can't ever be truly undone!"

"It takes effort, David, to keep a marriage on an even keel. You may be right about that lasting knot. Remember all the troubles Ulysses went through just to get back to his Lady Penelope?"

Davidovich heaved himself up with a laugh to answer the phone. It was Gabriel, saying he'd be back a little late and that we ought to proceed to the small restaurant where we were to dine in the old town.

Sat out in the mild air of the velvet twilight, the waiter serving us an aperitif of some aromatised wine as we waited for Gabriel, Davidovich looked at me a long, thoughtful moment over his glass before asking if I had ever heard Ursula sing. We had had more intimate moments but I had never heard her voice in song.

"No, I don't think I had that particular pleasure."

"Pleasant enough, clean, not much coloratura, though. A half soprano, or thereabouts. A good sense of melody and quite able in climbing the scales. It was in coming down that she often tripped. Something to do with her breathing, that voice teacher Marinetti couldn't satisfactorily correct. Which meant anything too operatic was out. Something like *O Mio Babbino*

Caro she could manage, even getting through the octave leaps. The melodic line is simple and the pianist can help out with a lighter touch. Beyond that…Armin of course knew her limits, yet hoped, unreasonably I think, that she might be able to tackle some more complex pieces. Hope, unfortunately, is no substitute for talent. Not meaning to belittle her…now that she's not with us. The truth was that she just didn't have it in her. Ugly ducklings turning graceful swans is only the stuff of fables.

"After training with Marinetti and the time in Vienna with a famous opera coach, more than two years later they came back here, to Armin's place, for about six or seven months. Armin asked me to go over once or twice a week, for practice sessions, to accompany Ursula through the repertoire he had chosen for her. It was plain he wasn't sure, at times quite nervous. After all, it was his head on the block. It was really about Armin von Göttner, his renewed presence on the stage. Ursula was only meant to throw new light and burnish his faded image. The songbird bringing to new life the once great maestro!

"I remember the afternoons sitting at Armin's Bösendorfer in the airy room upstairs. The accompanist can help or hurt the singer, it's an art by itself. I'd never done much accompanying and it was even more difficult with Armin sitting silent in a corner, listening to us. Afterwards, alone together, the two of us, he would ask, 'What do you think, David? Is she ready?' I should have, but didn't have the heart to tell him. It was oppressive. I began to have a sense of guilt. After all, I owed Armin much of what I'd been and achieved. Mentor and guide, but also a second father, if you will. To let him down now, make a fool of himself…"

"Was it that bad?"

"No, not bad. The difference between a decent weekend skier and one competing in a downhill event… Ursula, God bless her, was a good and simple soul at heart. To think of her being held up to derision and ridicule. Yes, she had a voice, good enough for the drawing room and amateur song contests. Not the professional stage. It made me cringe to think of the fate that awaited her. Still difficult to imagine, after all these years, how Armin, with music in his blood, could have entrusted her with what little remained of his name. He was one who could hear a mile away if a violinist's finger slipped on a string for a nanosecond!"

"Love blinds."

"Less love, more pipe dream. Don't wish to be too harsh, he's still around and might hear me! I think simply failure to see what ought to have been obvious. Mainly, failure to come to terms with reality. Men of attainment suffer from this, a mulish refusal to accept when one's time is over. Like leaders clinging to the throne, even when deaf and decrepit."

"Were you ever there, at any of her concert appearances?"

"I was." Davidovith nodded with a sombre look. "At the first one. And it wasn't entirely pleasant. An evening to remember, but best forgotten.

"Laurant somehow, don't ask me how, managed to convince the management of a small provincial theatre using Armin's name as leverage. *Specchio per le allodole,* they say in Italian. A mirror for the larks, is that right? The singer was an unknown, the public would be there for Armin von Göttner, a name that still carried echoes in older memories. There was also a second evening planned, up in the north, a town near the Austrian border."

Davidovich paused, with a quite chuckle. Armin in his heart of hearts, he said, had hoped for Ursula's debut in a more famed locale than a small provincial town known then as the world capital of ladies' tights. The place was near Parma, but the Teatro Regio of Parma was an impossible dream. Not even Laurant with all his connections could pull that off. The temple of Verdi, the Regio was also the cradle that launched some of the great vocalists of the century. It was a lion's den, not every tenor and soprano had come out entire and whole. Thumbs up from the unforgiving audience meant one was on the way to glory, thumbs down could set back a singer's career by years.

"Whatever else, however much he might rant or rage, Armin could also be a realist and knew when he was up against a wall. Pulling an elephant out of a rabbit-hole an impossibility, he accepted that Carpi was not a bad choice, after all. A pleasant locality, neoclassical, with a surprisingly immense piazza for a town of that size, the municipal theatre at one end. A charming little place, several tiers of loggia, seating a few hundred, lots of stucco work, an elaborately painted ceiling.

"Ursula didn't have a big sound and her voice would carry well in that limited horseshoe space. Better still, the local audience was likely to be less demanding. Aficionados of opera, as much of the population in the area, but without the cruel bite of the theatregoers in Parma and elsewhere. And then there was, so Laurant told me, a new lady *Direttore* of the theatre, only too glad to be kicking off her tenure with a name like von Göttner offered her on the plate for a very modest outlay. Armin himself would have offered the evening free of cost, but Laurant said no, a professional performance, unless for charity or suchlike, called for give and take, however small or large the fee.

"Armin thought Ursula needed to have a few familiar faces around her. So we had gone down for the evening, Laurant also keen to see at first hand how she'd fare, before arranging future engagements. Not that Ursula would be adding much wealth or lustre to his ARTISTES UNIS company. More a labour of love and loyalty for him, he owed it to Armin.

"Neither of us would be staying for the entire performance. He had to be back in Paris and had an early morning flight from Milan. I'd be taking the first train back, for a recital at a charity event in Lausanne the next evening.

"Miranda was with us there. She had come down with them, to lend a hand with Ursula's costume and see to things. I remember how excited she was. In all the years in his service, she'd never seen Armin on the stage. During our practise sessions in the house, one afternoon I found her outside the door, listening in. '*Hermosa! Tan hermosa! Como un ángel,*' she whispered in my ear. She had taken to Ursula from the start, treating her like a daughter, mothering and coddling, never letting her lift a finger. Seated with us in one of the forward boxes, she half-swooned when Ursula walked onto the stage, murmuring '*Oh, Señora!*' under her breath.

"Before the curtains parted the lady *Direttore* appeared for a brief presentation. She laid it on quite a bit, something to the effect of what an honour it was for Carpi to welcome the great Maestro Armin von Göttner, one of the living legends of the musical world. And no less a matter of pride for a modest municipal theatre to have been chosen for the debut of one of the new voices of the future, that surely would go onto fame and greatness. With that she asked the public to extend the warmest of welcomes to Ursula von Isenburg.

"Yes, Ursula had not only gone through a thorough makeover, Armin had also thought it best to put a distance between them, getting her to adopt a stage name, taking on her mother's family title. Apart from the fact that a husband and wife duo on the stage is sometimes a bit suspect…"

"Why suspect, David?"

"I mean, it gives off a whiff of conspiracy, collusion, covering up each other's shortcomings, that sort of thing. In practice all small ensembles, trios, quartets, do that, members coming to each other's aid in case of a hurried or skipped note.

"Also…," Davidovich looked at me as if from a distance. "If that way inclined, one could assume, I suppose, that on Armin's part it was a precautionary measure. He might not have wanted his name associated with her just in case the evening turned out to be a fiasco. A touch of malice there, but knowing the man…"

The evening could not have started better, the audience rising to its feet as one man to give von Göttner a thunderous applause when he made his entry, his presence alone, tall and imposing, in black with a crisp buttoned-up white shirt, filling the small stage already a bit crowded with a grand upright Bechstein. Provincial music-lovers who had heard the name but never seen the man in person and performance, his appearance there in their midst had for them the air of a milestone event.

Davidovich looked at the time. "Gaby is late. You don't mind if we wait another ten minutes, maybe? This place serves dinner till late." Taking a sip of his drink, he sat back.

"Italians tend to be free and generous with their salutation. Cheering heartily at weddings, fêtes and festivities, wholeheartedly clapping their hands even at funerals. Enough to make the deceased want to rise from the coffin and take a bow! But the applause that greeted Ursula as she came onto the stage could have raised the roof.

"It was a sight, I can tell you, probably with revisitation at night for many of the males present in the theatre. Got up in a scintillating metallic lame sheath from neck to feet, it was as if Anita Ekberg in the *Dolce Vita* had emerged from a bath of liquid gold in the Fontana Trevi. Figure and contours perfectly moulded, siren-like, everything where it belonged. Don't think it would have mattered if she'd not sung a single note. The applause went on and on, as if at the conclusion of a memorable evening. Might well have been better had it ended there, without her voicing a single line of song!"

It had started well, Davidovich mused, and ended less so. The evening's programme was divided in two, von Göttner cleverly choosing familiar territory for the first half, the cradle songs Ursula could have carried off with eyes shut, Wiegenlieds by Haydn, Mozart, Brahms. Also some popular classic ones,

Guten Abend, gut' Nacht, things of the sort. Pieces Ursula had sung to infants in her nursing days.

"Word perfect, melodic lines easy, Ursula carried it off well enough. A little nervous, faltering and side-stepping here and there. Understandable, after all it was her very first appearance in public. But it didn't much matter, the audience was well disposed and, in any case, not familiar with traditional German melodies.

"The trouble began after the interval. Armin had decided to give the public some home-grown stuff, nothing brilliant or demanding, *cavatine* from the Italian classical repertoire, easy enough on the ear but not without small complications for the singer. Simple things have their dangers, a good omelette is not the easiest thing to serve up. And then, Armin had wanted to end with a flourish, a handful of *canzonette* from Haydn's *Arianna a Naxos*. That's when Ursula came undone. Losing her nerve, diction faulty, half losing voice, unable to keep pace with Armin's accompaniment. He tried to help out, with small, subtle repeats and imperceptibly slowing down. But an accompanist can only do so much.

"As I said, Laurant and I were to leave a bit early, before the end. But even by then you could sense the public getting restive, shifting in their seats, murmurs floating up. No it didn't end well. We heard afterwards there were catcalls and some jeering. Not outright heckling, but no jubilation either, just small, sparse applause. Neither Armin nor Ursula reappeared after the curtains came down. And they deserted the after-concert dinner with the lady *Direttore* and the theatre management. Armin bullheadedly passed it off as mere stage fright. But no doubt about it, a proper debacle, that spelt ill for the future. In fact, the concert programmed in Trento was called off."

Davidovich saw nothing of the von Göttners for several months after that. "I was kept busy with major work readying the winery for the coming harvest season. And then, Gabriel and I had met recently. As you can imagine, new love demands time and attention. He had his own cosy place in Geneva and was more than a little reluctant to come and live here. Out in the country. Much too quiet for one used to the lively nightlife of a city. Nightlife, so to speak, that shuts shop and goes to bed by ten! That winter, with all the snow about, I finally managed to persuade him.

"Before that I had an invite from Armin. Sometime that autumn he had bought the place in Como and he wanted me to go down and have a look. Well, it was a grand piece of property, a fit retreat for an ageing lion king. I thought he'd give up the place in Geneva and finally settle down with Ursula in the new residence to a quiet life, writing, maybe composing a bit. Years earlier had had written several short pieces.

"Wrong again, of course! He did sell off the apartments in Geneva. But the quite life was anything but quiet! I didn't understand it then, that he was putting Ursula to grass, to graze in opulence and with all possible comfort. Always generous, but it was his way of repaying her for not having lived up to his expectations. For himself, he had other plans. Who was it… Socrates perhaps, who said the only wisdom is in knowing you know nothing. I'm not sure it made me any wiser, but I realized, once again, how little I knew the man after all those years."

Davidovich paused to call the waiter over to tell him that we'd be moving to the table, Gabriel joining us when he arrived. A slight nip in the air, he hugged himself glancing at the diners in the candle-lit interior. "Shall we? You must be hungry, after Céline's generous portions at lunch."

"No," Davidovich shook his head, passing me the menu. "Miranda and her husband didn't go over to Como. They'd put together a tidy sum and went back to Spain after Armin sold the place in Geneva. They run a B&B, somewhere in Andalusia, I believe. I've had half a mind to go down and see them sometime, but Gaby refuses. Too hot down there, he says. He's a cold weather soul."

A call from Gabriel informed us he was not far off, the delay caused by a minor road accident.

"Looking back now, I think Armin was more than a little embittered, wounded in spirit, as much as by Ursula's failure to keep his presumed faith in her, as by the depths to which he himself had fallen. Understandably. After the debacle of her debut, and then having to call off the concert date up in Trento, they'd gone to Prague. Like those itinerant musicians and composers of the Baroque era, travelling from town to town in the company of a lady love able to sing and dance, some received at a minor royal court, putting on a show or two for the locals, pocketing the purse and departing. Hardly the life for a once great heavyweight like Armin. Sad to think now that one day soon that's what he would become, a travelling journeyman offering his art to unlettered audiences in remote provincial capitals.

"That was to come later. In Prague that summer he touched bottom. Couldn't have fallen farther. There are those who delight in seeing the great and mighty held up to public derision and humiliation. I for one thank my God I wasn't there to see the sorry spectacle.

"There are several small theatres in Prague that put on hour long concerts for tourists. Sweaty visitors drifting in from the sweltering early summer afternoons in sandals and shorts to listen to the usual pop repertoire. A movement or two from the *Four Seasons,* a snatch of *Nachtmusik,* a warbling recital by some ageing soprano who never made it on the stage of the world. The players are from local ensembles, artisanal musicians, so to speak, good enough for the easy ears of the backpacker audience.

"I never learnt how things worked out in Prague, if Ursula managed to hold her own through the couple of concerts. In any case, Armin shouldn't have been there, sat at the piano in those halls. Not the Armin von Göttner the world had known. How the mighty fall! More than a fall, Prague was a sad requiem, the curtain finally coming down on an impossible illusion."

Davidovich snapped a breadstick with a sombre smile, just as Gabriel appeared at the entrance, pausing for a moment to look around the candle-lit tables.

2

"Odd that she never told you. After all…," Davidovich paused, as if to choose his words with discrete care. "After all, you'd been close to her most of this past year."

We had started out early, Davidovich unhurried and easy at the wheel, intending to reach the clinic before midday. He meant to stop over to see von Göttner and consult briefly with the doctors before lunch down in the village, after which we would make our way up the valley to the small Füssli family cemetery above the farmhouse.

The journey to the sanatorium was one he was destined to make monthly, a task left him by Ursula, part of the inheritance consigned in his care. Less a chore, more a labour of love and loyalty, he did not much mind. Having been close to a person in life, he remarked, conferred the right to be near in death as well, adding wryly, "Just that one like Armin never really dies!"

He peered up at the uncertain sky, the day moody with intimations of rain. "Rain? Don't think so. Though one never knows in these parts. Still, we might have chosen a better day."

"Is there ever a good day for visiting the dead?"

"Probably not." Davidovich turned to me with a boyish smile. "At least not with my mother. Going to see her once in a while, sometimes I have the impression she's going to slide out from under her slab of marble to scold me with a tug of the ear. Because I've not seen to the cellar doors loose on their hinges.

Or because Céline doesn't clean out the oven after every roast and bake.

"It was different with father. For years after he was gone, I had this dream of him standing at my shoulder saying, '*Metzuyan!* Well done, David.' I'd wake wondering what I'd done. In fact, in real life he'd say that at times, without particular reason. It was, I guess, his seal of approval, his way of expressing love."

"The dead can be burdensome, though," I said, perhaps inadvertently, thinking of my own recent past. "A ballast not easy to unload."

"Don't tell me!" Davidovich's short burst of laugh was without mirth. "Look what they've done to me."

What von Göttner and Ursula had done was to leave to him all their earthly possessions, sole heir to their estate, the villa in Como, several bank accounts and investments, some managed by Laurant, now willed to Davidovich.

"You see how we live," he said. "Gaby and I are not the sort to take luxury cruises around the world or winter in the South Seas. Gaby is not overworked but manages to get regular small-scale commissions. I'm, well, comfortable, shall we say. To tell the truth, I may have inherited a bit of the frugality of my mother's faith. 'Waste, and one day you'll want,' she'd mutter if I left something on my plate at table. And now, look what I've got on my plate!

"Fabbri will manage to sell the place, sooner or later. Meanwhile, we'll have to clear out the furniture and all the rest. Houses in Italy are sold unfurnished. Anyway, the Second Empire style is a bit passé, not to everyone's taste. But Fabbri thinks there are quite a few valuable objects around. Armin was not a collector as such, but he knew a good thing when he saw one. I'll get a friend at an auction house here to go down and draw up a list for valuation. And then there's all the paperwork, the processing of the will, lawyers and notaries. You're right, the dead can be burdensome. Not only the weight one carries around inside."

Davidovich looked up at the sky, squinting with a suspect eye. "I think we'll be seeing some rain, after all. Later perhaps."

Heading north, we had turned eastwards, leaving behind the larger towns and major centres, the road winding above valleys wooded with larch and beech, turning darker then with spruce and pine as the slopes steepened towards mountain ranges, small villages nestling here and there half-concealed by the dense green of the forestland. Sparse traffic on the roads, there was even less sign of life.

"This," Davidovich directed my gaze at the landscape around, "is what one might call the heart of darkness of the country."

Some things of the past, he said, still inhabited these lands, habits and way of life, frugality and faith. And a laborious silence. The local folk were good for a song and dance, making merry and getting high at fêtes and festivals. But the jollity was less light-hearted, more leaden and ponderous. Times were changing, but it was still very much a man's world, women a necessary accessory. Especially so in the small localities and among the farming communities.

This was the cradle in which Ursula was born. The area largely unfamiliar to him till now, having to come up more frequently of recent to see to arrangements for Ursula, for von Göttner at the clinic, looking around he had finally begun to understand Ursula better, peculiarities that had escaped him in life. He thought he now saw why she had always accepted to go with the tide, never protesting, never a word of complaint leaving her lips. A sort of mental and moral servitude. Never deciding on her own, never once mistress of her fortunes.

"As if, whatever befell her was the hand of *Karma*. Written, signed, sealed, and irrevocable, for her merely to submit and obey. Choice was never an option. I don't mean the passing peccadillo, the short affairs on the side. Moving Armin to the sanatorium was perhaps the only time she chose of her own, something weighty. Even so, less her will, mainly circumstances that forced her hand. The hand of *Karma* at work again!

"I'm, *per se*, not a suspicious person. At least, I don't think so. I'll not call a person a thief until I find his hand in my pocket! But I've to admit that I found it curious, the frequent trips up and down Ursula had started making from the middle of the summer. Before, she'd drive up to Zürich once in a while, on banking matters or to visit some people she knew there. Occasionally she'd stopover for the night at my place before going back.

"I confess, and I'm not proud of it, at first I thought her repeated trips might have had something to do with putting Armin down once and for all. But the DIGNITAS people are quite strict about putting anyone to sleep without their written consent and active participation. I'd heard, though probably just rumours, there was a small clinic operating somewhere up there which was a bit lax about personal collaboration in assisted deaths. In truth, it was difficult to imagine one like Ursula stepping into such muddy waters. To think of her as the killer nurse in movies pressing down a pillow on the sick man's face! After all, she'd cared for him for years and one had never heard her grumble or gripe… It seemed to have become the sole mission of her life, to be by his side as long as there was a breath of air in his lungs. Even as the good days of her own life went to waste. And then, one time when she'd dropped in to stay for the night, I saw a plastic folder sticking out of her bag. Written large across the front was the name of the Zürich University Hospital Cancer Centre."

"Of course, I didn't dare ask. Some things are just too private, too close to the bone. Anyway, I'd no idea if it had to do with her, with Armin, or maybe a friend. Having a tumour for some people seems a matter of shame. A cousin of my mother had it and, apart from his wife, no one else in the family was told. Until the liver died and he with it."

~~~

Not only had Ursula never made mention of it, in fact I had not seen her again since her abrupt departure, leaving behind merely a confused note delivered by butler Silvio. The message, vague and wandering in the wording, a veiled adieu if one chose to read it as such, ending with a line or two of darker syllables, about time passing and the impermanence of things. Read through several times but largely incomprehensible, the note put away, I puzzled for days conjecturing what it was she might have had in mind and what she had meant to say. Possibly to convey separation and parting, the end of our short season of love. Even so, much too hurried and abrupt, no less hurtful.

She had not been her familiar self of recent. That much was plain to see. Little trace of her often theatrical pose and posture, voice low and words distanced, quiet as often with a distracted air, the mind seemingly elsewhere. What weighed down her usual buoyant spirit one could not guess. But, sat out in the garden as the late summer days slowly tapered towards twilight, she had once or twice revealed briefly her seemingly newfound concern for Armin as he lay on the terrace, waxwork still as always, still animated in the far reaches of his being with some mysterious trace of life.

"*Ich bin müde, mein Freund. Sehr müde!*"

She did look and sound tired, a shade of waste shadowing her expression. It was a peculiar habit of Ursula's to revert briefly at times to her native tongue when fatigued or low in spirit, the words meant more for herself, not the listener. Reaching out a hand to mine, she had repeated, "Yes, tired. Very, believe me."

As Davidovich was to mention later, Ursula had a canny if not entirely conscious knack of revealing much about herself and her affairs, private and personal, events and experiences, some touchingly intimate, others of public domain more or less, but all too often leaving out some essential particular or detail. An omission that made the telling incomplete, at times made little sense of the scattered pieces. Like an intricate jig-saw missing the couple of cut-outs that made the puzzle recognizable.

One time she had in passing touched on her father's accidental death, without revealing in so many words that it was her mother's hand that had given the push over the cliff-edge. Not quite an accidental send-off towards eternity! Allusion and inference woven into the telling, understandably one came to doubt the veracity of whatever the act or event. More than once she had mentioned the abuse suffered at the hands of the head of the clinic where she had worked, never once mentioning her possible complicity and willing collaboration in letting the doctor have his way.

One listened and sympathized, but often enough an air of dubiety hung in the air. The theatre of her mind leaving unplayed some small relevant part of the act, the drama then resulted incomplete and confusing for the audience. Was her father the monster she had repeatedly implied, merely hinting at his incestuous sorties in an off-hand manner? Was the stormy affair with her tormented neighbour truly the resurgent passion late in life that had threatened to unhinge her marriage? The artful hieroglyphics of her narration often concealed some major element, like legal fine print.

"*Sehr müde.*" she said, and one believed her, the weariness less visible to the naked eye but apparent in the hearing, the words pondered, the air of a fatigue of the spirit draping her presence, the smile forced like the sun trying to break through the brume.

With the months I had indeed begun to notice alterations, little decipherable at first, if not for the pregnant pauses and long, thoughtful silences at times. Nothing had visibly changed in her day, the routine the same as ever, long mornings, before the heat rose, in the garden beside Armin, the coming and going of the two moonlighting nurses, the house quietly alive with Silvio and the maid going silently about their chores. But for the odd visitor, postman and tradesmen, Dr. Silvestri from the local hospital dropping in to check on possible, but little probable, changes in the patient's condition, David Davidovich was the only friend and familiar figure over from time to time for a short weekend. Once Ursula summoned me to meet Pierre Laurant, von Göttner's former agent and friend, affable and light-humoured, down from Paris on a working visit in Milan.

Often the early afternoons were a private moment for Ursula and me, she at my place, the warmth of the noon hour sapping energy, our love-making languid and deliquescent, a slower dance encased in a skein of moist heat, motion and pulsation measured. As perhaps befitted our age, I thought at times, but no less pleasurable and satisfying for that. The fumbling frenzy of the early months gone, lovers still but also companions out of the sheets, we knew something of each other, I less about Ursula with her winding and tortuous journey, feints and blind alleys misleading one through doubtful and, possibly, faux confessions. Comfortable with each other, but very likely we were not friends, friendship calling for affinity and empathy, and time, while we were in truth only passing lovers, drawn together by private grief and solitude, with idle hours on our hands.

As the summer wore on, her absences becoming more frequent, she was often away for days, no particular reason offered for the trips out of town, only with casual mention of small details that gave nothing away, as if she had merely been down to the lakefront for an afternoon. Discretion prevailing, I probed no further, nor was she any more forthcoming. Yet, the odd word escaping, one understood it had something to do with von Göttner. One day, then, the curtain parted a little, to offer a glimpse of the possible cause of her unsettled air.

Unusually downcast, she said, "What am I do with him. What will become of him should something happen to me?"

"Why should anything happen to you?"

She parried my words with a look of gloom, indeed misery, so unlike her and such as one had never seen. "There's always the unexpected around the corner."

She took my hand, to gaze at the upturned palm, as if to decipher what might lie ahead. "What a long life, Professor," she remarked in a tone of distracted affliction, tracing a finger across the web of lines. "Things do happen. Isn't that what life's about?"

Possibly nothing more than an hour or a day in the dumps, a passing interval in the trough, when the latitudes of living appear void of sense. Not uncommon in a life solitary and burdened, seemingly with no end in sight and prospects few. Possibly, too, attributable to the watershed of the midlife pause, the fertile plains of youth and prime left behind, the flatlands of age, barren and inconsequential, stretching ahead towards a horizon nebulous, indistinct to the eye of the mind. And yes, one could well understand the dilemma and uncertainty of an existence keeping interminable watch over a man dead for all purposes but refusing to release the last breath of life. The expectations that mark the dates on the calendar paused, what design and destination could she chalk out for the time ahead?

Even so, the joyless words were out of step with her accustomed self, perhaps merely the drip by drip accretion of a sense of confinement in a limbo without end. Of late she had even shed her nurse's uniform when sat out with Armin in the garden. With the merest particle of his mind still alive and wandering in the reaches of some remote universe, one wondered if he noticed his Nightingale denying him this last satisfaction of his once jejune predilection for the white coat and the nursing cap.

Imagination running riot in the hours of the dark, some nights, before sleep closed in, the mind hastily heaping together a castle in the air, as in a length of celluloid speeded up, conjured up the chimera of a life together. She and I, floating through an undefined space, drifting out of sight as the drowsy lids closed shut. The stuff of dreams, yet the thought persisted.

If not now, later, unburdened and free, with Armin finally gone, she would come across the waters to join me. A late union, but not overmuch, neither of us inordinately aged, with days and years ahead as yet, our tastes and appetites still reasonably alive to nourish us as bedmates and life-mates, wanting nothing more one from the other than the affection of a companionable presence, the warmth of a body alongside at night, a shoulder to lean on, a hand to hold. But like all flights of impossible fancy, the vaporous dreams of dark and dawn failed to reckon with the light of day. With no magic at hand to make von Göttner's ever-present spectre disappear in thin air, the square peg of nocturnal visions appeared not the fit the round hole of reality. And what, too, of Ursula herself, her heart's inclinations, needs and hopes. It brought to mind the humoured words of Davidovich at our first meeting, that were dreams to be taxed by the state, there would be far fewer delusions and disappointments, possibly self-inflicted mortalities even.

There then came a few short weeks during which the uneasy calm took an unexpected turn, as I watched and waited at the Villa Serena and Ursula disappeared from sight, without word or notice, for an entire fortnight. Nor had she asked me, as at times in the past, to keep an eye on the household, especially the attendance of the nurses, summoning Dr. Silvestri, should von Göttner's condition so need. Going over to enquire, I found butler Silvio less than forthcoming. Or perhaps he simply did not know and could not help. Not wishing to peer into her affairs elsewhere, I had never called Ursula during her absences. Deciding to do so now, I asked Silvio if I could reach her, to be met by his terse reply that Madam had a new phone and, less than credible, he had not been given the number.

Keeping anxious watch, one waited. Maria looked on wordless as I sat at table, half indifferent to the hearty nutrition she served up, as ever, her expression one of chiding and concern, her aged discretion withholding comment. This was not how it was meant to be. One had come here with a purpose, a year's rest and reprieve, to gain time and start anew, the new surrounds meant to refresh and reinvigorate, distance grief and help gain final acceptance of a seemingly irreparable loss.

Standing at the window, coveting the neighbour's wife could well have been a pleasant, if somewhat unseemly, diversion for the airing of a burdened spirit. See, watch, don't touch, don't taste, one had forgotten the ancient wisdom of keeping distance. Instead, not only drawn into the life of another with its tortuous byways, worst still, entangled in the intimacy of an affair that had silently begun to put down roots in the flesh and fabric of one's existence, raising puerile expectations, hopes and assumptions without firm earth beneath the feet, attention distracted and the work at hand neglected, adrift in a sea cluttered and confused by sensations and inclinations out of place and out of character, to end in a cul-de-sac of delusion and distress. More than a little surprising the faulty self-knowledge of having thought of oneself as a sober and rational being, measured and with reasonable good sense. Fables, it was thought, were for infants. Mature age was not, evidently, much of a defence against the designs of fancy and fantasy!

Back after several days in Verona with a friend and fellow academic come over for the summer vacation, with the welcome distraction of an evening at the Arena for an opulent performance of *Aida,* I had found the von Göttner villa silent, shut and shuttered, the grounds empty, without trace of life, the coming and goings of the nurses, butler Silvio and the maid disappeared from sight, Ursula's absence an echoing void.

"They've gone. *Tutti quanti,*" Maria informed me in her

usual laconic manner. More she did not know, having been at home the days I was away.

The next morning, catching sight of Fabbri pacing in the garden, his secretary Franca beside him, I went down to meet him. Cordial as ever in greeting, there was a thoughtful air about him.

"What am I to do with this place now?" he said, his eyes taking in the breadth and height of the mansion.

In these times there were fewer buyers for elephants of this size, he explained. Evidently the oligarchs, tycoons and sheikhs were somewhat thin on the ground at the moment. And then the clearing out, the furniture and furnishings, objects weighty and of some worth.

"But that's Mr. Davidovich's headache. You must have met him…" Turning, he saw my confused look, his gaze then quizzical. "You didn't know? She didn't tell you?"

"I've been away this past week."

"Oh. But…" His hand light on my arm, he walked me up the steps to the terrace, to join Franca intent on jotting notes on a small pad.

Ursula had been to see him only a few days back and it had come out of the blue, Fabbri confessed, when she told him that she and von Göttner would be moving out within days and that she wanted him to put the villa on the market. "At short notice, just like that! Surprising, very surprising." She was in a hurry, apparently. No details discussed, she had merely given him the number for contacting Davidovich who, she said, would follow up with whatever needed to be done.

"Just that. Nothing more," Fabbri nodded his head pensively. "I didn't ask the why and when. As you probably know, we weren't on friendly terms. But it was more than noticeable she didn't look well, didn't sound well. Not at all the person one knew. Quiet, subdued. Yes, subdued. I told her I'd do what I could. After all, it's not a little antique bedside table that you put on display in the shop window. Selling a property like this takes time, and time was something she didn't seem to have."

I walked down and out the gate with Fabbri, Franca at our heels. "In a way," said Fabbri, "this is a refugee town. All these immigrants massed at the frontier, in flight from misery, trying to get over the border in search of their fortune. And the fortunate, great and famous, coming over and settling down for a few years. In flight from the misery of wealth and fame! Soon you too will be gone, no?"

In flight not from riches and name, I thought. Rather, a brief season of illusion and vain expectations.

3

We had lunched at a small eatery in the village down from the sanatorium where von Göttner was lodged in the palliative care wing. Davidovich was satisfied that, though comatose as ever, he was cradled in the best possible comfort and care. Surrounded by pretty young things in starched white.

"It could come as quite a shock, were he to awake someday and find the bevy of beauties around him. Could be dangerous for his heart!"

"Death is a leveller, they say," Davidovich mused, forking an onion ring. "Maybe. But dying rich is not the same thing as dying without means."

He meant it did not come cheap at the Grünewald Klinik. Even so, the estate entrusted in his hands would suffice for as long as his maestro could draw a thin air of breath. He had outlived Ursula, younger by decades and, Davidovich added with a wry smile, "Never can tell, he might even outlive me!"

Too much a lover of food to be a true epicurean, Davidovich savoured the crusty custard pie in generous mouthfuls. Yet a distracted air of melancholy shaded his expression, as imperceptibly he shook his head.

"Still can't believe it," he said finally, picking crumbs from the underlip. "It came as a shell-shock when I heard the news. But even now, when I come here to see Armin, it's hard to believe, the speed with which it happened.

"The last time Ursula came to my place, I could see something was not right. Fatigued, unusually worn out, a bad headache tormenting her, she seemed to have put on a good five or ten years. Not aged as such, more sapped of her usual energy and spirit. Clearly there was something on her mind, matters weighty that made her distracted, strangely forgetful. I remember Gabriel telling her that he was renovating the facade of a medieval church near Nyon, then at the end of the dinner she asked if he was working on anything.

"Gabriel himself went to bed early that evening and the two of us sat out quite late after dinner. That was when she told me. As often, only half the truth. She said it had become increasingly burdensome to manage on her own and the time had come to place Armin in professional care. There was a new hospice wing at the clinic where she had worked. Normally they wouldn't have taken in one in Armin's condition. The doctor who had been head of the place during her time was still there, as honorary president. Somehow she managed to convince him. I've met this man, Dr. Krieger. Very old now, in his eighties, but a benign sort. Arrangements were already in place and Armin would be moved there in a week or two. Quite a surprise in itself, but there was more to come."

She had handed him several large, sealed envelopes. Weighty stuff, quite mystifying. Not to worry, she told him, only a precaution, just in case. Because she was booked in at the University Hospital in Zürich for a week of check-ups. One never knew, she had joked, trying to make light of it.

"Only by digging for gold did one find gold! Those were her words. Curious. At the time I made nothing of it. For a moment she was her usual self, a touch theatrical, impersonating some character from her gallery of dramatis personae. You could see it was a bit forced and I really didn't know what to think. But as she talked, it was clear that her main concern was for Armin, what might happen to him were she to go missing. Curious that, too. Here was a person whole and in health, more or less, worrying about the future of one with no future at all in the event of her own demise. Only later I learned she already knew that evening that her time was running out fast. So like Ursula. To retreat into silence, whatever the pain."

Some three weeks later, Céline had hurried from the house while Davidovich was seeing to the first pruning of the vines, to say there was an urgent call for him. It was the Zürich University Hospital, to inform him, as his name had been given as the main contact, that Frau Ursula von Göttner had passed away during the night.

"Ridiculous! I asked them to confirm the name. They did, giving some details and asking when I could come to see to things. I drove up the next morning in a complete fog. And there I learned what there was to learn, little and late. Ursula had been diagnosed with a brain tumour a couple of months back, very aggressive and inoperable for the delicate location. There was a possible ray of hope, however. The British had come up with a new experimental technique and the Cancer Centre got in touch with the hospital in London. The Royal something... Ah yes, the Royal Marsden. That's the name, I think. She'd be flown there after further checks in Zürich. That's when she had come to see me. The very last time. A few days later she was dead."

We rose to leave, Davidovich taking my arm as we gained the fresh early afternoon air. "She died alone," he said quietly. "Much as she had lived most of her life."

It was a further hour's drive through the dark heartland of stone pines massed like forbidding sentinels on the slopes rising towards bare mountain ranges, narrow-armed valleys opening up here and there with crystal waters flowing over pebbles and boulders. Leaving a small town behind us, winding up a narrow road for some ten minutes, towards a steep rise, finally parking the car on the open ground in front of an abandoned farmhouse, we took the path across a sloping meadow overgrown with tall blue grass and clumps of autumn cyclamen.

The cemetery was on a clearing at the top, rocky and undulating, several generations of the Füssli family entombed under ground, the tall weathered headstones subsided, askew and tilting, the names of the dead half erased by time. A tall wooden cross with Christ crucified, still upright, looked out over the chalet above the farmhouse and the little bridge across the rippling brook that demarcated the frontier, offering an open view of the broad valley below cradling the town and, at a distance, a small lake like a smudge in the gloom of the autumn afternoon.

Davidovich led me to the far end and, discreet as ever, left me alone to take my last leave. A few steps away from the older dead, as if to mark the generations, lay Ursula's parents under simple, rough-hewn gravestones, her mother's lineage in the name inscribed: Conradine Isenburg Füssli. Alongside, Ursula's headstone carried only the matrilineal title, as too the von Göttner name. Tall and in rust-red Sienna marble, distinct among the rest in the field of the dead, it seemed not to belong there.

Standing by a long moment in the sullen light under a sky leaded with grey, the air keen but somehow one had the sensation of laboured breath at the thought of the once warm and pliant flesh, touched, held and loved, now left to lie and decay under the stony earth, never again to pulse with the beat of life. A prayer unuttered, a farewell distracted, I turned to retrace my steps.

ACKNOWLEDGEMENTS

Grateful thanks to Ms Rosella Bongiovanni for her kind suggestions and assistance with with German names and terms. Thanks are also due to Giorgio Sibella for his constant help with ordering and setting the digital text.

For exclusive discounts on Matador titles,
sign up to our occasional newsletter at
troubador.co.uk/bookshop